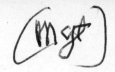

Adrienne McDonnell has taught literature and fiction writing at the University of California, Berkeley. *The Doctor and the Diva* is based in part on the true story of her son's great-great grandmother. McDonnell was inspired by hundreds of pages of family letters and memories of elderly relatives, long haunted by the story. She lives near San Francisco. This is her first novel.

The
Doctor
and the
Diva

Adrienne McDonnell

sphere

SPHERE

First published in the United States of America in 2010
by Pamela Dorman Books/Viking
First published in Great Britain in 2010 by Sphere

A CIP catalogue record for this book
is available from the British Library.

ISBN 978-1-84744-368-7

Printed and bound in Great Britain by
Clays Ltd, St Ives plc

Papers used by Sphere are natural, renewable and
recyclable products sourced from well-managed forests and certified
in accordance with the rules of the Forest Stewardship Council.

Mixed Sources
Product group from well-managed
forests and other controlled sources
www.fsc.org Cert no. SGS-COC-004081
© 1996 Forest Stewardship Council
FSC

Sphere
An imprint of
Little, Brown Book Group
100 Victoria Embankment
London EC4Y 0DY

An Hachette UK Company
www.hachette.co.uk

www.littlebrown.co.uk

For my parents,
Catherine and Phil McDonnell

A Historical Note: Although few readers may be aware of it, certain fertility procedures now considered "modern" were used by physicians—behind a curtain of secrecy—more than a century ago.

PART ONE

1

⁓∞⁓

BOSTON

1903

D octor Ravell had already missed the funeral. The body was being carried from the church as he arrived. Many of Boston's most prominent physicians descended the granite steps in a parade of canes and black silk hats, the modest old man in the casket the most esteemed of them all. Six or seven members of the von Kessler family—all of them doctors—served as pallbearers, and they shouldered the gleaming casket suitable for a king. Ravell wondered how many others, like him, must have deserted patients at their bedsides in order to join the procession.

He heard his name called, a black top hat raised and waved in his direction like a celebratory shout. "Ravell!"

It was Doctor Gerald von Kessler, a homeopath, who greeted him— the nephew of the man they'd come to mourn. His short wife stood beside him, with violets blooming in her hat.

The couple insisted that Ravell ride with them to the cemetery. In the privacy of their carriage, Doctor von Kessler leaned closer to confide.

"Can you help my sister?" von Kessler said. "This is what I am asking."

"We are afraid," his wife added, "that she has grown desperate."

Doctor von Kessler removed his top hat and placed it on the seat. "My sister's husband has become obsessed. He's dragged her to physician after physician, put her through every procedure and humiliation so that she can have a child. He won't relent."

"I'd be honored to help your sister," Ravell said, "in any way I can."

"We heard about your recent triumph in the Hallowell case." Gerald von Kessler gave Ravell a sharp, congratulatory nod.

"After nineteen years in a barren marriage," Mrs. von Kessler said, "thanks to you, they had twins!" The violets jiggled in her hat and her eyes shone at Ravell.

"My sister and her husband have wasted too much time consulting the old guard," Doctor von Kessler said. "They need a younger man—a pioneer in modern techniques, like you."

At the gravesite Ravell stood next to them, one hand clasped over his opposite wrist. He would never have guessed that before his thirtieth birthday, the von Kessler family would be relying on him. In the distance of a valley below, he noticed skaters skimming along a frozen pond. Cold air filled his lungs and he felt an odd elation—so peculiar to sense at a funeral—the buoyancy of knowing that his reputation was on the rise. Lately his practice had expanded at such a rate that he had been forced to turn patients away.

The last time he had seen the legendary physician they would bury today was at a professional dinner just two months previously. It had been the sort of event where eminent men toasted one another, half in jest; they had planted a crown of laurel leaves on Ravell's head to welcome him into their midst. That evening the revered old man had turned to Ravell and said, "You'll be appointed professor of obstetrics at that famous school across the river before we know it. Remember that I made that prediction."

Now the grand old man in the casket was being borne up and carried above their heads to his grave. Mourners settled into respectful poses—heads bowed, feet slightly apart—yet the minister seemed to be delaying for some reason. While they waited, snow flurries began.

Finally a black motorcar drove into the cemetery grounds. A shining black door opened, and a slender woman in a white ermine fur cape stepped out. Two violinists accompanied her. As she clutched her fur and headed for the gravesite, the crush of onlookers parted, making a wide aisle for her.

4

The woman in the white cape climbed onto a small platform. Above the congregation, she stood dressed entirely in white, and as she raised her oval face to speak, snow fell faster. Flakes dusted her hat and clung to her dark ringlets.

The deceased had been her uncle, she explained to the mourners. "The aria I am about to sing is not religious," she said. "But when my uncle heard me sing Paisiello's 'Il mio ben quando verrà,' he said: 'When they bury me, I want you to send me up to heaven with that song.'"

She loosened the white fur from her throat. For a moment she closed her eyes and gathered herself up, and then she sang.

The sounds were unlike any Ravell had ever heard. It was not an earthly voice; it was a *shimmering*. Falling snow melted on her face as he listened. In the valley below, on the distant pond, skaters circled the ice with the *legato* of her phrases. He wanted those ice skaters to keep going, round and round. He wanted the woman's iridescent voice never to stop.

Who is she? he wondered. Later, when he learned her name—*Erika*—it made him think of the words *aria, air,* as if she breathed melodies.

After her singing ended and the minister had spoken, mourners adjusted their silk top hats and knotted their scarves and shuffled past the open gap in the earth.

"I don't believe you've met my sister, have you?" Gerald von Kessler said to Ravell, and guided him toward the platform. The singer lifted her chin toward him and took his hand and smiled, the light on her face as radiant as snow. Almost immediately she turned to another person. Ravell knew that at that moment, he was nothing to her—only another doctor among scores of them.

2

Ravell watched from an upstairs window in his private quarters as Erika von Kessler and her husband made their way down Commonwealth Avenue. They would be his first appointment of the day. The husband, the one leading the charge to end their childlessness, walked several paces ahead of his wife. She lagged. The husband paused and waited for her to catch up, but when he spoke to her, she turned her head to observe the town houses on the opposite side of the avenue.

Ravell felt a tinge of excitement as he observed them. He was a man drawn to risk; nothing made him feel more alive than the nearness of a gamble. This might—or might not—become a storied case for him.

As the couple moved closer, Ravell saw that the husband, Peter Myrick, was a tall, elegant figure perhaps a few years older than himself. A sandy-haired man with pleasant features, Peter had a narrow face and a blade-thin nose. He looked like a young senator. Later Ravell would learn that on the way to their first meeting, Peter Myrick had urged certain advice upon his wife: *If you want this doctor to dedicate his best efforts to us, we must develop a special rapport with him.*

Ravell had just finished getting dressed, the strands of hair at his neck still damp from his morning bath. Before going downstairs to the street-level suite of rooms that housed his practice, he shook a few drops of musk-scented pomade onto his palms and combed back the wings of his dark hair with his fingers.

When the couple entered, Ravell rose from behind his mahogany desk to greet them. Given his conversation with Erika's brother during the carriage ride to the cemetery, Ravell had not expected to experience any particular warmth toward her husband. But from the moment Peter Myrick came into the room, he seemed lit by optimism, and Ravell felt fondness toward him. Peter was a man of refinement, and yet he had the air of an eager schoolboy.

Like a curious child, Peter glanced around the office. He recognized at once what interested him.

"I see you've got a Morpho!" he said in an accent that was unmistakably British. He lifted the magnifying glass from Ravell's desk to examine three glass cubes. A different butterfly of exquisite colors and dimensions had been preserved inside each.

"Did you capture these yourself?"

Ravell nodded. "A friend has a coconut estate on an island off South America. The wildlife is magnificent there."

"And that?" Peter Myrick pointed to a framed photograph of an anaconda entwined in a mangrove tree. "Is that from the same island?"

Ravell nodded.

"I'm an animal enthusiast myself," Peter said. "Someday I'll show you my collections and my little menagerie."

Erika Myrick (or the mezzo-soprano Erika von Kessler, as she was known professionally) had stepped into his office with the same proud carriage Ravell recalled from the day she'd appeared at the cemetery. Yet she looked very different today, as if she'd been crying earlier, her lids swollen and her eyes small. As she settled herself distantly in a chair, Ravell recalled other things Gerald von Kessler had confided during the ride from the funeral. ("Peter has become fixated to the point of tormenting my sister. If she didn't have such a glorious voice, all this might have destroyed her by now. It's music that has saved her.")

Peter Myrick offered a brief history of their struggles to conceive. They had been married now for six years. He mentioned obstetricians they had previously consulted—all mature gentleman, renowned specialists.

To reassure them that he might have something new to offer, Ravell spoke of his mentor from Harvard Medical School. Together they had designed a series of particularly elegant instruments that were beginning to yield interesting results. "Perhaps you've heard of the famous Doctor Sims? Some people call him 'the Father of Modern Obstetrics.' My mentor was a student of Sims.'"

"A figure of controversy, Sims—wasn't he?" Peter said.

Ravell nodded. Sims had been brilliant, but far too invasive in the eyes of many. "Fertility work is still—" Ravell hesitated. "Well, let's just say this must be handled with the utmost discretion. Few people should be aware of anything except the results."

Peter and Erika nodded. They understood. In a quiet tone she responded to questions about her menstrual cycles. Every gynecologist who had examined her had apparently found her female system healthy and unremarkable.

Ravell put down his pen and turned to Peter to suggest an intrusion that made many men balk. "In such cases, it's standard to inspect a sample of the husband's semen as well."

Peter gave a laugh, as abrupt as a cough. "I can assure you that virility is not of concern here."

"It might provide insight."

"That won't be necessary." Peter crossed one leg over the other.

Ravell knew when a man's dignity must be respected, so instead of pursuing the matter he led Erika von Kessler down a corridor into an examination chamber. Normally a nurse placed a freshly starched sheet on the table, but today he made it up like a little bed for her. She removed her hatpin and set her dove-gray toque on a chair, and smoothed her pompadour.

"I heard you sing at your uncle's funeral," Ravell said. "Afterward, the sound of your voice stayed in my head for days. It was so—so—"

She turned to him with interest. "Do you enjoy opera?"

"My father trained to be a baritone, but he gave it up long before I was born. He managed a large farm in Africa. When I was a little boy, he used to sing from *Figaro,* and I used to dance around and bump against the walls."

Erika von Kessler's lips parted in a faint smile.

A nurse stood in attendance while he examined her. As he reached under the drape of skirts and palpated, he kept his eyes locked on hers, as he had been trained to do, so that a female patient would feel reassured that a doctor had no intention of peering at her private areas. Her eyes were blue-gray, deepened by lavender shadows beneath the lower lashes. Unlike many women, she lay completely relaxed. Her uterus was slightly small—not uncommon for a petite woman—and it tilted to the anterior. The ovaries were healthy, properly positioned. Ravell kept his eyes on hers until she arched her throat backward and switched her gaze to the ceiling, as if returning his stare felt too intimate.

When the examination was over, the nurse left the room. He took Erika von Kessler's hand and helped her sit upright. Her hair had loosened from its knot, with a froth of dark curls sliding down her neck. He smelled whiffs of lilac soap.

As he turned to depart, Erika von Kessler called to him, "It's useless, you realize. My husband doesn't want you to know that every procedure you're about to propose, we've done before—many times. This," she declared gravely, "is the end for me. It's the end for me *of everything.*" The anguish in her words made him uneasy.

Yet she did agree to come to the office, accompanied by her husband, for regular visits that winter. Ravell assured Peter that his privacy would be respected; the moment he surrendered a sample of his seed, it would be quickly injected into his wife's body; no one would tamper with the precious substance.

And so, twice a week, Peter retreated into a windowless chamber where a book of photographs taken in a Parisian brothel had been left for him. When Peter Myrick finished, he covered the glass jar and left the specimen there. He then hurried out to the street where a carriage opened its doors and bore him away, wheels rumbling over cobblestones. An importer of textile machinery from Bradford, England, to the mills of New England—and an importer of Egyptian cotton as well—Peter traveled widely. He was a man in a hurry, with numerous transactions to oversee.

After Peter rushed off, twice a week Doctor Ravell completed the procedure on his wife. She was forced to lie for a half hour with her legs raised, knees and calves propped by pillows and bolsters, to allow her husband's seed to flow into her.

"It's hopeless," she said to Ravell every time.

❖

"I'm afraid that she plans to end her life." The wife of Doctor Gerald von Kessler sat in Ravell's office. The worried little woman wore the same crushed violets in her hat that she'd worn that day at the cemetery. "Something dreadful is going to happen to my sister-in-law, I'm certain."

"What makes you think that?"

"Erika asked me, 'If I did something that hurt the family terribly, would you and Gerald ever find it in your hearts to forgive me?' She's asked about wills; she says she wants all of her financial papers in order. She's given away beautiful dresses from her closet, saying that she won't be needing them. She's worried about her maid losing her job. Erika asked me, 'If something happens to me, would you promise to help find another position for Annie?' "

"Thank you for telling me," Ravell said.

He left the room, shaken, and stood behind a door down the hallway to collect himself. He'd once known a patient who had harmed herself under similar circumstances. That had happened during his days as a medical student, while he'd served as an assistant to another obstetrician. Ravell had never forgotten how cheerful the lady had seemed the day before she'd died by her own hand. When he'd passed her on a staircase, she'd smiled and called him by name. As she was leaving the building, she'd thrust her arm upward and waved to him with a flourish, and he heard her calling exuberant good-byes to everyone—the nurse, the head doctor, other patients and acquaintances seated in the waiting room.

The odd cheerfulness. That is what stayed with him most. Later another physician explained to him that a suicidal patient might appear suddenly uplifted just after she'd made her decision, thinking that she'd soon be free from whatever was causing her agony and sorrow. In a last note to her husband, the poor woman had written: *Since I have failed to give you the children you so dearly wanted, it seems only fair to leave you free to remarry more happily, and fruitfully. . . .* If Erika lost her life over this, Ravell knew the news would blind him with regret. He'd never wash the darkness of it from his mind.

❖

At Erika's next appointment, Ravell stepped away after examining her. "So you're having your period," he said. That morning, Erika admitted, she had hidden her bloodstained bloomers from her husband.

"You can tell Peter yourself," Erika told Ravell. Bitterness sharpened her features. "I'm tired of seeing the disappointment in his face."

She was his last appointment of the day. Ravell asked her to come into his office after she'd finished getting dressed. It always took an excruciatingly long while for a patient to rearrange her undergarments and rows of buttons, he'd found, before she was ready to exit with grace.

In the intervening minutes he slipped into the washroom, lathered his hands, and dried them. The small bathroom felt as private as a prayer cell. He tugged hard at the hot and cold water taps to shut off large drops that fell into the porcelain sink. As he combed his dark moustache with his fingers, he wondered what he would to say to her.

In the mirror he stared at himself—a slender man, shorter than most others he passed in the street. People said that if he weren't wearing a fine suit, he might be mistaken for an Arab sheik or a Tartar. His eyes dominated his face—dark eyes like his father's, thoughtful, deep-set. "It's those eyes," a lady had once said, "that make people want to tell you things."

Each woman, each patient, was her own mystery. He tried to listen until he saw distress ease or tears dry on a woman's face. Much depended on their trust in him. Some told him how they shuddered under the weight of their husbands' bodies, shunning and avoiding conjugal duties whenever they could.

When a rare husband or two had pleaded for his advice, Ravell had shown them diagrams and spoken with candor about the importance of a woman's enjoyment. At times he'd needed to be stern with wives, asking: *How do you expect to ever have a child if your husband finds that you keep locking the door to your room?*

❖

He heard a hallway door open. When he returned to his office, Erika was already there, walking around. From his desk, she picked up the glass cube with the big blue Morpho butterfly trapped inside, and she held it up to the light before setting it back down. Then she lifted the magnifying glass. Centering it above her upturned palm, she peered at the lines.

"Are you trying to read your palm?" he asked.

Erika gave a rough shake of her head and put the magnifying glass down, as if she did not believe in palmistry. The walls of his office could not contain her restlessness. She gave a noisy sigh.

When Ravell sat down behind his desk, she took the chair opposite him. "May I ask you something personal?" he said. "A woman's attitude is important. . . . Do you want to become a mother, or is this Peter's—?"

Closing her eyes for a moment, she then opened them and spoke with sharp resolve. "I used to want a child more than anything," she said, "but I've learned not to want a thing I can't have."

She looked sweet and solemn as she said this. Ravell watched her closely. If he did not interrupt and allowed a patient to continue talking, he'd found that she might reveal things she hid from a close friend or sister-in-law. Erika, however, said nothing else.

He leaned toward her, his forearms resting on his desk. "Erika, other people are worried about your state of mind."

She stared at him, then glanced at the closed door. Obviously there was something she was wary of admitting. "You must have a great many patients waiting," she said.

He assured her that this was his last appointment of the day—that he had plenty of time just now to counsel her—but she got up and began fastening her long purple cape.

To delay her, Ravell stepped between her and the doorway. "Don't do anything drastic—will you promise me that?" he said.

She was as tall as he was; her blue-gray eyes looked straight into his, her proud neck growing longer. "My life is my own," she said. "I can do what I like with it."

Had she already rehearsed a ghastly act in her mind? In the darkness of the moment he offered blind assurances. "This will all turn out happily, Erika. I'm certain of it."

"I don't believe you," she said. When she reached for the doorknob, he moved aside. Just before she turned away, he saw the sharp light of tears in her eyes. Drawing her wool cape tighter, she headed into the corridor, and when the front door opened, cold air blew into Ravell's face, lifting the hair off his collar. Long after she had gone out into the winter day, his mind held on to her. Long after the strand of bells jingled and the door banged shut, he saw her dark purple cape make a sweeping turn just above her heels.

Would she keep her next appointment? He worried that something awful would happen before then.

By the time his nurse filed some papers and left for the day, the sky had gone dark outside. Ravell extinguished the lights in his office, went down the corridor, and shut himself into a closet-like room. At medical school—at Harvard—he was hardly the most brilliant, but he had asked bolder questions than most. Since then, he had braved more and taken more risks; he had often gotten results where others had missed.

Now he was about to do something unforgivable. Ravell removed a glass dish from a drawer, set it on the counter, and removed the lid. Less than two hours before, Peter Myrick had departed from this room, leaving a sample of his semen; the specimen was still fresh. Ravell had used only a portion of it; on a hunch, he had saved the rest. Now he adjusted knobs on the microscope.

With nervous hands he took a pipette, and let a drop of fluid splash onto the slide. As he slipped the specimen under the lens, he felt moisture break over his face. He thought of Leeuwenhoek, a man from Holland who had first seen sperm through a microscope in the year 1677. A daring act of discovery then. Before gazing into the eyepiece, Ravell bent his head and held his breath, as Leeuwenhoek must have done.

At first nothing darted past his eye, only a blizzard of grayish-whiteness. He pulled away, changed the magnification, adjusted the focus, and peered again. The results made him feel snow-blind. He saw nothing there, no sperm at all.

3

"Your neck smells marvelous," Ravell said, laughing. His nose nudged the soft place under her earlobe.

Mrs. George Appleton was over forty—a decade older than he. On his bedside table she liked to keep a ring of candles burning while they made love. Wax ran from the tapers. His bedsheets felt moist after their exertions, the air humid with scents from her body and his.

Her hair was half-gray, but her speaking voice was low and deep, with theatre in it. Her laugh had the resonance of an actress's. Her own husband had not touched her in four years.

"I need to leave now," she said. She was a tall woman. When she got up from the bed, in search of the clothing she'd cast across a chair, he saw the large-shouldered, great-breasted silhouette of her, the long lean stilts of her legs, the absence of any tapering at her waist. Her backside fell flat like a cliff, like a man's. ("Where's my derriere?" she liked to jest, grabbing herself there.)

Ravell knew he was not the first man she had sought out, apart from her husband. He loved her hunger. Since he lived on the floors above his practice, he was careful to draw the shades before she came, and he shut every window. She was noisy while being caressed, and in her cries he heard more animals than he could name. When he told her this, she squatted on all fours and dived at his body, snuffling and rooting. That made him laugh. He had to shush her sometimes, because even three stories up, she might be heard from the street.

Prior to Amanda Appleton, he'd never had an affair with a patient.

The idea had appalled him. But from the day she first flung herself across his bed, he'd felt relieved and grateful for all she'd taught him. He'd never had a wife, and when it came to advising married couples, he'd felt secretly embarrassed by the limits of his own experience. He used to worry that he did not know all he felt he should.

She sat at the bed's edge and squeezed Ravell's knee. "What's wrong?" she asked. "You look troubled."

He frowned at the ring of candlelight that wavered on the ceiling. "I've been thinking about a patient. An infertility case." Ravell did not describe to her how he had stolen a bit of Peter Myrick's semen and how, with nervous hands, he had slipped the sample under a microscope. He only said, "It turns out that the husband is azoospermic."

"What's that?"

"That means he has absolutely no hope of fathering a child. He has no sperm in his semen, none whatsoever." Ravell sat up and punched a pillow lightly between his fists. "I don't know how to tell them."

❖

"I have no desire to adopt," Peter Myrick said. "It's not the same, although I admire people who do it."

Ravell and Peter had arranged to lunch at the Algonquin Club. They agreed to meet there as late in the day as possible, after most of the tables had been cleared, to ensure more privacy. They sat in a far corner and kept their voices down. Even their waiter sensed that he ought to stand at a distance, a crisp white towel hung over his bent arm.

Ravell wished he could be frank, but how could he simply blurt out what he'd learned? Peter had never given permission for his manhood to be inspected and counted under a microscope. As a physician, Ravell knew he had committed an invasion of an appalling kind: what husband would trust him in the future if it became known that he had violated a patient's privacy?

"Perhaps it's time we resorted to the dreaded semen analysis," Ravell said briskly.

"What good would it do?" Peter said. "Would it mean that we'd do anything differently?"

"It might help you to stop blaming your wife."

"I'm not finding fault with anybody."

"Do you ever worry," Ravell said, "that your wife may be feeling terribly despondent after all this? There are women who lose their will to live—"

"Not Erika," Peter said. "She has great zest for life. She's indomitable."

Was Peter blinded by his own optimism, by his own gusto? Ravell wondered. Did the man know his own wife at all? Ravell gulped from a glass of ice water, then fingered the tines of his fork. Their white plates shone, clean and ready. The rack of lamb they'd ordered seemed a long time in arriving.

"At this stage," Peter said, "I know some might suggest mixing my seed with another man's. But I won't have it. If I were interested in adopting another man's child, we'd have done that years ago. Besides," he reasoned, "why fool ourselves? If I've fathered a child, I want to know it's mine. I never want to wonder if it's somebody else's."

Their lunch arrived. The waiter replaced the cold white plates before them with hot plates laden with lamb that sizzled and steamed and ran with rich juices. Peter spooned dollops of mint jelly onto each bite with the delight of a boy who relished huge helpings of sweets. "Erika is giving a private recital at our home for my birthday," Peter said. "And she has promised to sing my favorite arias. We'd like to invite you."

Ravell longed to hear her sing again. Peter's enthusiasm welled up as he described the fine musicians he'd hired to accompany her, the turquoise damask dress he'd bought for Erika to wear at the event. "The dress is from Paris," he said. "From Worth. I owe it to her, after all she's endured. Besides, what could give me more pleasure on my birthday than to see my wife looking luscious?" He winked.

After the party, Peter would leave for Egypt, where he had dealings with cotton merchants. From Cairo he would head to England to purchase the latest textile machinery. He would be gone for two months.

Erika would not be joining him because she had singing engagements at the Handel and Haydn Society, as well as at the new palazzo Mrs. Isabella Stewart Gardner had recently opened on the Fenway.

Since he would be gone for many weeks, Peter suggested that he might leave semen samples on ice, ready to be thawed and used on his wife in his absence. "Before I leave"—Peter leaned across the tablecloth and spoke in confidence—"perhaps you might be willing to come to the house? Perhaps on the night of my birthday recital, after the guests are gone? I think my wife and I might be more relaxed there. Things might go better at home, in our own bed, than they have gone at your office. Erika could drift to sleep afterward, and not stir until morning."

The invitation to enter their home intrigued Ravell. The rooms that people inhabited, he'd found, always mirrored unseen aspects of their souls. He was curious to see the paintings they'd chosen, to hear his own steps creak along the staircase they descended every day. He pictured himself opening the lid of Erika's piano and brushing his knuckles across the ivories. He nodded as Peter talked. Ravell agreed to everything, the way one humors a child. What harm could come from pretending—at least for now—that the ghost of Peter's future son or daughter might actually become real? Why crush a man's hopes just before his birthday?

And so Ravell let Peter go on speaking and imagining.

"All I am asking is for a lucky thing to happen once," Peter said. "For one child, boy or girl—I adore small children, their spark. To me, they're like puppies. They're eager to know all they can about the world. Children are always staring," Peter went on. "Have you noticed that? They may stumble, but they pick themselves up and charge ahead."

Like you, Ravell thought.

"If I had a child, I'd never stop teaching it things. . . . Last time I sailed to Europe, a tiny Italian girl saw me on the deck. She must have been about two. She left her mother and came right over to me. I held her in my lap and she opened her little fists and pointed upward. You know what she was after? She wanted me to grab a bird out of the sky and give it to her."

"I have no doubt that you would make a profoundly good father," Ravell said.

They left the Algonquin Club in separate carriages. Ravell headed toward the hospital, Peter toward his offices on Congress Street. Ravell told the driver to let him off early, a few blocks from his destination, so that he could stroll for a few minutes through a park.

On the icy path Ravell's shoes slid against the glaze. A stout nursemaid in uniform wheeled a sleeping baby in a pram, mincing her steps to keep from slipping. Near the pond, two mothers kept watch over young boys who poked and pushed toy boats through the cold water with long sticks. Children ran in circles, their aimless zigzags serving to heat their bodies on this chilly March day. Seeing families on benches, he wondered why he had held himself apart from all of this.

Old dowagers sometimes patted his arm and asked, "Why isn't a handsome young fellow like you married, Doctor Ravell?"

"How can I marry?" he would say, smiling, in response. "It wouldn't be fair to a wife. I'd be up half the night, delivering other ladies' babies."

The truth was that he was fond of all women. He could never believe he had fallen in love for the last time; that was his failing. He looked forward to appointments with a patient so rotund that she barely squeezed through a doorway—because she blurted jokes that made him drop his stethoscope and laugh. Among his favorites were elderly ladies who no longer bothered to gaze at themselves in mirrors; they looked outward, gasping and rejoicing over lapdogs, children, blooming peonies. He missed young mothers whose deaths haunted him—patients whose wrists had gone limp in his hand as he'd searched in vain for a pulse.

How could he ever manage a wife, with so many patients? Their needs sometimes exhausted him. By day's end, he could not have gone upstairs to his rooms and listened to a wife's problems. At suppertime he occasionally took a book and carried his plate into his study just to escape the chatter of his housekeeper.

Still, he wondered if he kept himself from being fully alive by never marrying. At the park a boy held up a baseball glove to catch a ball and missed; the ball landed at Ravell's feet and he reached down and threw it back. Would he never watch his own child being born? Would he remain an observer, in service to others' lives?

He understood Peter's longings more than he dared to say.

4

"It's still a tad early, Doctor," the parlor maid confided in a rough, splintery whisper as she opened the door. "The musicians are upstairs, rehearsing with Madame von Kessler." In the entry hall Ravell took a seat on the velvet cushion of a carved bench. The maid put a finger to her lips as they both heard violins strike up overhead.

The stringed instruments soared in unison, in an exuberance of wings. Erika von Kessler's voice swooped in and caught the air currents of the violins, leading them heavenward. Phrases of the aria she sang—Handel's "Va col canto"—echoed down the wide black walnut staircase.

The thin parlor maid folded Ravell's coat over her arm, her wiry gray hair pinned tightly against her head. Then, with a whimsy Ravell would never have expected from a woman her age, she smiled and rose up on her toes like a ballerina and danced into a dim corridor, out of sight.

It was a stately house—narrow and vertical like the other brick residences on Beacon Street. The entry hall was unusually spacious, with dark wallpaper that had the sheen of gilded leather, imported from somewhere exotic—Morocco, perhaps. While Ravell waited alone, he reached out and touched the wall's leathery paper with its embossed filigree.

Just as the aria ended, Peter appeared from a side staircase that ran five stories from top to bottom of the house. "Forgive me," he said, breathless, pulling on his French cuffs before he clasped Ravell's hand. "When I heard the bell, I put my head out the window and saw you standing on the front steps—but I found myself standing three stories above you with not a stitch of clothing on my body!" He and Ravell both laughed.

After all the guests had arrived, they took their cue and headed upstairs to the music room, where Erika stood near the piano singing "Voi che sapete" from *Le nozze di Figaro,* her shoulders half-exposed in a dress that shimmered like pale turquoise water. She placed one hand on the piano, welcoming everyone with her other arm outstretched.

The fashionable white woodwork made the music room feel larger and more airy than anywhere else in the high, narrow house. As she moved through more Handel and Mozart, to "Caro mio ben," her eyes glittered and skimmed across the audience. *I always search for a face I can sing to,* Erika had told Ravell. Tonight he hoped that face would be his own. When she broke into a flirtatious "Havanaise" and "Près des remparts de Séville" from *Carmen,* she tilted her shoulders and swished her skirts at her husband, and then she glanced at Ravell, as if to say, *After the rest of the guests leave, it will be just us here—Peter, you, and me.* The giddiness in her expression was impossible to miss.

The enthusiasm of the audience was so great that they demanded encore after encore, until she finally refused to sing anymore. Rings of light shone on her half-bared shoulders. Her face was luminous, moist with exertion. How different she seemed here, Ravell thought, than when she sat in his consulting room. He imagined that if they extinguished every light in the house, her face would remain visible in the dark, incandescent. He wondered if she, like so many artists, suffered from periods of manic euphoria—followed by debilitating gloom.

They raised champagne flutes and toasted Peter's birthday; they ate mint ice cream and hazelnut torte. As the party wound to a close, her brother, Doctor Gerald von Kessler, lingered in the entry hall with Ravell. It appeared they would be the last guests to go.

Erika had already declared herself exhausted and she'd bid her brother good night and gone upstairs. For the sake of appearances, she'd also made a show of saying farewell to Ravell, although their business for the evening was hardly finished.

"May I drop you somewhere?" Doctor von Kessler asked Ravell, opening the front door for them to exit together.

Ravell glanced at Peter. Peter stared at him. They had made no firm plan, no excuse for him to remain after the other guests had departed.

"My place isn't far," Ravell told von Kessler. "Just over on Commonwealth Avenue. I'm in the mood for a little brisk exercise."

"I'll walk with you," Doctor von Kessler offered, clearly intent on further conversation. His wife had gone to New Hampshire to visit her sister, who'd recently given birth to a sixth child, so he was alone.

Ravell could think of no graceful way to refuse his company. Under a streetlight near the curb, von Kessler's handsome brougham waited. The driver had dozed off. Doctor von Kessler nudged the man awake, and instructed the driver to meet them over at Ravell's address.

As they walked, von Kessler adjusted his muffler. "So how is the treatment progressing? Are my sister and her husband—?"

Ravell avoided answering. At Clarendon Street, as a cart clattered past in the darkness, he put out an arm to caution his companion before crossing.

"I don't mean to pry," Doctor von Kessler said, "but it's dreadfully hard on Erika, prolonging things."

Ravell sensed the doubts and barely disguised judgments of the other physician. *If you don't feel capable of handling the case—just say so,* von Kessler might as well have been saying, *and we'll move on to another man in the profession who may be.*

"What's the prognosis? Is my sister able to conceive, in your estimation?"

"Your sister is as fertile as any woman in my practice."

"Then *why*—?" von Kessler said, frowning.

"Confidentiality is at stake here," Ravell said. "If you persist in conveying such impatience to your sister, it won't help matters."

Under a lamppost on Marlborough Street, von Kessler stopped midstride. A tall, large man, he loomed over Ravell in the darkness. "Are there techniques you haven't tried? Is there any cause for optimism?"

With all the bravado he could muster, Ravell caught himself uttering words he knew he should not have said. "Of course. Absolutely." At this, the other man's shoulders softened and relaxed, and Ravell felt he had just made an awkward promise.

By the time they reached Ravell's house on Commonwealth Avenue, von Kessler's rig was waiting at the curb. Once again they had to rouse the driver, a man who clearly had a gift for dozing anywhere. The other physician raised his hat to Ravell as they drove off.

The telephone was ringing inside his office as Ravell unlocked the door. He hastened to catch it before the caller hung up.

"Are you coming back to the house?" Peter said. "We are waiting for you. *Knock softly,*" he added, "*so as not to wake the servants.*"

❖

It was Peter himself who opened the stout front door as soon as Ravell's knuckles grazed the wood. Peter tightened the belt of his silk dressing gown, which he wore over pajamas. "I thought we'd never be rid of my brother-in-law," he muttered.

As they stole up the grand public staircase (the steps creaked less there than on the second, narrower staircase along the side of the house, Peter confided), Ravell wondered if he ought to be carrying his shoes in his hand. Peter led him into the family's private quarters, careful to lock the bedroom door behind them.

Erika lay on a peach velvet chaise longue in her own silk robe and matching gown, reading a ladies' magazine. "I see you've come to help us out," she remarked, sounding amused.

He'd never seen her hair fully unleashed from its pompadour before; it rippled and streamed across the back of the chaise, the strands reaching her elbows. Contrary to what she'd told her brother, she didn't appear fatigued after her performance. With her body outlined under silk, she looked ready to leap, quite impetuously, from her long chair.

A chambermaid had already turned down the fine linens of their great bamboo bed. The pillows lay smooth, the sheets folded back in parallel triangles, his and hers. The bed had been a wedding gift, built in Japan, they told Ravell.

24

"This isn't the sort of house call I usually make," Ravell said lightly. He thought of the great Doctor Sims. Back in the 1840s and 1850s, Doctor Sims had not hesitated to bring his newfangled instruments into a married couple's home and stand at the ready, behind a wall, to assist conception—an arrangement that shocked any number of people.

"I suppose we ought to begin," Peter said, his hands hidden in the pockets of his long robe.

The three of them looked at one another. Ravell brought his heels together and stood straighter. He reached into his black bag and gave Peter a special condom, telling him that he should use it with care so that not a drop of his precious seed would be lost. Ravell explained that he would reappear afterward to aim the syringe directly into the opening of the womb. The quick injection might prevent the sperm from tiring on their journey, and from going astray. The syringe might carry the seed more effectively—even faster into a wife's depths—than nature could.

Erika and Peter knew such things by now, of course. "Have you any other advice for us?" Peter joked.

"Enjoy yourselves," Ravell said. "And let me know when you've finished." He took his black leather medical bag and found his own way through the adjoining room, which happened to be a bathroom. From there he wandered into what appeared to be Peter's private study and latched the door.

To distract himself, Ravell picked up a stereoscope. He inserted photographs Peter kept of bazaars in Cairo, and of serpentine streets and arches that might be located, Ravell guessed, in Morocco. Held up to the light, viewed through the stereoscope, the scenes shifted in the brain and became three-dimensional, so that he felt himself step inside dusty North African towns where he had never been.

When he heard the quickening of her breaths in the other room, he put down the slides and the stereoscope and shut his eyes. The door was closed, but he heard them nonetheless. He could not focus on anything else. Not a sound came from Peter, only from her. Her gasps heated up in a mounting crescendo. Something thudded. (A foot or leg against the bamboo bed?)

Ravell walked the circuit of Peter's study, trying to mask the echoes of lovemaking with his own footsteps. He leaned closer to inspect a dozen framed images on the walls—a series of butterflies Peter had painted (Morphos, *Caligos,* extraordinary specimens)—all exquisite miniatures, absolutely true to nature, the colors applied with a hair-thin brush. Normally such paintings would have ensnared Ravell's complete attention.

But not tonight.

Peter's instincts had been good. He had predicted that after a performance, his wife's every pore would open in a kind of radiance. Privately Ravell had to agree: if there was ever a time to impregnate her, tonight was surely it. Was this the same woman who had complained to him—to the point of weeping—about her husband's obsessive tracking of her periods, his habit of picking up undergarments she'd dropped to the floor and turning them inside out, checking for blood?

How relaxed she had seemed tonight when he, her doctor, had entered the bedroom. He'd worried that she might resent his presence, but clearly she wasn't minding the intrusion at all. In the adjacent room, the bamboo wedding bed squeaked like an object vibrating on a factory chassis. Ravell envisioned it shuttling back and forth at a rate faster than the human eye could measure. His chest hurt from the effort of trying not to make a sound, as though something sacred were occurring behind that closed door.

She began to use her voice, issuing more than pants of pleasure. He heard hints of the music they'd all reveled in earlier, her back probably curved, her mouth open as notes leaped from her.

He couldn't recall ever having been in such a position before. In hotels, yes. But not as a physician. No other couple had ever suggested that he embroil himself like this.

Why had he come? He didn't really believe he could help Peter impregnate her, did he?

So why had he come—to torment himself? He rubbed his palm across his face as roughly as if he were washing it. It was unbearable to think, just now, of ruining their hopes. And the elation in Erika that he'd seen tonight—he wanted to keep sparks of that alive. Yet the fact was that Peter's sterility could not be changed. Ravell shut his eyes at the thought. *I will deal with the consequences of that later,* he decided.

In the corner of the study Peter kept a huge birdcage. Either Peter or one of the servants had draped a cover over the bars to help the creature sleep. Ravell lifted the cloth to peek. A gorgeous parrot balanced on a swing, its feathers saturated with scarlet, yellows, and cobalt blue. Ravell removed the cover completely to have a better look.

The parrot's clawed feet shifted on the bar. The cage trembled as the bird awoke.

"Kiss me!" it squawked. "Kiss me!"

Ravell threw the cover back over the bars and the bird went silent.

When Peter appeared, blinking hard against the light, he handed Ravell a small balloon filled with whitish liquid. "Did the parrot wake up?" he asked, incredulous. Ravell quickly turned away and reached into his medical bag, wiping his smile away with his hand.

Erika lay on the bed, fully draped in her silks. Her skin was moist, her cheeks and forehead flushed. The smell of sex filled the room, though she'd tried to disguise it by spraying herself with an atomizer that rested, half-full, on the night table. Her thighs were damp with the spray she'd flashed across them, preparing herself for the doctor. The fragrance was fruity with cherries.

Peter held a bright light for the doctor as Ravell prepared his instruments. He took the condom and siphoned its contents between Erika's open legs. Meticulously he completed his work.

In his dressing robe and slippers, Peter escorted the doctor through the dark house. At the front door, Peter rose up on the balls of his feet, looking pleased. "Maybe tonight will be the turning point," he said.

Ravell had taken care to save the condom that Peter had given him. In the small hours of the night, back in his office, he cut off the end of the rubber he'd tied so precisely, and extracted an unused portion of residue from the condom's interior. He smeared a few drops across a slide, and peered at this second sample. He squinted, watching for anything to float into view, but saw nothing that swam or wiggled or flitted past. The second sample, too, was as lifeless as water siphoned from the Dead Sea.

5

"I no longer wish to become a mother," Erika said. In his medical office she sat dressed in a smart blue-gray suit with velvet lapels, nipped and tailored to display her slim waist. On her head she wore a matching blue toque, pinned at a fashionable angle against her hair.

She's in despair again, Ravell thought. *She cannot really mean this.*

He listened. Her husband had gone away on business, she said, and when he returned, he would find his life forever changed. "I know I'm about to cause him great sadness," she added.

He kept his eyes on her for so long that she finally glanced away from him—out of embarrassment, perhaps. She tilted her chin upward as if to scan the spines of the medical texts on his shelves. Clearly she had made some sort of decision: he sensed an underlying cheerfulness in her, and that worried him. Yet he still could not be certain that she was a person on the brink of extinguishing her own life. Less than a week previously, Ravell had entered her bedroom and smelled her as she lay in her nest of silks. He'd heard her every inhalation of pleasure. She was a woman of emotions and appetites so strong that she forgot—at least for the duration of lovemaking—why her husband had ever irritated her.

"What are you planning to do that might cause Peter such sadness?"

She would not answer. There was finality in every sharp turn of her head. If she walked out of his practice today, he knew she would not return. (*"I warned you,"* her sister-in-law might rail at him later. *"And you did nothing."*) The prospect that he would disappoint Peter and Erika and all the von Kesslers—that these efforts might provoke a tragedy—sank through him.

Why had he lied to her brother in such a foolhardy way? Insinuating that he could cure what could not be changed? In the end they would believe the failure was his.

He had it in his power to save her life, if that was really what was at stake here. He could satisfy them all. It would be easy enough.

But I cannot do it, he thought. *I would never do such a thing.*

"So—" he said. "You are refusing to seek my help in trying to conceive? Is that what you mean?"

"I've come to say good-bye to you," Erika said.

He felt alarm pulse in his wrists. *I am at my best in times of trouble,* he thought. *At moments of greatest emergency.* Others depended on his ability to rush into a dark room where a dire scene was unfolding and react as if by instinct. It was a gift he had: he could decide a thing quickly, in a flash of light from an opening door. In this way he had pulled forth babies from wombs that might soon have become graves; he had revived half-conscious mothers and staved off more deaths than he could remember.

A doctor is supposed to save lives, he thought, *by any possible means. Erika has been tortured by this situation long enough,* he decided. His leg muscles flexed; he prepared to rise from his chair. Above all, he must keep her from walking through the door and disappearing.

"Erika," he said, and leaned across the desk. "Are you depressed?"

She stared at him. "Of course," she said. "About all this? What else am I supposed to feel?"

"Peter has left frozen samples of his semen," he reminded her. "We've all agreed to work on this in his absence."

She twisted her neck to one side, as if to relieve a crick.

"This is hardly fair to Peter," Ravell argued. "I made a promise to him, and I feel a certain loyalty to the agreement, not only as a physician but as a friend. When Peter returns—if we haven't had any good fortune by then—maybe we can discuss the situation and reconsider matters then.

"I've already thawed the sample for today," Ravell added. "It wouldn't be right to waste it."

At first Erika appeared unmoved, and then a quake of exasperation went through her. "All right," she said, sighing. "But it's futile. And this is going to be the last time."

A radiance carried him then, and his heart beat hard, knowing that he was about to take a terrible chance. *Whatever happens,* he decided, *I'll cope with any unpleasantness that arises.* He ushered her to the examination room where she began, with a few resentful mutters, to undress. Her chest thrust forward as she arched her back and shrugged off her jacket with its velvet lapels.

"I'll be back in a few minutes," Ravell said. He hurried to the closet-like chamber where he kept his microscope and locked the door. The dish containing Peter's specimen waited on the counter. Ravell turned on the tap and carefully washed away every trace of Peter's semen. Then Ravell shut off the light and loosened his suspenders, unfastened his trousers and underwear, and let everything drop to the floor. He took himself in his own hand. Madness! He would never have condoned such a thing before, but now he had no time for self-doubt. He had to hurry. When Peter stood in this space, he'd been given a book illustrated with Parisian prostitutes, but he, the doctor, had no such luxury. He kept the chamber dark, and remembered how her breasts had moved, loose, unleashed under peach silk.

The nurse rapped sharply on every closed door in the corridor, searching, calling his name in a bewildered tone. "Doctor Ravell?"

"Yes!" he managed to answer.

"We're ready for you."

He groped in the darkness and found a dish he knew would be lying on the counter, and replaced Peter's seed with his own. He flicked on a light and buttoned his trousers. His tongue felt swollen in his mouth.

Dutifully the nurse remained in the exam room, a reassuring, motherly presence. Ravell took the dish and suctioned the pale substance into a long instrument. He lifted the drape covering Erika's lower body.

The nurse stood by, a sentry in a corner. She was supposed to serve as a guard of sorts—but what, she and Erika might have wondered, did they need to guard against? Doctor Ravell was a reputable man; he had never done such a thing before, and surely never would. Part of the drape had slid from Erika's thigh, exposing her there, but she did not bother to cover herself.

With his shoulders, Ravell blocked the nurse's view. No one could see inside his mind, but he worried that they might hear how loudly he inhaled and exhaled, the harsh beat of his pulse inside his ears.

"Don't mix mine with another man's," Peter had said. Peter who had read so many articles and obstetrical books.

Ravell had done no mixing. He used only his own.

6

"Come early," her voice teacher had encouraged her. "We can have sherry and a few good laughs before the famous lady arrives."

So Erika went early. Attired in her blue-gray suit with its velvet lapels, she walked several blocks through the Back Bay. The suit was new—she'd worn it only twice before, once to Doctor Ravell's office—and its style and trim fit pleased her and invigorated her step. On her head she wore the matching blue-gray toque adorned with a flat satin bow. The bluster of the wind forced her to keep one hand pressed to her hat to prevent it from being snatched, pins and all, right off her pompadour.

When she reached her voice teacher's town house on Marlborough Street, the glass in the bay window assumed the purple cast of dusk, as though the panes had been glazed. The front door swung open. Sixty years old and handsome still, Magdalena Hasselbach beckoned Erika into the solarium, where a grand silver tea set and a walnut cream cake had been placed. Anticipation lit her teacher's movements. Magdalena touched her queenly white coiffure, fluffing and smoothing it in excitement. Inside Magdalena's broad chest, laughter welled up. She laughed easily, and beneath her breathlessness, Erika heard familiar wheezes. Asthma had ended Magdalena's singing career.

"So, *mein Schatz,* my treasure," Magdalena said, "are you ready to meet America's most famous diva?"

"The *most* famous?"

"On an international scale, she's the most well-known singer New England has ever produced."

The voice teacher had met the legendary Lillian Nordica long ago in St. Petersburg, where they had performed together for the czar. "We'll have to think of an excuse for you to sing for her," Magdalena said.

"You promised her that she wouldn't be coming here to audition anybody."

"In any case," Magdalena said, regretting her ruses, "it's essential for you to meet her. And if I still had a voice—a voice like yours—I would not be bashful."

"I'm not going to risk annoying her," Erika said.

"If the opportunity presents itself, you might try 'Caro mio ben' or one of your lovely Handel arias."

"Not unless she asks me," Erika said.

"Don't fool yourself into thinking that she'll hear you perform at Isabella Stewart Gardner's palace. Believe me, she won't be listening to the singers that precede her. She'll be hiding somewhere, preparing for her own grand act."

Magdalena strode over to the dark purple velvet drapes to scan the street for signs of Lillian Nordica. When a brougham approached and a stately lady with a great ostrich feather in her hat stepped down from the carriage, Erika and her teacher hurried downstairs.

❖

"Surely the life of a great soprano has its difficulties," Magdalena said. "Don't you sometimes feel that people romanticize—? Don't they overlook the hardships of a singer's life?"

"Indeed." Madame Nordica gave a nod. "Few have any inkling of what a lonesome life it can be. One finds oneself in a sterile hotel room . . . or one ends up spending the night in a Pullman car traveling between Kansas City and Minneapolis."

"Or enjoying Paris?" Magdalena said.

"Or fighting seasickness on a boat between Dublin and Liverpool," Madame Nordica finished, dismissing any nuance of glamour. "The important thing is that one must be a trouper. People say that prima donnas

34

are temperamental creatures. Let me assure you, I'm so busy making certain that my gowns will be fresh for the next performance . . . or keeping scarves wrapped around my head to prevent colds . . . I don't have the slightest energy left over for histrionics except onstage."

While seated in concert halls, Erika had never realized what a physically massive person Lillian Nordica was. Onstage she appeared the size of an ordinary woman, but in the intimacy of this solarium, seated on a Turkish sofa surrounded by potted palms, Madame Nordica appeared taller than Erika's own father. The diva had wrists as thick as a man's ankles.

"What sort of advice would you give to a young woman who wishes . . . to further her operatic career?" Magdalena said, and moved her eyes meaningfully toward Erika.

For the first time that evening, Madame Nordica shifted her knees and regarded Erika, who was seated next to her on the sofa. A thousand times before, no doubt, the diva had been asked to guide aspiring singers. Counsel flowed from her like lines rehearsed.

"Go to Italy," was the first directive she had to offer. "The first step, as I would advise anyone, is *to get yourself to Italy*. Select a reputable teacher, start studying repertory there."

Erika sat up straighter and slid closer to the sofa's edge. Only to her voice teacher had Erika already confided the plan that had been taking wing in her own breast. For months now, she had been intending to leave Boston, to leave Peter and move permanently to Europe for the sake of bettering her voice and expanding herself professionally.

"You wouldn't consider a move to Paris?" Erika asked.

"The French language ruins the voice," Madame Nordica declared, the ostrich feather on her hat shaking for emphasis. "Italian is far easier for singing. Besides, the cost of living is lower in Italy than in France or Germany. Also, in Italy you have more than eighty small towns where opera is performed. In Italy, even poor farmers attend opera. To them"— she extended her velvet sleeves horizontally, with theatrical flourish— "opera is a necessity."

As a young girl, Madame Nordica had trained at the New England Conservatory, where Erika herself had studied. Among Bostonians, the story of Lillian Nordica's ascent as an opera star had spread far. At twenty, Madame Nordica had journeyed to Milan, chaperoned by her widowed mother. In Italy, in a minor city, Lillian Nordica had sung in her first performance. On opening night, all her arias were encored. Eight curtain calls followed Act I. At the death scene, middle-aged men in the audience wept. The very next morning a hundred people swarmed in the street below her hotel room balcony, and they had cried, *"Nordica! Grandissimo talento!"*

The three women paused to taste the walnut cream cake Magdalena had sliced. Madame Nordica drew the empty fork from her mouth and tilted her head dreamily as she chewed. In a generous gesture, she reached over and patted Erika's knee.

It dawned on Erika that Madame Nordica probably mistook her for a woman much younger than she actually was. *Does she think I'm a sprite of eighteen?* Erika wondered. *A girl who can simply pack her bags and sail off to Italy without remorse or consequence to others' lives? Without summoning up a terrible courage?*

Detractors said that Madame Nordica, now sliding toward fifty, risked losing her upper register. At her most recent engagements in Boston, however, the ovations had lasted fifteen minutes. The public had thrown carpets of blossoms at Lillian Nordica's feet. Yet at this moment in Magdalena's solarium (and who would have dreamed such a meeting could happen?), the three of them sat so close that as the soprano swallowed her tea, Erika could see the wrinkled skin move on the great diva's neck.

The three women had been conversing for an hour when Madame Nordica brushed crumbs from her lips with a napkin and stared with sudden interest at Erika. "Doesn't she have a lovely-shaped face?" the opera singer remarked to Magdalena. "If she decides not to sing, she can always become a hat model or something."

The comment left Erika feeling both flattered and diminished. As

Magdalena refilled their cups, her eyebrows arched with inquiry: "Cream? Sugar? Lemon?" Her lips closed together in a humorless line, and Erika realized that her teacher did not especially care for Madame Nordica. Magdalena squeezed sour lemon into her tea until the cream separated and curdled.

"The thing I don't understand," Erika said, "is how an American goes from being a student to being a bona fide diva in Italy. She just auditions everywhere, is that it?"

Madame Nordica rested a heavy-boned hand on Erika's arm, as if to impart something essential. "In Italy your teacher will arrange your debut. Your teacher will know an agent who selects artists and creates companies. An impresario from Acqui or a lesser city may come to a teacher seeking singers for *Norma* or *Ernani*.

"But let's suppose," she went on, "that the student dreams of doing *Traviata* or *Sonnambula*. The impresario may agree to alter the repertory, but only if she reimburses him to the tune of two or three hundred lire—"

Magdalena's spine flinched and became erect with indignation when she heard this. "And you advise the young woman to pay such a sum?"

"Yes," Madame Nordica replied. "It's only fair to the impresario. Think of the risk he takes. He supplies the theatre, and he hires the orchestra and the rest of the cast. He lets this unknown foreign student assume the limelight in a role of her choice. Why should he agree to let this foreigner succeed or create a fiasco?

"Think of the expenditure as an outlay for training," the diva advised. "Opera is an expensive profession. And if you're successful," she added, with another pat to Erika's knee, "you'll have a chance of getting a genuine offer."

And if the debut were a failure? Erika wondered. That was a scenario Lillian Nordica did not consider, any more than she recognized that the "young lady" to whom she offered counsel was nearly twenty-nine, already encumbered with a husband and a five-story town house filled with servants.

Upon departing, Madame Nordica stood in the foyer wearing her lapis lazuli necklace and a fur coat that made her look like a hunter's grizzly. She placed a crisp white card in Erika's hand with the address of her personal agent printed in raised letters upon it. "Should you ever need the name of an eminent teacher in Italy," the diva said, "do write my agent. He will gladly name you several."

When the door fell shut behind the famous singer, Erika felt a draft of cold night air pass over her head. "She did not so much as ask to hear you sing," Magdalena said.

Hurrying home on foot, Erika touched the sharp edges of the card in her pocket. Under a lamppost on Dartmouth Street, she held it up to the light to see the agent's name. The letters had been embossed like Braille onto the card; she could read the name with a finger.

She had forgotten her house key, so she had to ring the bell. For weeks now, her husband had been away doing business in England and Egypt. One of the servants let her in.

"We've kept your supper warm for you, ma'am," the cook said.

At the long mahogany table where Erika found herself alone on many nights, the servant set the meal before her—slices of pork with sautéed apples, creamed onions, mashed potatoes.

"Will you be needing anything else, ma'am?" the cook asked.

Erika shook her head. "It's late now. Why don't you get some sleep? I'll leave the dishes in the butler's pantry when I'm finished."

The cook nodded, wiped her hands on her apron, and left. Erika cut her meat into small pieces and paused to sip the burgundy that was the same color as the room's flocked wallpaper.

"It must be hard on you," friends sometimes observed, "that Peter travels so much."

The fact that she was often alone meant that she had to fill the hours and her heart with something apart from him. Especially during his absences, her voice had bloomed. Music invaded her with wildness, overtaking everything. It consumed more hours of her life than a husband or a child could ever have done.

The servants were accustomed to holding her dinner late while Peter was gone. Sometimes Erika did not eat before ten o'clock at night because she had been sitting at the piano, not wanting to stop until she had sung through an entire opera. The notes under her fingers led her onward. She conversed with the music, with imaginary characters who sang in reply.

In just a few weeks Peter would be back. Usually when his homecoming neared, she felt a small dread, knowing that soon she must sink back into the limits of wifely routine. Dinner at seven, bed by the early hour of ten. No more running off by herself to attend evening concerts. No lingering by the gramophone, listening to Nellie Melba past midnight. When Peter was home, she felt she ought to awake with him at six, and take breakfast with him before a carriage bore him off to the office.

Peter had noticed (how could he fail to notice?) that her voice was gathering acclaim. More offers for recitals and concerts had come, including engagements with the Handel and Haydn Society. A man from London had urged Erika to let him manage her career.

"Promise that you won't leave me?" he once murmured as they lay in bed. "Not even when they try to lure you away to Covent Garden or La Scala?" He meant it as a little joke, but to her, the vision of having a larger career felt real.

Peter did not want a wife who lived apart from him in Europe. Whenever she had broached the possibility, he had become dismissive. He was tall, with princely good looks that made ladies pause in the street to stare at him. A man of bullish enthusiasm, he had a knack for bending others to his way of thinking. He often won her over with his body.

Within minutes of his homecoming after a trip abroad, he would bound up the staircase with her, locking the door against overly attentive servants, drawing the shades. She'd hardly missed him at all, she thought, until he'd appeared in the foyer and she'd seen him again—the glint of many colors in his hair, strands of russet, bronze, and gold. As he removed his jacket, she saw the taut muscles in his slim hips; she knew their shape even before she placed her hands against them. In the bedroom she quickly kissed his face, and found his cheek perspiring. Her lips came away with the taste of salt. She could never pack trunks and get away to

Italy with Peter present in the house. The pull of him was as hard as an undertow; she could drown in it.

Like a pair of athletes, they were often collapsing, spent, with pumping hearts and glistening skin against the bed. But if it were not for the physical, without that, what did they have in common? She with her scales and cadenzas, he with his ledgers that recorded clever bargains he'd made for shipments of cotton from the Minet-el-Bassal?

What did they have, really, to talk about? He barely cared about music. If not for lust, would they even be friends?

While he was absent for long stretches, she almost forgot that he was part of her life. During the weeks he'd been away, as her throat vibrated with song and her fingers trembled over the ivory keys, she, too, had gone to another place.

And she loathed the thought that when he returned, he'd resume his zealous quest to conceive a child. Why did he need a child so much? It used to depress her, too—their lack of children—but no longer. She had sung her way past it.

❖

That night Erika was too elated and too full of plans to sleep. She enjoyed having the bed to herself. When the bed was all hers, she could lie diagonally across it, arms flung overhead, toes resting against the bamboo footboard.

If she meant to make a new life in Italy, she knew she ought to book her passage and leave before he returned. She would be twenty-nine on her next birthday. She could no longer allow Peter to silence her.

"In the great design of fate," Madame Nordica had said tonight, "there are no accidents. It is fascinating to look back at obstacles and realize how they were overcome. I have an absolute belief in destiny."

Tonight's instructions from Madame Nordica would alter her own life, she felt certain. The diva's words had been like a finger pointing to the moon. Erika now understood—unequivocally—where she must head.

7

On the day she was scheduled to sing at Isabella Stewart Gardner's grand new palace, Erika telephoned her voice teacher and begged: "Can you listen to me sing this dreadful note?" Erika held the receiver as far from her mouth as possible, and let the phrase escape through open lips.

"Nothing in that aria is beyond you," Magdalena assured her. "Before you leave this afternoon, try to take a deep, hot bath. After that, I want you to place a butterscotch candy on your tongue and keep it there—just to relax the muscles—while you sing the same note you just sang to me."

During its years of construction, the palazzo Isabella Stewart Gardner had been building over on the Fenway had been closed off like a secret. Not even Mrs. Gardner's closest friends had been permitted to view what lay behind its fortresslike walls until she had every statue, every orchid, every painting, every Venetian balustrade, perfectly positioned. On New Year's Day in 1903—just a few months previously—Mrs. Gardner had finally opened the doors to the most eminent of her acquaintances. They had driven up in their carriages at nine o'clock in the evening, and the next day newspapers burst with accounts of what her guests had found there.

Since then, several concerts had been given at Fenway Court. On the afternoon when Erika first entered Mrs. Gardner's palace, the musicians and soloists were invited to wander freely through the grand rooms, as if the private art collection belonged to them.

Erika's trepidation about the performance vanished as soon as she stepped inside, for she had never known a place that soothed her so. The great courtyard with its arched Venetian windows opened before her, welcoming her with its fountain, its vast shaft of light, its potted mimosas and stone urns and softening ferns. A glass ceiling protected everything. Tonight she would sing one aria in the courtyard, while standing on the Roman mosaic tiles near a tiny sarcophagus. Other soloists would be stationed on the upper balconies so that their voices would erupt from various levels of the building, like surprises.

As Erika walked through the Raphael Room, the Dutch Room, the Titian Room, she felt as if she were inside a private home rather than a museum. Mrs. Gardner now resided on the palazzo's uppermost floor. Erika could hardly believe that one individual—a widow in her sixties—had fought so relentlessly to gather things she loved from around the world and bring them all here. Mrs. Gardner, everyone said, had fussed over the placement of each object, setting a vase or a small painting next to a window to make it gleam.

Although Erika had never met her, she had glimpsed Mrs. Gardner twice in a brougham on Beacon Street, riding past.

Standing at an arched Venetian window that overlooked the courtyard, Erika was startled by the sounds of birds, a glance of wings flitting against the stucco walls. Mrs. Gardner must have ordered them released from cages to add a dash of whimsy.

Erika could not decide what captivated her more—the art or the architecture that housed the collection. In nearly every room, she wandered from the paintings to the balcony windows, drawn to look upon the courtyard gardens from above.

I could already be in Italy, Erika thought as she leaned her forearms against the balustrade and drank in the light, the archways, and the delphiniums.

Three stories below, the musicians were tuning up. For the few remaining moments before the rehearsal began, she lingered at an open window. Tonight Madame Nordica would perform here. Erika and the other soloists would emerge, one by one, in a kind of preshow tribute to the renowned diva. Two hundred guests would arrive and wander through the public rooms, surveying the art prior to the concert. No one could be present in the palace, with its arched windows open to the courtyard, without hearing Erika's aria. For the few brief minutes when she was singing, her voice would be everywhere, as pervasive as air and light. Everyone would hear her—even the great Nordica, whether she cared to listen or not.

Afterward, at precisely nine o'clock in the evening, the two hundred guests would file into the Music Room at Fenway Court for a formal concert. The Cecilia Society would sing, and as a sumptuous finale, Madame Nordica would spread her arms draped in wide sleeves of velvet, and the famous soprano would dazzle them all.

The strings sounded fiercer now, a signal for Erika to clutch her skirts and hasten down two flights. She took her place next to the sarcophagus. It was a strangely small container—no body larger than a very young child's could have lain inside it. As she closed her eyes, quieting her heart, preparing to sing, she recalled what everyone in the Back Bay knew: Mrs. Gardner and her late husband had only had one child, a son who had died of pneumonia before his second birthday. Erika opened her eyes and glanced at the child's sarcophagus again—no lid on its stone. The coffin lay open, and empty. A baby might have risen from it and gone through the skylight to heaven, leaving Mrs. Gardner with no one to mother— and all this to create.

If I had children, Erika thought, *perhaps I would not be here, nor would I be on my way to Italy very soon.* She was certain that Mrs. Gardner had placed this infant's sarcophagus in her courtyard for a reason.

Let there be music here, Mrs. Gardner must have said.

The conductor signaled to Erika, and she nodded. As the violins began their stately preamble, the sounds swelled inside her until her arms lifted away from her body. Her mouth opened to let Handel's spirit out. She sang:

"Lascia la spina, cogli la rosa . . ."

After the last note trailed skyward, after the last vibration of sound had passed over her tongue, she lifted her face to the palazzo's uppermost level. Four stories overhead in the penthouse, a small, frail figure appeared at an open window, listening. Isabella Stewart Gardner extended her arm toward Erika, and gave her a wave like a blessing.

8

That same day—just hours after Erika had finished rehearsing—
Ravell arrived alone at Fenway Court. Night had fallen by then, and
the whole Venetian palace glowed, illuminated by torches and candles
and red Japanese lanterns that festooned the courtyard. Two hundred
guests wandered along the arcades, most viewing the palazzo for the first
time.

As Ravell entered that evening, his eyes took a moment to become
accustomed to the luminescence of hundreds of candles. The courtyard's
graceful mimosas cast their own silhouettes against the stucco walls.
Along the arched windows in the upper stories, figures passed like shadows. Overhead, Ravell saw guests pause to lean their elbows against bal-
ustrades and stare down into the courtyard.

Ravell knew that Erika was somewhere in the palace. Most likely the
vocalists and musicians were being sequestered until the time came for
them to perform. Yet as Ravell climbed a staircase, his hopes rose; he
half-expected to encounter Erika on the landing. Or she might be hidden
in the next gallery. . . . He felt it possible that he might come upon her
suddenly—she might look away from a masterpiece by Raphael and notice him, and her upper lip would twitch in surprise.

As he stood gazing at a painting in the Veronese Room, his hands
joined behind his back, a woman cried out his name with a squeal.

"Doctor Ravell!"

He whirled around.

A patient, of course. He collided with them everywhere. As the woman reached toward him in greeting, her fat upper arms strained the seams of her green satin gown.

Knowing all this particular woman had endured, he felt pleased to see her mingling freely in public, so obviously happy. She insisted on introducing him to her sister, to her cousin, to four friends. They smiled politely. None of them quite understood why this woman looked as if she'd melt with thanks at the sight of Doctor Ravell. Only she (and presumably her husband) knew that Doctor Ravell had removed the greatest blight for her. Before treatment, the affliction would never have killed her, but it had certainly ruined her life. Women did not confess or exhibit such a thing even to their closest female friends—not if they could help it. Long before he met her, she had pushed a baby from her womb with such force, over so many hours, that her uterus had fallen and hung out of her body. When she presented herself to him, she could hardly walk. Gravity and tumescence had left her with an organ dangling between her legs like an elephant's trunk. She could not leave her house, not with any dignity, not comfortably. He had designed a pessary for her, and finally restored her with surgery.

"I thank you every day," she murmured into his shoulder. "You are always in my heart and my prayers."

She grasped his sleeve, until he smiled and nodded deeply, and finally got away.

The grand rooms glowed with hot embers inside their hooded hearths, and the burning logs made the air smell like a forest. By firelight Ravell could see every halo and earlobe in the paintings.

"A good fire adds a certain medieval quality, doesn't it?" remarked a gentleman standing near Ravell.

When Ravell strolled to a window that surveyed the high-walled courtyard, there was still no sign of Erika. At every level of the building, candles wavered like spirits.

Where was she? Erika had explained to him that she was not part of the main concert. Instead, she would emerge to sing one quick aria, serving as a curtain-raiser for Madame Nordica.

His heart clenched. He panicked for a moment, worried that at this instant, she might be performing in some tucked-away room. What if he had missed her singing completely? He leaned over the railing as far as he dared, but he detected not a single note.

In the Gothic Room he felt someone's hand glide across the back of his trousers. It was a deliberate caress. He jerked back quickly and stepped away when he saw her: Mrs. George Appleton stood there, older and taller and more mischievous than he. She smirked at him. "Hello there," Amanda said. She had lain in his bed that very morning, and he imagined that he still smelled his own damp sheets wound around her body. He glanced across the gallery, nervous that someone had seen her pat his woolen pants, but all backs seemed to be turned, all faces raised toward the framed pictures.

"Have you seen Sargent's portrait of Mrs. Gardner?" Amanda asked. "The one that caused such a scandal?"

Her breath carried its familiar scent, reminding him of warm, dried apples. She led him across the room to inspect the regal figure of Mrs. Gardner posing in a black velvet gown. In the portrait Mrs. Gardner's décolleté dress dived into a deep heart shape. A double strand of pearls encircled her tiny waist.

Although the artist had accentuated every curve of her figure, he had also painted Byzantine halos around Isabella Stewart Gardner's head—as if she were a saint and a queen and a vixen.

"Captivating," Ravell decided. "A masterpiece."

"Sargent's a genius," she said, laughing softly, "to have spun gold out of such a homely little creature as Mrs. Gardner."

Again Ravell glanced over his shoulder, hoping no one had overheard.

More visitors poured into the gallery. He saw Mrs. William Farquahr—Caroline—come through the doorway. She recognized him before there was time to avert his glance.

Many months had passed since he'd last seen her. Now she headed straight toward him, with her husband straggling behind her. Her gown was dark blue, the color of Mrs. Gardner's courtyard delphiniums. Fortunately her husband halted for conversation with acquaintances.

"Doctor Ravell," she said, smiling and extending her gloved hand.

He had no choice but to introduce her to Amanda. "This is Mrs. George Appleton. A patient of mine."

Caroline Farquahr smiled and nodded. Her hair was as blonde as ever, coiled and pinned against her head. He had always been wary of Caroline, because he suspected that she used her good looks as a kind of whip, and she delighted in dominating others. Whenever she noticed his attention to her drifting, the muscles around her eyes tightened, and she edged closer. It hadn't been easy, fending her off.

"Tell me," she said, and leaned toward Amanda in a confidential manner, as if they'd known each other all their lives. "What do you really think of all this?" With long-gloved arms, she gestured at the walls of the palazzo. She beckoned Ravell and Amanda to follow her into a corner where the three of them could speak more privately.

"Some people have called this place a junk shop," Caroline said. "I don't necessarily agree with that. But I do wonder what the good people of Venice think of her. What gives a rich American lady the right to buy every marble column and stone balustrade she can find in Venice, and bring it here to build a monument to herself?"

"Some people think all this art ought to be returned to the countries she's taken it from," Amanda said.

He had made an error, Ravell felt, by introducing the two of them. The two women began to discuss the Sargent portrait of Isabella Stewart Gardner from halfway across the room. Back in the 1880s when the painting was first unveiled, Amanda recalled, the image stirred so many malicious comments about Mrs. Gardner that her late husband had never wanted the portrait exhibited again in public during his lifetime. But now that Mr. Gardner had been dead for five years, Caroline pointed out, his wife displayed it with prominence alongside her masterworks by Giotto and others here in the Gothic Room.

"Mrs. Gardner claims it's the greatest portrait Sargent has ever done," Caroline said.

Ravell excused himself, saying that he needed to meet a friend elsewhere in the building. The sight of those two women together, Amanda and Caroline—one outfitted in violet, the other in dark blue—felt odd. Whenever he happened to encounter Caroline, awkwardness weighted down his shoes as he sought a way to elude her.

Finally he escaped. Walking through a passageway, he wondered why Mrs. Gardner excited such envy and controversy. Nowhere, he thought, did another house of art like this exist. A century from now, visitors would wander through this palazzo and sense her presence in the sculpture garden, in the fountain waters, in every gilded picture frame. Long after her demanding personality and her homeliness had been forgotten, Mrs. Gardner's spirit would linger, and she would be remembered for what she had created here.

❖

A sudden commotion began in the courtyard. Musicians were entering with stringed instruments. On the second floor Ravell rushed to an open window and bent over the balustrade to view things better from above.

A great torch had been lit near a small, empty sarcophagus. Out of the darkness Erika appeared and stood next to it. Her gown was white, like that of a Roman goddess. She looked almost terrifyingly small—until she began to sing.

Then the sounds that came from her soared and penetrated behind every potted tree and carved archway.

"Lascia la spina, cogli la rosa . . ."

When her far-too-brief aria ended, Erika fled into the darkness. The audience, stunned, did not react for a moment, not quite believing that after only one Handel aria, she was already gone.

"Such a voice!" exclaimed an elderly woman who shared the balcony window with Ravell. Her hand, ridged with age, flew to her windpipe and she held it there. Applause resounded from every level, every arcade. Candles wavered and blurred; Ravell blinked away the moisture in his eyes. Guests clapped until their hands stung and male voices bellowed for the singer to reappear, but Erika did not show herself again.

("I didn't want to delay the performance," she told Ravell later. "There were so many more singers yet to come. Not to mention Madame Nordica.")

The elderly lady next to Ravell put a knotty hand on his arm, and motioned upward with her forefinger. "You see Madame Nordica up there, listening." In Mrs. Gardner's penthouse far above, a statuesque woman stood half-hidden by a velvet drapery. "Madame Nordica must be staying with Mrs. Gardner," the old lady remarked.

Three other soloists sang after Erika. The other vocalists stationed themselves on various balconies, calling to one another like figures in a play. To Ravell's ears, they all sounded shrill or flat compared to her.

When the time came for the formal concert of the evening, the slow-moving crowd made its way into the Music Room. Ravell followed almost reluctantly, because Erika had told him she would sing only once that evening. Mrs. Gardner's Music Room surprised him in its simplicity— its white purity, its straw-bottomed chairs and light wood floor. At the rear, Ravell saw to his discomfort that Amanda and Caroline had found seats together, along with their respective husbands. The pair of women had remained together, still chatting fast. Their husbands, who had obviously just been introduced, had fallen into conversation, too. Ravell nodded to the two ladies, though not to their husbands, whom he had never met. A glance told him that one husband (Amanda's) was bald, and the other (Caroline's) sported a thick blond moustache. Though Ravell had always entertained a curiosity about those men, and while he might have wished for the opportunity to observe them better if he could have remained invisible, he hardly dared to look at them. He hunted for a seat near the stage, to distance himself from them all.

Most people were already seated as he wriggled toward an unclaimed chair. Two grandmotherly types reached for his wrist as he sidestepped down the aisle. "Doctor Ravell!" they exclaimed, and petted his hands. The gray-haired ladies offered him fond looks and knowing winks, and he smiled back, although he could not recall whether it was their grandchildren he'd delivered or their infections he'd cured.

Then the conductor announced that the star of the evening (the celebrated Madame Nordica) had requested that Erika von Kessler sing another aria before the main program began.

In the darkness of the stage Erika appeared again, the sleeves of her white gown diaphanous. The acoustics of the Music Room were so pure, the resonance so intimate, that the audience might have been enclosed inside one perfect, wooden instrument. He could see the stage light reflected in her eyes.

> "In quali eccessi, o numi, in quai misfatti
> orribili, tremendi, è avvolto il sciagurato! . . ."

Ravell recognized the aria from *Don Giovanni*. He could not understand the exact lyrics, but he knew he was hearing the war cry of a woman betrayed, the anguish of a woman who loved and pitied an amoral man.

Erika was so close that he saw the perspiration across the bridge of her nose. He saw the color of her blue-gray eyes, and wondered if she would turn to look at him. She did not do so. He knew he was staring at a woman who might be carrying his child, though she had no inkling that this could be so. For the only time in his life, he had deliberately tried to impregnate a woman. Three times during Peter's absence, Erika had visited the office, and Ravell had persuaded her to cooperate. ("But I've promised your husband—") Three times since Peter's departure, Ravell had placed his own seed inside her.

Even a raped woman knew what had happened to her. Erika had no suspicion.

In the mad, gorgeous music that possessed her, he heard strains of his own goodness and evil. How often did a man gaze at a woman, having done what he had done, without her possibly knowing?

He wondered what compelled him to take such a risk. The dread of disappointing the von Kesslers? The need to impress them? That was part of it. Soon—through no fault of his own—they might cast him aside and move on to another specialist. He told himself that her suffering would deepen the longer it went on. But another truth was this: he did not want to give her up. He wanted to keep her from leaving him.

Onstage she sang of the doom she foresaw: the world was closing in on her lover, a man entangled in unspeakable crimes. Outraged fathers and husbands hunted him, ruined daughters and wronged women wanted revenge. The welling up of injustice shuddered through Erika.

Suppose, under the white veils of her dress, his child now grew? No one must know—not even twenty years from now. He blinked in sudden terror for himself. If anyone learned the truth, no patient could ever entrust herself to him again. Such a thing could never be forgiven.

> *"Mi tradì quell'alma ingrata:*
> *infelice, oh Dio! mi fa. . . ."*

He had never heard her sing an aria so dramatic before. He closed his eyes for a moment, trying to recover from his flash of fright.

She left the stage wrung out, her hair falling from its pins.

❖

At the evening's close, Madame Nordica sang "Let the Bright Seraphim" for an encore, the same chestnut she'd been feeding her worshippers for many years. The diva's hard, polished voice left Ravell cold. He hurried from the concert room as soon as he could and found Erika at a side door, where a circle of enthusiasts surrounded her. She smiled and reached over strangers' heads and tucked her hot hand inside his, just a fleeting squeeze of recognition before she pulled it away.

She smiled at everyone and no one. She looked dazed, as though she couldn't decipher the words being spoken to her, her eyes unfocused by candles and torches and the glory of the evening, her head still ringing with Mozart, perhaps. And why shouldn't she be elated? Madame Nordica had requested that she sing.

"Are you coming to the office next Thursday?" Ravell called out. "I'll see you then."

She called back to him over the heads of others: "Oh—there's something I must tell you—I'll tell you on Thursday." More bodies crushed together in the passageway, and other musicians and singers pressed her to join them for a private celebration. Before she disappeared through a doorway, Erika sent a fleeting wave in Ravell's direction. He wondered if she already sensed—as women sometimes did—that she had a child inside her, but that seemed unlikely. It was really too soon for her to know.

❖

As he turned from Erika, he noticed another figure standing nearby in the hallway. It was Caroline Farquahr. After rushed excuses to her companions, she must have followed him in hopes of a private exchange.

With the ice of resentment in her eyes, she looked at him, and Ravell wondered what she had just witnessed. The quaver in his voice as he'd called out nervously to congratulate Erika on her singing? The worshipful hunch in his shoulders? The heat in his face? Caroline had clearly caught hints of something.

Ravell tipped his hat to her, raised one arm in greeting, and without stopping he followed a herd of dark overcoats into the night.

9

❧

On a May morning Erika sat on the bed's edge, pulling on her stockings, her head ripe with plans. She caught herself singing fragments of another Handel aria, over and over again.

> *"Oh, that I on wings could rise,*
> *Swiftly sailing through the skies . . ."*

She was due to depart for Italy in just nine more days, and she decided she must go that very afternoon to her father's house and inform him of what was to come. She had booked her passage on the White Star Line's *Canopic,* intending to flee before Peter's return. Until now she had not found the courage to tell her father or her brother or any family member that she meant to leave her marriage and find her future on another continent. Only her voice teacher, Magdalena, knew that years might pass before any of them saw Erika again.

Even the servants had no inkling that anything extraordinary was afoot. For weeks Erika had been walking to Magdalena's house every day, smuggling a few items at a time—a satchel filled with undergarments, a parasol that would shade her from the Tuscan sun, a costume bag containing a long cape she might need for winter in Florence. From a dressmaker she had ordered an Eton suit with a white satin collar, as well as a Princess gown in burgundy chiffon velvet. She had arranged for these things to be delivered to Magdalena's Beacon Street address, where Erika had packed them into brand-new trunks she kept hidden there.

She wanted Papa to know that she did not mean to abandon him. Although he still practiced medicine and looked remarkably robust for a man of his age, his blond walrus moustache and sideburns had gone white and his heart was weak. Other men with similar circulatory ailments sometimes left the house in the morning and fell onto the pavement, dead of apoplexy before they rounded the front gate. If she sailed for another world, Papa might not be there to greet her ship upon her next visit.

As Erika turned the key and let herself inside her childhood home, she saw that things remained unchanged. Papa had not yet returned from his rounds at the hospital, though the maid informed her that he would appear soon. She looked around, trying to memorize a place she did not expect to see again for years. The immense furniture felt rooted in the rooms. As always, her late mother's Spanish fan dangled from a knob on the foyer mirror. On the floor of Papa's study, a pair of men's Chinese slippers rested in the corner—the same style of slippers he'd worn for a quarter century.

Shortly after Erika's seventh birthday, her mother had died. Her own memories of Mama were distressingly few. Her mother used to lie on a wine-colored chaise longue writing letters. Erika could no longer see her mother's face, yet Mama's hands were imprinted in her memory: long, tapered fingers that smelled of gardenia soap. While Mama braided Erika's hair, Erika had sat erect, savoring the lovely chilly feeling as the strands were drawn upward, and she felt Mama's cool breaths upon her nape.

For several years Papa had wished to keep things exactly as they had been prior to his wife's death.

"Where are her magazines?" he had demanded of the chambermaid one evening. As a child, Erika had watched from a doorway as he stumbled around like a man who returns to find his house burglarized. "Where are her powders that used to be on the bathroom shelf? Where are the perfume bottles from her vanity?"

The chambermaid, thinking she was doing the widower a gentle favor, had concluded that it was time to stop dusting a dead woman's cosmetics.

"I've taken it all in boxes to the attic, sir," the maid had said.

From the doorway Erika had noticed how Papa drove splayed fingers across his scalp, leaving his hair in unruly spikes. In a pained voice he told the chambermaid, "I want everything replaced. Exactly as it was."

❖

Her father was a doctor who treated members of the Back Bay's most prominent families. His practice was located on the ground floor of his house, distinctive for its twin archways. Patients entered under the right arch, family under the left. These days his consulting room was typically filled with elderly widows dressed in black, their white silk hair slipping from under their bonnets. Patients sometimes noticed Erika on the side-walk as she came to visit her father. They caught her hand and rolled it in their own, as they had been apt to do ever since she was a child. (Poor, motherless daughter of Doctor William von Kessler!)

"Your papa," one effused, "can describe every symptom I've been ex-periencing without my even telling him."

In winter, wreaths of apples and evergreens—anonymously given—hung from their front door. At Christmas, Papa's doorbell would ring and a fruitcake would appear on the steps of fresh, unshoveled snow. A carriage would pull away quickly, leaving no sign of who'd left it—except for footprints in the snow from a lady's heeled galoshes.

❖

"Erika," Papa said. "Forgive me for my opinion, but this plan may be the greatest mistake of your life."

Her father blurred before her. Tears melted like hard bits of ice in her eyes. "Don't tell me that someday, with luck, I'll have children," she said desperately, "because you know that won't happen."

"But how will you live," Papa asked, "without a husband to sup-port you?"

"I can manage on the income from the Bell Street property that Mama left to us. I can live simply. Gerald can mail me a check for my share of her estate, just as he does now."

Papa lit his meerschaum and puffed calmly on the carved ivory pipe. "Why not take a summer in Milan?" he suggested. "Immerse yourself in all the opera you'd like. Go every night to La Scala. Why not?" he said. "After all you've been through, I'm sure Peter would understand. Perhaps he'd go with you."

"I am not yearning for a long holiday—I am embracing a career!"

She got up and opened one of the long drapes and looked down at the stunted saplings planted along the mall that divided Commonwealth Avenue. She let the drape fall and turned to her father again.

She pressed her fingers against her windpipe. "Your daughter," she whispered at him fiercely, "has been given this voice for a reason."

❖

"So," Magdalena said, "how did things go with your father yesterday?"

Dripping, Magdalena stood up in the bathtub. Her maid took a hand mitt foaming with special soap and rubbed the older woman's thighs and buttocks with a hard, massaging motion. Magdalena believed such rubdowns lessened *peau d'orange*—the lumps and dimples that marred a female's lower body.

"It was unpleasant," Erika said.

Apart from professors at the New England Conservatory, Magdalena was the first and only voice coach Erika had ever had. Magdalena was also the first woman Erika had ever seen naked. The summer she was nine, when she first arrived at Magdalena's town house for her morning vocal lesson, the older woman would often be running late. During her career as a diva, she had gotten into the habit of falling into bed very late, and being slow to rise. "Come upstairs, don't be bashful," Magdalena used to call down the stairwell to Erika. "Come up and keep me company while I'm getting dressed."

Today, just as she had done long ago, Magdalena sat at the vanity table and combed wet tendrils upward with her fingers and locked them against her head with tortoiseshell pins.

The dressing gown slipped from her shoulders as Magdalena stood, and she discarded it across the bed. Magdalena strode around the bedroom with the same athletic self-assurance that she had exhibited as a much younger woman, oblivious to whatever assessments her maid or Erika might make as they observed her unclothed sixty-year-old body. "I like to delay as long as possible before I lock myself into a corset," Magdalena said. "Not that I approve of wearing no corset at all—but for a certain period every day, I think a woman's skin should *breathe*." Magdalena was European, and Europeans had a reverence for skin.

After Magdalena got dressed, they went downstairs to the solarium, a room shaped like a glassed-in gazebo—their favorite place to talk. The room was as humid as a tropical forest with its orchids, moist potted soil, and Kentia palms that brushed the ceiling. The solarium windows wept steam.

"Have you seen my amaryllis?" Magdalena touched the petals like long tongues. Even in winter when the solarium was cold, they sat here— Magdalena in a wool cape, Erika in black fur. They would cover their laps with crocheted blankets, while hot bricks toasted their feet. Through a hexagon of windows, they watched snow slant and melt against the brick sidewalk.

When Magdalena heard how Papa had responded to Erika's news, the older woman shook her head. Earrings shivered like raindrops on her lobes. "This is the great difference between your father and me," she declared. "He's a conventional man, not a person who understands that to be a true artist, one must burn all one's ships."

As a child Erika used to dream of her father and Magdalena together. If only Magdalena's husband—that long, thin businessman who walked with legs like two stiff canes—if only he would become ill with tuberculosis, as her mother had; if only that husband of hers would die!

As a child, Erika had longed for Magdalena to throw open the doors in the dark, shadowy corridors of the house where she and Papa and her brother, Gerald, lived; she imagined that Magdalena would replace the black walnut woodwork and lighten the walls with fresh paint. Just as in Magdalena's town house, light would be reflected from mirrors, and there would be long windows everywhere. . . . Or perhaps Papa and she and her brother would come to live at Magdalena's home on Beacon Street, among the jungle of orchids and Kentia palms, in a house that resonated like the inside of a piano.

Now she detected something in Magdalena's impatient remarks about Papa that made her think that the older woman had once considered the same possibility. Perhaps after Magdalena had finally been widowed, several years previously?

"Tell me something," Erika said, "now that I am going away." Her fingers caressed the sofa's velvet curve. "Were you ever the least bit in love with my father?"

Magdalena inhaled so deeply, Erika could hear the underlying wheeze, the old struggle deep in her lungs.

"We had a romance."

Startled, Erika felt her ears rise, as if they were lengthening, opening. "When?"

"Long ago. The year after you first became my student."

How had she missed this? Erika wondered. Memories rushed back, clues that now made sense. As a girl of nine or ten, she had settled herself squarely in her father's lap, thinking it odd that she smelled the scent of Magdalena's lily-of-the-valley sachets on Papa's cheeks, on his shirt cuffs.

As a girl, Erika had arrived at the Beacon Street house one afternoon for her lesson just as Papa was descending Magdalena's brick steps with his black medical bag. Was her teacher ailing? Papa made no excuse about why he'd come to call at her voice teacher's home. Instead, he'd fished out his engraved pocket watch and opened its etched filigree cover and peeked at the time with the edge of his eyes. He'd cupped Erika's small chin in his huge hand for a moment, given a reluctant sigh, and departed.

"Did you ever consider marrying my father?"

"Never," Magdalena said. "Your father and I could never have lived well together. But we've shared many things. Like you, for instance. There was a period when he was a wonderful secret in my life, and he said that I was a gift for him."

Erika considered the timing of when this had all occurred. When no chambermaid or adult had been around to stop her, she used to wander into her mother's old bedroom and peer into bureaus and jewelry boxes. Curious, she had pulled open a drawer and slid a long satin glove over her hand. Her own short fingers only half-filled the empty tubes; with her other hand she pinched the limp finger ends, hoping to discover a square folded note or something left by her mother inside, but there was nothing.

Around that time Papa used to whistle arias that Magdalena taught her. One day she had gone into Mama's former bedroom and noticed that her mother's clothes had finally been taken away. The dark violet Chinese dressing gown Mama had always worn no longer hung from the armoire door.

10

At the hospital a nurse led Doctor Ravell with terrible haste down a corridor toward a young woman who was lying on the floor in a crescent, knees bent toward her chest. The staff hovered around her, draping her arms over their shoulders as they helped the young woman hobble—doubled over and emitting coarse moans—to the nearest bed.

Her pallor was extreme. When Doctor Ravell touched her flat belly, she flinched. Yet she had no fever. Strands of her hair felt as dry as hay when his palm brushed against her forehead. He lifted her upper lip with his thumb and saw a telltale blue line across her gums.

"She has swallowed lead," he told the nurse. "She's going to abort very soon."

Later that evening, when her struggles had ended and the young woman rested in quiet isolation, he stopped by her bedside. No doubt she was poor—it was always the poor who presented themselves at hospitals, desperate for free care and a place to give birth apart from the dank, tenement rooms they usually shared with many others. Affluent patients had servants; the rich could afford to pay physicians to attend them while they gave birth at home. But for poor women, the hospital was the only sanctuary where they could be assured of starched sheets, and nurses who could sponge them clean and bring soup to their lips. How many a destitute mother, especially one who already had several children, could find anyone to bathe and spoon-feed *her*?

He knelt beside her, and kept his tone grave and muted. "You've taken a great risk," he said. "I've seen women dead—I've examined the corpses of women who've done to themselves what you did." He paused. "If this ever happens to you again, come to me first."

The young woman's head barely moved on the pillow, and her voice was faint. "You'd have tried to convince me to have the baby."

Ravell kept silent for a moment. A series of crisply tucked beds adjacent to hers happened to be vacant, surrounding them with a measure of privacy.

"You'd have refused to help," she said.

He leaned closer to her, his forearm braced against his knee. "There are other, safer means."

"Like what?"

He had to be careful. He did not mention apiol, a substance extracted from parsley seeds. He did not speak the name of a pharmacist he knew on Water Street—a friend who over-innocently explained to a woman that if she took three tablets of apiol, the medicine would help to regulate her periods. If she *happened* to be pregnant, however, and if she *happened* to swallow twelve tablets at once, she'd lose the baby within a week.

"If you ever need help," Ravell repeated, "come to me as quickly as you can."

❖

"I shudder," a well-coiffed matron was saying, "when I think what my daughter might endure on her honeymoon."

At Ravell's private practice, the matron sat on the opposite side of his massive oak desk, and she had been talking for somewhere between ten and fifteen minutes.

"And what is it exactly, Mrs. Philbrook, that you wish me to do?"

"I thought you might have a talk with my future son-in-law, to warn the groom about *excesses*."

The egret feathers on the matron's hat shook with emphasis. According to her, according to the tales she'd heard, the enthusiasms of a young groom not only exhausted a young woman; such honeymoon exertions were apt to result in fever, miscarriage, sterility, illness, and, on rare occasions, the death of a bride.

"I thought you might impose certain limitations," she declared, "and set forth rules."

"If you hope to regulate the frequency of their intimate relations," Ravell said, "I am afraid that is a matter for a young couple to decide between themselves."

The egret feathers drooped. Ravell stood up, a signal that the appointment had drawn to a close. A puddle had collected on the floor below the tip of Mrs. Philbrook's umbrella, and Ravell thought of Erika outside in the rain, hurrying toward his office at this very moment.

"Think of all the ladies you know who have survived their honeymoons," he said.

❖

All afternoon he'd only half-listened to patients, aware of the fury of rain pelting his office windows, the rain that had surely become part of Erika's day as well. He pictured her shielding herself with her umbrella, lifting her ankle to step over a puddle before it soaked her feet and discolored her shoes. All afternoon he'd attuned his ears to the jangle of bells hanging from the office's front door, a signal that one patient had departed or another had arrived. Every shimmering sound of the bells marked the passing of the hours that brought him closer to her, his last appointment of the day.

He knew, as one who counts the chimes from a church tower, exactly when it must be she who pushed open the front door. He peered down a corridor just as her skirt and the back of her rain-soaked hood were disappearing into the waiting room. This was the final occasion he would see her before Peter returned a week from Thursday. Enough time had elapsed by now for Erika to know the sobering results; what news might she bring him? For a moment he stood in the vacant corridor, half-terrified to face her now that the hour had finally come. Yet he savored the chill air she'd carried into the corridor, the tang of excitement.

Thirty years he'd been alive. Until now, he'd been prudent, careful to spill his own seed onto sheets or taffeta skirts. He'd wet his own hands with ghosts of children he'd been cautious never to father.

True, he had placed sparks for a child inside her. . . . But apart from that, he had never touched her or spoken to her with impropriety. He prided himself on this.

When she swept into his office, her rain hood lowered, drops of water glistened on the ridged folds of her cape. He could tell at once that she had something important to tell him. She paced and moved like a figure onstage.

"Let's remove that damp cape, shall we?" he said. He came around from his desk and caught a whiff of lilac from her hair as he slid the cape away from her shoulders. He hung it on a coat rack.

She did have news to tell him, but it was not the announcement he'd counted on. "I'm completely serious about a singing career," she said. "And I won't be coming back."

Her pupils were enormous, as large and dark as those of a lady who had ingested belladonna, and he wondered again if there were something unstable about her. She would sail for Italy in four more days, she announced. Her curls and her pearl buttons and the tiny turquoise bracelet at her wrist brightened before him like the markings of a flower. Even her speaking voice sounded like a song.

Yet something emanated from her—flashes of fire—that scared him and warned him not to come any nearer, not to object to a single phrase she was uttering.

Within five minutes she had thanked him and was gone.

Ravell sat for a long while in his oak chair and watched rain glaze the pavement in the alley. He had wondered, of course, if the imaginary child he might have given her would possess her talent for music. He had expected to observe his own child's upbringing from afar—a truth that could never be told, or it would ruin him. He had expected a connection to her that he had never felt toward any woman—but to her, what had he been? Only a technician.

11

The endless preparations depleted her, as well as the strain of her father summoning her to his house twice to argue with her. ("I won't live forever, Erika. . . . If you leave your husband, if your aspirations come to nothing—do you realize how *alone* you will be in this world?")

She had to banish Papa from her concerns as she ran from the dentist to the shoemaker, and to the milliner to order more hatboxes. She filled half a trunk with heavy linen feminine napkins, as if Florence were not a civilized city, as if Florence were not a place where a modern woman could be assured of finding what she would require for her personal hygiene. Guidebooks were crushed into her overstuffed baggage. In the middle of the night, she rose from the bed to scratch a note to herself that she must order yet another trunk. What relief such extra space would bring—not having to cram more clothes into the impossibly small walls of her luggage. She felt an easing inside her chest at the prospect. Her own respiration had grown tight from planning what bordered on the impossible: to reduce her worldly possessions from what fit inside a five-story house into what might fit inside a pile of latched boxes.

At yesterday's appointment, she should have asked Doctor Ravell about replacing a douche bag. . . . Suppose she visited a pharmacist in Florence but could not manage, with her limited Italian, to ask for such a thing? The servants understood that she had been studying conversational Italian with an old woman from the North End, but everyone presumed that Erika did this to fine-tune her pronunciation of librettos.

In the deep of night, she awoke again and her eyes roved in the darkness. Famished, she descended the servants' staircase to the deserted cellar kitchen, an area of the house she seldom visited. Every servant was asleep under the eaves five stories above. No point in ringing any bells or rousting any of them from their dreams. Within two or three hours, the kitchen would become the noisy hub of deliveries from the iceman, the milkman, the grocery boy. Until the late morning, she would lie in bed three stories above this ground-level kitchen, trying to recoup the sleep that eluded her now, while dimly, at the edges of her pillow, she'd hear the ragman yelling as he peddled rags and bottles from his cart, and the laundress laughing to someone in the alley as the woman strung bed linens between posts.

The instant Erika flicked on the pantry's electric light and saw the fruit bowl, she felt herself swoon. She lunged for a banana with mounting panic, ripping the skin from it and shoving its smooth flesh against the roof of her mouth. Greedily she bit down. After a few quick swallows, her stomach settled, and the terrible hollow feeling was gone. She relaxed then, convinced that she was not sick, and reassured that she would indeed embark on Friday morning and make the voyage as planned.

Upstairs in the master bathroom, just steps from her grand bamboo bed, she'd set a box of heavy linen napkins near the toilet. Twice in the past few weeks she'd felt aches and congestion in her lower abdomen—sure signs that her period verged on descending. Yet it had not come. The stress of planning for travel and for an unknown life, Erika reasoned, had upset her normal rhythms. The box she'd brought out she now tucked into a cabinet and packed away. How long had it been since she'd last menstruated? Before or after the concert at Fenway Court? She could not recall. . . . She could only remember how before she sang that night, she'd carefully strapped a linen napkin between her legs, just to be certain. Suppose she'd sat on a stone bench in Mrs. Gardner's courtyard and stood up to feel mortifying scarlet drops across the back of her white diaphanous dress?

It seemed a blessing how that part of her body had shut down temporarily. Her mind must have begged her body to postpone the inconvenience of menstruating while she bustled frantically from the drugstore to the dressmaker to the shop where she stocked up on musical scores. Of course, the moment the White Star Line's *Canopic* set sail, it would probably come, but she would have little else to worry about during the long ocean crossing. Already she saw herself rinsing her undergarments in the stateroom basin, her bloomers floating in water tinted pink. While the vessel tilted and leaned and drove through the waves toward Europe, she'd have plenty of time to fuss over such things. For days they'd see nothing except birds. For days the band would play to distract them all from raging boredom. The passengers would crowd the ship's rail as the seaweed thickened at the Azores and they neared land.

❖

On a Tuesday evening just three days before she was to embark, she took a sheaf of paper and filled up a pen and settled herself at Peter's wide desk to write him a proper letter, a last letter, the only explanation she intended to leave for him. There was much to say. She gripped the pen and wrote the date. Then the pen fell from her hand and her head felt too weighty for her neck to hold upright.

The date. That was all she wrote.

She willed herself to go on, but it came over her then like a fever—a fatigue so extreme that she had to leave the desk and slide her body onto the Turkish tufted sofa, one cheek against its mohair upholstery, her left arm dangling loose over the side. What illness was this? A flu? A severe anemia? What was happening to her strength just when she most needed it? It was impossible to move from the sofa, impossible to raise her head. A tiny invisible bullet must have felled her, though she had heard nothing, had seen nothing, and could not recall being shot.

She groaned until the door opened. Call Doctor Ravell, she told the maid. If he is not there, call my father.

After he'd examined her, after he'd sent the maid away, Ravell drew his chair alongside the bed and pillows that bolstered Erika's back.

"How long since you've menstruated? Weeks now, isn't it?"

His face was close to hers. He was a slender man, his eyes deep-set and almost black, like a person from Persia, or Egypt.

"You don't think—?"

"You're pregnant."

A cry broke inside her windpipe, a sound that splintered into many sounds. "A baby?" she whispered. "When will this baby come?"

"Next winter," Doctor Ravell said. "Around the first of January."

Erika clutched her head in her hands. The dreadful weakness had evaporated as suddenly as it came. She opened her eyes as wide as she could and gasped, "Why should this be happening now? Why, after so many years—why now?"

He receded from her then, saying nothing.

"Peter will be happy." Her tone was loud and careless.

"What about you?" the doctor asked. "Does this make you happy?"

"Everything is ruined now. Everything I've planned for."

He did not blink when she said this. He only watched her. His eyes, encircled by smoky shadows, held the history of all the homes and lives he'd entered during his career of doctoring. Nothing, it seemed, could shock him. He must have forgiven woman after woman for saying what she felt.

He fiddled with his cravat, loosening the knot, and drew a finger between his neck and collar. "Erika." He brought his face close to hers again. "Only two people know what has happened—you and I. So I want you to tell me frankly: do you want to have this child or not?"

She stared back at his dark, unblinking eyes that dared her to say words no woman in her position was supposed to speak. She stared at his neatly trimmed goatee, his lush red mouth—a mouth almost like a woman's—and at the faintly Semitic curve of his nose.

"Yes," she said, her tone flat and steady. "I want the child." Reason told her that for many years she had wanted a child, so she ought to be grateful that she'd finally been given one.

"All right, then," he said. He pushed his hands against his knees and stood up. Then he went into the bathroom, folded back his shirt cuffs, and lathered his hands, rinsing them vigorously. He did not hear her as she tossed off the bedcovers and tightened the belt of her dressing gown and came up barefoot behind him, wanting to ask him something.

When she noticed his reflection in the mirror, she forgot what she had come to say. Bent over the washbasin, he appeared as slightly built as an adolescent—hardly taller than she was—and the abiding calm was gone from him. In the mirror his features twitched and he looked anguished.

12

Ravell removed his suit coat. On a humid July evening he sat finishing paperwork in his suspenders and shirtsleeves long after his practice had closed for the day. He'd just returned from attending the birth of a robust baby boy at a residence on Clarendon Street, and the effort had left his collar soaked, his hair separated into damp strands behind the ears.

The sky was dark as the window rattled behind him. He assumed at first that someone had seen the light and come around to the back alley with a medical problem. When he tugged the window farther open, Caroline Farquahr rested her arms on the sill and angled her face at him. Her lips looked painted.

It was the first time she had visited the premises after hours. Without any prompting from him, she walked around and let herself in through the screen door at the back.

"Well," he said. "What brings you here?"

"Boredom," she said. Her neck appeared to lengthen, her head rising higher as it swiveled and she peered around his office with interest.

Once again, she was back to haunt him. "You look as if you're on your way to the theatre," Ravell observed. Her dress was ice blue; it cooled him just to look at it. As she batted at her neck with an ornate Japanese fan, the blonde tendrils flew. Her small diamond earrings captured and refracted the light.

He slipped his suit jacket back on, like protective armor, to convey a certain formality. Then he escorted her into the rear hallway, where they would remain unseen from the street. "Actually, this isn't the best time for you to have stopped by," he said. "I'm expecting someone." A small lie, but he felt uncomfortable remaining alone with her.

The dimness stirred her. She took hold of one of his suit coat buttons and tugged it gently. He backed away, but she sidled close again and gave a giggle. "That evening at Mrs. Gardner's palazzo, you liked that young singer, didn't you? What was her name?"

He stepped backward, appalled, and shook his head. "I don't recall."

"I thought I overheard you ask if she'd be coming to the office."

He shrugged, reluctant to tell her anything.

With one fingertip Caroline touched his tie, and with a hint of a smile, she complimented him on its color. Then she placed both her hands on his shoulders, and brought her mouth close to his ear.

"Let's go upstairs," she said. "You should give me a little tour. I'm always curious to see where people live."

Ravell smelled sweet mint on her breath, and it alarmed him to realize that he felt tempted—just for a fleeting moment. "I'm not in the habit of taking patients upstairs to my private rooms," he said.

"Why not?" Her head dropped to one side.

"Because I don't want to be that sort of man," he said, trying to sound firm.

She laughed, and said, "And what type of man do you intend to be? A man who lives without passion?"

"I didn't become an obstetrician to ruin other people's marriages."

He felt a pang of hypocrisy, saying that, because of Amanda Appleton—but their affair, if anything, had helped her marriage continue, because it allowed her to overlook her husband's loss of sexual appetite. She still felt loyalty toward the man.

When Ravell's time with Amanda ended—as they both understood it inevitably would—he believed that they would part with grace. But his arrangement with Amanda was rare. He'd have to be half-mad to take up with Caroline. To juggle more than one mistress? His conscience and his nerves could never bear it.

The screen door at the rear of the building remained open. A light il-luminated the back stairs. He and Caroline both turned their heads when they heard the crisp clack of heels as an unseen person (a neighbor's ser-vant, perhaps?) passed through the alley.

"Someone you know?" Caroline lifted her eyebrows in jest. "Another patient to whom you've given a private key?"

It was a Monday evening, the night when Amanda Appleton usually found herself free to visit Ravell, due to her husband's regularly sched-uled card game with friends at the St. Botolph Club. Ordinarily it might be Amanda crossing through the yard at this hour, heading for the back entrance to Ravell's private quarters. Amanda did indeed have a key. But tonight Amanda and her family were away in Bar Harbor, Maine.

He made no reply. Caroline gave a rough tug to his right lapel and moved her nose closer to his. "Another patient?" she accused in a sharp whisper.

"What's that supposed to mean?"

She rested one shoulder against the wall. "Women talk among them-selves," Caroline said. "That's one thing a man like you never counts on. Amanda and I have become friends, you know."

He suspected that Caroline knew very well that Amanda Apple-ton was away with her family, that this was the night of the week they usually met.

"Whoever would have guessed," Caroline said, "that a lady of Aman-da's generation could be so . . . frisky?" Her shoulders twitched with mirth. From Caroline's tone and airy manner, he realized that she was amused by the notion that he had become entangled with a woman so much older than himself.

He placed a hand lightly on Caroline's arm and guided her toward the formal exit to his practice. If she lingered here much longer, would she brush her lips against his face, or nip his neck? He could not predict what she might do.

13

Peter stretched out his arms as he stood and modeled the new boa constrictor he'd acquired during his travels. He'd coiled the snake around his neck and let it dangle the way a woman might show off her long pearls.

"Gorgeous, isn't he?" Peter said. "When I spotted him in a market in Tangier, I had to have him. I couldn't resist."

The snake delighted Ravell. When he let Peter drape the thing around him, he felt the reptile's sinuous weight fall against his shoulders. Before the mantel mirror Ravell posed with the boa's patterned skin twined around him like a royal decoration. In the mirror Ravell saw his own irrepressible grin.

"I want you to have him," Peter said suddenly. "As a gift."

"God, no. I couldn't—"

"Please," Peter said. "After all you've done."

"You be responsible for his upkeep, and I'll visit him," Ravell said.

In his personal library Peter walked over to the wall where his collection of painted butterflies hung in fourteen individual frames. He selected the largest and most intricate one, a dazzling Morpho that Ravell had previously admired.

"Then, I want you to accept this instead." Peter lifted the frame from the wall and handed the miniature painting to Ravell.

"But this must have taken you weeks to do!"

"Take it," Peter insisted.

Someday, Peter said, he and Ravell ought to travel together to that island off the coast of South America, to that coconut plantation owned by Ravell's friend. Ravell had described in ravishing terms the abundance of flora and fauna on the island. From there, Peter suggested that they might take a boat trip down the Orinoco River together, and explore the wilds of Venezuela.

"Yes," Ravell said, "if I can ever steal away from my medical practice."

"I'll serve as your excuse," Peter said. "Tell everyone that you've promised to make the trip with me."

❖

Returning home from a middle-of-the-night delivery, Ravell pulled a plate of cold lamb the housekeeper had left for him from the icebox. He ate, wondering with terrible unease if anyone else knew what he did—that Peter could not possibly father a child. Suppose another specialist whom Erika and Peter had consulted in the past had lapsed—just as he himself had done—and out of curiosity had slipped a slide under a microscope and peered at the truth?

Now that Erika was pregnant . . . how could such a thing be explained? Suppose another physician, driven by a sense of righteousness, were to confront him and make an oblique yet insinuating remark?

A pregnancy might arise from more than one scenario, of course. An unfaithful wife . . . A secret agreement reached between a couple and their doctor to infuse the wife with an anonymous man's sperm . . . If accused, Ravell decided that he must remain aloof, noble, and silent—as if his patients' confidentiality were sacred to him. He would stare at his accuser until the other man turned away.

Suppose someone told Peter, sent him an anonymous letter? The chance of that was very remote. No doctor would wish to be suspected of violating Peter's privacy.

Ravell put his empty plate in the sink, ran a little water over it, and retreated to the parlor. He poured himself a glass of brandy and sipped, hoping to relax, or he'd never be able to sleep. He kicked off his boots and sank into a fringed chair, his ankles crossed, his stocking feet resting on an ottoman.

Nothing terrible would come of it, he told himself . . . only the sweetness of a small child. . . . He took a long swig and let the brandy run deep and warm his ribs, almost certain that he would be able to swallow the secret.

❖

As dusk shadowed the bedroom, the two men hovered over the bamboo bed where Erika lay. Her white blouse had been raised like a curtain to expose her belly, and Peter and the doctor leaned toward her navel, their heads nearly touching. Doctor Ravell gave an eager nod, unhooked the stethoscope from his ears, and passed the instrument to Peter, who frowned at first, detecting nothing. Then he jumped back with a yelp and tore the tubes away from his ears.

"He just told me his name is Oliver," Peter joked. "What a ghastly name."

"Let me have a listen," Erika said, reaching out.

Strangers and passersby on city streets would not have guessed just yet that she was with child. She herself could not completely believe that a living creature actually existed inside her, and that made her particularly curious to hear a heartbeat.

She heard nothing at first, and wondered if a hoax was under way. She felt like a skeptic at a séance. What signal, precisely, was she expected to perceive—a faraway moan, a rap behind a wall?

"Try here," Doctor Ravell said, adjusting the stethoscope for her, moving it lower on her abdomen.

The sounds pumped through the bones of her own ears—the first message sent by a ghost from the future, an unseen person who floated and thrived in a netherworld.

"By God!" She laughed, her fingers fanned over her mouth to stifle her own surprise.

The thumps might have been her own heartbeats, only wildly quicker. The marvel of it raced through her.

The three of them listened, passing the stethoscope back and forth, over and over again. Even Doctor Ravell, who must have checked such heartbeats many times every day, appeared affected by hearing the rapid, underwater whooshes—the whip crack of the child's heart. As he put the stethoscope back into his black medical bag, his eyes glimmered wetly.

"He's a sentimental man," Erika said, after the doctor had gone.

Peter nodded. "He's in the right profession."

❖

"It's a postponement of your plans, that's all," Magdalena said upon first hearing the news. The older woman folded her arms and paced, as she was apt to do when disappointments surfaced. "In a year or two, you'll hire a nursemaid and take the child to Italy with you."

Take this child from Peter? Erika thought. *He'd pursue me from Milan to every small hillside village in Umbria or Tuscany, hunt me down like a kidnapper.*

Her vocal training continued to be focused and productive. In the mornings she headed to Magdalena's house for a formal lesson, and then she returned home to practice. As long as she fed herself bits of apples and cheese and oranges to keep her energy level, she could pitch away far into the afternoon. She'd end in exhaustion. A deadline loomed before her: only five more months remained, and soon it would be four, then just three. . . . What would happen to her life, her voice, her aspirations of Italy, after the little creature came? Surely it would be eons before such perfect stretches of solitude were hers again.

Books about Italy, unpacked from their trunks, lay in piles around the house. These days she could not bear to look at them. If she had not gotten pregnant, where would she be at this moment? Trying to secure a fine vocal coach in Florence? Auditioning? She pictured herself having found splendid rooms overlooking the Arno, where two long shuttered windows could be flung open.

Instead, she found herself climbing Beacon Hill. In her fourth month, before any stranger might have noticed a suspicious curve to her middle, she headed upward toward Louisburg Square, passing the stately brick homes, following the narrow streets she knew so well. She had always been a hearty walker, but now as she headed uphill, the muscles of her belly tightened, resisting every step. Each stride was cut to a third of its normal length, and such a faltering pace depressed her. The baby she carried could hardly have been larger than her own thumb. . . . So why must she mince along, as helpless as an invalid? It made her want to sob.

For twenty-eight years, her body had been her own domain, but no longer.

The sky darkened as she descended into Charles Street. The stores had closed; she passed storefronts with blackened interiors. Before a locked photographer's shop she paused to inspect a portrait displayed in the window. An electric light illuminated the face of a blond boy dressed in a sailor suit. He must have been about two years old, and the sight of him made tears seep into her eyes. Whose face would she see in two years—the features of a little boy or a little girl? Reflected in the glass storefront window, she noticed her brow clenched in distress. Who was this person who stole her oxygen and reduced her crisp steps to an old lady's creeping gait? How humbling, to bow before the needs of a being she had never seen.

❖

Together Erika and her cousin Phoebe strolled through the Public Garden, wheeling a carriage that held Phoebe's fourth daughter, who had entered the world at the staggering birth weight of eleven pounds.

"Twenty-eight years I've been alive," Erika said musingly, "and my body has never made a baby before. It's never grown all the parts for a little boy, if I have a son. I watch all the changes and wonder: how does it know?"

"Yes." Phoebe gave a soft laugh. "How does the body know?"

They wheeled Baby Judith to an area shaded by rose trellises. Under an arbor they sat down on a wooden bench. In the distance children rode swan boats propelled by paddle wheels, their cries as faint as fingerprints on glass. In the carriage's nest of pastel blankets, Baby Judith kicked her bent legs and twitched her tiny hands.

"Since the birth," Phoebe blurted suddenly, "something dreadful has happened." Her husband had insisted that she leave their New Hampshire home and come down to stay with Boston relatives "for a rest."

Everything had been fine, Phoebe confessed—until the labor. "I am going to tell you things I haven't told anybody else."

With her daughter three weeks overdue, Phoebe said, nature had done nothing. Nature might have let the baby fatten inside her forever—if her doctor had not intervened. He had sparked her labor with a substance called ergot. As she writhed on a bed with her legs open to fate, she had felt the doctor's nearness, and everything had disappeared except for him. To him she had screamed warnings: *My legs are tearing away from my body.* . . . Love, that's what she had felt for her doctor when it was over. A love as extravagant as her terror had been. The doctor rejoiced because her baby was the biggest he'd ever delivered alive.

Before her departure for Boston, Phoebe happened to meet her New Hampshire physician on the street. It was the first time the doctor had seen her slender. "He dropped a package he was carrying!" she whispered intently. "I was so shy, I couldn't say anything. I know he expected something. He seemed disappointed. . . ."

Since her arrival in Boston, Phoebe had begun writing a letter to her obstetrician, and she wanted Erika to tell her—frankly, please—if sending the letter would be an act of madness. The doctor was a good man, engaged to marry for the first time in November. She had no wish to ruin anybody's life—she wasn't asking for much, just another meeting, and perhaps a kiss. . . . "I just want to draw him close and smell him," she said.

Heartache made her voice weak. Cousin Phoebe kept a clipping from a New Hampshire newspaper hidden in a large satchel. It featured a photograph of her obstetrician at an awards ceremony. In the middle of the night she'd sit and stare at the doctor's photograph. While her four children and her husband slept, she'd weep.

"Tell me," Cousin Phoebe said, "if you think I ought to send the letter."

"Suppose this man declines your proposal?" Erika pointed out. "You'll feel the pain of rejection. Suppose his response is positive? What would that reveal about his character?"

"I know what you're saying," Phoebe said. "I just need an outsider's voice to say it to me."

As they headed out of the Public Garden, Erika steered the baby's carriage.

"You wouldn't believe how often this happens with expectant mothers and their obstetricians," Cousin Phoebe said. "The lady across the street felt the same way toward her doctor. And my oldest sister, the same thing."

❖

The waiting room was crowded. A young asthmatic, huge with child, wheezed in her chair, and her jaw hung open as she struggled for air. Erika surveyed the mix of ladies, ranging from expectant girls of twenty to aging widows dressed in black silk. In amusement she wondered how many of these patients harbored an unspoken fondness for Ravell.

An opera ought to be written, she thought. A whole harem of sopranos and mezzos might sway on a stage, some writhing in the throes of childbirth, some penning letters of passion to their favorite medical man. *The Doctor of Women*, such an opera might be named.

She smiled with sealed lips, as though she were privy to an understanding few women in this waiting room had. Someday she might ask Ravell about his experiences.

Twice Ravell rushed past an open door. He wore a rose-colored cravat. When he finally noticed her in the waiting room, he snapped to a halt, his hands catching the sides of the doorway. "Erika! I didn't realize you were coming today."

The doctor liked to check the baby's heartbeat every two weeks. He led her down the hallway. "Have you felt the baby move yet?"

When she nodded, flickers of interest brightened his eyes.

❖

One morning as Peter got up for work, the dawn light showed his nude silhouette as he crossed in front of the gauzy draperies. He had a long torso and a backside so muscular that she wanted to cup his buttocks in her hands.

Suppose she had actually gone to Florence or Milan? She had not wanted to consider how her body might have fared without his. Magdalena said that once a woman has experienced physical intimacy, she finds it almost impossible to live without.

From the bed Erika watched Peter button himself into a pair of pinstriped trousers. Shirtless, he bent over a bureau and jotted a note, a reminder to himself. His naked back formed a lean bridge of muscle. Erika smiled because he was hers, her lover. Others might admire his moustache or the tan calfskin shoes he'd purchased in London, but she had rights nobody else had: she could rise from the bed, walk over and bite his shoulder like an apple, rub her nose against his flesh and take a sniff if she felt like it.

❖

In the middle of the night she could not understand why her eyes had come open in the dark. She lay there, then felt it: someone gliding through soft waters within her.

During those sleepless spaces in the night, she was no longer alone. With her palms placed against her midriff, the unknown creature's stirrings soothed her. She had never had a companion like that, so close and silent in the night.

Her fingers parted in order to catch every rippling under the bones of her hands. All she knew of her child were these vigorous wanderings, not the face, nor the sex, nor the voice. Only the movements hinted at what this secret person must be like.

One evening in Magdalena's parlor, as Erika gave a private recital for a small circle of friends, the silky billows of her magenta dress began to move. She wanted to pause—mid-aria—and hiss down the front of her dress, "Behave yourself! Not now!"

When viewed against the long sweep of a woman's whole life, these were rare months, and she told herself to notice everything. So one morning, trying to savor the otherworldliness of it all, she reclined on the chaise near her bedroom window. She'd just finished bathing.

Light circled her belly as she pulled open her dressing gown and peered over the horizon of her midriff. She had to wait a long time before anything moved. Quivers came near her navel—what caused those? A punch? A foot? She studied her belly like the pure curve of the earth. The motions could only be observed the way one stands in a field and knows, in retrospect, that one has just seen a white dart of lightning.

Then something rolled like a ball under a rug. She gasped. A head. A human head, inside her. Shock slapped her heart. Then it was gone, submerged. During the rest of the pregnancy she never saw that head again.

Regarding the baby's gender: she savored the mystery and was glad not to know. For much of her life, she had longed for a daughter as a confidante, but ever since the pregnancy began, perhaps as a means of preparing herself, she had imagined it to be a boy. She envisioned sniffing his damp, salty scalp after a bath, her boy swaddled up and clean as she carried him from room to room. Her visions of him grew so real that she wondered at the loss she would surely feel if Doctor Ravell handed her a girl after the delivery: "But where is my son? That son, my son?"

Not knowing, she held all possibilities in her womb. To know would be a loss of something.

She grew fond of them both, the dream son, the dream daughter.

❖

In her seventh month, a flicker of concern traveled over Doctor Ravell's face.

He touched Erika's abdomen tenderly, and with a shrug of dismissal he started to stroll off, but then he stopped, uncertain about what he had just seen. "Let me measure you again." Since her previous examination, whatever was inside her had not grown.

"Unless you're hiding it—" he said doubtfully.

Curving his palms around her belly, he kneaded a bit. "It feels like four and a half pounds, but I can't quite tell how much the baby weighs by feeling." A triangle of worry formed between his brows.

He suggested that Erika keep a record, a precise count of how many times the baby moved inside her during a given hour every day. Although Ravell did not speak his fears aloud, she knew that a baby could languish, fail to grow, or even die inside a mother.

At home she locked her bedroom door and stood in front of a full-length mirror, her clothes removed, and looked at herself. Facing the glass frontally, she tried to envision how a whole person could fit in there. On the bed she lay in a crescent shape, lifted her blouse, and found the creature stirring, the movements different now that the child was larger, the rolls and swivels slower and more deliberate. With her palms resting against her smooth flesh, her fingers opened, as sensitive as a blind person's passing over a page. She tried to imagine what the child must be doing now. A heel (or was it a tiny fist?) circled her navel, but just as she touched the bony knob, wanting to grasp it, that part of the baby sank away.

"Twenty movements in one hour are very good," Ravell had said. "Three or fewer would give us cause for alarm."

The child's vigor relieved her: fifty-eight motions in an hour. Fifty-eight.

❖

In her ninth month, he came to the house to examine her. "This is reassuring," Doctor Ravell said, glancing at the chart she'd kept. "A baby who isn't doing well doesn't move this much."

Lying on her Japanese bamboo bed, Erika lifted her blouse to expose her midriff. The sight made him clutch the mound of her womb with such sudden intensity that her hips nearly jumped from the mattress.

"You," he cried, "are *not* going to have a small baby." He kept his hands on her with a glee that said, *Eureka, I've discovered something here.* His eyes, dark as those of men in the doorways of Cairo, stared shockingly into hers and his grip was confident. Ravell was not shy about pressing his hard, strong palms around that unseen creature she and Peter were timid about hurting.

The doctor's face loomed over hers. Her child's body, her whole belly, was drawn up into his hands. Jubilant at his discovery, he looked as though he might lift that small ripe baby right out of her. The child was his to grab and to feel—her child, her center, the essence of her.

"There are at least six pounds of baby here," Ravell declared. "A few weeks ago, I couldn't be certain. Now I am. You are simply *all* baby."

She tried not to notice the loving arrangements of his hands as they framed the baby. The doctor tilted his head with sentimentality—not because she was a favored patient, she reminded herself, but because she was a woman in her ninth month, ready to expel her infant, and that was the sort of tender, parting blessing Ravell felt an obstetrician should give. It was so similar to the sort of fatherly, proprietary adoration that Peter had shown during all those months of gestation—a breathing of affection over the full moon of her belly—that she dared not let herself think about it. The man had hundreds of patients and he probably offered those squeezes of love to the ripe wombs of every one.

Still, she wanted to be special to the doctor in some way. "My husband suggested that you might join us for dinner some night before my confinement. This Thursday, perhaps?"

"Thursday would be excellent."

❖

On Thursday, however, Ravell was delayed so long at a laboring mother's bedside that they had to postpone dinner past nine-thirty. When he finally arrived, apologizing and stomping snow from his boots, the smell of icy air escaped from the crevasses of his coat, and the buttons squeaked with cold. His hat had crushed his hair, and he looked exhausted.

"Let's have Erika sing a bit," Peter offered, "and we can relax while the servants warm up our supper."

As they entered the music room Erika asked Ravell: "How many infants do you deliver in a given year?"

"On average? I would say a hundred." Ravell dropped into a chair, and looked as if he might slide into a thick slumber. Peter handed him a glass of port and the doctor took several thirsty swallows.

Peter settled at the piano to accompany Erika. "Mozart wrote this aria when he was still in his late teens," Erika explained to Ravell as she took up her position next to the piano. She had found—as pregnant singers often did—that the pressure of the baby supported her diaphragm and actually strengthened her voice. The aria she sang was as tuneful and simple as a lullaby.

Ridente la calma nell' alma	Let calm arise, smiling in
si desti,	my soul,
Né resti un (più) segno di sdegno	And let no hint of anger or
e timor. . . .	fear remain. . . .

As she sang, Ravell turned his face sharply toward the wall. He spread one splayed hand over his eyes. She wondered if he slept or listened.

"Thank you," he said when the aria ended. He slapped wetness from his face, laughing at himself. Peter laughed, too, at Ravell's swell of emotion, and Erika smiled. Ravell shook his head tiredly, as though after his madcap day running from house to house, the brief song had provided a corner of peace.

The pork roast tasted dry and overdone by the time it was served, but Ravell ate ravenously, as if it were the first meal he'd paused to consume that day.

"Once our baby is born," Peter declared from his end of the table, "I'm going to write a letter. The medical community ought to be apprised of your success in our case. Four doctors we consulted before coming to you—including two fertility specialists. And you were the first to have achieved any result."

Ravell put down his glass of port, his face reddening, and pressed his napkin to his mouth. He shook his head hard and held up a hand in protest.

The telephone resounded through the house. Erika started in her chair, wondering if the rings might awaken those servants who had already gone to bed.

The maid who had stayed up to serve them announced: "It's a call for Doctor Ravell."

Ravell never tasted the pecan pie that had been baked for him. He shoved his arms through the sleeves of his overcoat and rushed down the icy steps, hastening toward another suffering woman on Boylston Street.

14

O n the last night of the old year, as Erika's labor began, the telephone
rang and rang in Doctor Ravell's office. The rooms were entirely
dark except for a bright rectangle of streetlight that fell across the green
blotter on his desk. The telephone shrilled in the darkness, and went
unheard.

"I've tried his office," the switchboard operator told Peter. "Now I'll
ring his residence."

Next the operator said, "Let's try him at the hospital."

Later it was: "Doctor Ravell still isn't answering. Shall I try his young
assistant—Doctor Markham?"

Ravell could not be traced because at that hour, he lay spent and satisfied
in his mistress's bed, the mist of his own perspiration cooling him from
scalp to toe. Amanda put her lips against his sternum in a finishing kiss,
and gave his private parts one last, grateful pat.

Her husband had departed to bring in the New Year with rounds of
whiskey and whist with his male friends at the Club. No doubt it would
be three or four in the morning before her husband staggered home. The
previous year as New Year's Day dawned, a maid had found two inebriated men, stiff and nearly lifeless, on the carpet at the Club. One of them
had been Mr. George Appleton, Amanda's husband. The maid had
nudged them awake with her carpet sweeper, saying, "You gentlemen
should be ashamed of yourselves."

Amanda's children were grown and lived elsewhere, and the servants were out reveling, so she and Ravell savored the rare quiet of a town house deserted by everyone except them. Ravell almost never came to her home. As an alibi, he'd brought his black medical bag. If anyone startled them by knocking on the locked door, they would explain that Amanda had summoned Doctor Ravell to treat her for a violent onset of abdominal cramps.

With their heads cradled against pillows, they listened to the crunch of footsteps pass on the brick sidewalks below. A recent storm had changed the landscape of the Back Bay, leaving rooftops lathered in snow, and ropes of ivy hanging like whitened nets across red brick façades. Outside, passersby linked arms and celebrated Boston's First Night by singing "Auld Lang Syne."

Ravell got up from the bed, pulled on his trousers and shirt, and crouched at the windowsill like a boy, peeking through the draperies to admire the scene illuminated by streetlamps. Amanda joined him, swaddled in a warm robe, and she knelt and rested her chin on the window ledge. They huddled like two children awed by the wintry sights. On the strip of parkland that divided Commonwealth Avenue, someone had sculpted an enormous dragon from snow, and dyed its long body with splashes of green food coloring. Icicles ran in spikes along the crest of the dragon's spine.

"A marvel," she whispered, "isn't it? I watched them yesterday as they built it." By the streetlight, her hair shone like frost that grew at the corners of the window. He had never before slept with a woman whose hair was as white as hers, yet she always flew at him with vigor, her legs long and sturdy as two lean trees.

A pounding came from below. At Amanda's front entrance, someone hit the door hard with the wrought-iron knocker. The noise was so insistent that Ravell sprang to his feet. He scrambled for socks, vest, suspenders, detachable collar and cuffs, throwing them onto his body, tying his shoes.

It had begun, he realized at once. It had to be. No servant of Amanda's, no husband of hers, would bang like that. Not that incessantly. ("If Erika von Kessler should happen to go into labor," Ravell had instructed Doctor Markham, "alert me at once. My housekeeper will know where I am.") When Ravell had slipped away to Amanda's house, his housekeeper had still been out, so he had left a note on the servant's pillow, telling her where to find him.

His heels hardly touched the stairs as he headed downward, toward the banging.

On Amanda's doorstep, his housekeeper stood with her gray hair slipping from a woolen hat, and her snub nose looked red, shocked with cold. "Doctor Markham has telephoned several times," his housekeeper reported. "I didn't see your note on my pillow until I got ready for bed."

They rode together in the brougham. After the horses paused before his house to let the housekeeper off, Ravell continued. His breaths were broken, his nerves unsteady, his knees and shoulders jostled by the motion of the carriage. Suppose he had already missed the birth? He winced at the foolishness of having lolled in Amanda's bed on such an important night. Suppose the baby mirrored his own features so exactly that as he entered Peter and Erika's house, everyone turned to him, mouths open, their faces aghast? Suppose there could be no hiding his treachery?

Through the carriage window he watched as they passed icicles that glinted from trees. To be born on First Night, amid clear, cold air that enlivened the mind and circulation. It seemed an auspicious sign.

How many minutes left before midnight? Ravell reached into his vest to check the hour, only to discover his pocket watch gone.

Worry flared in his chest. In his haste he had not checked around Amanda's bedroom as carefully as he should have. Earlier in the evening, he had unhooked the pocket watch from its chain, intending to place it on the table next to her bed—just to keep track of the hour. The watch had been securely in his palm at the instant when Amanda had hopped onto him, straddling him from behind, pushing him onto the mattress. He did not remember what had happened to it after that.

Suppose her husband discovered it? Suppose his bare foot grazed it, wedged under a tunnel of twisting sheets? Mr. George Appleton would toss back the bedclothes and scoop up the round, silver timepiece and hold the weight of it in his fist. He would flick on the electric light. George Appleton would turn the watch over, examine the Roman numerals that marked the hours, and he would see Ravell's initials engraved in silver filigree across the back.

"Turn around," Ravell yelled to the driver.

The light was still on under his housekeeper's door when he rapped his knuckles against it, panting. *"You must go back and ask for my pocket watch,"* he said.

The housekeeper understood everything. She stuffed her feet back into her boots, and found her muff and hat and woolen coat. If anyone other than Mrs. Appleton answered the door, his housekeeper was to explain that the doctor had treated Mrs. Appleton earlier that evening, and he needed his pocket watch at once in order to time a patient's contractions. The housekeeper looked sleepy. Inside Ravell, a voice also barked instructions for Amanda: *Scour the room, search the carpet. Rip the sheets off the bed and shake them. Don't give him cause for suspicion, even if he lands in your bed drunk!*

The housekeeper rode beside him in the carriage as they reversed course and headed back several blocks to Amanda's home. The driver parked around the corner, and Ravell waited in the brougham while the housekeeper approached the front door alone. He cursed every minute his oversight had cost him.

The housekeeper reappeared with the silver watch almost at once, as though Amanda had stood by the door, expecting him to return for it. Ravell replaced the watch gratefully in his pocket. "Ring Doctor Markham," he told the housekeeper as the carriage paused to drop her off. "Tell them I'm on my way."

❖

Peter appeared weary as he answered the door, his feet in sheepskin slippers, his striped dressing gown belted and neatly drawn shut. "So you've come at last." He gave a crooked smile. "She's still in the early stages of labor. Doctor Markham told me to take a nap, but I'm afraid I haven't had much success."

The house was quiet. Hours earlier, the servants had gone out, and most had not yet returned from their First Night festivities. On an upstairs landing Peter and Ravell parted ways, with Peter retreating to a bedroom down the hall.

Before Ravell entered the darkened chamber where Erika lay, he stopped in the adjacent bathroom and changed into a clean shirt he'd carried in his bag. That very morning he'd pared his fingernails, and now he scrubbed them with a brush, using a tincture of green soap. Then he lowered his hands into a bowl of alcohol to disinfect them.

Doctor Markham, a thin and boyish man of twenty-six, opened the bathroom door and entered to confer with Ravell. The younger man spoke in hard, terrified whispers—at least they were intended to be whispers, but harsh tones broke through. The door was ajar and Ravell was certain that Erika, who lay just steps away, heard every frantic muttering.

"I had the heartbeat half an hour ago," Doctor Markham said, "and now I think I'm going deaf. I can't hear a thing. Neither can the nurse."

Ravell swept past him. His necktie flew over one shoulder as he rushed into the dim room where Erika lay on her side. The nurse and Doctor Markham switched on every electric light they could find. Erika turned onto her back and faced the ceiling, her expression stoic.

"I thought I felt a movement a little while ago," she said.

"Where?" Ravell asked. "Where did you feel it?"

She pointed to an area near her hip bone. Ravell pressed the stethoscope against the mound of her womb. He jerked his elbows too high as he shifted the instrument from side to side, searching. For months he'd caught the heartbeats easily, every time. Only two days previously, he'd checked on the unborn child here in this very room, on this bed—and he'd heard the sounds immediately then—the quick and steady lashes of an underwater whip. But now no heartbeat came. Nothing.

Ravell raised his gaze to the ceiling, and then closed his eyes. He bit his lower lip so hard that he thought it might bleed.

He shook his head firmly. *I am NOT going to perform a Cesarean,* he thought. *Not if there's no sign of cardiac life.*

He tore the stethoscope from his neck and slapped the instrument down onto a table. His mouth filled with water and his face twisted with tears, but he quickly forced himself to straighten up. He drew his heels together, knowing that he must inspire calm and certainty. "I think we should proceed with the labor," he declared. "Let her go on and deliver in the natural manner."

The nurse pressed her knuckles against her mouth to smother a sob. Markham turned his back, his shoulders vibrating, for he must have been crying, too. Only Erika remained tearless. She sat up, noble and composed, and looked openly at Ravell. From the sadness and regret in her face, Ravell saw that she understood what must have happened, what they all feared. "Tell my husband to come here," she said.

Markham went to find Peter.

When Peter pulled up a chair alongside the bed, she squeezed her husband's hand and assured him gently, "I'll give you another child someday, I promise."

Peter flung back his head and howled like an animal then, and Ravell shuddered as if the sound came from under his own sternum.

"Let's give them a moment alone together," Ravell told Markham and the nurse. They all fled into the hallway, but Ravell hurried alone down another flight into Peter's library. He turned the door key, granting himself privacy.

Ravell glanced through the window at the islands of snow on rooftops. Ice shone on the street. Only nine years previously, he had worked at Boston Lying-in when the first Cesarean was performed there. A Cesarean was still a rare and dangerous operation. And in Erika's case, what purpose would it serve? A long time had passed since anyone had heard a heartbeat; the child must be dead. And he'd done enough damage, hadn't he? Without invading her further and risking infection, without marring the pure globe of her womb with a desperate, possibly murderous incision—on top of everything else he had wrought? Surely she would survive the usual delivery. The infant was small enough. He was not a churchgoing man, but as he stared out the window, he saw everything, as clear as the icy air on this first night of the year. This was the Lord speaking, the Lord's comment on what he had done. The judgment was absolute and irrefutable. No one—certainly not the woman upstairs who would now struggle for many hours to expel the dead child—must ever know his own part in what had happened here.

Erika was still sitting upright in the bed when he returned. The electric lights burned sharply in the room. "When this is over, I want to see the baby," she told him. "Don't try to hide the child from me."

He was surprised by how firm she sounded, and by the command she retained over herself. Other patients he had attended under similar circumstances had required quick sedation or they could not have gone on laboring. But Erika did not weep. It must have been due to her years of training as a singer; she knew how to muster fire and steel before she stepped onto a stage.

"Give me something," Erika told Ravell. Amid the commotion, her contractions seemed to have ceased. She added, "Whatever you need to make this faster and more painless, I want you to do."

He reached for his medical bag, relieved to resume a definable task. To nudge her labor into motion, he gave her a dose of ergot, but not too much, lest it set her contractions galloping. When Erika's labor pains resumed, the nurse handed him a tumbler. Ravell dropped a cotton ball soaked with a dram of chloroform into it and he made Erika hold the glass over her mouth and nose. Soon her hands faltered and she sank back against the pillows, and before he or the nurse could catch it, the tumbler had rolled off the bed and skipped along the carpet.

❖

For eighteen more hours the labor continued. Daylight came, then night again. Each time Erika felt the next round of pains burning through, like a match struck against her tailbone, she called out to one of them—the nurse, or Peter, or Ravell—to douse a cotton ball or a handkerchief with more chloroform so that she could sniff its vapors. If she dozed between contractions and waited too long, the burning match became a torch that raged inside her.

Doctor Markham hurried off to deliver other, living babies, but Ravell never left the house.

❖

At seven-thirty in the evening, on the first day of the year 1904, Ravell announced to the nurse, "Dorsal position."

They made Erika turn onto her back and brace her heels against the bed's footboard as Ravell rolled his shirtsleeves above his elbows.

"Forceps?" the nurse asked.

"The low ones," he said.

"Do whatever you need to do," Erika cried, reaching toward him in surrender before she fell back against pillows.

Their faces were solemn as Ravell maneuvered, turning and angling his own shoulders and head as he brought forth those of the child.

What were they seeing? Erika wondered. A tiny demon? A monstrous confusion of organs and limbs? What sort of creature had died inside her? For a long moment no one made a sound.

"It's a little girl," Ravell said tonelessly.

Peter stood at Erika's shoulder. "She has your nose," he said with curiosity.

That gave her hope. Perhaps she was about to view a happy, living child who resembled an ordinary child, nothing hideous after all. Silently they carried the infant to a far corner where they ministered to her, swaddling the baby in a white blanket. *Oh, bring her,* Erika thought. *Just bring her to me.*

"Here she is, a pretty lass," the nurse said, planting the wrapped package of her into Erika's arms.

"Ringlets like yours," Peter said. "And like your brother's."

The little girl was dead, of course. *Dead,* Erika thought, *and yet she's as perfectly formed and sweet an infant as any I've seen.* The baby made no sound, her scalp awash with waters from the womb, and dark squiggles of hair stuck to her head. Her eyes were shut fast, underlined by deep half-moons, and Erika saw her own nose, with its high, straight bridge and rounded nostrils. Ravell had lured the baby from the birth tract with expert skill; the child's head was wondrously symmetrical and not damaged by the doctor's instruments in any way.

"Lovely," Erika said. "She was a lovely thing, wasn't she?"

Already Erika found herself speaking of her daughter in the past tense, in an effort to become detached. The blanket held the nest of the newborn's heat. She noticed the curl of the baby's fingers, and there was a succulence in those fingers that Erika could almost taste.

When Ravell told Erika that she would need stitches, Peter took the infant in his arms and left with the nurse. Only Ravell remained in the room as he finished sewing her up like a tailor.

"Forgive me," Erika said.

Ravell dipped his hands in a bowl of carbolic acid, disinfecting them for a final time. He held his fingers suspended over the bowl, dripping. "Forgive *you?*" he said.

"Forgive me for not wanting her at first," Erika said. "Later I did want her; I did."

"Of course," he said. His voice sounded distant, his face expressionless, as he left the room.

When Peter returned, he and Erika sat alone with the baby. With the swaddling blanket unwrapped, they set her down on the mattress and had a look at her, with her skin still warm from Erika's body. The baby's head tilted back and her mouth opened in a flash of red gums. They examined the perfect knobs of her shoulders, the creamy substance that lined her left ear. Hidden inside her, a miniature womb must have already existed, a place to ripen babies she would never bear. Their daughter would never know a moment such as this.

Peter said, "I don't think she suffered. Look how peaceful she seems."

The baby's sealed eyes lay in deep coves. If those eyes opened, Erika imagined they would be large. She wished she knew their color, but the baby looked so serene that Erika repressed any thought of pushing a lid upward with her thumb; she wanted to let the baby lie undisturbed.

Neither she nor Peter wept as they studied her; they were too full of awe. As the minutes passed, the baby's bent legs and arms grew colder and tauter. Flecks of blood had dried on her temple.

A tap at the door. "Do you need more time?" the nurse asked. "Or shall I take her now?"

"You can take her," Erika said.

The baby's skin had taken on a lavender cast, but Erika wanted to remember her as a warm thing, almost alive. Already the tiny fists were tightening, hard as stones, and she did not want to watch the little body stiffen.

They had not decided on the name they would christen her, so Peter made one up. "Good-bye, Dorabella," Peter said softly.

"Good-bye, Dorabella," Erika said. Dorabella . . . a character in a forgotten Mozart opera, considered immoral. Dorabella's arias were unknown, and yet exquisite.

Before surrendering the baby to the nurse, Erika kissed the soles of the child's feet.

❖

In the private library where Peter caged his boa, his parrot, and his toucan, Ravell waited. *Bring the baby to me,* he'd told the nurse, *when Peter and Erika have finished.*

He had told the nurse that he wished to examine the infant.

The moment he had pulled the baby from Erika's body, Ravell saw that the little one had his mother's mouth. His mother had died when he was nine, and her mouth was one part of her face he could still remember.

When mourners came to view his mother in her casket, he'd asked his father: "May I stay?"

"If you're well behaved," his father had said.

His younger brother, pouting, had been led away almost at once. Ravell had not wanted the same to happen to him. All afternoon and into the evening he had hardly fidgeted, and he did not allow himself the release of a single sob. The bereaved, especially the ladies, had paused to admire him from time to time, seated in his chair.

He's so good.

Such a little gentleman.

Impeccably mannered.

Some mourners never spoke. The bones of their faces glistened, and they reached into pockets and shook out folded handkerchiefs, applying them to their eyes. Some ruffled the hair on his head, and an older man slipped him a piece of candy to make up for his loss.

At one point during a lull in the flow of visitors (had it been dinnertime?), he found himself alone in the room with his mother. He walked over and stood before the casket. To see her better, he stood with his shoes on the padded cushion where people knelt to pray. That made him taller. Balanced there, he placed his palms over her joined hands, and felt the chill of her.

Close to his mother's casket, he studied her face. She'd been laid out in a blue velvet dress with a white lace collar, her hands folded over her chest, fingers interwoven. Her long, heart-shaped upper lip had been plumper than her bottom lip, her mouth curled at the corners. At some point they would close the casket lid and take her away, so he had stood there memorizing her features.

He'd leaned over as far as he could and put his lips against hers, thinking he might be the last person to kiss her.

The nurse tapped on the library door. She gave the baby to Ravell and went out again, closing the door with discretion.

He brought the baby over to the Turkish sofa, sat near the fire in the hearth, and laid the child across his thighs. He kept his face close to the little girl's.

Speckles of black and blue appeared on the baby's chest, signs of hypoxia; the child had died struggling for air in the womb. But why? Just for a few minutes, had the baby twisted too far to one side? Had the cord pulled too tight? He had delivered hundreds of infants with umbilical cords around their necks—loose, just as this baby's had been—yet most of them had lived.

Peter and Erika would press him with questions, but he would have no answer to give.

The baby's hair had dried since emerging from the damp womb, and by the firelight, her matted curls had glints of auburn, like Erika's hair. Ravell held the child closer to the fire, and as he did so, her skin felt more warm and supple, as though she might be revived.

He held her small heels in his hands. He rubbed the creamy lobe of her ear between his forefinger and his thumb.

The nurse waited outside in the hallway, no doubt impatient for her duties here to be finished. She expected him to emerge. Ravell bent his brow over the child's. And just as he'd done when he was a boy of nine, he kissed his mother's mouth good-bye.

15

After the doctor had gone home, it was eleven-thirty at night. The nurse brought a tray into the same bedchamber where Erika had labored, a roasted chicken dinner with mashed potatoes and sweet green peas and buttery rolls, the first meal she had eaten in thirty hours.

"You've been the strong one," the nurse observed. "You've got to let yourself cry about this."

How peculiar that sounded. *I am the one,* Erika thought, *who weeps onstage, or sobs in the bath.* But at this moment she did not have any impulse to cry. She grasped the drumsticks and gnawed at the crispy flavored skin, as glad as a woman who has crawled on hands and knees and gotten herself out of a burning, besieged city. She was eager for each swallow of milk, glad for the normalcy, glad for the food.

By midnight another nurse came to replace the first. The fresh starched sheets the nurses stretched across the bed felt cold against Erika's legs. The nurses had advised Peter to let his wife sleep alone here tonight, undisturbed, so he collapsed into sleep downstairs on the library sofa.

The new nurse hovered over Erika, kneading her womb. "The doctor has ordered a sedative for you," the black-haired nurse offered. "If you want it."

"I don't need it," Erika responded. After the nurse left, Erika pulled the lamp's chain and snapped off the light. Willingly, thickly, she slept.

Around three in the morning, her eyes came open in the dark. She remembered the baby and how the little girl had died.

The child had lived closer to her than anyone. The baby had slept right under her heart. Erika recalled how she had not even wanted the child at first. The truth made her weep. But because it was all too much to consider then, she shut her lids and slept.

16

Through the window of his kitchen door he saw her—blonde hair tucked under a trim hat, her dark plum suit with its fine tailoring. Caroline Farquahr carried a satchel of offerings—sherry, a baguette her French cook had baked, Stilton, dried pears and apricots. Ravell had not seen Caroline since that summer night when she'd appeared at his office six months previously.

"Amanda tells me you've been despondent," Caroline said. "I've not come here to play Madame de Pompadour. I've come as an old friend."

So he let her into his apartment. His boots drying near the fire, he moved about in his woolen socks and resumed his seat in a leather chair. "I'm here," she went on, "because I'm concerned about your state of mind." She set the bag on a round oak table and drew forth groceries, tearing a baguette into pieces and spreading Stilton on the bread, preparing a little plate for him.

"You don't have to tell me about the case," she said. "I know you wouldn't divulge anything to Amanda."

Caroline placed the platter and a glass of sherry before him. He left the food and drink untouched.

"No matter what happened," she said, "don't persist in blaming yourself. Infants die. Mothers die. Every physician loses some patients." She sat down at the oak table and poured herself a glass of sherry and drank with a kind of frankness. "Let's suppose it was a young mother. . . . Do you keep imagining you could have saved this person?"

Ravell had gone over and over that day in his mind, and could not see how he could have drawn a living child from Erika's body. Yet his mind persisted with self-blame.

If only I had not gone to Amanda's bed that night. . . . *If only I had not forgotten that silly engraved pocket watch.* . . . The mind railed at itself. But even if he *had* arrived at Erika's bedside sooner, as Doctor Markham had done, he would have been powerless to save his own child; that was the horror of it.

Such deaths sometimes happened during labor. He had seen it often enough. If he *had* been standing in Markham's shoes, using a stethoscope to do a routine check on the baby every twenty or thirty minutes, the child's strong heartbeat would still have disappeared—abruptly, inexplicably.

No instrument had yet been invented that could be used during labor to warn that a child's heartbeat was about to falter. No physician could open a small window and peer into a womb to catch sight of a baby at that crucial instant when she turned, tightening the umbilical cord around her neck; or at that instant when a little girl suddenly clutched the cord with her own tiny fist, squeezing off her own air supply. He recalled once delivering an infant born with the umbilical cord clamped between her gums, as if biting it. In utero, a baby could suffocate in three minutes, before she ever opened her eyes and saw the world.

In his mind Ravell wanted to go back to that day and rest his ear against Erika's navel, keeping a scalpel at the ready, braced for that sudden minute when the heartbeat was lost. But her labor had gone on for twenty-seven hours. No doctor could have kept listening to every heartbeat, without cease, for that long.

He had done all he could, and yet . . .

Caroline tilted her head and glanced sideways at him, trying to cajole him into talking.

"No," Ravell answered finally. "There's no one I could have rescued."

"Then *why*—? If it was something hideous . . . certainly you've witnessed dreadful things before. The nightmare of it will wash away with time. Am I right?"

He gave a ceremonial nod.

"Look at you," she whispered hard. Her eyes narrowed in their scrutiny of him. "You haven't combed your hair. That's so unlike you."

She got up and rearranged his hair with her fingers, then resumed her seat. Caroline lifted her glass and swirled the sherry, admiring its translucent color.

Ravell loosened his cravat and pulled it off, then detached his starched cuffs and collar and placed them on the mantel. Words scraped his throat, but he spoke anyway. "I can't tell you how hard it is for me these days," he said, "to attend a normal birth. To hold a living baby."

Caroline gazed at him, stupefied. "You need a rest. Go to Cape Cod—or take the waters at Baden-Baden. You must do something to relieve such feelings. How will you perform your functions, if you've been so badly affected?" She put down her glass and folded her arms, shaking her head at him.

Ravell closed his eyes, longing for just such a respite. He stretched himself across the tufted leather couch, and propped his stocking feet on the sofa's fat arm.

"I can't understand it, really," Caroline said. "To be so vulnerable, so traumatized—after all you've seen. After so much experience, and so many years." Though the platter of baguettes spread with Stilton remained uneaten, she busied herself with creating another serving of delicacies. From the satchel she drew a cylinder of Boston brown bread and sliced off a few thick rounds, then slathered each piece with cream cheese studded by chopped dates.

How long had it been since he'd eaten? she wanted to know.

Many hours, he admitted, so she urged the sweeter fare upon him. Ravell took the molasses-flavored bread she held out to him. He bit into it like a hungry boy. When he'd swallowed every morsel, he licked traces of syrup and chopped dates from his thumb and forefinger.

Smiling, she reached out to hold him like a mother, ready to cradle his head in the bends of her arms. She slid against him on the leather couch. As her blouse pressed against his face, he inhaled the scent of fresh ironing, the slightly burned aroma in the starched fabric. Her hair was the soft yellow of pineapples. For a moment he closed his eyes and sank into her, imagining Erika against him, Erika in the masses of Caroline's blonde hair.

Then, abruptly, he wrestled loose and stood up. "Caroline," he said. "I can't—I can't let this happen."

Reddening and flustered, she got up, too. Leaning her back against a wall, she looked at him, a glint of bitterness in her stare. Many men must have melted at the sight of her prettiness; was he the only one who'd ever rebuffed her? A light rain tapped at the windows. She swaddled herself in her wraps and stabbed the air with her umbrella as she rushed off into the night.

❖

"So Caroline came to visit you," Amanda Appleton said. "She told me that she stopped by."

Ravell said nothing. Amanda walked through his flat, looking around at the doorways draped by rope portieres, at the clawed feet of his oak table, and at the pillows plumped on his bed.

"She says she's worried about you," Amanda said, "but I suspect she has designs on you."

Ravell shrugged. Amanda did not ask for an accounting from him. In fact, she appeared amused by the notion that Caroline had been here. Amanda turned on the glass Bordeaux lamp, and she stepped back to admire its jewel colors—the topaz and orange, and the royal purple of the stained-glass grapes. She asked if Caroline had noticed the lamp: had he told Caroline that the Bordeaux lamp had been a present from her, from Amanda?

When Amanda kissed him, there was an edge of spite to the kiss that had not been there the previous week. She locked her legs around him and pushed her bones against him with a kind of greed, as though she were sparring with somebody. She may have scrutinized the pillow next to his for extra creases made by another woman's head. This only sharpened her lust.

"They must all want you," Amanda said. "Your patients."

"Hardly," Ravell laughed.

"They lie with their husbands and think about you."

"When they hear my name, they remember the agony of childbirth," he said. "They hope I'll never darken their doorstep again."

After this, Amanda came more frequently to his private residence. She had a key, and whenever he came up the stairs, he could not predict if she would be waiting for him. One evening he arrived to find Amanda seated in his leather chair, wearing nothing but a corset laced so tight that her breasts seemed to swell and overflow from the top of it.

"I've been here for ages," she said.

"I've got an infant to deliver in less than an hour," Ravell lied. "I've just returned home to grab a couple of cold pork chops from the icebox."

Amanda pulled at his suspenders, lowering them from his shoulders.

"Did you hear what I said?" Ravell brushed her hands away. "There simply isn't time."

She fell back, stung. "I've become tiresome to you, haven't I? Is it my age—is that what bothers you?"

"Age has got nothing to do with it."

One Monday evening when he expected that Amanda would be coming, he walked the streets of the Back Bay until it grew so late he knew she would need to leave. After nightfall pedestrians became anonymous; the row houses lit up from the inside like stage sets. No one noticed him as he strolled along the strip of parkland that divided Commonwealth Avenue. While passing Peter and Erika's home, he slowed his gait, his breaths suspended as he gazed at five stories of windows that glowed from within. At a third-floor window he caught sight of Peter's silhouette near the toucan's cage. Peter lifted his elbow, his arm extended to offer a perch for the bird.

Ravell took care not to lurk; he moved past slowly but steadily. He wished the season were not winter, but summer. If it were July, their windows would be thrown open, and the vibrations of her voice might be heard.

Dear Hartley, he wrote later that evening to his boyhood friend who owned the coconut plantation near the coast of South America. *Perhaps in November, I will embrace your long-standing invitation to visit your part of the world. Lately I have witnessed a good deal of sadness in my practice. It has become difficult to shrug off the sorrows I've seen. Besides, the needs of certain members of the fairer sex can exhaust a man's spirit. . . .*

A hand clattered against his back-door window. He dropped the pen, glanced up, and saw Caroline Farquahr flash a wave. She had no key, and he had not seen her since the evening she'd fed him brown bread sweetened by molasses and dates. Ravell snapped his head down, rereading what he had written to Hartley, sorry that he had glanced up and met her eye. Why had he not drawn the curtain over that window?

Caroline saw how he stalled, reluctant to open his door to her. She knew that he had not returned her smile with his own—she noticed how he had jerked his head away, and that only made her smack the pane harder.

Finally he got up to answer. As soon as he unlocked the door, she turned her body sideways to fit through the narrow opening, and she sliced past him. He closed the door behind her. She opened her lips, ready to spit flames.

"First you threw me over, and now it's Amanda."

He ran one finger under his tie, loosening it, not responding.

He heard a snag, a pause in her hard, enraged inhalations. Caroline paced for a moment and halted. "There's somebody else, isn't there?" She placed her palm on her jutting hip. "Could it be that singer we heard last spring at Mrs. Gardner's palazzo? I remember how eager you were to run to the stage door for an extra glimpse of her."

Stunned, he stared at the floor. With open hands he rubbed his face and wiped his features, as though to cleanse himself. "To be completely honest, I'd prefer to be alone at this time in my life. Celibate."

"You?" she scoffed. "Celibate? From what Amanda tells me, you won't be happy staying celibate for long."

17

During the days that followed the baby's birth and death, memories replayed in Erika's mind, spreading like fire across a night sky. The scenes burned through her sleep and woke her while the moon was still up. She watched the same nightmare hour unfold over and over—the one with a very young doctor yanking the stethoscope from his ears, declaring that he must be going deaf; the sound of Ravell's tread on the stairs; the tie that flew like a long tongue around Ravell's neck as he raced into her bedchamber.

She saw the little girl again, the weary half-moons under the baby's closed eyes after her long day of being born and dying. The baby's head fell back in surrender, her tiny lush lips parted.

Peter's memory flared with similar scenes, and at night he molded himself protectively around Erika. Whenever she slid from the bed, his body jerked awake. His hands followed her waist and he whispered anxiously, "Where are you going?"

"To the bathroom," Erika said. "Only to the bathroom."

When her eyes opened in the dark on the second night, she sat up, startled by sensations her body had never known before. Milk spurted from her nipples, droplets wetting her midriff and her forearms. Milk soaked the sheets. She dabbed at the leakage and licked it from her fingers and found the substance strange—sticky and sweet.

She pulled the chain and snapped on the lamp next to the bed and woke Peter, knowing he would be as amazed by the sight as she was. "It's the milk," she said, staring down at nipples that wept and left her torso glistening.

Her breasts had never been so ripe, so enormous. She might have hired herself out as a wet nurse. "Do you want a taste?" she asked Peter.

A look of curiosity passed over his face. With one finger he wiped opaque drops from her arm, and he tasted. "Sugary," he observed.

❖

Papa came to visit while the fresh horrors of labor flashed through her still, and she spared him no detail. Her father listened with the tender interest he showed his patients.

Magdalena came to call, her arms laden with gladiolas and chocolates and Caruso's latest recording, which she promptly set upon the gramophone. Magdalena had never borne a child. Every time Erika alluded to her ordeal, Magdalena interrupted with a funny anecdote.

"Have you heard that Dame Nellie Melba is suing a newspaper over a bad review of her singing?" Magdalena said. "This time I must say she's got a good case. It turns out that the newspaper published a review of a performance that had been canceled. The critic had written his terrible review in advance!"

Erika had difficulty concentrating on Magdalena's words. *How, she wondered, could Magdalena speak of such frothy things? Doesn't she realize,* Erika thought, *that two days ago a dead baby was wrenched from between my legs and taken from my body?* Her mind was crowded with those visions, and her thoughts could not make room for anything else.

❖

Her recollections were violent, and through the haze of scenes, Ravell moved unforgettably. A thousand times she watched the shock freeze his features as he rushed into the bedchamber and saw her lying there. Erika held the warm swaddled bulk of the baby against her chest, murmuring,

"Oh, she was sweet—" Ravell went away wordlessly, not wanting to linger at the scene.

He had not become an obstetrician to pull dead, lavender-faced babies out of women's bodies. Knowing him, she suspected that he went home, sat on the edge of his bed with elbows on his knees, and hung his head.

The next morning he entered her bedroom very early, as a father might do, and stared at the closed drapes. *In about two months I will examine you again,* he said. *By then everything will be clearer, and we can discuss the future and whatever decisions we ought to make.*

❖

All her life she had been curious to know what pregnancy and childbearing would be like, and now she knew. Her womb had held a baby who was perfectly made. That gratified her—to know that her body had given root to all the proper parts of a child.

A miracle to have grown her, even if the little girl did not live. What was missing? As the weeks passed, whenever Erika saw parents with baby carriages during a stroll in the Public Garden, she was baffled. What had sparked their offspring to breathe, to squirm? The daughter she and Peter had had looked the same as those infants, yet their daughter had no more life than the Chinese figurine on the mantel whose porcelain black hair required dusting.

❖

Only three weeks after the delivery, Erika stood before a tall oval mirror and cinched a pink belt snugly, her waist as narrow as it had ever been. So this was to be her consolation, then: the little girl had been kind to her body. No one would have guessed that she had ever been pregnant.

She was free now to book her passage for Italy. ("You've got your chance back," Magdalena pointed out. "Why not seize it? Just raise the sails, and get away.") During the labor, when the baby's death first became apparent, for a few shameful seconds relief had passed through her, because all the freedom she had loved so well had rushed suddenly, miraculously back. But the relief had lasted only that long—seconds.

Now that her womb had been emptied of the child that had kept her from all her plans, it was no longer Italy she thought about. Only the devastation of it filled her—the shock, like a rape. Fate had robbed her, left her reeling—not quite a woman until she got back what had been taken from her.

Now she wanted—as desperately as she had ever wanted anything—to go back and do it properly. She knew she had the power of it inside her, buried deep. Given another chance, she felt she could make it come out right. How could she devote herself to anything else until she had finished this, until her womb made a living, laughing baby?

❖

As she walked down Commonwealth Avenue, about six blocks from her home, she paused on the frozen strip of land across from Ravell's office. She envied the female patients who came and went.

It would not be proper for her to enter his office, not until her appointment in several more weeks.

She sat at the piano and sang Schubert's "Erlkönig" over and over, like a madwoman, her fingers galloping over the keys like a horse scrambling at night through a storm. She sang about the terrors of a child who verged on being snatched by Death. She repeated it so many times that she expected the servants to enter the music room and make her quit, but nobody did. She played and sang until her vocal cords grew sore and her shoulders collapsed.

Perhaps the Lord was a Great Artist who designed the plots of people's lives, she thought; perhaps when old age brought her a more aerial view of things, she would understand why this had happened. For now she could only guess. *Maybe this will enrich my voice, my art,* she told herself, after she'd pulled her fingers away from the ivory keys. That was the irony: for an artist, the worst and most painful thing could also be a gift.

18

Four men waited on the sidewalk outside his practice as Ravell returned from attending a birth. It was just past seven A.M. and the office was not due to open for another half hour. He had been looking forward to ducking upstairs to his apartment for a swift change of clothes before the first patient arrived. He had hoped to enjoy a scone with honey, to rest his head against the back of his leather chair—just for a few minutes—and close his eyes.

The moment he saw the four men, he understood that something was amiss. One gentleman raised a cane and pointed it at Ravell, and the other three, all dressed in black overcoats and top hats, turned to face him. With their feet apart and their hands behind their backs, they blocked the sidewalk. White breaths issued from them like steam from the mouths of dragons.

An air of importance and high social position emanated from all four of them. Their hats and gloves were impeccable, and the smell of quality wool hung about their damp overcoats. The eldest of the foursome, a bald man nearing sixty, had hands that trembled. He appeared in need of a stiffening drink. Ravell recognized him as George Appleton, Amanda's husband, but the man had never appeared so unbalanced, or so sickly, before. He could hardly look at Ravell. Next to him, a younger man whose hair was slicked with pomade glared at Ravell, the menace in his facial muscles unmistakable: the younger one was Caroline Farquahr's husband.

"Doctor Ravell?" The tallest gentleman stepped forward. "We wish to have a word with you."

Ravell unlocked the front door and led them through the stale air of the vacant waiting room into his office. His nurse had not yet arrived. As he went behind his desk, he motioned toward a coat rack and three chairs ranged along the wall. Ravell offered to bring another seat to accommodate the fourth man.

"That won't be necessary, thank you," the tallest of the lot said. "We'll keep our business here brief." He explained that he was an attorney, and he pointed out that the man to his left was the brother-in-law of the governor of the Commonwealth of Massachusetts. "We appear here with regard to a matter of great personal concern to all of us. At one time or another, each of our wives has been a patient of yours.

"You stand accused of repeated attempts to seduce Mr. Farquahr's wife," the lawyer announced, "and though Caroline Farquahr has managed to resist, it seems that Mr. Appleton's wife, Amanda, has been subjected to the same type of advances. In fact, Mr. Appleton's wife admits to having succumbed."

Ravell's collar felt soaked at the place where his hair touched it, but he did not dare to take a handkerchief and wipe the back of his neck. He stood before them and said nothing. He did not move.

The attorney went on talking as Caroline Farquahr's husband gave hard, sharp nods of satisfaction, his eyes never leaving Ravell's face. Obviously her husband regarded this as his rightful bounty—to enter this office and watch the reaction of his prey.

How long had they been lurking outside his office this morning? Ravell wondered.

Even before the lawyer described the proceedings they intended to initiate against him, Ravell foresaw how absolute it would be, the shunning. He understood at once that this encounter was only the beginning. He heard only random words and phrases as the attorney went on speaking in dire terms: *investigation . . . censure . . . Board of Obstetrics . . . American Medical Association . . . your license revoked . . . the possibility of criminal charges . . .*

He saw how patients would vanish from his waiting room. Even if female patients remained loyal, their husbands would forbid them from submitting to any examination by him. Even if he moved to another city or state, the vengeance and righteousness of men like these would follow him.

The foursome departed just as the first patients arrived. Passing through his waiting room, the four gentlemen gave the arriving females concerned, regretful glances—as though they disliked entrusting any woman to Ravell's care, even for another day.

After they'd gone, Ravell fell into his desk chair and turned to the window and watched the color blanch from the sky. In their indignation these men did not even suspect the worst breach Ravell knew he had committed—but God had already punished him for that.

He suspected that it had been Caroline, not Amanda, who had sent the posse here. An arsonist—that's what Caroline was, and she would not be satisfied until she'd hurled torches through the windows of his practice.

Amanda's frankness had always been a risk; she had no talent for lying. When confronted by her husband or a group of inquisitors, she must have found it difficult not to speak the truth.

Dear Hartley, he wrote in his mind, *Please disregard my recent letter about a visit next fall because you may be seeing me on your island of coconut palms far sooner than that. Everything has changed for me since I mailed my last letter. My career as a physician has unexpectedly ended. I must begin a new life as far away from this one as possible.*

19

⟨∞⟩

The barbershop smelled of men—the pungent spice of Havana cigars and rum and aftershave. White towels protected men's clothing like bibs. Peter savored the camaraderie he felt whenever he stepped into the place. It was not simply an establishment where one paid one's fifteen cents for a shave; the shop was more intimate than the Club, really. Men came and went daily and fell into reclining leather chairs and spoke their opinions and released their cares to barbers whom they trusted to draw sharp-edged blades across their jaws and throats.

As Peter entered one morning in early March, he noticed one customer engrossed in a copy of the *Police Gazette*. Another rather portly gentleman pressed his belly against the counter as he trimmed his cigar with a device that resembled a miniature guillotine. The fellow puffed with relish before settling into a chair.

A wall held dozens of shaving mugs, each one bearing an individual customer's personal insignia. The barber pulled down Peter's mug and had him swiftly draped and lathered up.

"I suppose you're aware of the troubles with your friend Doctor Ravell," the barber said, his expression grim.

Before Peter could express his perplexity, the cigar-smoking fellow in the next chair gave a hard cough that sounded like a laugh. "That one," the fat man said. "That's a doctor who enjoys reaching up the skirts of half the wives in the Back Bay!"

The man reading the *Police Gazette* glanced up from his pages. "Let's hope they put him behind bars. Quite an earful we'll all get after his trial."

"Trial?" Peter winced. "Are you talking about Doctor Ravell?"

"It's all allegations at this point," the barber said.

As the barber and the two other customers recounted bits and pieces they'd heard, Peter thought he might choke. In the mirror his jaw looked white, painted with whipped cream. He wrestled his way to an upright position and turned to face them.

"I happen to know Ravell quite well," Peter declared, "and I don't believe a word these women are saying. They've made it up—like those young girls in Salem, pointing fingers at witches. . . . God knows, a man in Ravell's profession must be vulnerable to all sorts of female hysterics."

The barber stepped back, silent and cautious as he wielded the straight-edged razor. He waited for Peter to recline in his chair. Then he dipped the badger brush back in the mug and continued to stir.

"Well," the portly customer added more quietly, "I could never be a doctor of obstetrics myself. Too many temptations, if you ask me." He flourished his cigar in the air.

"Ravell is a scientist," Peter went on. "A brilliant one. He's meticulous in his techniques. . . . If you don't believe my opinion, I suggest you ask a couple who were childless for nineteen years of marriage. Under Ravell's care, the couple managed to have twins. That wasn't luck—that was the work of a superlative physician."

The barber, of course, knew about the little daughter Peter and his wife had lost just two months previously. In the mirror Peter noticed how the barber glanced sternly—warningly—at the other clients. To sharpen the long-handled razor, the barber drew the blade with slow strokes—almost meditatively—over the leather strap that hung from a post. He waited for the redness and fury to drain from Peter's face before he began the actual shaving. The barber said nothing as he completed his work. Peter sensed doubts behind the barber's reserve—the man was clearly surprised that Peter would rush to defend a doctor who'd delivered a lifeless child.

20

∞

"I'm ruined here," Ravell told Peter and Erika. "You must see that."
"Where will you go?" they asked him.

"My friend in Trinidad has asked me to manage one of his estates. I plan to start a new life."

The three of them had gathered before the fireplace in the library, where Peter unlocked a portable case that held crystal decanters. He poured shots of whiskey for himself and Ravell. "Why," Peter asked, slapping two coasters against a table, "should a couple of women be allowed to wreck a superb doctor's career?"

"I have to blame myself for what has happened," Ravell said. "I'm sorry to inform you that I'm no saint."

"You're an unmarried man," Peter said. "Maybe it's nobody's business what occurred or didn't occur." He opened a box of cigars, offering one to Ravell, taking another for himself. "If George Appleton's wife seduces a man, is it entirely the man's fault? Or is it also hers?"

Erika removed her high-heeled shoes and sat on the horsehair divan with her legs tucked under her. "When?" she asked quietly. "How soon will you be moving away?"

"In six days."

Six days! She closed her eyes, suppressing the liquid that welled under the lids, but it was no use. When her eyes blinked open, her vision blurred. Slow tears ran into the corners of her mouth, and her tongue licked salt and wetness. Peter got up and slid onto the divan next to her.

He pressed a clean handkerchief into her hand and stroked the folds of her skirt, patting her covered knee.

"I'm useless to you both at this point," Ravell said. He went to a window and looked down at the street. "You don't know what it's like. It gets worse every day." Ravell took a seat on an ottoman close to the fire. He unbuttoned his vest before continuing.

"A man chased me down Marlborough Street yesterday afternoon," Ravell said. "He came after me with his cane raised." Ravell sounded helpless, perplexed. "I delivered four of his children, and his wife's last confinement was exceedingly difficult. For three days I kept returning to their house, and for those three nights I hardly slept. He and his wife seemed terribly grateful at the time. . . . Now the husband chases me with a stick."

"We'll come visit you on your coconut plantation," Peter offered.

"I'd like that," Ravell said.

❖

Before Ravell left, he promised to write down the names and addresses of other specialists for them to see, and he said he would leave them his boyhood friend Hartley's address as well. The day before he was due to sail, he stopped by the house to drop off an envelope. Peter was still at work. The maid led the doctor into the music room, where Erika sat at the piano singing Mozart's "Ridente la calma," which she had sung like a lullaby throughout her pregnancy. Sometimes the melody and lyrics soothed her, but at other times the aria reminded her so acutely of the baby that she had to stop singing it.

A hundred things remained for Ravell to do before he left the following day, he explained. He did not have time to stay for dinner, nor did he have time for tea. "It's just hello and good-bye, I'm afraid," he said. He paused for a last, lingering look around the music room, at the striped wallpaper and the lacquered piano. The pink fringe that hung from a lampshade trembled as his elbow brushed it.

"I won't forget the night of Peter's birthday." He gave a faint smile. "Hearing you sing here."

She nodded, prepared to escort him out. Just before he reached the music room door, his head fell to one side and he seemed to buck in frustration as he asked, "Is there anything you want to *say* to me?"

Her chest went concave with helplessness and she raised her right arm toward him in a limp salute. "I'd like to give you a hug," she admitted.

Eagerly he bent, his arms opening to catch her waist as he pulled her against him. She whispered against his ear, "You were so wonderful and so warm!" Her arms reached up, casting a loose wreath of love around him.

Sounds of relief came from him, and this surprised her. Had he thought that she would hate him, blame him for the baby's fate? For an instant he drew himself away to warn, "You're going to make me cry." Under his dark brows, his lashes batted together. During those blinks he reminded her of a four-year-old boy who stood bashfully at his mother's knee, permitting himself to be hugged.

"You were so good through the entire ordeal," she said. Once again her body washed up against him, her wrists joined at his nape, urging him closer to her. It was only kind and human, she told herself, for a doctor to hold a patient in her grief.

He hesitated, and then something exploded from inside him—an exhalation as he moved forward, absorbing her against his dark blue vest and suit coat. He murmured into the earrings tangled in her hair, "You will have another child—trust me." She was amazed that he, who usually carried himself with a certain formality, had come unleashed. He had never flirted with her before. Now it was as if they had lost a baby together.

He backed her up, a little waltz. As he held her and held her, her hips slid flush against him so that his genitals could be felt right through her dress. She had never flown against any man other than her husband with so much passion before, but it was not just she—it was the doctor, too.

With his hands at her waist, hers around his neck, they fell together naturally, as though they'd been married for years.

Her consciousness then came awake. There was something untoward in how long the man was embracing her. In the dining room directly below, she heard two maids polishing silverware. A drawer slammed shut, the utensils jostled with the ring of coins. Overhead, a chambermaid rolled the carpet sweeper across the bedroom floor. It was hardly proper for any doctor to be this physical with a patient. Certainly he was an emotional man, but . . . Always before he had guarded himself.

How often did he indulge like this? she wondered. How often did he give a calculated pivot at the door and ask his postpartum ladies, "Is there anything you want to say—" and then wait for them to throw themselves against his chest? This was a safe moment, after all, with no husband present. Once he stepped through the door, he'd be neatly, sweetly rid of her.

Were his accusers justified in banishing him from Boston?

Between him and her was the rare thing, though: a dead baby. His body sighed against hers, and in holding each other there was sadness, forgiveness, desire, a sensual relief.

In the soft, warm fusion of embraces that went on too long, she and the doctor made their peace. If it continued much after this, things could slide in only one direction, and they both knew it.

"And your husband," the doctor said at last, as if to remind himself, gulping, pulling back, "is he helping you?"

"Yes." She let her head drop in a reluctant nod.

At the guilty mention of her husband, they broke apart. The doctor took a large and deliberate step backward, and the sudden desertion made her breath catch. Her fingers slid down the length of his navy woolen sleeve until she found his hand, and she held on to it.

Until now she had always been cautious not to be seductive with men other than her husband—but now, oddly, she lowered her eyelids and gave a coquettish stir of her hips. He had seen the ugliest things happen to her, but this man had brushed his lips against her hair.

The notion that the doctor and she had lost their senses like that struck her as faintly comical, and she could not hide a smile. She faced the window. "Look—more snow is falling." The flakes obscured the view.

"Well." His tone switched then, and became more loud and brusque, taking on a ring of practicality. "I should have worn my galoshes."

How could she possibly say good-bye to him? She threw a stray arm around his neck again.

His body went rigid and he glanced over his shoulder at the door. She winced, knowing no married lady ought to be doing this. Her hip gave one last nudge against his.

"All right," he murmured, a signal that he intended to open the door. "All right." His voice grazed her hair, assuring her that he did not deny what had happened, but now it had to end.

He fled down the carpeted staircase, not looking back. In the foyer, just before opening the front door—just before leaving her house, a place that he would never visit again—he fished something from his pocket and called in a high, bright tone to one of the maids: "Would you give this to Mrs. von Kessler?"

The door opened and shut, taking him away, bringing a gust of winter into the house that chilled Erika's legs even under her long gown. She stood, stunned, at the top of the stairs. The maid trotted up the steps and slipped the envelope into Erika's hands—the same one that had prompted Doctor Ravell to call in the first place. Erika carried it into the library and slit the envelope with an ivory-handled letter opener. She waited for the flush of dizzying impressions to settle before extracting the slip of paper from the envelope.

In flowing blue ink Ravell had written his friend Hartley's address in Trinidad. Peter had also asked Ravell to recommend other fertility experts, but Ravell had left no names. Erika placed the page on Peter's desk blotter. She went to the window and peered into the swirl of darkness and snow, wondering if she could still catch sight of Ravell, but he was gone.

It was odd, of course, that he had not offered any referrals. Peter would make excuses for him, pointing out that in the haste of leaving Boston, particularly under the threat of professional expulsion, Ravell's mind must have been scattered.

But Erika saw it differently. Perhaps it saddened Ravell to imagine her being cared for by another physician. He wanted to do it himself, and have the next birth turn out more happily. He was hoping they would come to Trinidad.

21

That night, for the first time since the delivery, intercourse gave her no discomfort. "Does this cause you pain or tenderness?" the doctor had asked while examining her. *No, no.* She relaxed, remembering his expert hands.

While her husband brought his body against hers, it was the doctor who made love to her.

With her whole belly drawn up into his hands, his palms gripped the child, his face over hers, his eyes peering into hers. His eyes were huge and dark, rimmed in charcoal shadows.

On the bamboo marriage bed, she opened her legs to him.

While her husband made love to her, she heard the doctor exhale in relief as his chest fell against hers. She was one of thousands of women he had touched. A favorite concubine.

In the doctor, too, there was that yearning to scavenge something lovely from the wreck. The doctor pushed his heart against hers. He wanted to hover over her another nine months with his instruments and erase the failure absolutely. The doctor wanted to draw a fresh glistening baby from the recesses of her.

❖

Her husband's body was trim and vigorous—more virile, in truth, than the doctor's slight-framed body. After the doctor had blended into every touch of her husband's hands, after pleasure had rinsed through her . . .

The glare of electric bulbs went on, and she was back at the delivery, just as it was ending. The truth, the final judgment, then: the child was dead.

Cradling the moist, lifeless child in her arms, she lay on the bed and turned to the doctor. He did not look back as he opened the door and went away.

If she had surrendered herself to the doctor earlier, if she'd not been so reluctant to have the baby, perhaps her womb would never have become a grave.

In the darkness her shoulders shook.

"Did it hurt?" her husband whispered, alarmed.

"No," she answered. The doctor, in making love to her, had reached into her most sorrowful space. In the darkness she took the hem of the sheet and wiped her wet cheeks so that her husband would not detect what he suspected—that she was weeping.

PART TWO

22

⚜

Peter wrote:

My dearest Ravell,
Ten months have passed since what was surely the saddest day of our
lives, and alas! Since you left Boston, yet another fertility specialist
has been unable to help us. Only you, dear Ravell, came miraculously
close to succeeding. . . .

It will hardly surprise you that Erika and I intend to book our pas-
sage to Trinidad in the hope of visiting you shortly. . . .

Ravell wrote in reply:

. . . It would be best to wait until February or March to visit the coco-
nut plantation, when the season is drier and the worst tropical down-
pours have passed. Until then, I shall be so busy supervising the
clearing of the land, that I fear I'll be too distracted to welcome the
two of you with my full heart. . . .

But by November Peter could not bear to wait any longer, and he was
not the sort of man to be daunted by weather or any sort of obstacle. Peter
ignored Ravell's entreaties to postpone their journey by a couple of
months. Just days before he and Erika embarked on the SS *La Plata*, he
sent word to Ravell that they would soon arrive.

The first night after they sailed from New York and headed for the big island of Trinidad, ice crusted the rigging and snow whitened the decks. All the next morning the crew took up shovels and crowbars and labored to loosen frozen debris, and while the men worked, Peter settled into the stateroom he and Erika shared. He spread his maps across pillows and blankets, and opened a small notebook against the table that fitted neatly alongside the bed. He held the end of his pen between his teeth, the nib pointing upward at a jaunty angle as he formulated plans.

He placed the tip of his finger on a map and showed Erika how tantalizingly close Trinidad lay to the great continent of South America. If Ravell could be persuaded to abandon his work for just ten or twelve days, Peter figured that he and Ravell might venture into the interior together. They simply had to cross the channel known as "Serpent's Mouth," and follow the Orinoco River into the wilds of Venezuela.

"And where do you plan to leave your wife," Erika asked, "if you and Ravell head off on an expedition?"

Peter shrugged. "In a lovely hotel in the capital." This did not seem to trouble him.

On a notebook page, under the heading "Orinoco River Trip," he jotted: *See Venezuelan consul at Port-of-Spain to obtain visa. For proof of vaccination, roll up sleeve and show my big, scarred arm. Pack pistol.*

Under the page captioned "Collection of Specimens," he wrote: *Hire experienced boy to take me into the woods. Bring jars and nets.*

Under the page marked "Conceiving a Child," he reminded himself: *BUY ICE, LOTS OF ICE, no matter how costly it may be in the tropics. Leave the rest to Ravell.*

❖

Awnings appeared a few days after they left New York, and passengers packed away the somber gray woolens of winter and changed into white clothes, for they had entered the tropics. Ladies propped up parasols and men sprawled across the deck like starfishes drying under the sun.

Erika spent long hours standing at the rail. The night the ship passed Martinique, she saw how darkness made the island invisible, and an eerie, red glowing ribbon of lava marked the volcano there. After the island of Martinique was gone, she lingered at the rail and felt breezes finger the fringe of her shawl. She felt Ravell's presence beside her. In her mind he was always listening.

On the deck Erika lifted her face toward the stars. She wanted the doctor to enfold her in his navy woolen coat and rock her slowly in his arms. She imagined he was the only man on earth who could understand what she had felt through all these past eleven months. Just after the baby was lost, Peter had been forthright in his grief, but soon he, like many men in such circumstances, had crawled into a trench of silence. It hurt him to hear her mention their baby—his chest heaved and he held his breath warningly.

One evening she watched a gale from the bow, and when Peter insisted that she seek shelter, she refused. She liked the rough water pouring down on her, and she found that one could hear instruments in the wind—an oboe, a cello, a bassoon—if one listened.

Alone on the deck, she sang into the storm, closing her eyes as though in prayer. She was still determined to move to Italy, but until she had given birth to a living child, she could not say when that day would come.

❖

Anchored off Barbados, the ship took on a crowd of deck passengers— Negro men, women, and children piled on board with their colorful personal cargo of parrots, boxes, and bananas. Each deck passenger was assigned a canvas chair where he or she was expected to sit and suffer through all manner of weather, and survive a week without a change of clothing. The ship furnished their food.

Erika paused near the group from Barbados one morning to observe a child who was not quite yet walking. A dark-skinned mother wearing a red kerchief stood behind the child, holding her two tiny fists, trying to balance the toddler.

Eleven months, Erika thought. *If my daughter had lived, she'd stand there with locked knees and wobble like that.*

23

Upon reaching Trinidad, the steamer had to anchor at a great distance from Port of Spain. A rim of royal palms marked the island's perimeter. While passengers waited for a tender to take them ashore, officials came aboard, including a gentleman who approached Peter and Erika and introduced himself as Mr. Hartley, Ravell's friend. Due to an outbreak of illness among the plantation workers, Ravell had been unable to get away, so he had asked Hartley, who lived close to the capital, to welcome their ship.

"I've received a bit of confidential information of rather serious concern," Mr. Hartley told Peter. "May I speak to you and your wife privately on the upper deck?"

Mr. Hartley owned several large agricultural estates on the island. Associates of his had alerted him to the news that yellow fever was rampant in Port of Spain. New arrivals were particularly vulnerable; eight who had landed by the last steamer had since died. His informants had advised him to keep quiet about this in order not to spark panic; still, they had encouraged him to warn any friends of his of the grave risk.

"Landing here would be dangerous," Mr. Hartley emphasized. "Especially if you and your wife intend to stay in the capital. Why not stay on board and consider traveling to another island?"

Hartley was a fellow of sizeable girth with russet hair and a sun-bleached moustache. As he frowned, his eyebrows pulled together, thick and thatched. The concern was evident in his pale blue eyes.

Their predicament was so unexpected that Peter did not know what to do. As a result of the fever, the Queens Park Hotel had closed. Disconcerting, of course, for the Queens Park Hotel was the very place they intended to stay.

Peter glanced at Erika. "Shall we land here or continue on?" he asked.

She stared at him, unable to speak. Finding their way to Ravell again—for the past year, that was what they both had lived for. Peter had dreamed of coming to this island for longer than she had—ever since Ravell had described its butterflies and hummingbirds and fabled animals; ever since Ravell had unwrapped a twenty-foot anaconda skin across the Oriental carpet of their Boston drawing room.

"We've come to see Trinidad," Peter told Mr. Hartley, "not any other island. And we've come to consult our friend Ravell about a serious personal matter. I think we should go ahead and risk the fever."

"In that case," Mr. Hartley said, "I insist that the two of you stay as guests with my family at Tacarigua. My residence is up in the hills about ten miles out from Port of Spain. The danger would be far less at my estate. Mosquitoes are rife here in the lowlands—particularly in the evenings, when the air in Port of Spain becomes covered by mists."

"We accept your offer most gratefully," Peter said.

Relieved that they had decided to land, Erika took Mr. Hartley's hand as he helped her descend and climb into the tender. Within days, Mr. Hartley said, the island might come under quarantine. If they'd arrived a day or two later, their ship might have been turned away.

"Perhaps the two of you could take the train into town in the early morning for a tour," Mr. Hartley said, "when the danger is less."

Thanks to Hartley's well-placed acquaintances and connections, their luggage passed with great speed through the Customs House. Within minutes they found themselves seated in a victoria, being driven to Hartley's estate, which he called Eden.

During the carriage ride, torrential rains prevented them from viewing much of the countryside, except for the bamboo groves and giant balata trees that flanked the roadside. The downpour proved to be short in duration—typical of most tropical rains. By the time they reached

Hartley's gracious home with its white porticos set against the foothills, the air had become dry and hot.

It was not the grandeur of the grounds or the house's generous archways that sent a pang of envy through Erika. It was the sight of Mrs. Hartley, a plump lady in white, strolling across a vast lawn to greet them. Four young children surrounded her, and in her arms Mrs. Hartley carried a newborn that would be christened on Sunday.

❖

From the moment the victoria pulled up in front of the house, servants in saris appeared. Hindu males spirited away their luggage. A large proportion of Trinidad's population was made up of coolie people, and Erika could almost imagine that she had arrived at a country estate in India.

"Open your palm," Peter told Erika after they were shown to their room, and she obeyed. "Three grains of quinine per day will guard you against the fever," he said, and handed her a glass of water to help her swallow the tablets.

While Erika unpacked, Peter slipped down to the garden where he chased lizards with the Hartley children. Through the open windows, she heard him laughing. Erika stepped onto a balcony to observe the scene. Three small boys and Gladys—a girl of about seven—ran after Peter. The little girl's sash had come undone, two long tails flying behind her.

"These lizards are too swift for us," Peter called to the children. "Let's try to court them with whistles."

The children were so young they had not yet learned to whistle, so they hunched their small bodies furtively and trailed Peter, following the flutelike notes he formed with his lips, the sweetness of his trills. He bent over to peer closer at something. Suddenly Gladys, the girl, squealed and bounced upright and pointed.

Peter waved to Erika on the balcony above. "It's working," he declared. "The lizards pause and change color when I whistle. They switch from green to blue."

A knock came at the bedroom door, and Erika turned to answer it.

A tall and very young coolie woman had come for their laundry. The servant, perhaps no more than seventeen years of age, entered with a basket.

Erika was struck at once by the tall girl's beauty, by her long, polished limbs and tawny skin, but the rare thing was this: the coolie girl had green eyes. Erika stared at those eyes, transfixed by their color. How was it possible for a person whose ancestors came from India to have such eyes? The irises seemed paler than the hue of her skin, and for a moment Erika wondered if Peter's whistling had altered them, too. Did the light of the tropics affect eye color, the way light changed opals?

It was rude to stare so long at any human face. Erika turned to open the trunks. It relieved her to heap all their soiled garments into the girl's arms—the sour smells of the ship's damp corners still lingered in the wrinkles and folds, ripe for the work of a washerwoman.

The coolie girl wore silver bands around her ankles that jangled lightly as she stepped. Her sari smelled of sandalwood. Around her toe she had fixed a thin ring.

When the laundry had been gathered up and the servant was ready to leave, Erika leaned her head sideways with interest. "What's your name?"

"Uma," she said.

"Thank you, Uma." Erika gave a nod.

When she returned to the balcony, the lizard hunt was over; the boys had gone. Only the little girl remained with Peter. They were sitting on a stone bench. He was showing her something in his flattened palm—a petal, or maybe a caterpillar. The sight of him there with the Hartleys' little daughter pained Erika. It was a harmless, ordinary sight, but it saddened her.

❖

"Ravell and I met in an English boarding school," Hartley explained over dinner, tucking a big napkin under his neck. "Like brothers, we are. Our fathers lived in British colonies—Ravell's father was a farmer in

Kenya, and mine lived here in Trinidad." After he'd finished huge helpings of every dish, he leaned back in his chair and patted his ample midsection. He had to unbutton his vest.

Uma, the same tall coolie girl who had come for the laundry, served the meal. She seemed to be a favorite housemaid of Mrs. Hartley.

"Those eyes," Erika declared as a door swung shut and the servant had gone temporarily. "She has *green* eyes."

"Uma is a lovely girl," Mrs. Hartley agreed.

"It's uncanny, don't you think?" Erika said. "For a Hindu person to have eyes that color?"

Mr. Hartley laughed and shrugged and gulped his wine. "Must have been those marauding tribes north of India."

"Uma had a harrowing childhood, I am sorry to say," Mrs. Hartley murmured. She refrained from saying anything more as the servant girl returned to collect a remaining platter.

After dinner Mrs. Hartley drew Erika aside. "Why don't you help me tuck the little ones into bed?"

Erika gave a strained smile, but she did not wish to be rude. As Mrs. Hartley lifted her skirt and headed up the staircase, Erika followed with dread. Upstairs they moved from room to room as Mrs. Hartley pulled one boy's wet, wrinkled thumb from his mouth, patted another's bottom with affection, and kissed all her darlings good night. After drawing doors closed, Mrs. Hartley led Erika into a room that smelled like a closet filled with too much sweet powder, too many hot breaths, milk that verged on souring. "I don't believe in hiring wet nurses," Mrs. Hartley said as she lifted her prized infant from a crib. She fell into a rocking chair, unfastened her shirtwaist, and pressed her breast against the newborn's upturned mouth. Erika sat on a loveseat opposite them.

"How did you and your husband happen to meet our friend Ravell?" Mrs. Hartley asked.

"I was a patient of his," Erika said, surprised that Ravell had divulged so little to his friends.

"Ravell's doctoring days appear to be over," Mrs. Hartley said, sighing. The nursery was dim, the walls so close that they might have been riding together in a carriage. "Ravell has forbidden my husband and me to mention anything to anyone on the island about his past career."

"Did he deliver your baby?" She glanced at the newborn.

"No," Mrs. Hartley said. "He didn't wish to do it. Besides, he has so much responsibility at the plantation."

Erika stood up abruptly. "I must get some air. I think I'll head downstairs." Mrs. Hartley looked faintly hurt by her departure.

With relief Erika joined the men in the grand parlor. At the fireplace Peter stood with a cigar in one hand, his elbow against the marble mantel. He slid his other hand into the trouser pocket of his three-piece suit. Erika found a seat on an ivory chintz settee, by a fringed lampshade. Mr. Hartley poured golden liquid from a cut-crystal decanter into glasses so clean they were nearly invisible. For privacy, he drew the parlor's twin doors shut.

"You inquired about Uma," Mr. Hartley began. He settled into a chair and rested his index finger against his cheek, as though considering where to start the story.

"Uma's parents worked for my parents here on the estate," Mr. Hartley explained. "Her mother was a strange creature. In the middle of the night, the woman used to have fits of caterwauling. The sound made me bolt straight upright in bed. You couldn't lie back down and go to sleep, for fear you'd hear her again. Have you ever heard a howler monkey?"

Peter nodded, but Erika shook her head. "You'll hear them," Mr. Hartley said, "when you visit Ravell at the coconut plantation. Uma's mother could have had a dozen howler monkeys inside her. The sounds could not have been more distressing."

"A victim of lunacy?" Peter said.

Mr. Hartley gave a nod. "One night we smelled smoke and had to rush from our beds. She'd set the kitchen wing on fire. We're lucky that we didn't lose the entire house."

He swallowed golden liquid from his glass and grimaced, as if the dregs tasted bitter. "Naturally you can't keep a disturbed soul like that on the premises, endangering everybody. My father had Uma's mother taken to an asylum where she eventually died."

"A sad story," Peter muttered.

"That wasn't the end of it," Mr. Hartley went on. "Rajiv—Uma's father—wasn't the most sane fellow, either. He held the whole thing against my father. One evening the other servants warned us that Rajiv had put poison in my father's soup. Rajiv was the main cook on the estate, so this wasn't hard for him to do."

Mr. Hartley slouched at an awkward angle in his chair. "I remember that dinner rather well. When Rajiv brought my father's bowl in, my father asked if the soup was any good. Rajiv said yes. So my father pulled a revolver from his pocket and held it against Rajiv's head, and Father made *him* eat the soup."

"And what happened?" Erika leaned forward, both hands braced against her knees.

"We held the funeral here at Eden—the very next day. Uma was a tiny thing then. I don't think she remembers her parents, though she certainly must have heard stories. We've kept her on ever since. My wife tries to be particularly kind to her."

Erika remembered the servant girl's erect posture, how long and refined Uma's fingers seemed, her slim arms like polished wood. "Uma would appear to be very different from her parents. She seems quite dutiful and composed."

"She doesn't talk much," Mr. Hartley said. "Never has. But she does seem gentle. With the children, she's gentle."

❖

Early the next morning, when the mosquitoes retreated from the lowlands and the danger of yellow fever temporarily lessened, Mr. Hartley took them to see Port of Spain. As might be expected in any British colony, they found order and cleanliness. It was odd to see a great Gothic church flanked by royal palms. A fine tramway service glided past the

Queens Park Hotel, which now sat eerily empty. The cement roads were so cleverly engineered that as soon as the wild tropical downpours ceased, the roads drained, lost their shine, and became dry within minutes.

From the carriage they saw the Savannah, a vast park where horse races were sometimes held and where cattle were permitted to graze. The Savannah lay at the heart of everything, a verdant expanse. The governor's palace overlooked it, as well as the Queens Park Hotel and the town's finest residences.

"Let's visit the tailor first," Erika said. It was nearly Peter's birthday, and she wanted to choose gifts for him.

While the tailor stretched a tape along the length of Peter's leg, Erika stroked a silky handful of ties, deciding to purchase a mauve one because it reminded her of a cravat Ravell had worn.

"My wife dresses me," Peter called over his shoulder to Mr. Hartley, who remained in the doorway watching a sudden shower wet the streets.

"And I'm very good at it," she added. "Really, I ought to go into the business of dressing men."

Peter was handsome, easy to decorate. She made the tailor drape a swath of charcoal pin-striped fabric across Peter's chest to see if it would distinguish him. The prices delighted Peter. In Boston he paid fifteen dollars for a suit, but here the tailor charged one-third that price.

While Erika lingered at the tailor's, finalizing her selections, Mr. Hartley took Peter to introduce him to gentlemen at the Trinidad Union Club. In the end she ordered eight suits for Peter, plus ties and shirts. All would be quickly sewn and delivered to the Eden estate.

Eight suits. The abundance might startle Peter, but she was buying them for herself, wasn't she? She'd be the one who would grasp the slippery tail of his tie and draw his moustache closer. At the end of the day, when he fell playfully against the bed, still fully clothed, she'd bury her nose in the fine pin-striped wool of his jacket.

Since the stillbirth, she had turned to her husband's body again and again for relief. But the tumult inside her was never quite quelled, and she felt she'd grown more distant from Peter than she'd ever been.

When she touched her husband's body with all that pleasure, why did her mind fly toward Ravell? She thought of the doctor daily, often hourly. She could hardly wait for the next day, Sunday, to arrive. Following the christening of the Hartleys' newborn, a celebration would take place at Eden, and Ravell was expected to attend.

After she'd paid and prepared to leave the shop, the tailor looked at her worriedly. "Another foreign visitor died in San Fernando this morning," he warned. "You and your husband really ought to finish your business here quickly. The two of you should leave Trinidad as soon as possible."

Erika nodded. So little protected Peter and her from the worst—just three grains of quinine daily. That evening she'd tell Peter that they should increase their dosage to six.

As she stepped into the street, the smell of the recent but vanished rain rose from the pavement. She had arranged to meet the men around noon, so she had an hour to herself yet. Through the searing air of Port of Spain, she walked toward the lovely Savannah. If mosquitoes were apt to appear later in the day, where did they hide at this hour? She halted, propped a parasol over her head, and listened for the sound of a mosquito drilling past her ear. She detected no sign.

Cattle roamed on the Savannah. Mr. Hartley had mentioned that the coolie people were unusually gentle with animals, and now Erika witnessed a touching scene. A cow and her calf loped toward a coolie woman with almost a rhythmic love. The woman, clearly their owner, raised a curved arm in greeting, as though the pair of animals were family to her.

Later that day when Erika and Peter returned to Eden with Mr. Hartley, a message from Ravell awaited them.

Dearest friends,
Unfortunately, I am still tending to ill workers on this side of the island. Regretfully, I won't be able to attend tomorrow's christening and

*garden party. I do look forward to Peter and Erika's imminent arrival
at the plantation.*

Erika's spirits plummeted, reading the lines he'd sent. Now that she
and Peter walked on the island where Ravell lived—they smelled the same
soil, their skin touched by the same fragrant air and temperature—he still
seemed a hemisphere away.

❖

"I'm afraid you have a rival," Peter remarked to Erika the following
morning. "Another lady in this house seems quite smitten by me."

Gladys, the Hartleys' seven-year-old daughter, waited on the landing
as Erika and Peter emerged from their room and started downstairs toward breakfast. The little girl sat on a window seat, feeding her teddy
bear chocolate creams. She sprang up when they appeared and ran at
once to Peter, slipping her hand into his.

Apart from being the day of the christening, it was Peter's birthday.
By noon a dogcart arrived at Eden, bearing the eight suits and other
birthday gifts the tailor and his assistants had finished.

Erika scurried up the staircase and rapped her knuckles against the
bedroom door, two sharp knocks of anticipation. When Peter opened the
door, she whisked the rustling packages into the room.

"Don't peek yet," she warned. Her arms laden with bundles, she swept
past him and arranged the goods, wrapped in paper, across the bed. How
beautiful his gray eyes had just looked, all liquid, silver. . . . Then she
realized there had been tears in them.

What had prompted those tears? It might have been a child's toy he'd
just seen lying on the stairs, or a glimpse of Gladys brushing her doll's
hair. In an instant Erika understood why he wept, even before she asked
him. After all these months he—like she—still suffered these private,
silent spells of sorrow.

She turned to him. "Were you thinking about the baby?"

He nodded. At such rare moments, she felt unspeakably close to him.

At the church christening a few hours later, Peter wore presents she'd given him: the ivory suit that would keep him cool in the tropics, a tie that shone like a textured silver fish. A long man with beautiful shoulders, he held himself well.

At the front of the church, families held their infants and stood in semicircles around the baptismal font. Seated side by side in the pew, Erika and Peter listened as one baby's shriek carved into the air. Water rose in Peter's eyes again, shining like his tie, though he stared straight ahead at the altar and nobody noticed except her. She folded a handkerchief into a square and slipped it into his hand.

❖

All afternoon families drove up to the Eden estate in their victorias. Carriage doors opened and children spilled from them. Children swarmed on the lawn, boys dangled from limbs of trees, girls ran and hopped until their hair bows unraveled. In the garden Mr. Hartley held a lime drink in his hand and introduced Peter and Erika to everyone. Hartley insisted that Peter join him for a hunt in the northern hills the next day, with hounds hired to lead the charge.

Two ladies—Mrs. Hartley and a friend—were coming slowly down a path in Erika's direction. No doubt Mrs. Hartley's companion would soon shake Erika's hand and inquire, "Do you have children, Mrs. von Kessler?" That was the question that every stranger posed.

Erika glanced at the sky, as though scanning for rain. Then she fled.

She went upstairs to the bedroom balcony and called Peter's name, beckoning impatiently to him. As she paced the room, the floorboards creaked.

When he came upstairs, he looked at her with concern. She locked the door behind him.

"Are you ill? What's wrong?" he said.

Through the open window she gazed down at the garden full of guests. "Look at them," she whispered roughly. "Do any of them deserve children more than we do?"

Expressionless, Peter looked down at the party below.

"Mr. Hartley and his wife have four little ones—and now they've got another baby. *Five* of them."

While Peter remained at the window, she slid behind him. Holding herself from view, she pressed her breasts against his back. She stroked the fine threads of his ivory suit coat, and dug her hands into the depths of his trouser pockets. She pulled him onto the bed. They shed their shoes. They lay on top of the bedclothes, her skirt rucked up, and to the eager sounds of children who hung from trees and squealed, she and Peter had more of the pleasure that made her want to squeal, too, though she kept it tamped down, like a stone stuffed in her throat.

"Promise me you won't go hunting with Mr. Hartley tomorrow," she said. "Tell him we need to leave. We've got to see Ravell."

"All right," Peter said. Before the mirror he patted his hair and shook creases from his ivory suit. Then he went back to the party.

24

Erika could hardly believe that within hours, she would see Ravell again. During the train ride east to Sangre Grande, she took out a tiny mirror and straightened her pearl earrings; she folded a clean hand-kerchief and blotted the perspiration that shone above her upper lip. At the station, as she and Peter stepped onto the platform, she was disap-pointed to see that it was not Ravell who had come to meet them. Instead, the estate's overseer, a man named Gibbs, welcomed them. Ravell, he explained, was still caring for a couple of fever victims.

Gibbs was thoroughly British, rather military in appearance. With his white mushroom helmet, riding breeches, and leggings, he carried him-self as straight as a brass-tipped cane. To the station he had brought two buggies—enough for an extensive family—as well as a wagon for their luggage.

Along the coast they traveled south, enjoying an unforgettable drive on a beach so hard that people used it as a road. For fifteen miles, from Manzanilla Point to Mayaro, Mr. Hartley's coconut plantation bordered the sea, its perimeter marked by a wall of cabbage palms. Coconut trees—thirty thousand of them—had been planted wherever the tropical forest could be pushed back and cleared.

The tide was high, so for much of the ride, the carriage wheels churned through water. Erika hung her arm over the side of the buggy so that the ocean's drops wet her fingers. She tasted. Surprisingly, the sea was not very salty.

"We're not far off the South American coast," Peter observed, "and the Orinoco River is so powerful, its freshwater may dilute the sea."

"What do you call those?" she cried above the noise of waves and water splashing under the wheels. She pointed toward what appeared to be blue and magenta jellyfish bobbing along the surface like balloons, with streamers floating beneath them.

"Portuguese men-of-war," Peter called loudly back. "If you touch one, you'll get a nasty sting."

Finally they reached the estate, a place referred to as the "Cocal," meaning a coconut plantation. Their buggy turned as they came upon a lagoon with a great forest behind it. Near the lagoon they noticed a man out with a gun. He, too, wore a white mushroom helmet, and at first Erika hardly recognized him, transformed in his white tropical clothes. Ravell had been out hunting ducks.

He turned toward the carriage and put down his gun. He seemed like an apparition standing there. Under the helmet, his dark eyes went straight toward her—looking into her face with an intensity that she'd not seen prior to that day they'd embraced in the music room.

"Hello, old friend!" Peter leaped from the buggy to thump Ravell's back. The two men grasped each other's hands.

A great nervousness came over Erika as she descended from the carriage. To guard her composure, she turned toward the lagoon, admiring the mangroves with their great roots in the water. She looked everywhere except into Ravell's eyes.

"You travelers must be hungry," Ravell said to Peter. "Would you like oysters for dinner? They grow here on trees, you know."

When Ravell offered to show Peter how oysters could be gathered from the mangroves' roots, Peter was predictably willing. As Ravell led her husband away, he told the overseer, Gibbs, to drive Erika to the house and unload the luggage for her.

The one-story house was similar to others in the countryside. It was enmeshed in blossoms and vines. The rooms rambled one into the next, as though someone had kept adding to the maze of it. The front door was open.

"Munga!" Gibbs startled her by shouting. To her, the word did not sound like a person's name at first. A reed-thin male servant with skin the shade of brown parchment came to the doorway and bowed to her. In the days that followed she learned that a whole coolie village lived here under Ravell's charge, yet the cry most frequently heard at the Cocal was the name of this servant, "Munga!" It was Munga who served meals, cleaned boots, fixed doorknobs, did everything.

Munga hurried toward the wagon to remove steamer trunks and escort Erika inside.

Upon first entering Ravell's house, she noticed that it did not have the sparse look of most bachelor abodes. The foyer had potted palms that brought the forest inside. Ravell had lived in many places in the world before this, and he had acquired unique and artistic furnishings. Besides the usual grandfather clock and rocking chairs, the parlor had a quilted Turkish leather couch. A mammoth turtle shell rested like a cradle on his dining table, with mangoes and bananas and alligator pears placed inside it. Instead of the predictable portieres, the doorways were draped in carved ebony and ivory beads, with African idols cut into them.

The room where she and Peter were to stay had French doors that opened onto a courtyard. The long curtains were white, the fabric so sheer that the room was extraordinarily bright even when the drapes were closed. Erika took a silver-backed brush from her bag, stroked her hair, and adjusted her crescent-shaped pompadour comb.

The ride had not tired her, and she felt no need for a rest. She was eager to explore everything.

Opening the twin doors, she stepped into the courtyard. Hummingbirds hovered around the flowering shrubs. They flew so rapidly their wings looked transparent. Like bees, they moved from blossom to blossom. Trinidad was known as "the land of the hummingbird," and Peter said twenty varieties existed on the island. The ones she observed now were ruby-crested, and their silent, vibrating wings emanated different colors like fiery opals catching the light, now reddish flashes, now gold.

"No need to dress for dinner here in the hinterlands," Peter reminded her that evening, as he opened his trunk.

Erika had already changed into a dusty-rose gown whose ruffled, low-cut neckline gave the illusion of petals draped over her bosom and shoulders. Standing before the mirror, she fixed a double choker of pearls around her throat, and then removed the necklace, not wanting to appear too formal. Her husband sat on the bed lacing his shoes. She went over and smoothed his collar with her hands.

Ravell met them in the parlor. He held his eyes on her a moment too long, as if the sight of her décolletage unbalanced him. Then he busied himself by pouring cocktails. "Would you care for a green swizzle?" he asked, handing her a glass

"Green swizzle?" Erika repeated cheerfully. She sipped hers and pronounced it delicious. "You'll have to describe the ingredients to us."

"I mix falernum and water with a dash of rum and Angostura," Ravell said.

"Falernum?" Peter asked. "What's that?"

Falernum, Ravell explained, was a sweet, tropical syrup he liked to concoct himself, blending the flavors of almond, lime, vanilla, and ginger. He let the falernum stand in wood for a month, then added milk to settle it.

The dinner began with the oysters that Ravell and Peter had harvested from the roots of the mangrove trees in the lagoon. The oysters were exceedingly tender. At every bite, their soft juices exploded with flavor and dissolved against the heat of Erika's tongue.

During dinner Ravell spoke very little. Earlier she had overheard him chatting with Peter in the garden, and Ravell had sounded at ease then, but in her presence, a strange reticence came over him.

He seemed relieved when she talked, however—not so much because of her remarks, she sensed, but more to have the excuse to rest his eyes on her, her garnet ring, her ruffled neckline. She wondered how long it had been since he had spoken to an educated woman.

"Are you always so quiet?" Erika teased.

"Not always," he said with a trace of amusement.

The oysters were followed by crab-backs, which Peter declared one of the most succulent dishes he had ever tasted. Other local delicacies followed—turtle steak and guinea fowl. Finally, the ever-present Munga brought forth finger bowls. The meal ended with a liqueur of peach brandy.

"My dear fellow," Peter said to Ravell, "clearly you know *how* to live. Here we sit, fifteen miles from any habitation, and we've consumed the sort of meal one hopes to find in a good restaurant in Paris."

Ravell appeared pleased, but said nothing.

"Mr. Hartley reminded us that you've lived on various continents," Erika said.

"Yes," he replied. "I've lived on several." He crossed his legs and turned sideways in his chair. "And what about you? Have you always lived in Boston?"

"Always," she responded, telling him briefly of her childhood and her mother's long illness.

"Did your mother ever recover?"

"No," Erika said. "When I was seven, my mother died."

The look in Ravell's eyes deepened. He appeared on the verge of asking something else when Peter interrupted.

"Would you care to stroll down to the beach?" her husband proposed suddenly. "Mr. Hartley says the nights here are very beautiful."

Not far from the shoreline, the men wandered slightly ahead of Erika. The night was so warm that both men had removed their jackets, and they strolled with shirtsleeves rolled to midarm. Their suspenders resembled dark harnesses against their white shirts.

Following the water's line for a distance, the three of them listened to the long-backed breakers. The black sky looked sharper here, awash with stars. Across the sand, crabs were moving in exodus from the lagoon down to the ocean. "They only travel at the new moon," Ravell pointed out. "In October and November—around this time of year—their migrations are heaviest. On some nights it's impossible to ride or step across this beach without crushing them."

This intrigued Peter, although when he crept toward crabs, they ducked into holes. Soon he cried out with a discovery: by rolling palm seeds between his hands, he managed to lure the crabs to poke out of their holes for a curious peek.

"My husband is as irrepressible as a boy," Erika remarked to Ravell as Peter wandered farther away, playing hide-and-seek with the crustaceans.

She turned to face the sea. It amazed her how the ocean's waves always stayed in motion, always alive, spilling against the shore and retracting, even when no one stood there to observe the show. It would go on, undiminished, even while they slept.

"Did the ship that brought your furniture anchor here?" Erika asked.

"No," Ravell said. "There are quicksands here. It wouldn't be safe. The last time a schooner stopped here, its bow soon tipped into the water. The anchor disappeared until finally they had to sever the cable."

He took a Havana from his pocket and asked if she minded if he lit it. She shook her head. The fine cigar fragrance mixed with sea air and entered her senses in a pleasant way. He seemed more relaxed in her presence now.

"Did your father ever remarry?" Ravell asked.

"No," she said.

"You grew up essentially motherless, then?"

"Not entirely. There was an older woman—my voice teacher Magdalena—with whom I was very close. In fact, I still depend on her."

Receding waves made sizzling sounds and left residual foam in the sand. Crouching low, Erika touched the froth with two fingertips, and as she extended her hand she recalled her mother's long fingers.

Soon Peter walked briskly toward them, his arms outstretched in the darkness, the sleeves of his white shirt filling with wind. "I could live here," he cried out to Ravell. "I could join you here, old friend!"

He looked ready to embrace the night sky, the beach with its army of crabs. Erika knew her husband meant those words. Surrounded by this wild place, Peter could be quite happy.

Ravell laughed and turned to Erika. "What about you?" he asked. "You'd miss the city, wouldn't you?"

"I'm afraid I couldn't live without an opera house nearby," she said.

"Yes," Peter said. "That's the thing. Erika could never stay here very long." With his hands plunged into the pockets of his loose white trousers, he did not seem displeased by her remark. He turned and started back toward the house, with Erika and Ravell following.

From the rear she watched her husband. As always, he strode with vigor, and he walked like a man who had a plan.

❖

When they returned to the bungalow, Ravell clearly hoped to prolong the evening. He invited them into the parlor for a drink.

"It's late," Erika observed. "We should let you get some sleep."

"It's early yet," he said. "Besides, you haven't sung for me."

"Tomorrow I'll sing," she said. "I'm a bit tired now."

He unscrewed the glass knob from a decanter and poured Cognac for them. "Tonight when you go to bed, you must leave a light burning. We have vampires here."

"You actually have bats?" Peter put aside a book he'd been browsing.

"I'm afraid so. Last summer a man named Jotham was a guest here, and he neglected to leave a light burning. Needless to say, when he awoke, he found himself and the sheets all splattered with blood. During the night, a vampire bat had gotten hold of one of his toes. The bedroom looked like a murder scene."

"How wide is the wingspan?" Peter wanted to know.

"Some have a span nearly a yard wide."

"I imagine that would keep the victim rather quiet," Peter said, and laughed.

The Cognac swirled through her, and after a few quick sips, Erika found herself giddy. She laughed and spoke in rushes—louder than usual, knowing that before they all closed their eyes and ended the day, Peter would make love to her, and Ravell would slip into the room bearing his medical bag and his syringe. ("No point in wasting a single day," Peter had warned her.)

Ravell settled into an overstuffed chair that was upholstered in red horsehair, while she and Peter took the couch. At one point she crossed the room to admire a Congolese wall mask. When she turned, she caught Ravell taking a furtive glance at her midriff.

Peter noticed the piano. Impulsively he leaped up, flipped open the lid, and struck one chord, followed by another. The sounds were so horrid that Erika cringed and slapped her hands over her ears.

"Stop!" Ravell begged, and laughed.

"Pianos in the tropics always sound execrable," Peter declared. "I was wondering how you could manage to keep it in tune."

"I tried tuning it myself," Ravell said, "but it's hopeless. It's the moisture, you know, which swells the wood." Opera scores lay in piles on top of the piano: *Rigoletto, La sonnambula, La traviata, Don Giovanni.*

Before midnight Ravell brought a lamp and guided them through the shadowy corridor to their room. He left the light burning beside their bed and departed.

"It's hard to believe that we're here at last," Peter said. He removed a shoe and threw it noisily onto the floor.

Erika pulled the thin drapes shut and changed into a lilac dressing gown. As she lay on the bed, she worried that it might be strange to make love in a room where lamplight bleached the walls, where she half-expected bats to swoop down upon her from the four corners of the ceiling. Outside the house, the forest breathed its eerie noises. Wind riffled the palm leaves and red howler monkeys roared, sounding strangely like lions.

"Rather terrifying," Peter said, "if you didn't know they're just monkeys."

After the howls died away in the distance, she murmured, "I wonder how Ravell stands it here. He must live the existence of a monk."

Peter said, "Oh, there are women enough here to suit Ravell's purposes."

"What do you mean by that?" Erika asked, fascinated.

With his head nestled on the pillow, Peter shut his eyes and smiled with closed lips. His hand sought her knee, then her breasts.

While they pleasured themselves, Ravell waited elsewhere in the house. Green parrots lived in the forest at the back of the lagoon, and Erika heard their sounds. She kicked off the sheets and twisted in silence on the mattress and let the birds of the night cry out for her.

When they were done, Peter left the bed and called Ravell into the room. She had wondered if she would be nervous, or shudder, or weep when the doctor touched her again, but it all seemed natural.

"My hands may feel a little cold," he warned, and touched her thigh.

His hands felt as mild as the night, not cold at all. She glanced at his features—impassive—as he aimed the syringe. Peter held the lamp for him, and the men's faces glowed with light before they retreated into shadows.

After the doctor left the room, she lay with pillows stacked under her knees. For a long time she remained on her back and did not stir while Peter slept beside her, breathing rhythmically. The air in the room smelled the same as the garden, a mingling of jasmine and honeyed scents of blossoms she could not name. Why did flowers seem to release their fragrances more vividly at night? At night, in one's bed, the world became slower, and one noticed things more. Her nostrils drew in the essences of the garden, and as she inhaled more deeply, the scents felt almost piercing.

Erika found herself wondering why Ravell had not married. He must be in his early thirties. In a remote environment like this, how likely was it that he would meet women of his own class? With a pang she supposed that Mrs. Hartley or her friends would try to find a wife for him.

She thought of her piano far away in Boston, the keys left silent in her absence while snow fell like feathers past a nearby window. Already she missed her music. Given the chance, she'd still sacrifice everything—her life with Peter—to stand on worldly stages and sing as radiantly as she could. But first, she had something else to finish. For now, she was not unlike the animals hidden in the forest that surrounded Ravell's bungalow. Only by luring a man into her body, only by wrestling and grappling, could her need be relieved.

After the required half hour had passed, she left the bed. She took a chance that no bats would fill the room for a moment or two while she dimmed the lamp and went to the window, drawing the white curtain aside. On the opposite side of the courtyard, Ravell's bedroom was illuminated. Behind the sheer drapery in his room, she saw his silhouette. She watched him pace and move.

She could have opened the French doors and passed through the garden and slipped into his arms within seconds. But now that a ship had carried her across the equator and finally brought her this close to him, Ravell still seemed out of reach. He moved away from the window and she saw only the whiteness of draperies. She could no longer see him.

❖

In his room Ravell removed his fob watch and set it on a table. He sat on his bed, elbows on his knees, and ran the fingers of both hands through his hair. They had voyaged to another hemisphere to see him, and he wanted to please them. "These are the only weeks we have," Peter had taken him aside to say, with a beseeching look one man rarely shows another, so Ravell agreed to do whatever he could. But he had promised himself not to delude them this time, not to spite God or interfere with the natural course of things. He would use only Peter's semen.

The procedures would be worthless, of course. He could not stop their sorrow, the sadness he had only opened wider and made wilder. He could not bear to demolish Peter's hopes—and why shouldn't this husband be optimistic? Peter believed in the possibility of another child the way all human beings believed in the sun or the moon (the man had seen the thing with his own eyes!—hadn't he already succeeded in fathering an infant?). After yet another fertility specialist in New England had failed to help—why wouldn't they have crossed the equator to find him?

Why shouldn't Peter believe him brilliant?

Now, more than ever, Ravell could not bear to speak the truth to Peter—if you place your semen under a microscope, you will see there is nothing; no more hope for you to impregnate your wife than if I load a syringe and fill her womb with pure air.

❖

When Erika left the window and returned to bed, she realized that her throat and mouth were parched. She had no water by her bedside to sip. She had meant to ask Munga to leave a glass of water next to the bed every night, because she could not sleep when she felt thirsty.

From the bedside table she took a lamp and wandered into the corridor. Her feet were bare against the floorboards, but no matter how silently she tried to move, the old wood creaked underfoot. Her fingertips touched the dark wall with uncertainty as she made her way into the kitchen, closed up now, servants gone, kettles and skillets put away. A pitcher stood on a table. She filled a tin cup and tossed her head back, drinking, gulping, wetting her fingers with the glory of the water, wiping the spillage from her silk dressing gown. The tin cup made the water taste of metal.

A light moved closer and wavered against the doorway, brightening. Someone was coming. Ravell appeared, still fully dressed in the white clothes he'd worn earlier in the evening, when they'd strolled along the beach. He was still harnessed into his suspenders.

"Erika?" he asked. "Are you not feeling well?"

"I was thirsty," she said. "I came for a glass of water to keep by the bedside."

"Rainwater," he said. "That's what we have to drink here."

He found a proper carafe and filled it, and gave her a clean glass. When he turned to leave, she stunned herself with what she did next. She lifted an arm and said, "I want to thank you for all you've done," and—as simply and easily as if he were Peter—she flew against him and embraced him just as she had that day in the music room.

How natural it seemed to hug the doctor. . . . She pushed her nose against his cheek and gave his sideburn a kiss and sniffed musk on his damp and faintly perspiring face. His fingers—fleshier than Peter's, and more fatherly—were suddenly entwined in her own. This man had endured the most awful sorrows with her, and they had hugged with wild sadness before.

In the doorway Ravell winced. He pulled back, and in that one grimace she saw a man struggling with himself. Violently he jerked away and hurried off.

Returning to her room, Erika closed the door. She set the lamp and the glass of water down on the night table. Revolted and confused by what she had done, she clutched her head.

Peter slept on, oblivious.

❖

When Ravell took the two of them for a tour of the plantation the next morning, his manner was brisk and businesslike. He addressed his comments more to her husband than to her.

Ravell showed them the drying sheds along the beach where coconuts were cut open and their kernels dried in the sun. This was called copra, he explained, and the oil pressed from it was shipped to Denmark and sold as a replacement for butter.

Several times she asked for the buggy to stop so that they could step down. There were so many things she wanted to see. Coolie men wielding machetes climbed to the feathery tops of coconut palms. She watched in fascination as a man hooked a vine hoop around his waist and a tree. He proceeded to walk straight up the trunk, moving the hoop upward as he climbed. With a swipe of his machete, nuts rained down.

In the forest coolie men were cutting trees, clearing new lands for cultivation. Monkeys pestered them, and they had to pause in their work and throw stones to scare the monkeys away. In the buggy Erika's shoulder jostled against her husband's, and they laughed at the sight.

Giant balata trees grew in the forest, their dimensions unbelievably huge. Ravell said that balata wood never decayed. Their felled trunks would lie in the jungle for centuries, never rotting. The coolies, he said, believed it easier to remove a balata tree if they crept out with their saws and took it down by the light of a full moon.

The carriage drove on. Toward the southern areas of the plantation, Ravell showed them the new drainage system and an expanse of newly planted trees. When the buggy could venture no farther, the three of them hopped down and walked. Normally Ravell arose at four in the morning to supervise the work. He seemed quite proud of the improvements.

"If you come back in three years," he said, "these trees will be bearing coconuts by then."

Together she and Ravell walked ahead to view the saplings while Peter lagged behind, on the lookout for birds and butterflies.

"It's a wonder Mr. Hartley does not live here himself," Erika remarked. "He seems to regard the Cocal as the most beautiful land he owns."

"He would live here, I expect," Ravell said, "except for the distance from town and the Club, where he conducts his business affairs. Besides, his wife very much enjoys society. I imagine Mrs. Hartley would find herself isolated here."

"And you don't?" Erika asked.

"No," he said. "The solitude pleases me."

The sky changed from a pearly gray to a charcoal hue. When Erika raised her face, wet drops hit her cheekbones. The rain quickened and Ravell's wire-rimmed spectacles became splattered with water. As they hurried back to the carriage, Erika picked up her skirts. By the time they reached the buggy, Ravell's glasses were steamed and her white shirtwaist was streaked with rain, her shoulders quite wet.

"The marvel to me," Ravell said, "is that the delicate orchids and plants of the forest aren't crushed by the violent downpours here."

She drew her shoes farther under the seat, away from the brow of the carriage roof, which was dripping. Ravell rubbed at his oval spectacles with a handkerchief, then tucked the glasses inside his shirt pocket. From the sides of his dark eyes he looked at her.

Crackling sounds came from behind the buggy. "Is that Peter?" she asked. "Where has he taken refuge, I wonder—under a tree?"

Ravell made no pretense of being concerned about her husband. He continued to study her. "Peter tells me that you've stopped singing."

"I've taken time off from performing so we could come here. I haven't stopped singing."

He had a face out of the Old Testament, she thought, and wondered if he knew how foreign and mysterious his eyes seemed. Most likely he did, and perhaps that was why he did not pull his spectacles from his pocket. He seldom wore them in her presence.

"Do you regret—" he began. "Do you ever wonder what might have happened if you had gone—"

He was referring to Italy and her dashed plans, she was nearly certain, but he did not know how to phrase it. If he hadn't entered their lives with his instruments, with his face like a holy man's, she'd be in a room overlooking the Arno by now. She'd be standing on a balcony, and arias would flow from her.

"I continue to train and sing," she answered. "Back in Boston, with my piano in the music room."

"What is the point of having such a voice," he asked, "if you stay limited to one city . . . if that keeps your gift from—?"

"I'll live in Italy someday," she said. "*After* I've had another baby. *After* I've conquered this."

A pause. He picked up a glove that had fallen. "I hope I'll have the pleasure of hearing you sing," he said. "You can't imagine how lonesome I get for a fine voice sometimes, living here."

A muffled yell came from the woods, whoops of greeting as the cries moved closer. The buggy bent to one side as the weight of a foot pressed down upon it. Peter climbed into the turnout, his clothes sodden, thin ribbons of hair wet against his forehead and scalp.

"One of the coolies was showing me a cabbage palm they just felled," Peter explained, hard out of breath. "The top had decayed and they found a macaw's nest in the trunk with a bunch of young ones about to fly. They offered me one."

"And you didn't take it?" Ravell hiked up an eyebrow.

"I didn't dare, old friend. That bird could die during our winter voyage back to New England." In the buggy Peter looked as if he were perspiring raindrops.

❖

On the way back, the rain lifted, and they stopped at the plantation's little village because Erika was curious to see how the coolie workers lived. Hanging hibiscus baskets festooned the outside of the huts. Ravell ducked his head and led them inside a cottage where two young sisters lived with their elderly grandmother. Erika recognized the young women as servants she'd seen in Ravell's kitchen.

The grandmother had black hair with a streak of bright white running up the center of her head, like a rare pelt. The older woman slapped disks of white dough between her hands and fried the circles of bread for Ravell and his guests. *Na'an,* she called the bread, and when a piece grew puffy, she fished it from the pan and offered them delicious bites.

The hut was a humble place with a dirt floor, but it was extremely tidy. It pleased Erika to linger inside its walls, the air thick with spices she had never smelled before. When Ravell eased toward the door, nodding his thanks at the coolie women, she felt reluctant to leave. She would have preferred to remain there, listening to the clink of the women's bracelets on their delicate wrists.

When Ravell took Peter and Erika to another building that served as the plantation's hospital, she hesitated at the doorway, afraid to enter. "Isn't there a risk of contagion?" she asked.

"You have more to fear from mosquitoes than from these men," Ravell answered.

Inside two feverish men lay on cots. When Ravell appeared, relief washed over their faces. He set a cool palm on one man's forehead; he took each man's pulse. For one he prescribed quinine; for the other, Epsom salts. The wormlike lines of worry in the coolie men's foreheads eased as he ministered to them.

As they exited the village infirmary, an elderly woman approached. She took both of Ravell's hands and placed them on top of her head. "*Sahib,*" she said, calling him her master and bowing low.

The aged woman's daughter had nearly been lost in childbirth, Ravell explained after they'd walked away. "For some reason, she credits me with saving her," he said, and shrugged, his hands joined behind his back.

"Well, old friend," Peter remarked, "I see that you're held in rather high esteem around here."

25

After lunch, during the hottest part of the day, Erika sat on a wicker settee reading a magazine, and as she leafed through the articles, she hardly knew why she felt so agitated, or why a revolt was building inside her. It was a leisurely afternoon, but she wanted to leap from her chair and fling the magazine at Ravell.

At the opposite end of the front porch, Ravell sat with a sheet draped over his chest and shoulders while Munga shaved him. They'd brought Ravell's small oak shaving cabinet outdoors where breezes cooled the air. Munga used a soft badger brush to work up lather in a shaving mug, and he honed an ivory-handled razor on a leather strap. As the servant scraped his master's jawbone clean, Ravell lifted his head higher. Munga then slapped Ravell's face with a musk-scented lotion from a blue glass bottle. For his master's hair and moustache, Munga used pomade.

When the ritual of the male toilette was over, Munga held up a wooden hand mirror for Ravell to inspect the results, and Erika put down her magazine and walked into the house's dark interior, glaring hard at Ravell as she passed. He looked up, surprised.

Inside the house, Peter was napping. He'd dropped his shoes on the floor and lay fully clothed on the bed. Erika took some oil of citronella from inside a bag. Down by the lagoon, where she planned to go walking, mosquitoes were rampant. She tilted her chin upward and rubbed the lemon-scented oil across her nose and cheeks, and finally her arms. A red patch on the back of her hand itched, and she scratched it. Citronella did not deter the *bête rouge,* and a few had burrowed under her skin, but she hoped to seal her skin against as many mosquitoes as she could.

She thought of Ravell sitting on the porch while the servant painted his jaw white with cream. As she sat down on the bed, her weight shifted the mattress and Peter opened his eyes. Out of guilt she touched her husband's face. With a finger she marked the horseshoe of his jaw and caressed the soft place where it ended, under his ear.

"I'm going for a walk down by the lagoon," she murmured, and he nodded almost imperceptibly before closing his eyes.

She took a floppy hat and wandered. The lagoon's surface flashed silver here and there with tarpon, and the mangroves grew thick along the water and showed their roots. Behind the lagoon the forest was alive with the chatter of parrots.

A horse and its rider came up behind her. It was Ravell, on his way to supervise coolies clearing more forest. He got down and tied his horse to a tree, his hair still glossy, wet from the pomade. The sight of him made her upper torso tighten.

"Erika?" he said. "Are you upset about something?"

"You know why I'm angry." Her tone was low and curt and she walked onward, not looking at him.

Alongside her, he took two nervous steps to her every furious stride. "Why are you acting like this?" he asked. "How am I to know if you won't tell me?"

She spun around. "I should think that you, of all men, would understand a woman's loss."

His arms hung at his sides. He was clearly confounded.

"You think that I'm wasting my talent," she said. "You think that I should have forgotten about having a baby by now. Even you don't believe that I'm likely to become pregnant again."

Ravell let out a blast of a sigh, and turned his face toward the lagoon.

"You think that by now I should have rallied and taken myself to Milan or Florence. I should be singing my scales to the green river that washes under the Ponte Vecchio—" She took off her hat and flourished it with a wide arm.

Ravell stared at her as she went on.

"I know several other women who've had miscarriages or who have lost babies this past year," Erika said. "We've formed a kind of club. We meet for tea. Every lady has her war story to share. Her personal horror. Sometimes as I've rushed toward our meetings through the sleet and the snow, I think: Nobody except us can ever truly know. . . ."

"Do you think I'm not haunted by such tragedies myself?" he asked.

She retrieved a long stick that had fallen on the ground and bent it like a whip. She hit some shrubbery with it.

"I've had eleven periods since the baby died," she said in a cold whisper. "Do you know what it's like when a period comes? I feel the crush of tears starting up."

Ravell paced. He picked up a stone and sent it skittering across the lagoon's surface.

She glared at him, her shoulders squared. "Every friend of mine who lost a baby . . . By now, every one of those ladies has gotten pregnant again. Except me."

As he stared at her, a strand of hair fell onto his brow. "I am doing everything within my power," he pleaded. He untied his horse and mounted it, glancing at her uncertainly before he rode off.

❖

"We ought to do something adventuresome tonight," Ravell said. Dinner had ended, and Munga had cleared away their plates, but the three of them lingered at the table, enjoying the green swizzles Ravell had poured.

"What sort of adventure do you have in mind?" Peter unfolded his legs and looked alert.

"We could go for a midnight buggy ride."

A starry drive along the hard beach, with carriage wheels milling the water . . . that sounded diverting. Peter helped his wife into the turnout,

Ravell took the reins, and Erika found herself seated between the two men. A breeze swept in off the Atlantic, and they felt it chill the back of their necks.

A drive in the tropical moonlight was not a thing Erika would soon forget. For miles and miles they drove along the beach, until its hard surface changed and softened.

Ravell's excitement grew, and in the moonlight his teeth shone like ice.

"There are quicksands here," he cried above the sound of the surf. "We've got to be careful. In certain spots, these quicksands could swallow a whole team of horses." They approached certain stretches with trepidation, and Ravell urged the horses quickly forward.

"Well done, old friend!" Peter shouted as they eased past one dubious patch, and their wheels sped onward. "It would never do to tarry here."

After they moved beyond the dangerous areas, they turned for the next part of the journey through the woods. Vampire bats swooped and hovered above the buggy, their flapping sounds crisp and distinct. From tip to tip their wings must have measured two or three feet.

Peter said, "I suppose these vampire bats are hoping that we'll decide to take a nap by the roadside."

Erika felt Ravell's hip touch hers as they rode side by side on the black leather seat. When the buggy returned to the beach, they left the moonlit forest and the bats behind. Not far offshore Erika noticed a vivid light on the water. It was not a ship, nor a firefly, nor a spangle of moonlight. When she pointed it out to Ravell, he peered with interest and told them that he had witnessed this same phenomenon on two previous occasions.

"Watch it carefully," he advised. "The light will remain keen and steady for some minutes, and then it will disappear."

He halted the carriage. Just as he had predicted, the streak of light on the water extinguished itself, and the sea became dark again. "No one as yet can explain this," Ravell said. "Another peculiar thing is that on any night when I walk the beach hoping to see that light, I never do."

Mysterious happenings were often reported on the island of Trinidad, he said. Three times he had seen buggies disappear on the beach at the Cocal. "I can assure you," he added, "there's no greater skeptic in the world than I. Each time I've gone over very coolly to inspect the areas where the carriages have vanished, and I notice marks from the buggy wheels in the sand, but then the marks stop—there's nothing beyond them. What do you think?" He nudged Erika, who shrugged and widened her eyes.

"Quicksands?" Peter suggested.

"Quicksands actually do their treachery slowly. Besides, we have no quicksands at the Cocal. The beach is extremely hard—you know this yourselves."

"Then, who can explain it?" Peter thrust his hands into the air.

"Certainly not I." Ravell shook the reins and the carriage started up again. As they neared the Cocal, he seemed to trust the horses to find the way back without his actively guiding them.

As Ravell extended his hand to help Erika from the buggy, Peter hopped down and wandered ahead, his back to them. As she descended, Ravell gave her a long look, and he released his fingers slowly from hers.

A groom appeared to take the horses and carriage away. As they walked back to the house, she stopped and removed her shoes. Under her feet the sand was gritty and cool. She lifted her skirt to her knees and swayed her hips, humming as Peter walked ahead and Ravell followed her.

Just as they reached the house, she broke away from them and ran. The sea shimmered. Closing her eyes while breezes played at her hem and sleeves, she drew in the salt air, tendrils of hair loosening at her temples. The sound of the breakers became her orchestra as she let the song out—a naughty little "Havanaise":

Vente, niña, conmigo al mar,	Come with me, little girl, to the sea,
Que en la playa tengo un bajel;	For on the beach I have a boat;
Bogaremos a dos en él,	The two of us will row in it,

Que allí sólo se sabe   For only there do they
amar. . . .   know how to love. . . .

Later Ravell told her that he thought she'd been singing something from *Carmen*. It had a similar head-tossing, hip-shifting rhythm. Barefoot, with her shoes dropped on the ground, she stood on the bluff and danced a small dance.

While she sang, she felt the old surging joy come back, and with it, familiar ambition. Moonlight widened across the water as the men listened, and the music rinsed through her bones. She wanted her song to tame the waves, to shush the wind in the palms, and to make the fish pause under the dark water.

She longed for a baby, and she still wanted to live in Italy. The clash of those two things terrified her. If she *did* have another child, the force of wanting a full career would return; she knew it would, and all her difficulties would only worsen. But she could cope with only one problem at a time, and for now, becoming pregnant was all she could worry about.

"What a voice!" Ravell called out when she finished. "As lovely as anything ever heard at Covent Garden."

Peter gave a rousing shout of praise and clapped in the dark. The wind gusted under her skirt; she had to press her hands against her legs to keep the swirling fabric down. The men hurried toward her. Her husband took her by the wrist, and lifted her arm, holding it triumphantly high in the air. He caught Ravell by the sleeve and pulled him closer, too. The three of them joined hands, all dancing for a mad moment in a circle on the bluff while the ocean banged against the sand. All of them were laughing. Suddenly Erika halted and dropped her hands from theirs. She gave one last, frivolous twirl, and then she ran back toward the house.

26

In the woods, as the two men walked with butterfly nets, Peter broached his idea. To him, the coast of South America felt irresistibly near.

"Why don't you join me for an expedition on the Orinoco River?" he said to Ravell.

"I'm afraid my freedom is limited," Ravell replied. "We've got the clearing of the land for cultivation under way. I can't simply leave the Cocal." The preparation of land for planting new palms was difficult; the old hardwoods were often enormous, entangled in creepers, and sometimes impossible to remove. He felt he should be present to supervise the undertaking.

Good-naturedly, Peter nodded. He adjusted his white mushroom helmet as they forged onward. With his usual optimism, he intended to return to his proposal and keep talking about it to Ravell throughout the day. He knew when to let a conversation fade and when to resume it, how to nudge a subject along, how to persuade. He counted himself as a man who could bend fate in ways that suited him.

That morning they entered a valley where the air flickered with "big blues"—a species of butterfly with a striking dark border, the ones known as Morphos. It startled the eye to see these large blue butterflies on the wing, for they moved erratically, yet swiftly. Such specimens were plentiful but not easy to nab with a net. If pursued, Morphos fled to the depths of the woods.

After a hard chase, Peter finally caught one, and he and Ravell fell, breathless, to the ground. The two men sat up and drew out a flask of hot kola and drank from it to celebrate, licking the chocolate flavor from their lips. They opened a bag and ate a fruit called pawpaws, which had a creamy flesh that tasted like bananas. Ravell repeated that he was sorry about not being able to get away.

"We wouldn't be gone long," Peter said. "Just as far into Venezuela as the capital, Bolívar. Just there and back. We'd be gone no more than ten days at most."

Ravell shook his head. "I'm afraid such a journey would require at least a couple of weeks." During his first year as manager of the plantation, Ravell believed that he owed it to his friend Hartley to work especially hard to increase revenues. Again he insisted that he could not afford to be absent.

As a businessman, Peter took keen interest in the figures Ravell shared with him. A thousand coconuts brought in fifteen dollars, and the Cocal produced five million coconuts per year. Three thousand new trees were being planted. If each tree, on average, grew sixty or seventy coconuts annually . . . Mentally Peter calculated the potential for increased earnings, and the numbers flew like sparks in his head.

It turned out to be a good day for butterflies. In the late morning Peter spotted a *Caligo*, with its distinctive eye mark under the fluttering wing. The most interesting sighting of all was an unnamed butterfly that clicked as it flew. When the "clicker" flattened itself against a tree trunk, Peter tiptoed closer to inspect its gray and blue marbled wings.

Around noon Peter said, "If you can't get away, perhaps I ought to make the Orinoco expedition alone."

"What about Erika?"

"Unless you have an objection, I thought she might stay at the coconut plantation. I could leave samples of my sperm. You could treat her as before."

Ravell looked aghast. "You can't leave your wife at the Cocal."

"Why not?"

Ravell stared at the tip of his boot. Then he glanced up through the treetops and winced at the sun. "Because it wouldn't be proper."

"Who's to notice? Munga? The other servants? You live miles from any sort of habitation."

"I'll send word to Mrs. Hartley that your wife requires a place to stay while you're off exploring," Ravell said.

Peter halted. He removed his white helmet and rubbed sweat from his forehead. As he shook his head vigorously, droplets of water swung from his matted hair. "Not at the Eden estate. Erika can't bear to be there—she'd refuse to go back to the Hartleys' place."

"Why?"

"Because they've got children. They've got a *baby*. Don't you see?"

"Of course." Ravell waved his words away in apology. "Most insensitive of me."

Peter bent to observe an army of parasol ants. "Look at these," he murmured. The ants had made a track that ran fifty yards through the grass. They'd formed two parallel lines. In one line, each ant carried a tiny leaf like a parasol on its head. A second line, moving in the reverse direction, headed from the nest toward the source of leaves. En route the ants had to cross a stream where a fallen tree branch bridged the water. One line of ants—the ones bearing the parasol leaves—followed the top of the fallen branch, while the returning ants traversed the log's underside. Not a single ant experienced the least confusion. When Peter jabbed their nest with a stick, the warrior ants burst forth with their large nippers to counterattack. They bit his fingers—sharply.

"These warrior ants," he remarked to Ravell, "have no job, except to attack."

Ravell squatted to study them, his forearms braced against his thighs. He pointed. "Look how some of the ants dawdle. You see how the warriors act like policemen to push the slow ones along."

When the two men came to a river, they settled near a cluster of calla lilies and ate their lunch.

"Maybe I'm superstitious," Peter said, "but last time when I was away on a journey and we tried this—the artificial insemination—it worked very well." A glow of hope came into his voice.

Ravell held a piece of mutton, but he stopped eating it then and wrapped up the remainder and put it away. "Peter," he said, holding himself quite still for a moment. He turned to Peter and looked directly into his face.

"Peter," he said again, with so much gravity that Peter half-expected the other man to grip him by the shoulders. "I was run out of Boston by men who don't trust me with their wives."

"Well, I have an entirely different opinion of you—obviously, or I wouldn't be here. And I'm entrusting my wife and our fate to you."

Ravell stood up. He looked around at the forest and blinked as though he felt lost.

"I feel more respect for you and more confidence in you than I can say," Peter went on. "I've never had a brother, but if I did, I imagine that I'd feel the same closeness to him that I feel toward you."

Ravell resumed his seat on the ground. Along the riverbank the trees were festooned with creepers. Some were partly submerged, and blue herons and white egrets sat upon their exposed roots. The two men spoke of ice.

"Ice is horribly expensive in these parts," Ravell said. "It's like gold here, you know."

Ice would be required, as Peter well understood, if a man intended to refrigerate his own seed and leave some behind for his wife while he went off to explore.

"I'm not a poor man," Peter said. "And I won't be daunted."

He noticed a curious thing then—a line of ants moving up Ravell's back, along the other man's suspenders. The ants disappeared inside Ravell's white collar, and emerged, half-drowning in the sweat on Ravell's neck.

Suddenly Peter felt the jungle crawling in his own underwear. He jumped up and grabbed his groin. The hairs on his legs were teeming with ants.

Ravell let out a curse.

They realized that they'd sat down in the middle of a nest of ants, too engrossed in their talk to have noticed. Peter heard himself yelling, laughing. As he yanked his white shirt over his head, a swarm of ants fell into his hair and crossed his scalp like moving flakes. When he blinked, ants caught in his eyelashes. Ants crawled into the whorls of his ears.

Beside him Ravell barked and swore and laughed, too. They slapped the backs of their necks and brushed their faces with handkerchiefs. They ripped off their boots and turned them upside down and shook them. They flung their boots at a boulder, then put the footwear back on again, both of them sprinting for the only thing that could save them now. They plunged in fast, the two of them, giving themselves up to the deepest part of the river.

❖

They dined that evening in their pajamas. Two strangers on horseback arrived at the Cocal just as they were sitting down—travelers coming from Manzanilla in the north, bound for Mayaro. The visitors were in search of water. After Ravell filled their flasks, he invited the men to join in their meal. That was the custom in these parts: you furnished strangers with anything they might need—a meal, a bed, the loan of a horse.

One of the men, Smoot, was an experienced woodsman. Peter and Ravell planned to venture into the heart of the tropical forest the next day, and Smoot offered to come along.

Erika was bored—and restless—from staying in the house, so she insisted that she wanted to explore the far reaches of the forest with them. Smoot, who agreed to serve as their guide, did not approve. They would not get far, he felt, if a lady came along.

But Erika persisted. The next morning they outfitted her with a mushroom helmet and an old pair of Ravell's trousers rolled up at the ankles. Munga brought a small coolie man's boots and placed them at her feet.

They moved through the tropical forest in deliberate order, with Smoot in the lead, armed with his gun. All of them had cutlasses. For mile after mile, they raised their blades and hacked through creepers and vines, crossing a tropical forest floor that never quite dried. Very quickly they sank in mud up to their calves. To everyone's surprise, it was not Erika who slipped first. That honor went to Ravell, who keeled over laughing, legs sprawling, into a thick pit of muck.

Why, Peter wondered, did Erika not feel the exhaustion? The woods exhilarated his wife—he could tell from the way she gazed upward, smiling at a scarlet ibis winging past. Her face shone as though rain had fallen, and her lips looked swollen in the heat. The men glanced at her, expecting her to wither or whine, but she trooped onward, seemingly tireless, less in need of periodic rests than they. Peter counted himself blessed to have the sort of wife who continued intrepidly.

A waterfall of orchids spilled from the immense trees and blocked their path. *Ah, the extravagance of nature!* Peter wanted to shout. Smoot lifted his cutlass to make a great killing swipe. "Don't cut that!" Erika cried in protest. But she spoke too late. One minute a curtain of stunning orchids stretched before them, but by the next, it was gone.

For five miles they traveled by compass; they staggered and sliced their way. Thorns hung everywhere, some like needles, others curved like the tips of steel knives. At one point Smoot gave a yelp and ripped off his shoe. A sandbox tree thorn had pierced through Smoot's leather sole and gone straight into his foot.

The compass and guesswork led them to a swamp, but it was too late to turn back, so they lunged forward in water and mud that filled their boots.

When at last they heard the sound of breakers not far off, Peter tore the helmet from his head, and the others did the same. When they reached the beach, Ravell opened coconuts for them to drink. Peter felt the sweetness flush through him as he swallowed. Smoot poured a coconut's juice over his head.

After Smoot tossed the empty husk aside, he gave a hoot and ran toward the Atlantic and threw himself in, clothes and all. The other men followed. Erika, too, walked straight into the surf. After a moment she shot upward from the waves, her hair streaming over her face.

That evening they dined in their pajamas again. Erika came to the table in her peach silk dressing gown, her rinsed curls loose and damp.

While they ate, Peter knew the men were watching his wife. They stared at her as she lowered her eyes, plucked an oyster from its shell, and slipped it onto her tongue with her fingers. Smoot marveled aloud at Erika's stamina. Ravell's eyes rested too long on her.

Peter's head filled with the fumes of his drink, and he was more pleased than anyone, because she was his, while the rest were half in love with her.

I will do anything to keep her, he thought. *Anything.*

27

A groom arrived one day at dawn to drive Peter to Sangre Grande. From there he'd take a train to Port of Spain, where a steamer would carry him across to Venezuela and the Orinoco. In two weeks he would return, he said. After Peter's departure, Erika lingered under pillows and sheets until late morning, afraid of herself, afraid of what might happen when she got up from the bed.

Ravell had been long gone from the house, she knew. He went to sleep early, and began his work by four or five. Hard rains had resumed— drenching, tropical bursts that beat the roof hard.

At midday she sat in the parlor writing letters to her father and her brother. By that hour Ravell had returned to the house and finished the late breakfast he always took at eleven in the morning. He entered the parlor dressed in a helmet and rubber rain gear, ready to go out again. He stepped toward her, his hands clasped respectfully behind his back.

"Peter told me that you're menstruating."

She nodded. She sealed her letter and moved to a rocking chair near the window that had been left open. The covered porch directly outside prevented any rain from soaking the sill, but the torrent could be clearly heard, the curtains stirred by intermittent breezes. It was pleasant to remain inside the house, protected from the downpour, and still feel the force of it.

"In Boston, what would you be doing on a rainy afternoon like this?" he asked. "Listening to Caruso singing 'Una furtiva lagrima' on your

Victrola? It's a pity that we haven't got the magic of electricity here at the Cocal."

"I don't mind," she said.

"I worry that you'll be bored here," he said gently. "Perhaps in a few days—" He hesitated, knowing her feelings. "Maybe I'll have my overseer, Gibbs, put you on a train, and you can visit Mrs. Hartley at the Eden estate."

Erika shook her head in refusal. She rocked in the oak chair, peered through the slit in the lace curtains at the rain, and asked, "Why did you decide to become a doctor?"

He took a seat on the Turkish sofa and removed his helmet, turning it round and round in his hands. "Because my mother died when I was young."

She stopped rocking. When she had described losing her own mother, he had not mentioned this. "How did she die?"

"My mother died of puerperal fever after the birth of her third son," he said.

"Did the baby survive?"

"No," he answered.

She nodded solemnly. The breeze through the window—the welcome coolness usually brought by the rains here—only chilled her now. Under her white sleeves, her shoulders felt clammy. They listened to the driving rain for a moment, and then he asked if she had everything she needed, and if there was anything he or the servants might do for her.

"Actually—" Erika rose from her chair. "I've discovered something very strange." She led him to the bedroom she'd been sharing with Peter, where that morning, to her horror, she had opened a portmanteau and found that the clothes in the very center had become mildewed. Overnight, a pair of her boots had become covered with green mold. "Even clothes I hang up—" Opening the armoire, she showed him a white dress with filth growing on the cuffs.

"It's the extreme humidity," Ravell explained hurriedly. "It's a neverending fight. We'll have your things washed and bleached immediately."

He hurried down the corridor, the walls echoing like a tunnel as he shouted Munga's name.

❖

That night Ravell retired to his quarters by nine o'clock as usual, but when she retreated to her own bed, Erika lay stiffly on the mattress, listening. The rains had stopped. High in the trees beyond the house, howler monkeys let out roars that left her shivering.

She had forgotten her book in the parlor, and thinking she might read herself to sleep, she took a lamp and went to get it. Returning through the hallway, she almost collided with a tall figure—the Negress who cooked their meals. They both froze, each startled to see the other. The black woman was nearly six feet in height, and she looked down at Erika. The cook's great shoulders and statuesque presence gave the impression that she might have been carved from a giant balata tree. In her arms the servant carried a set of neatly ironed bed linens.

Back in her room, neglecting all her usual precautions against bats, Erika extinguished the lamp for a moment. The red howlers had grown silent, but she kept listening. She heard the Negress open Ravell's door to enter his bedroom. From the opposite side of the garden, the Negress's voice could be heard, and a short laugh from Ravell. The curious sounds drew Erika to the window, where she parted the drapes for a peek.

Within minutes, the Negress emerged from Ravell's quarters, pulling the French doors shut behind her. She hurried through the courtyard, returning to the village where the workers lived. In her arms she carried soiled bedclothes, pillows, crumpled sheets.

Erika wondered why Ravell had summoned for help at such a late hour, and why he'd wanted his bedding changed. Had he wanted to sweeten his sheets for a reason? Did he plan to sleep with her?

A lamp still burned in Ravell's quarters, his drapes still open. She saw him stride, fully dressed, into his room. He was alone.

She wondered if the French doors to his room would soon open, if he would cross the courtyard and ask her to join him on his freshened bed.

A river of brightness from the moon poured through the slit in her curtains and fell across the floor. She returned to her bed and hoped and waited, but Ravell did not come.

❖

Her period had finally ended, she told him.

"Well, that's cause for celebration," he said. "The tide is low enough to use the beach as a road," he pointed out. "Would you like to go for a buggy ride and visit the coconut oil factory near Mayaro?"

The sun flared as they left the house, and she felt nervous. This was the first time she and Ravell had gone anywhere alone together. She wore a white shirtwaist that smelled of the jasmine soap his servants had used to wash it. She'd put on her walking skirt, with the hemline just above her ankles. Freed from the cumbersome linen napkins she'd been wearing, she stepped into the carriage and relished the air that played between her legs.

When Ravell shook the reins, the buggy lurched forward, and he, too, appeared nervous. He glanced around the hard beach as though the terrain were unfamiliar to him.

When they reached the Nariva River, they found that the ferryman—a person known as "Happy Jack"—had fallen asleep in the noonday sun. For a full ten minutes Ravell's voice thundered and bellowed across the water, trying to awaken the man.

Finally Happy Jack wobbled to his feet, laughing at himself, and soon waved them aboard with apologies.

"He's always like this," Ravell told Erika. "Always happy. Always seeing the humor in things."

When they arrived at the coconut oil factory, Erika felt Ravell put his hand lightly against the small of her back as he guided her inside. His eyes met hers as they entered the building. His gaze did not waver. The intimacy of his stare felt almost unbearable and she looked away, relieved when the factory manager appeared. The man began to explain how his workers took copra, the dried kernel, and pressed oil from it. From a thousand nuts, twenty gallons of oil could be squeezed. Coolies poured it into their hands and rubbed its moisture into their skin. The oil could be used for cooking. When Erika dipped her finger in a vat and tasted, the flavor was rather pleasant.

"Why do we use lard?" she said. "Such unappetizing stuff. Why not use this?"

On the way home, Ravell asked if she cared to see a place where monkeys gathered—an encampment of sorts—so they stopped the buggy and he led her into the woods. With a cutlass he slashed a tunnel for her to follow him through. Palms and creepers and veils of orchids fell.

When they reached the site, it was apparent that monkeys must have recently deserted the area, because they'd left half-eaten balata fruit strewn on the ground. Sunlight slit through the trees, but not a single *Cebus* monkey showed itself. While she and Ravell walked around, twigs crackled underfoot. He followed so close behind her that she sensed that at any moment, his hands might steer her hips.

They did not speak about the monkeys' absence. No word passed between them at all. He still did not touch her. Finally she spun around to face him, but he had lifted his eyes toward whatever creature was whipping through foliage at the tops of trees.

She had her pride. *Last time I embraced him, he pushed me away,* she thought. *I will not be the one who reaches for him first.*

They continued to meander around the site before Ravell said, "So you still plan to live in Italy one day."

She nodded. "Yes, I do."

Ravell frowned, cast his eyes upward, and then looked down again, shaking his head. "It makes no sense, your wanting a baby. You should go to Italy now, while you're free."

Erika's hair had loosened, drifting to her shoulders. She paced around the clearing with fierce, strong steps.

"You remind me of myself," he said. "With these risks you plan on taking. The best and worst parts of myself."

"What I want is impossible, it seems," Erika said. "But that won't stop me. In the end, I'll figure out a way."

As they started back, it began to rain. Every stem and petal they brushed felt thick with moisture, filling her with sudden thirst. She wanted to suck a little water from the leaves. Instead, she closed her eyes and stuck out her tongue and caught a few drops and swallowed them. Ravell smiled faintly. A blue and yellow macaw floated past, and Erika noticed two yellow-breasted toucans seated on branches. Sober as judges, the toucans surveyed the forest with their hard, stern bills.

As the rain accelerated, she and Ravell quickened their pace. *Nothing can happen between us now,* she thought, *not with the rain scattering everything.* They passed a colony of green parrots that screeched so terribly, Erika put her hands over her ears for a moment. Rain soaked her white shirtwaist sleeves and pasted them to her arms and shoulders, her flesh showing through the thin fabric.

The showers let up as they drew close to the shore. Ravell, who'd been leading, stopped under a ring of palm trees and turned to her. His dark hair had flattened, the wet strands separated and stuck to his forehead and nape. He'd halted completely, his chest moving hard for breath. Again, he looked openly at her.

Then his mouth was upon hers, their tongues wet with each other's, and they tasted rain. They kissed for so long that she drew back, finally. As they paused for air, she listened. The sounds seemed as intimate as everything about to come: the hiss of rain on leaves, the emission of liquid pouring through a tiny nearby stream, the teeming in the forest behind her, the violence of the Nariva River they'd crossed, the thunder, the lapping of waves.

They found a place where the ground was sandy and their knees fell upon it. They could see white curling surf through the palms. When she lifted her skirts, she saw him falter and hesitate.

"I've not come prepared," he said.

"I don't become pregnant very easily."

"You did."

"Only once in eight years," she said. "It would take you eight years of trying."

While her back twisted against the hard sand, she felt the life she'd known was over now. Their cheeks rubbed, damp against damp, his moustache against her ear. Drops fell from her jawbone. He licked the rain off her face. She heard sounds of suction as his clothes stuck to hers. His trousers had become glued to his thighs, and she watched him unpeel them from his body. His shirt, unbuttoned, fell open, and she saw that he was as taut and lean as a very young man. She traced his ribs, and she touched his chest hair, wet and dark as it curled around her fingers.

As he entered her, blinks of sun emerged, and she shut her red eyelids against it. Soon she heard the surf splitting apart, and felt a pleasure so sharp that it flashed to the arches of her feet.

When it was over, they lay sprawled on the beach, the sun drying them. Natives of Trinidad believed that it was supposed to bring quick death, to go from a tropical drenching to letting the sun bake the moisture from your clothes.

Instead, everything felt blessed here, even the grit of sand in her hair, and the looseness of her bare feet, her heels falling in opposite directions, the breakers pushing a breeze against her soles.

28

A jaguar swam across the river.

Peter had risen at daybreak, keen to watch everything. By night the small stern-wheeler had carried him across the Gulf of Paria and Serpent's Mouth, and by dawn they entered the delta of Venezuela.

The waterway through the tropical forest was narrow at first, and the air swirled with noises of animals he could not see, such as wild pigs. Troops of monkeys swung from creepers high in trees. He had never seen so many birds in one place. Cranes and herons poised on roots exposed in the water, along with kingfishers, and to his amazement, none of them stirred as the little steamer passed. As he gazed at them, they watched him. Occasionally a single, hungry bird dived into water and disappeared.

But the jaguar was the sight that most gripped him. The animal was large and muscular, with every tendon stretched as he swam toward what he was after.

If he had not persisted, Peter thought, if he had not gotten the ice and convinced Ravell and Erika that they should follow his plan, he would not be moving freely across this river, entering a continent where he had never been. He wanted to possess it all—every scarlet ibis he saw through his field glasses, every dolphin that splashed upriver, every experience.

The forest throbbed with song and the snap of a thousand wings. He had every reason to hope that all his wishes would be realized, that Erika might be pregnant by the time he returned.

It was a strange thing he had done, leaving her with Ravell—no question of that. He had considered the risks carefully, weighed them in his palm like stones.

Suddenly an Indian glided past in a dugout, spearing fish. The hairs on Peter's arms stood up, seeing him. The Indian was nearly naked, his body sturdy and compact, and his red-brown flesh shone like a tree unsheathed from its bark. The Indian had no tension in his movements. All was easy and silent. He threw the spear and got his fish and pulled it up into his boat. He did it smoothly, just as he had taken a tree from the forest and carved it into a dugout canoe.

When the Indian passed close to the stern-wheeler, he glanced up at Peter, who waved. The Indian lifted his paddle in greeting. They did not smile at each other. If Peter had been able to tell him his situation, he suspected the Indian would have understood.

A man heads in the direction he needs to go. A man captures what he most wants, and lets the rest drift away.

❖

As the stern-wheeler left the delta, the Orinoco River widened, and they passed a place where Indians lived. Each dwelling consisted of four posts that supported a roof of palm leaves. Hammocks hung underneath, but the Indians seemed to own little else.

Next they passed an Indian burial site. The dead bodies had been raised several feet off the ground and rested in hammocks, the corpses covered by palm leaves.

All passengers on the steamer appeared to be armed, and quick and reckless about drawing their guns. Peter had brought his revolver, too. When they happened upon layers of blue-gray alligators sunbathing on a bank, with one alligator draped over the next, rifles lifted. Almost before the explosion of shots, the alligators slipped under the muddy waters. A mass of screaming green parrots fled from the high trees, joined by macaws that bolted with such a strong storm of wings that men snapped their heads upward and lowered their guns.

"Bolívar is a place of lawlessness," the captain of the stern-wheeler told Peter. "The whole of Venezuela still is."

The latest revolution had occurred just a few years earlier. In Bolívar, the captain said, lampposts and buildings were still pocked with bullet marks. Recently, eighteen men had risen up in some kind of protest. Those eighteen had been given no trial. They'd been taken to a sandy island in the Orinoco and shot. Nobody was allowed to touch the bodies as they floated downriver.

The map marked Bolívar with a great black dot, indicating that it must be a large and important place, but as the steamer drew close to its banks, Peter realized how dreary it was. No wharf existed. Passengers stepped across a plank to come ashore.

At the Hotel Decorie—the best in Bolívar—the landlady showed him to his room. Peter stared hard at the bed, the mattress bare with stains upon it.

"Are there no bedcovers?" he asked.

"You didn't bring your hammock?" the landlady said to Peter, surprised. She pointed to hooks.

Everyone here traveled with a hammock, it seemed.

The hotel had only one story, its rooms divided by partitions that did not quite reach the high ceiling. Each room had a window with no glass, only shutters. The landlady led him to the bath—a cement structure in the rear yard. He stared at the water and wondered how many had bathed in it, and how long it had been since the water had been changed.

He decided to rely on the sponge in his valise.

Through a kitchen doorway he caught sight of the cook hunched over a kettle, the strands of her long black hair almost dragging in whatever she was cooking. The cook's hair was so filthy that it looked as if she'd rubbed it with lard. When soup went around the table that evening, Peter noticed the grease and unidentifiable black specks that floated to the top.

He left his bowl empty and passed the soup to the next man, who hungrily fished a potato from it.

❖

Peter wanted to leave Bolívar but found he could not—at least, not for many days. No carriages existed here, no roads that led anywhere. The only ways to explore the country were by mule and by river.

He walked the steep streets of Bolívar, where gutters ran down the middle, and noticed that no women appeared on the street. Ladies stayed inside houses, where they sat at barred windows; their dark eyes glittered and observed him as he passed. Like him, they seemed imprisoned here. The ladies wore so much powder that he imagined reaching through the iron grill with his handkerchief to dust their cheeks and noses.

Erika could never tolerate their lives.

He knew he'd come very close to losing her. At home in Boston he had once opened a drawer and found a receipt for a passage she'd booked to Naples. She'd hidden it under a box of stationery, but he happened to stumble upon it. He'd noticed many gowns missing from her armoire. He suspected that she must have packed them. Yet not long after she had discovered herself pregnant, he'd opened the armoire one day and found that her favorite dresses had mysteriously returned.

A child was the thing that would bind her to him. Otherwise, how could he be certain that she would remain in the brick town house where he kept her like a butterfly in a jar? If he gave her no baby, what was to prevent her from signing on with a manager who would carry her off to the Teatro Colón in Buenos Aires, or the Sydney Opera House?

Unless she had a baby, he sensed that she was ready to step out of her shoes and soar away like a bird.

In the afternoon Peter returned to the Hotel Decorie and found that a bottle of rum he'd bought had been uncorked. Perhaps a maid or the houseboy had been drinking from it. Every time he left and came back, he found more of the rum gone, and yet he had drunk nothing from the bottle himself.

Since the walls between rooms were only partitions, one overheard every conversation and smelled every overboiled aroma from the kitchen. He did not sleep well at the Hotel Decorie. He shed his boots and lay down on the bedcovers that he'd finally persuaded the landlady to supply him with, and he tried to ignore the sweat of strangers that he smelled in the sheets. At home he rarely permitted himself naps, but here in the gloom of Bolívar, he closed his eyes and tried not to miss his wife.

As he sank into sleep, he saw Erika, the belt of her silk robe unfastened as she reclined against pillows. She bent her knees, her bare thighs parting as her legs fell open. A man held up a candle, looking down at her. The man was naked, aroused, his skin the same warm golden hue as hers, and as he came closer, Erika took his member in her hand. Peter chased the stranger. Outran him through the woods. Suddenly the fellow was fully clothed, wearing the suit of a gentleman. When they got to a remote place, Peter struck the stranger hard and repeatedly, until the man fell to his knees. Peter grabbed hold of the man's lapels, pushing him between rocks until blood poured from the man's ear. When the man turned his face, Peter realized it was Ravell.

Startled awake, Peter sat upright at the Hotel Decorie. He felt terror hidden in all four corners of the room.

Why have I dreamed such a thing? he wondered. In his mind, Ravell felt as dear as a brother.

Peter lay with both arms crossed over his heart and waited until the wild beating calmed. *Ravell will do exactly what I expect him to do,* he assured himself.

He adjusted an old, stained pillow and made himself go back to sleep.

29

❧

"How many estates does Mr. Hartley own?" Erika asked.

"Four," Ravell said. "Three cocoa plantations, as well as the Cocal."

As they rode through the moonlight toward Esmeralda, an estate Mr. Hartley had only recently acquired, their buggy passed huts that reverberated with the sounds of coolies chanting and beating their tom-toms. They passed one Hindu man seated in a doorway, his knees hugging his drum, his head ready to shake from his neck as his palms slapped his tom-tom's leathery skin.

Look how much pleasure he derives from it, Erika thought. *Lost in his rhythms, his trance.* She knew that feeling, as close as her own drumming heart.

They had to drive far to Esmeralda, fifteen miles toward the center of the island. Moonlight marked their route and poured with the whiteness of milk through the dense trees.

Finally they reached it. In a small clearing in the woods, a rough house stood. After coming through the dark trees, they might have been shifting from the darkness of midnight to the brightness of noon, for in Trinidad's pure atmosphere, the moonlight was incandescent.

At Esmeralda the house was lifted high off the ground by poles made of balata, the wood that never rotted. A tall flight of steps led to the door.

Out of the woods, a coolie boy appeared. He bowed low and set a plate of pawpaws on a table for them. While the boy swept the floor and made up the beds, Ravell went to work clearing bats from the house. Erika waited outside, as still as a tree, a thin shawl around her.

Then the boy was gone. He ran through the undergrowth and evaporated into the forest, and they had the house to themselves.

It was a curious structure, built like a hexagon. The house had no glass windows, only hinged shutters that Ravell propped open by means of a stick, so that the sides lifted like wings. The entire room became a sort of veranda, open to the air. After eating the dinner they'd brought along, they sat there encircled by the forest and listened to the songs of the night—the strange agitation of wind, the cries of lonely animals. They stared into the dark and watched the blink of fireflies.

"How long will you live on this island?" she asked.

"I don't know."

"Do you suppose you will ever marry and have a family?"

"I expect not," he said.

She did not ask why he thought this. Instead, she asked him about his youth in Africa. At the age of fifteen, he had made love for the first time with a black woman from the town who liked whiskey and dancing on tables, and one night he saw her break a chair. "I have this to say about her," Ravell confessed. "She was more alive than any person I've ever known."

In the moonlight Ravell's collar was crisp white. He wore no jacket, only a dark vest and white shirtsleeves rolled up to show his hard forearms, marked by well-developed veins. Erika studied his face, wanting to take her finger and trace the fine curve of his nose. She got up and stood behind him, and put her hands on his shoulders.

"What are you thinking?" He glanced up at her.

"How bright your shirt is." Gently she tugged at his collar and smoothed the pointed flaps. "It's the color of the moon."

Ravell pushed away from his chair and stood. His arms hung rigidly at his sides and he stepped back; she sensed he meant to keep his distance from her.

"I don't understand," she declared in amusement. "You've brought me all the way here. Don't you want me?"

He laughed and took hold of her by the waist. They fell against a bed, and tossed their garments, one by one, until each thing landed on the floor: vest, suspenders, camisole, corset, parachute of skirts. The smells of the forest were strong, and as they grew dizzy with lovemaking, the house on stilts seemed to turn like an open-air carousel.

Lying underneath him, she imagined that he must have touched many women, and she felt herself becoming all of them—an East African woman who danced on tables and broke chairs, coolie girls with rings on their toes. (*"There are women enough here to suit Ravell's purposes,"* Peter had said to her, smiling.) His accusers from Boston blended into Erika's senses, too—blonde Caroline, and gray-haired, leggy Amanda.

With her nose against his face, she smelled musk and remembered that day when Munga painted Ravell's jaw white with shaving cream. She winced from pleasure, and heard the sound of her own sharp little screams.

"Shush," he said with a jest in his tone.

"Why should I 'shush'?"

"The animals of the forest," he laughed. "You might scare them."

❖

"Taste," Ravell said. He'd sliced a piece of fruit open, and she bent her head and filled her mouth with the sweet pulp from one of the pawpaws the servant boy had left. The fruit made a good breakfast, along with hot kola, which had the flavor of steamed chocolate.

Ravell loved to rise early—at four in the morning—so they got up then, and walked through the woods before the moon was gone, just as the sun was emerging for a new day. Their movements roused parakeets and other birds.

"If your husband were here," Ravell remarked, "here's a sight he would be very interested in." He pointed to a carpenter bird boring holes into ripening cocoa pods. "Those holes will breed worms," Ravell explained, "and the bird will come back to eat them."

Why mention Peter? Why revive thoughts of him now? Something tightened under her ribs in annoyance. As they walked, her legs ached. Not since the earliest weeks of her marriage had she been so sore.

"Are you all right?" he asked, noticing her reluctant pace.

She nodded. At last they reached the road where they'd parked the buggy.

Driving home toward the Cocal, they met women in saris and coolie men en route to their daily labors, each politely calling *"Salaam sahib"* and *"Salaam memsahib"* in greeting.

It was not yet ten in the morning when they noticed a familiar silhouette heading on horseback in their direction. It was Munga racing toward them. Just from the lopsided way he rode—with one arm held high, flailing—they recognized that he carried a terrible message.

❖

Munga led them to a coolie settlement miles from the Cocal, where Ravell jumped down from the carriage and ran along a dirt path to a hut. Erika tried to follow, wondering if she might assist in some way, but as they came to the little house, ducking under baskets of hibiscus at the entrance, they saw a bloody handprint on the door, and more blood trailed over the threshold. Inside the house, a woman wailed.

Ravell made a fast pivot and gripped Erika by the shoulders. "Go back," he said. "Go to the carriage."

Munga took up the buggy reins. Neither the servant nor Erika spoke as he drove her back to the Cocal.

❖

It was evening before Ravell returned.

"Tell me," she said.

"I'm not telling you anything," he said. "There's no reason for you to know."

To calm himself, he walked to the beach that night. She left him to his thoughts for a time, and then she went to find him.

He sat on the sand, his knees drawn against his chest. From his pocket he removed a flask and took a swig of whiskey.

"It was not a pretty scene," he said. "Not a thing you should have witnessed."

The wind lifted strands of her hair, blinding her until she brushed the tangles from her eyes. She sat down and shifted her hips, the sand forming a saddle underneath her.

"When I left Boston, I vowed to do no more doctoring," he said, "but that's proved impossible. Am I to stand by and let a woman die at the hands of a country midwife?"

He drank more whiskey, capped the flask, and put it away. He hung his head.

"Did the mother—?"

He cut her off. "In Boston I had colleagues with whom I could discuss a traumatic case. Here, I'm alone. I practice in isolation."

She slid her hips closer to his, inching nearer in the sand. She sensed that he did not want anyone to touch him, not at that moment. "You can tell me," she said.

"In a village not far from here," he said, "there's now a newborn baby who has no mother."

"She bled to death, didn't she? That's what you're afraid to have me know."

"If I'd arrived sooner, she might not have had any problem at all." His lips formed a grim line. He stared at the breakers, crashing like glass. "In these rural parts, you've got midwives who plunge ahead and show terrible ignorance."

"What did the midwife do?"

"Certain untrained persons believe that as soon as an infant is born, the placenta ought to follow immediately. They're impatient. They don't wait the extra minutes for Nature to expel the afterbirth slowly."

He brought his fist against his mouth and kept it there, silencing himself, shutting his eyes. He would not say anything else.

Erika heard the rest of the story the next day. One of the kitchen servants had been present in the hut during the delivery—she was the one who had summoned Munga. While this older woman was describing the scene in a shrill, wild voice to the other servants, Erika entered the kitchen. The servant was reenacting how the midwife had pulled the cord and tugged with such violence that—

The servant stopped talking when Erika appeared. Two young coolie women were seated on stools, and they'd been preparing cassava, which were like yams, for supper. The Negress had been rubbing dough across a wooden board, exercising her strong, flour-covered black fingers. They had the air of sisters talking, but suddenly they hushed themselves.

"What happened?" Erika stepped closer.

The older servant hesitated, and then went on to demonstrate how the midwife had yanked the cord with such violence that she had pulled out the mother's womb.

Erika turned and ran from the house, down to the beach. She bent in half, her arms crossed over her midsection, then dropped down onto the sand. She sat there and writhed, her hair hanging over her face, sorry she had heard it, sorry she had asked.

30

∞

"I'm worried about Peter," she said. "Three and a half weeks have come and gone. Don't you think he should have returned by now?"

Ravell brought out a calendar and counted the days. He, too, felt alarmed. Venezuela was not always safe territory for a traveler, he admitted. It was strange that they'd received no word to explain the delay.

"It's so unlike him," Erika said.

Ravell decided to send a message at once to Mr. Hartley, who could go directly to Port of Spain and make inquiries.

Yet less than a day afterward, Peter appeared, as hearty and ebullient as ever. He drove up in a wagon, and when he saw them, he spread his arms and jumped from the height of it, landing on both feet. After his steamer had arrived at Port of Spain, he had gone to the Club and run into Mr. Hartley, who had invited Peter to stay at Eden for a few days and join him for a bit of hunting.

"How did you explain our situation to Mr. and Mrs. Hartley?" Erika asked when they were alone and Peter was unpacking his things.

"What situation?"

"The fact that you'd left me here."

"I told them that Ravell had you on strict bed rest, fearing a miscarriage."

"You told them I was pregnant?"

"It isn't any business of theirs what we do. These are private matters. We'll be leaving Trinidad soon."

She sank her hips down on the bed and sat there, dismal at the thought.

Peter was bent over a trunk, rifling through clothes. "There it is." He held up a pistol, relieved. "The authorities confiscated my other revolver when our boat arrived at Port of Spain. They realize everybody coming from Venezuela must be armed."

"Peter," she said. "My period is coming back."

He hesitated, brushing a scuff mark from his shoe. "I see," he said dully.

She let him think that she was menstruating. She could not bear the lie of it, to sleep with two men at once. During these last days on the island, until the ship took her away, she wanted to open her body to only one man, and that was Ravell.

❖

At Ravell's house, her husband looked quite tall. His hair grazed the tops of doorways, and his height seemed unfamiliar to her. When Peter's feet touched hers in bed, there was the sensation of ice. She pulled her legs away from his.

When he perspired into the bedsheets, the air became tainted by a smell she did not recognize. What bitter foods had he eaten in Venezuela? What sour water had he poured from a pitcher and drunk? When Peter unpacked the rum he'd brought back from Bolívar—the one luxury produced there—she took a little on her tongue and tasted, grimacing. She put down the glass and pushed it away.

It isn't Peter who has changed, she realized. *It is me. For me, everything is different now.*

When Peter left to go swimming at dawn, Ravell came into her room. They stood naked together in the light. She wore nothing except a necklace, a wreath of tiny, tear-shaped garnets. He stood with his shoulders no higher than hers, his eyes level with her eyes.

❖

On the morning of the day they were to leave, she woke up and found the mattress empty beside her. Sunlight warmed the walls, and Peter was suddenly, inexplicably gone.

They were supposed to load their luggage into a wagon and set out by buggy that afternoon. Mr. and Mrs. Hartley had invited them to spend Christmas at Eden, and Ravell was included as well.

She sat up in bed and realized what had awakened her. Gunshots rang out on the beach. She shoved her arms through the sleeves of her dressing gown and ran from the house, barefoot, the wind filling her robe like a cape. More shots. Peter was shouting in frustration, and shots came again. With each burst of bullets, her heart split apart. She tripped and fell hard, her whole weight coming down against her outthrust palms. Sand grated her knees and she got up, still running, until she saw Peter and Ravell, both of them alive. Peter was aiming his pistol and shooting at the beach itself. With each bullet, sand spit skyward and sprayed.

He'd been unable to catch the specimens he'd wanted to pack in alcohol and take back to New England. Portuguese men-of-war had washed up in brilliant color across the beach, with their long turquoise and violet streamers, but they were not the quarry Peter was after. It was the strange four-eyed fish that captivated him, the ones with divided eyes. Those fish could see simultaneously above the ocean's surface and below its depths. Every time Peter felt on the brink of capturing one, the four-eyed fish eluded him, and so he'd decided to stop them with something faster than his hands.

"My goodness," Erika said. "You have no idea—how much you just frightened me." She pressed one hand against her stomach; the other hand flew to her forehead as she stood there, recovering.

During their last hour at the Cocal, Erika sat under a grove of palms and listened to the fronds crackle as she watched the surf. She made Ravell bring her a chilled coconut. He'd drilled a little hole into it and put a straw inside. "This is the thing I want to drink," she said, laughing, "just before I die." She dug her toes deep under the sand until her feet touched the place where it grew damp and cool, and she sipped the clear juice from the coconut and felt the sweetness flow and spread inside her. *I will never see this place again*, she thought, and sipped slowly, trying to make it last.

When they climbed into the buggy to leave, Munga and the other coolies gathered around to say farewell. Bowing low to Peter and Erika, Munga placed their hands upon his head.

❖

The presence of the Hartley children no longer tormented Erika. The thunder of their small feet on the spiral staircase as they chased one another was part of the surroundings—like hibiscus, or hummingbirds. Even the Hartley baby did not matter. Instead, she thought about Ravell.

While Peter and Erika were guests at Eden, Ravell decided to stay at the Queens Park Hotel, which had recently reopened. He told Mr. and Mrs. Hartley that he had business to take care of in town.

The day before Christmas, Peter and Mr. Hartley took their guns and left the house very early to hunt deer. While Erika still lay under the bedcovers, she heard a horn in the distance, which triggered thrilling barks from the new hounds in Mr. Hartley's kennel. In the bed she hugged a fat pillow and smiled to herself, knowing that day she would be able to escape to town to see Ravell.

"I have shopping to do," she told Mrs. Hartley.

❖

Since they'd come to Eden, Peter had asked Erika, rather gently, if her period had finished yet. She told him half-truths. For days, she told Peter, she had feared that her period might be on the verge of beginning, but so far it hadn't. She hinted that another baby might be struggling to take root; if they made love, they might risk jarring a baby's tenuous hold.

At this, Peter gave a delicate smile. She felt a pinprick of shame, toying with his hopes. Peter backed away from her. He regarded her from a slight distance, almost reverently.

❖

On Christmas Eve, to her own surprise, she felt shivers of joy as she helped Mr. and Mrs. Hartley sneak into the darkness of the children's rooms, placing gifts under their beds while they were sleeping. The eldest boy only pretended to have his eyes closed when they crept in. As soon as the grown-ups finished, he woke all the others and the upper floor exploded into happy pranks and havoc.

In the parlor, after a midnight dinner, Peter held forth, telling all the guests about the unusual sights he'd witnessed during his Orinoco trip. He described how women in Venezuela fenced off areas of the river so they could launder things in safety, and not be attacked by alligators or electric eels or other biting fish.

"Things are a bit more civilized here," Mr. Hartley declared. He sipped the last of his eggnog, and set the goblet down. "In Trinidad and Jamaica, we've got laws against shooting birds, for example—whereas in Venezuela you've got terrible slaughter going on."

"For the feathers," his wife added. "For ladies' hats."

Ravell excused himself and went upstairs. From the distant reaches of the second story, the flush of a toilet could be heard.

Erika lingered for a time in the parlor, then slipped away. In the hallway upstairs she caught Ravell by both wrists and pulled him into the darkness of a linen closet.

"Has your period come?" Ravell whispered. "You said you saw signs of it?"

"Not yet," she told him in delight. "Any hour it might come, but not yet." The linen closet smelled of mothballs and cedar and woolen blankets and starched sheets on the shelves. She pulled pillows down so they could cushion themselves against the floor, and she unleashed her breasts from her corset. They had to be hasty, just a fast lift of her skirts, the licks of heat continuing until she swallowed her moans, her pompadour loosening, the pins coming unhinged.

No one saw. No one heard. No one who mattered, at least. Ravell emerged from the closet first, and started down the stairs. Erika waited a moment before following, but as she gathered up her skirts and slipped from the closet, a servant was heading down the hallway with folded bedding in her arms. It was the green-eyed servant girl, Uma. She paused and stared strangely at Erika, and pointed, finally, at Erika's hair. It had fallen to one side. Erika hurried to her room, where she stood before a mirror, straightening herself. With her elbows raised, she smoothed her pompadour, and wondered how long it would take for the flush of high color in her face to subside.

❖

"You cannot leave this island without seeing our famous horse races," Mr. Hartley told Peter and Erika. "The celebrations go on for three days."

All the people of Trinidad filled the roads and headed for Port of Spain for the event, which always occurred just after Christmas. En route to the festivities, Erika could not keep herself from staring at the travelers they passed. From across the island, dilapidated, rickety carts all moved in the same direction, carrying entire coolie families: the men in white, the women and children sheathed in silks that stunned the eye—a saturation of amethyst, topaz, emerald, and marigold.

On Port of Spain's Savannah, where the races took place, a mounted escort delivered the Governor to the grandstand. Behind bamboo stands, coolies peddled curries and potato-filled pastries.

Peter and Mr. Hartley and other friends cheered the riders. Their ears grew pink as they shouted for the horses they'd bet on. Erika studied the crowd of spectators. The races did not interest her so much as the staggering array of colors that fanned across the perimeters of the Savannah. As women in saris brushed past, Erika stared at the rosettes of gold pierced through their left nostrils, and she counted the earrings—at least five—that outlined each woman's ear. They were outfitted like princesses, and as they walked, one heard the sound of money. Coolie husbands often invested all their savings in their wives' adornments, in the gold and silver bracelets that clinked from wrist to elbow. The wives' anklets, too, jingled as they stepped.

Suppose one of these women deserted her husband? Erika thought. He would lose everything.

192

Ravell wandered off to say hello to an acquaintance. When he made his way back through the crowd, he insinuated himself behind Erika and squeezed her lightly at the waist. Nothing seemed quite so delicious as that moment, his hands upon her, then gone.

He was standing next to her when the one horrible event of the afternoon came. A nimble jockey, as slight as a child on the back of his horse, rushed into the lead, upsetting all predictions, surprising and thrilling nearly everybody. The hordes opened their mouths. Silk handkerchiefs flashed in the air as he won. Hearing the roar, Erika's eyes smarted with tears: it reminded her of those times when she'd sung so well that the audience had been lifted to their feet.

Afterward Erika kept thinking of those cheers, the last sounds the jockey must have heard. At least that rising of voices reached his ears. For just after he won, the jockey's horse ran into a post and the man fell to the ground, dead.

31

As a lighter carried them to the steamship anchored offshore, she and Peter waved to Ravell until their arms ached, and he became a fading figure on the wharf.

"We'll visit Ravell again next year," Peter said. Erika noticed that her husband, like her, seemed a little bleak and mournful.

On the steamship *Trent*, Erika and Peter had been given the best stateroom, the one vacated by Trinidad's Governor, who had recently returned from England. But she did not want to go to their quarters yet. At the Captain's invitation, Peter hurried off to the bridge to survey the panorama of the Caribbean while she remained at the stern. With a sense of stabbing loss, she stared back in the direction from which they had come.

The island of coconut palms sank away and Ravell disappeared over the edge of the earth, like a setting sun.

The previous night at the Eden estate, she and Ravell had stepped out into the garden and stood behind a tall hedge, knowing these would be their last moments alone together. In the darkness they made promises to write to each other, and she told him she would send a friend's address (Magdalena's, perhaps?) where he might send her private letters. He held her so tightly and for so long that she had grown nervous and worried that the others who remained in the house might question their absence. As she began to pull away, his shoulders trembled, and she felt shudders of sadness moving through him. His cheeks were wet when she kissed his face. She squeezed his hands hard before she broke away from him—afraid that she'd cry, too—and hurried back to the house. It was a long time before he followed her. When he finally returned to the parlor, he wore an overcoat, waved a brusque good-bye to everyone, and departed quickly.

Seabirds followed in the steamer's wake, fluttering behind the boat like tiny pennants, caught up in invisible drafts of air. She did not want to turn around and face north, so she stood there, wind-whipped and numb. For several moments she bowed her head and sobbed hard in silence. Fortunately no one passed by, so no one noticed. Only when a hard gust sucked her parasol inside out did she grab the handle and fight to set it aright, and then she went below.

❖

Near the Bahamas they awoke to a day that was deceptively clear. They were coming to the end of the tropics, yet seaweed still lay thick on the surface, and flying fish still erupted in spurts. Everyone had shed their whites and dug through their trunks for heavier clothes. By tomorrow they would stand at the rails shivering.

Peter and Erika sat at the Captain's table, along with Mrs. Bickford, a widow traveling with her daughter Prudence. The two ladies had been visiting Mrs. Bickford's brother, the American consul in Barbados. During lunch Mrs. Bickford said that she felt quite appalled by the card playing and gambling on board—even the four Colombian priests had been at it. After lunch she intended to head directly down to her stateroom and write a letter of complaint to the Company.

As she spoke, such a heavy roll moved under the steamer that it overturned Mrs. Bickford's bowl of curry soup, spreading a stain of violent yellow across the tablecloth. That was the first sign of the weather to come.

At a nearby table, Germans sat with their napkins tied around their necks like bibs. When one man leaned back gently, the front legs of his chair lifted slightly. As the sea pitched again, the German fell right over, his black shoes pointed toward the ceiling.

By three o'clock the skies had darkened. Standing on the ship's bridge, Peter saw a wave reach up and break a chain that held a set of deck chairs. Half the deck chairs washed into the sea; the other loose chairs were sent hurtling with a force that could kill a man.

The crew hands rushed to tighten doors and batten down whatever they could. The storm shifted the cargo—coal, bananas, thousands of bags of cocoa, a herd of Hereford cows—and made the ship list badly to port. Peter could feel the imbalance in his hip and shoulders, as if one of his legs were shorter than the other. The steamer butted hard against the sea. His heart took a wild leap as he watched a wave crash higher than the ship's funnel, because it looked so terrible, and so glorious.

❖

Erika braced herself as she moved down the corridor, her arms horizontal, her palms pressing the walls as she lurched from side to side. A man threw open the door to his stateroom and pointed to water sloshing across his floor. His mouth was agape.

The purser, carrying a mandolin, staggered and stumbled toward the music room, where he hoped to calm the passengers by playing a few tunes. The sea heaved him hard against a door, and he fell backward. Erika winced at what she saw next: the purser's mandolin, smooth as a red-gold gourd, hit a wall, and its neck snapped. When the purser turned the wooden instrument over, the front had been bashed to splinters.

When he glanced up, she saw the anguish welling up in his eyes, and she knew what she must do.

❖

In the music room the Colombian priests lay stomach-down on the velvet window seats, their heads hanging over the sides of the long benches.

She went to the piano, planted her feet firmly against the floor, and accompanied herself as she sang in Italian. Her fingers hit the notes quickly, her throat on fire, with her voice leaping across two octaves, outrunning the waves.

Agitata da due venti,	Buffeted by two winds,
freme l'onda in mar turbato	the waves shake in the turbulent sea
e 'l nocchiero spaventato	and the terrified steersman
già s'aspetta a naufragar.	already expects to be shipwrecked.

More passengers appeared, drawn to the furious music. Caught in stairwells, afraid to remain in their staterooms, they made their way toward the sound of Vivaldi. Mrs. Bickford's daughter Prudence entered and dived against a bank of velvet pillows. Others held fast to whatever they could.

❖

In her stateroom, after finishing her letter of complaint to the Company about the gambling on board, Mrs. Bickford found it impossible to nap. Fear roused her from her bed. Her daughter had gone to the music room, and Mrs. Bickford decided that she did not want to die alone. She put on her best emerald necklace and tucked two pickles, for which she had a great fondness, into her pocket. Just before she closed the door to her stateroom, she heard an explosion of glass and water behind her; she turned to see that a tremendous wave had punched through both portholes, and the sea poured in as if through a fire hose.

Mrs. Bickford headed for the stairwell, feeling she ought to report this. She gripped every rail, making her way upward. Overhead, she heard havoc in the saloon—the smashing of what must have been stacks of white dinner plates.

❖

On the bridge the Captain said, "We are now out of communication, I'm afraid."

"How do you mean?" Peter asked.

"About an hour ago," the Captain admitted, "the gale smashed our wireless apparatus to bits."

It was as though a giant had lifted the ship in his arms and kept shaking it, so that they would all rattle and break.

❖

Singing was a form of prayer, her voice teacher Magdalena always said.

Erika sang "Agitata da due venti" four times, five. At the Conservatory it was the aria she most feared because of its rapid *passaggi*. Now she sang it as if it were the only aria ever composed, the only piece of music she could remember.

Would it be the last song any of them would ever hear?

At this moment Ravell was probably riding a horse along the beach at the Cocal, never imagining that she was here, pounding at a piano, arching her throat heavenward, hoping not to drop like a stone to the Atlantic floor.

The linen napkin between her legs was still dry—the only dry thing on this ship, it seemed. Suppose, in the hold of her womb, a baby as small as a pearl was now rolling inside her? Another baby's life over, just as it was beginning . . .

If she abandoned this piano and headed upstairs to search for Peter, the storm might hurl her against a wall and shake the baby loose from her. But maybe there was no baby, only her in a room full of people, all wondering how much worse it might become.

She sang:

Dal dovere da l'amore	By duty and by love
combattuto questo core,	this heart is assailed,
non resiste e par che ceda	it cannot hold out, it seems to give up
e incominci a desperar.	And begins to despair.

As the gale whistled through the boat, she felt the ghost of Vivaldi pass through her. In the music room one man fell completely over another, and the two of them somersaulted toward Prudence, who hugged a velvet pillow and let out a scream.

❖

On the bridge the windows blurred, awash. Peter could barely discern a figure in black on the deck below. It was a stout woman he saw—Mrs. Bickford in fact, a miserable spectacle of drenched hair and skirts. Mrs. Bickford was making her way haltingly toward the bridge, no doubt to issue a complaint.

"All passengers must stay below," the Captain bellowed to one of his men.

As Peter descended into the violence of the weather, holding on as best he could, he decided that he must turn Mrs. Bickford around and lead her below. Afterward he must find Erika. He hoped his wife had stayed in the stateroom as he had advised.

On the deck between him and the dark, soaked figure of Mrs. Bickford, Peter saw a bizarre sight: the ship's pig had gotten loose—the sweet, crazed pig ran, its split feet useless for balance on the slippery, tilting deck. The pig was being saved for a feast on their last night at sea. It was entirely possible that *this* might be their last night, Peter thought ironically.

The pig had slid from the arms of a Negro crewman who was trying to capture it without getting himself drowned. As the little beast twisted and turned, its curly pink tail jiggled. The animal skittered to a ledge and hung there.

Given the choice, Peter thought wickedly, he would prefer that Mrs. Bickford be washed overboard rather than the sweet, helpless pig.

"Come," he shouted into the wind, grasping the widow by her upper arm. "None of us passengers are permitted to be enjoying the scenery just now."

❖

"I cannot believe I am hearing such a gorgeous voice, in such a storm!" an old man cried out from a corner of the music room.

Nobody dared to leave the room once they entered, not even when a table that had been screwed to the floor got loose and flew.

The melody of "Agitata da due venti" was the only lifeline God had tossed them, it seemed. The priests and Prudence were still splayed across velvet benches and pillows, the Germans no longer wore their bibs, and the purser cradled his bashed mandolin. They all hung there listening to Vivaldi's music, as if it contained the only passage that could lead them out of this.

❖

"We all might very well have drowned last night," Peter said during lunch the next day. "The engineer tells me that we rolled to the absolute limit."

By dawn the weather had turned serene. Repairs were already under way. Hammers flailed and mallets pounded; new screws were being driven into the teakwood ladder that had been battered. A starboard rail had been ripped away by the rush of high waters, and crew members were tying ropes around the replacement beams.

"We're lucky to have survived," Mrs. Bickford said. She helped herself to more chicken croquettes and an extra pickle.

Erika turned to the purser. "Are you going to eat your beef?"

"Actually, I'm not," the purser said. "It's a bit tough. Too much exercise for the jaws, if you ask me."

Erika eyed his plate. "Would you mind if I ate it?"

"Certainly not," the purser said.

To everyone's astonishment, she lifted her fork high and aimed the prongs straight into his filet, and took his portion for herself. She tore a large piece of bread with her teeth. Soon everyone at the table except Erika had finished, their silverware resting on their plates.

"Would you like to have the rest of my hash?" the Captain offered, extending his plate toward Erika.

She gave him a quick smile, and a nod. Erika's fork and knife were soon at work on his potatoes, too.

During the storm, her stomach had been strong, but when the sun was bright and the ocean as smooth as a lake, she felt so weak she could barely stand. Peter worried that despite all the quinine they had consumed, the fever might have caught her just as they left Port of Spain. He worried that, due to quarantine regulations, they would not be allowed ashore in New York. The authorities knew they were coming from a yellow fever port.

She went from being ravenous to not being able to hold herself upright.

Mrs. Bickford knocked one morning on the door of their stateroom. Peter had already gone upstairs to breakfast in the saloon. When the older woman entered, she found Erika hunched over a chamber pot with her mouth open to retch, but nothing came out.

"I've just come to look in on you, dear." The widow gathered Erika's hair into a loose knot to keep it from falling into the bowl.

Later, Mrs. Bickford brought Erika little saltine crackers and biscuits and a large pickle to settle her stomach.

❖

Mrs. Bickford shifted the shawl around her shoulders and flagged down Peter as he was leaving the dining room. He wanted to duck away when he noticed her coming, but there was no pole to hide behind, no alternate avenue to take. The memory of her in her drenched black skirts during the gale reminded him of the ship's pig running loose on the deck—the poor creature had been knocked dead by the storm. The pig had always been skittish, terrified when anybody tried to hold it. The only person the pig trusted was the butcher, whom it shadowed and followed like a pet.

Since the storm, they'd enjoyed plenty of bacon and pork chops. The widow's upper torso looked fatter, as though the unfortunate pig had become a visible part of her. As she stepped close to Peter, lowering her chin, two prongs formed between her brows, and he braced himself for a reprimand.

"Your wife," she said, her tone low and knowing, "can only be suffering from one thing."

"And what is that?"

"A pregnancy."

❖

Shortly after their return to New England, Erika walked across the white expanse of Boston Common on a silent, muffled winter morning. As she drew in breaths, particles of clear, cold air sharpened like crystals in her lungs. With glee—with the toe of her boot—she wrote in the newly fallen snow:

I AM EXPECTING A BABY

32

"I'd never seen such a gale," Peter said. "Even crossing the Atlantic— even when we came within sight of an iceberg—I was not so terrified." In the months afterward, at social gatherings, Peter liked recounting what they'd witnessed during the great storm at sea. He told the story again that summer, as he relaxed on his business partner's veranda on Cape Cod.

Erika overheard him through an open window as she lolled in an upstairs bath. His business partner's children ran outside, little people alive with shrieks as they chased the evening's first fireflies. The nights Erika had longed for had come, when she could rest her palms against her abdomen and feel the baby's movements.

For their weekend on Cape Cod, she had brought along a special bar of jasmine soap. Something within her had changed and evolved, but as the scent blended into the bathwater, she remembered wet orchids dangling in a forest, and a house on stilts, after-dinner lime and rum swizzles. She remembered Ravell taking hold of her face and rolling her head between his hands until her senses swooned. When Peter made love to her, she let her mind fill with Ravell because that picture brought blue sparks, pleasure, madness. Then it was over. In just a few minutes, it was always over.

Below the window where Erika bathed, Peter and his business partner and his portly wife murmured in contentment on the porch. Their wicker chairs squeaked as they rocked.

In the bath, the water grew cooler. Erika watched the child inside her roll, as smooth and slow as a hill that shifted position, her midriff higher on the right side until the baby reversed and rolled left.

This little one's movements seemed more tranquil than the last one's. The infant floated serenely, having crossed oceans to come here. A water child.

Now that the child had grown larger, she liked to frame the moon of her belly with her arms and encircle the tremblings.

"Should we write to Ravell, and tell him?" she'd asked Peter.

"Why don't we wait until the baby's born?" Peter said. "Just so we can assure him that everything has turned out well."

❖

In late August, when Quentin was born, the doctor held him up in triumph, as if he'd just leaped, glistening and shining, from the sea of her womb.

Erika never tired of gazing at her baby. Hour upon hour, there was always something new to see. His hair was dark, like Ravell's. The child had delicate features, petite crimped nostrils, very small lips through which he poked a tiny kitten tongue. Quentin laced his fingers together with exquisite poise.

One evening while Magdalena was visiting, Quentin awoke in Erika's lap, ready to be nursed. While she and the older woman spoke, his newborn eyes stared, as blind and black as a hamster's. His rooting mouth did the seeing for him. He tongued her sleeve. When his gums clamped—with blind success—onto her nipple, an electric current went through her.

After Quentin had nursed enough, his head fell back, his arms outstretched, milk oozing from the corners of his mouth, his eyes closed. He looked like a man intoxicated.

From week to week Quentin grew more awake and alert to the world. When he was two months old, while Erika and the nursemaid bathed him in the wide kitchen sink, he stared up, astonished at the noise of water running from the faucet. Stray droplets fell, and he licked them.

"Don't you just wonder," Erika said to the nursemaid, "what he's going to *say* when he learns to speak?"

Wrapping the freshly bathed baby in a white towel, Erika packaged up the child and brought him to show Peter. A terry-cloth hood framed Quentin's face like that of a miniature monk, his baby skin moist. At no moment did their son look more perfect than just after he'd been bathed.

Peter drew the child snugly against his chest. "A warm little loaf," he said. "He smells like he just came from the oven."

Even after their baby boy's birth, she did not write to Ravell. She decided she did not want to shatter everything—Peter's rapture over his delicate-limbed and dark-haired son, and, above all, the little boy's position in the world. If she began a letter to Ravell, she was afraid there would be no end to all she wanted to tell him. With every phrase that poured from her, bricks would loosen from the walls of the Back Bay town house she shared with Peter. She imagined her son might be turned out into the streets, shunned because of what she had done. *He is only a small boy,* she reminded herself. *Peter must continue to love him. He must be protected.*

When correspondence arrived from Ravell at Christmas and on other occasions, she left it to Peter to respond. She never asked if Peter had told Ravell about the child, although she presumed he had.

PART THREE

33

BOSTON

1905—1910

Returning from attending an opera one evening, Erika headed straight to the nursery. The room was dim, but her son, outfitted in white flannel, glowed as she lifted him from his crib. With the heat of him pressed against her satin dress, she sat down in a chair and nestled his head against her neck.

All evening, under the influence of glittering costumes and singing, the orchestra and the Opera House's chandeliers, she had been remembering that other life she had once planned for herself. She had been imagining things that were blasphemy.

With the baby balanced against one arm, she took huge breaths and tried to calm herself. She pulled pins from her pompadour and let the strands fall down. She put her lips against Quentin's scalp, sniffing him, hoping the salty baby scent would center her and stop the agitation of her heart. *This child is a gift. He is all I could ever want. And yet . . .* Tears seeped from under her closed eyelids and wet the baby's ears. She bent her head until it was touching his, and drowned him in her hair.

❖

On a winter's night in Boston, hot air rose from the heating register, the iron grill set into the floor. The windowpanes became opaque with steam. In the darkness of their bedroom, she and Peter danced, their bare feet moving across the creaking floor. He had just returned from a trip, and, as usual, they reached in greed for each other's bodies. By day, she pretended that the baby was really Peter's son. By night, when she and Peter could not see each other's faces, she pretended that she was back at the Cocal.

It was not the low curve of her husband's spine that her fingers stroked, but the fine fringe of hair that grew at the hollow of Ravell's back.

When she and Peter fell against the bed, their bodies damp and recovering, she imagined that if she opened a window, she'd hear the rough whisper of palm fronds in the wind; she'd see phosphorescent streaks across the water—not brick sidewalks crusted with ice.

The trouble with having taken a lover was this: he never left your bed once he'd been in it. But she could never have remained at the Cocal with Ravell. How long could she have stood on a bluff and sung to the waves and the fish?

In the morning the baby sat upright in his crib and turned and stared at her with Ravell's dark eyes. She wondered how her life had evolved into this: for the sake of her son, she must say nothing. Quentin's happiness and his future depended on her silence, the weight of a solemn lie.

When she was alone at the piano, she leaned back her head and closed her eyes and heard it in her singing: the desperation that lay beneath everything.

❖

Peter accompanied her to a concert hall one evening. Dressed in his tall silk hat and starched collar, he was as high-spirited as ever, waving to their acquaintances. And she thought: *On our honeymoon, he took me to see pyramids; thanks to him, I've walked through rain forests. He has given me everything. Now we even have a child, and yet . . .*

In the bedroom they continued to approach each other with the eagerness of two tennis enthusiasts, their bodies limber and ready for the match. But almost from the moment their bodies separated, Peter looked past her. He pulled a sheet of paper from the bedside table, and jotted notes about appointments, or about matters of complaint regarding shipments of machinery that had not yet been delivered.

She lived in a world that did not matter to him. At the concert hall, he sat beside her with visible indifference. When the orchestra began an overture, his face looked numb, his expression dull. He slept with eyes wide open and waited for the performance to be over. He simply did not hear the music at all.

❖

During the first year after the baby's arrival, she rarely sang in public. The gorgeous gift in her windpipe felt smothered; like a painful lump in the throat, it swelled and grew. It hurt to feel the voice there, silenced and useless.

Then one afternoon while her son napped and she lay on her chaise, her vision blurred, and she could not tell the lace of her curtains from the snowflakes that fell behind them. Squeezing her eyelids tightly, she held her breath against the deadness she felt. She threw off the light knitted blanket that covered her legs, jumped up from the chaise, and paced the room. How could she allow her small, sweet son to end everything? Had she given Quentin life only to find that he had taken what was most real to her?

She resumed her voice lessons with ferocious intensity. She gave a major recital. When Erika entered the stage to begin the performance, people stifled coughs and stopped rattling pages. As she sang, she noticed how the audience held its breath. These had always been her most passionate moments. Performing brought the deepest transport, a form of touching. Only during lovemaking had she felt anything close to the chill of pleasure sweeping through her as the audience listened.

"Your voice is richer than before," Magdalena said afterward. "At your age, it has ripened to its fullest power."

Peter brought her a newspaper, pointing to a review of her recital. The critic praised her technique and wrote that her voice was "like burning sugar in its sweetness and dark colorations."

Buoyed by those words, she sprang up the steps to the nursery. Quentin had learned to walk by then. She knelt beside him and pulled her son's tiny rib cage against her own. She hugged him in apology, as though the child could hear her thoughts.

Her own motherhood had been so long in coming that she was ashamed of her ungrateful feelings. Possibilities occurred to her that no mother was supposed to consider. She covered her son's cheek in guilty kisses. How fresh a toddling boy's skin was. How soft and new.

Impossible to leave him. Impossible to fly away on the wings of her voice.

❖

"No, Mama, no!" Quentin snatched back the shoe she'd taken from him.

"You're putting that shoe on the wrong foot," Erika said.

"No!" At two years of age, he slapped her hand.

I am bored by the petty spats, she decided. *By the fastening and refastening of small shoes. I am not alive; I am only marking time until he grows old enough to recognize his left shoe from his right.*

It was a tedious thing to spend one's day trailing after a small child, though nobody she knew admitted it. Most ladies she knew simply sighed, and handed over their young to nursemaids.

She became one of them, gone from afternoon into evening, rehearsing for other appearances and recitals. She attended countless performances at the Opera House. Sometimes she took supper with Magdalena, glad for the intimacy of their old tête-à-têtes. Erika often returned to the house long after Quentin had been tucked into bed.

Up late, she slept late, too. Whenever Peter was away, she asked the servants to place Quentin on a small bed in the room adjacent to hers. Mornings were her time with him. The little boy slept as late as she did. He did not climb from his pallet until he heard her stirring. Then he came with his teddy bear and plunked its fur down on her mattress and stood there, his breaths noisy while he waited for her to open her eyes fully. "Mama? My wanna milk," he'd say.

"All right," she'd say, pulling him into bed with her. She hugged his small, plump shoulders, and gave his nape loud, smacking kisses. He giggled and ducked his head as if being tickled, and then waited for her to do it again. After they both grew breathless and sore from laughing, she rang for the nursemaid to bring his milk and porridge.

❖

One evening as Erika was changing her clothes before going out to the theatre, Quentin stood in her bedroom in soft pajamas, his feet encased in sheepskin slippers. She had just slipped a coral dress over her head. The driver would be coming around with the motorcar in fifteen minutes, and she was running late.

Her dress—donned at the last possible moment—became a hideout to Quentin. As she turned to reach for a hairbrush, he lifted her skirt and ducked under it, giggling as he held on to both of her legs.

"Quentin!" she said, laughing. "Get out of there!" In all her life, no one had ever darted under her skirt before. At two, he was short enough to stand upright between her legs. As she tried to walk forward, she saw his head protrude against her smooth skirt. "What do you think you're doing under there? Being born?" She laughed again.

❖

During a week when the nursemaid left to tend to her ailing mother, Erika took care of Quentin herself. On their way to the Public Garden one afternoon, she was stunned as her two-year-old reached out to examine dog excrement on the sidewalk.

"No!" she cried, amazed that she should have to explain why he must never touch such a thing.

At supper he took a fistful of bananas and flung it with exuberance toward the ceiling, saying: "BYE-E-E-E!" Erika choked on her own dinner, laughing at the sight. That got him pitching faster.

Quentin followed her into the parlor. Guests were expected soon, and the maids had filled silver bowls with salty nibbles. Quentin grabbed fast, knowing he'd be stopped. He shoved handfuls of crackers into his mouth, crushing the crumbs against his lips.

The cook had set a coconut cake on the dining room table. Quentin climbed onto a chair and dived—his full body nearly landing on the white icing—until Erika caught his squirming torso, and lifted him horizontally into the air while he kicked.

All the scolding, fighting, and explaining overwhelmed her. But every night at eight o'clock sharp, Quentin went down blissfully. He was an easy child then, a very solid sleeper. Erika wound up his wooden music box, carved in the shape of a sheep, and darkened his room. In a chair she rocked him, tucked the rubber nipple of a feeding bottle into his mouth, and stroked his straight hair. Her lips touched his forehead and she whispered: "You know Mama loves you. . . . All our fights mean nothing. . . . You know Mama loves her boy. . . . Mama will always love Quentin."

His lips opened as he broke suction on the bottle to respond, "Yes, Mama." They nodded together.

❖

Quentin always wanted to be with her. He slipped away from the nursemaid and followed Erika wherever he could. She had to teach him that he should not accompany her into the bathroom, because adults needed privacy. While she used the toilet, she told him he must wait outside the closed door. Across the floor he lay down on his stomach, peeking under the door crack to see his mother's shoes.

"Hiiiii—" he called. His tiny fingers slid under the door, waving to her. Nearly his whole little hand fit through. Playfully she lifted the sole of her shoe, pretending to step on his fingers. The hand disappeared as he giggled, and then the fingers came into view, wiggling at her.

"Hi, Mama," he repeated hopefully, leaning his cheek against the floor, pressing his little mouth close to the crack.

"Hello, my little monkey," she said, slowly opening the door.

❖

At a dinner party, seated with guests around the fireplace, Peter charmed everyone with stories of his latest trip to Morocco. Whenever Peter finished his business with cotton traders in Alexandria, he liked to visit remote and fabled places. Outside Tangier, he'd traveled by mule with a guide named Hadj. They had wandered along cliffs overlooking the Atlantic, gazing far down at the green sea.

"We came upon a signal station," Peter recalled, "where an Englishman—a kind of hermit—lived behind a white gate with a garden. On the gate a sign read LLOYD'S AGENCY. The hermit was delighted to see us. His job is to peer through a telescope and watch for vessels on the horizon." The man wired messages to tell people in London exactly which ship had just passed Morocco.

"Just days after I met him," Peter told the guests, "I found myself on a boat passing through the Strait of Gibraltar. I peered through my glasses at the cliffs and I saw a tiny white blur. I gave a wave, because I knew my friend must be up there, watching me."

The guests were amused by everything Peter had seen and done. While listening, Erika toyed with the fringe of the Spanish shawl he'd brought back for her. She wondered why he—a man—was allowed to go away and leave his child for weeks that grew into months at a time, whereas she was bound to the house, tethered to the Back Bay. Why must she be the one to stay, while he was free?

If she remained in a backwater like Boston, she would never have a real career.

❖

She had a plan, she told her husband finally. The plan was this: she would take Quentin and a servant with her, and they would go to Florence to live. Whenever Peter crossed the Atlantic, he would come to stay at the apartment she'd rented for all of them.

"You must be raving," Peter said. He sat on the side of the bed and stared at her. A pair of socks dropped from his hand. "How many years did it take for us to have a child? And now you want to live apart? You want to take my son from me?"

"You come and go as you like, don't you?"

"Am I supposed to provide for my family another way? The bulk of my business is conducted here in Boston."

Peter snatched up the fallen socks and pulled them over his feet. He stood and pulled his suit jacket from the back of a chair, shoving his arms through the sleeves.

"I cannot believe you would even consider such a thing," he said. "Quentin isn't a lapdog you can tuck under your arm. He'll be attending school soon. The best schools for Quentin are right here in New England."

"The greatest kind of education would be to grow up abroad—"

"The family is here. His grandfather, aunts, uncles, cousins . . . You intend to cut him off from everyone? I won't allow it," Peter said. "You won't ruin Quentin's life, and you won't ruin mine."

After breakfast, he left for his office. From an upstairs window, she watched him go.

❖

Peter was in England, visiting the mills in Manchester, when Quentin contracted diphtheria. He was four years old by then. At first her son complained of a sore throat and hoarseness. When his swallowing grew painful and his neck swelled to unbearable fullness, she realized what it must be, even before the doctor told her.

Knowing the dangers, Erika sat up at night with him. Beside her sick child, she fell asleep, sliding sideways in a chair. She understood that children could suffocate from the bacillus; it could inflame and weaken a child's heart. It was March, still winter then, and she told the servants to bring her clean rags that had stiffened with ice while on the clothesline. She wrapped the half-frozen cloths around his feverish neck to lessen the swelling.

"Does that feel better?" she murmured, bending close. Her breath blew wisps of dark hair from his forehead.

Quentin did not open his eyes, but he heard her, and nodded. His throat had narrowed; he could not speak.

"Drink this," she said softly, and held up a glass filled with hot water, lemon extract, and honey. "This will soothe your throat. It's sweet."

As her son's head lay in helpless surrender against the pillow, his eyelids closed and moist, his features had never looked so delicate and perfect to her, like a child's face captured by an Old Master's brush. His chin reminded her of Ravell's, the shape of his lips.

One morning when she woke, the light of dawn filled his room, and Quentin was struggling to breathe.

"Call the doctor," she told the maid. "Call my father, call my brother! Tell them to come at once."

Quentin may die, she thought, *before Peter returns.*

When she heard a motorcar drive up, she ran to the window, lifted the shade, and saw three men get out. She pushed the window open and called to them. Her father and brother looked up and waved. Downstairs, a maid waited to let them in.

She thought of Quentin prancing in high spirits through the Public Garden, raising his legs in goose steps. Why did a child appear in one's life, if he were only fated to die, and melt away like winter?

Her heart sore with worry, she waited for the men to file into the room. Her little boy's breath had developed a peculiar, unpleasant odor. While the specialist bent and fitted a tube down her son's tiny throat, she held Quentin's hand. The physician, who had come twice before, administered a larger dose of antitoxin serum this time.

"My wife wants you to know that she's praying for him," her brother, Gerald, paused to tell her softly. Just before he left, he squeezed her hand, which was unlike him. But by that afternoon, Quentin's breathing eased. By evening, he sat up and asked in a loud, cracked voice if he could have some ice cream. She leaped from her chair and rang for a servant.

Later she wrote to Peter, *Quentin has rallied. He is going to live.* She wept as she wrote it.

❖

As Quentin slowly recovered, Erika spent long hours with him. When a maid came to relieve her, Erika went to her own bed but could not nap. Peter had acquired a new toucan. In the adjacent room the bird was making dreadful screeches, its wings batting and clamoring against the bars of its cage. When Erika lifted the cage door, the toucan hopped out, flew straight into the mantel mirror, and banged its head.

One day she opened both windows in Peter's study and set the unhappy bird on a ledge. It was spring then. The temperature was mild. *I will tell Peter that someone accidentally left a window open,* she decided. Erika let the toucan fly straight out above the rooftops of the Back Bay, and she felt herself going with the creature, its wings lifting to catch updrafts of air until the exotic bird became smaller and smaller, and blended into the sky.

❖

When Quentin was cured of his diphtheria at last, Erika took him to the Boston Public Library with a friend of his. The boys got their books and raced ahead of her down the great marble staircase. At the place where the stairs turned, the boys patted the great marble lion's backside, just as thousands of hands had done before theirs, polishing the lion's bottom.

At the Public Garden, as Quentin and his friend skipped and ran far ahead of her, Erika felt her old restless yearning to move to Italy returning. *Why must I trail after my son for the next eighteen years?* she wondered. In the summer he would turn five; Quentin already needed her less. Soon school would take more hours of his day. In the end, a son grew tall and shrugged off his parents and went away.

Whereas music was hers, it would never part from her.

If only I had been born without this voice, she thought. *It would have been simpler for everyone.*

❖

"Let me be frank," Magdalena said. "If you are serious about achieving an international reputation, you shouldn't wait. For a woman, the voice reaches its full glory in her thirties or early forties, but then—" Resting an arm across the back of the divan, Magdalena gazed through a window, perhaps recalling theatrical stages where she had sung in St. Petersburg or Milan, triumphant evenings that would not come again.

"The problem is this," Erika said. "I can't afford to wait all the years for my son to grow up, and Peter refuses to let me take Quentin along."

"Can you survive by yourself? Financially, I mean?"

"I've got a small income from my mother's estate—enough for one person. I haven't the means to hire a servant or support a child."

Magdalena sighed. "You'd never manage on your own. Not with a five-year-old child in tow." The older woman sank against the plush burgundy cushions on her divan. She passed a box of marzipan to Erika, and then chose a piece for herself.

"What makes me desperate is knowing that this voice I've been given cannot possibly last." Erika patted her throat.

"A great voice is like any other living thing," Magdalena said. "It weakens and ages and develops breaks and loses its upper register— sooner for some of us than for others."

❖

Time, time. It was the press of time that pushed her and made frantic feelings circulate through her. If she waited ten years, any splendor in her voice might be gone.

An hour after she put Quentin to bed one evening, Erika tiptoed into his room again, just to stare at him. Nothing looked holier than a child asleep.

A coonskin cap hung from the bedpost. She took away the rabbit's foot that her little son cupped in his hand, and set the trinket on the windowsill. She saw nothing of herself in his features, really. The twitch of his nose, the way his lips drew into a pucker as he made his mouth smaller— even his gestures were Ravell's. At times she thought: *Peter must see it.* How could he fail to see Ravell in the black waves that fell, slightly uplifted, from the child's temples?

At moments Peter studied their son with such sadness in his gaze that she thought: *He knows. He knows, but does not want to know.*

She glanced around at the objects in the nursery. A thirteen-foot-long stuffed crocodile curved along the baseboards and encircled half the room. Peter had purchased the crocodile from an old Egyptian peddler on the steps of Shepheard's Hotel in Cairo during a business trip. It was the first thing visiting children chose to sit upon, and it had soon become a tattered, mangy thing.

At the age of five, Quentin was very much Peter's boy. No one in his life had proven quite as exciting as Peter, who returned from transatlantic crossings and opened trunks and pulled out treasures that made the boy hop back in awe. Peter read to Quentin, took him fishing, showed him how to capture frogs and hold them between his thumb and forefinger. At a soda fountain, after eating ice cream, Quentin would slide from his mother's lap and climb onto Peter's.

"He's trying to get warm," Peter observed, amused. "And I've got the larger body mass."

Just before she left her son's room, Erika drew the covers higher over Quentin, draping the sheet like a collar under his chin.

In her own bedroom she sat at the vanity table and leaned closer to the mirror, uneasy at what she saw. She took a pair of tweezers and plucked several silver hairs from her head, and then rubbed rouge onto her pale cheeks. These days when she performed in costumes and jewels, her face looked paler, aged. Yet the voice was resplendent, everyone assured her of this—the singing trumped all petty loss of beauty.

As she watched other things fade, the voice was growing better. The voice still soared.

❖

Erika brought Peter into the music room, relying on its fine cream-colored upholstery and good light and airiness to keep him calm, but in no time at all, the volume of Peter's response magnified. She felt the beating of her own blood rise behind her ears.

"It's entirely possible," she said, "for a child to have a happy life without a mother living in the house."

"Is it?" Peter looked at her, incredulous.

"I grew up without a mother, didn't I? After Mama's death when I was seven years old, my father gave me all the love I needed."

He glowered at her. "Quentin isn't seven. He's *five*."

Peter paced the room slowly, with emotion heightening the color in his face and neck. "It isn't as if your mother had a choice about dying, is it?" He paused to wipe a drop of spittle from his chin. "How do you expect a boy to live with the notion that his mother has decided to abandon him?"

Erika replied almost in a whisper: "I'm not abandoning him."

"What do you call it, then?" Peter asked. "Moving permanently to another continent, with no intention of coming back?"

She told Peter that she meant to return, but he did not believe her. To go away just for a year, or two or three, to see how she fared—that was her plan, with a couple of long visits in between. If she flourished by her efforts, she might shuttle back and forth. In the meantime she would send her son gifts, and letters twice a week. He might come to stay with her in the summers. Anything was possible. Nobody she knew had lived the life she was prepared to embark upon, the route unmapped, the road unlit. It was all a great risk.

"If you desert us," he warned, "I shall have to divorce you. And I'll take custody of our son."

Was he really speaking as loudly as she thought, or had her own distress turned up the volume? This could not go on much longer, because she sensed that her plans were pushing him toward being something he had never been—a man who verged on doing her harm. As Peter stalked across the carpet, his arms brushed the long draperies and she expected him to rip the hanging fabric from its rod.

"There's nothing more to discuss, then," she said, and ran upstairs to lock herself in the bathroom. She went to the tub and turned on the taps, welcoming the roar of water as she prepared the hottest bath she could stand.

As steam rose, misting the mirror, condensing on the wainscoting, Erika thought about all the years she and Peter had fallen asleep together, spines touching, and yet her husband hardly understood her. She thought of Ravell, the night they'd spent at the Esmeralda estate where they'd sat on the tall steps of the hexagonal house. As she sat on the stairs and sang, Ravell had listened more closely than anyone ever had. He'd heard what propelled her, what was now taking her away. He would not have fought her like Peter. Ravell would have nodded, knowing how long this had been in the making, and together they might have made a plan.

❖

It was after that conversation that she stopped loving Peter. It had drained away gradually, of course—everything she'd once felt for him. Now silence stretched between them every evening as they sat opposite each other in the dining room. As she stared down into her plate, the air filled with sounds of him chewing a piece of beef, or sucking on a pear. Their lack of conversation made her want to writhe under her clothes.

Inside her, the discomfort was building like an illness. When she left the house, she dreaded returning in the evening and mounting the stairs to her own front door. If Peter was near, she chatted with the servants or escaped to the nursery, where she squatted beside Quentin, petting his dark silky hair while he opened his small fists to show her two cat's-eye marbles he'd found on the grass at the Public Garden. If she passed Peter on the stairs, she turned sideways, so that her body would not graze his.

One evening Peter came into the music room and sat down on the davenport as if he had every right to be there. "You were in a frenzy to have a baby," he said, "and now you're in a frenzy to run off to Italy. You find motherhood tiresome."

Peter leaned his head back. His eyes searched the ceiling, his Adam's apple sharpening in his neck. "You gave birth to a little boy and now you don't even love him," he said.

She wailed then, *"I do love him, I do."* On the carpet she walked in half-circles, and hit the sides of her skirt with her fists. "Why can't we all move to Italy?" she cried out.

Peter reminded her—as though she were unaware of this—that for the past eighteen years, he had been cultivating a network of business interests among mill owners in New England, textile machinery manufacturers in Bradford, England, and cotton traders in Alexandria. "I don't see how Italy fits into that picture," he said coldly.

He pushed himself from the sofa and stood up. "Why can't you sing here? Boston is a musical city."

She made a face.

His tone softened as he pleaded. "I've given you this house," he said. "A beautiful life. Your son will—"

"But it's not what I most want," she said.

For a moment he looked helpless, devastated by her words. Then his mouth tightened. "Am I supposed to let my business collapse because of your—your illusions that you'll arrive in Florence and be *worshipped*? There must be a thousand foreign singers who land in Italy every year—"

She glared at him. "You hope I'll fail."

"Yes," he said. "For Quentin's sake, I hope you'll fail."

❖

On a Thursday she arranged for her passage to Naples, but within an hour, shudders of self-blame passed through her, so she went back to the agent and asked for a refund of her ticket. It would be a deplorable act to leave Quentin. She could not do it.

That evening when Peter arrived home from the office, a layer of light rain rested on his sandy-colored hair. Before he had even removed his overcoat, she confessed what she had done.

"I hate my lack of resolve," she added, and showed him the torn receipt. Later she wondered why she had admitted such a thing to him. Had she hoped to make him drive her from the house?

His eyes became huge, daring her. "If you want it so much, why don't you just go ahead and desert us?"

Near midnight, Peter burst through the doorway of her bedroom. She'd been sitting up in bed, reading. He came toward her with such a wild look that she wondered if he might strike her, although he had never done so before. She tensed, ready to pull the servants' bell and wake the whole attic full of them.

"You love nobody except yourself!" he shouted, and suddenly his eyes watered.

Even three stories above, no one could have failed to hear the thunder of his voice. She pictured the servants shaken into consciousness, sitting upright in their beds.

From the room directly overhead, they heard another sound: Quentin had awakened, and was sending up a thin wail. The echoes of a little boy's sobs shamed them into silence.

Peter opened the door and bounded up the staircase to Quentin's room.

She shut off the lamp and pushed her face into a pillow and wept in the dark. *I should board a ship and stop threatening,* Erika thought. *My indecision is tormenting us all.*

❖

She waited until September when Peter was gone on business, so that he could not stop her. Then she stepped into Quentin's room one evening, and ran her hands over the bedcovers to feel his small legs before she kissed him good night. She put her face close to his and said, "Tomorrow I am going away."

"Where?" he asked.

"On a long journey far across the ocean. To Italy. I'm going to sing opera there."

He looked so alarmed that his head lifted off the pillow. "When are you coming back?"

"Not for a long time," she said. "But you must write me letters and tell me all about school and your friends, and I'll write to you. I'll even send you little presents."

"Is Papa going with you?"

"No, he'll stay here." *Except when he's traveling,* she thought. *Except for the long months when he'll be off buying Egyptian cotton or textile ma-chinery in Manchester.* But it would be best not to make the child anxious by mentioning that.

"I want to be the best singer I can be," she said. "Italy has many the-atres and audiences love music there, so that's where I must go so that more people will hear me."

"You want to be famous. That's what Papa says you wish for."

"Shall I sing you another lullaby?"

"When are you leaving?"

"In the morning."

Quentin sat up and tightened his arms around her neck. He pressed the sharp bones of his face against hers. Did he mean to hug or hurt her?

"Sing for me, Mama," he begged. When she finished one soft little song, he asked for another—a funny one, and then another. He tried to keep her singing to him as long as he could. When she slid toward the door and opened it, he beckoned her to sit near him again.

"Mama? Will you be here when I wake up?"

"Yes, in the morning. But not after you get home from school. My ship will sail at noon."

"Mama? When are you coming back?" he asked a second time.

To this house? she thought silently. *Never back to this house. Not to live with Papa. He swears he'll divorce me for leaving.* But she did not speak those words to her son.

How long . . . ? How long would it be before she stroked the little notch in his chin again? She didn't know. She didn't have a date she could promise him.

Quentin moved his hot breath closer to her ear. "Please don't go away."

She could have lost all courage at that moment. Her eyes grew wet, but she couldn't let Quentin see that, so she caught her tears with her thumb and rubbed them onto the sheet. "Maybe you'll—" she said. "Maybe you'll come to Italy and hear me sing."

The previous week she'd taken Quentin to the beach for one last out-ing together. Hand in hand, they'd run along the edge where waves met land. Whenever she looked back at their footprints in the sand, water was filling the cups of their heels, mother's and son's, and washing them all away.

She pressed her nose against the top of his head and sniffed deeply, trying to hold the scent of him inside her. As he lay back down, she kissed him again, folding the blanket around his small shoulders as though it were already winter. "Remember Mama loves you," she whispered. "Even while she's far away, Mama always loves you."

"Yes," he nodded. They nodded together, yes and yes and yes, until Quentin's eyes closed.

PART FOUR

34

❧

ITALY

1910—1911

On a sheer moonlit night, a steward rapped on her stateroom door and woke her, alerting her as they passed one of the Azores. To view it, Erika hurried up to the deck in her dressing gown and slippers. Under a generous moon, she saw the island of Pico in silhouette, its solitary peak seven thousand feet high. She imagined Ravell beside her. Like him, she was leaving one land for another, and he seemed alive in the salty tang of sea air, in the pressing onward of the ship, in the slapping weight of waves.

They passed Gibraltar, where the people could not drink water from the rock they lived upon, so rainwater had to be collected in huge tanks. African shores appeared, and then Sardinia.

When at last they came to the Bay of Naples, the fourteen hundred Italians in steerage waved their arms at the sky and sang in celebration of the voyage's end. The great tossing crowd pressed against the rails with babies and bundles. When a school of porpoises glided past, the Italians pointed and cheered. The grand sight of a smoky Vesuvius unleashed the last hint of restraint in them and made them wild, their loose garments flapping, their hair flying as they danced.

A ghostly fog threaded through Erika's hair as she watched the shores of Italy coming closer. She thought of Lillian Nordica and Geraldine Farrar, American divas who had sailed to Europe to seek fuller careers. Both of them had arrived here so young that their mothers had accompanied them as business managers and chaperones. It was their mothers who had shaped ambitious futures for them, their mothers who were determined that their daughters would appear at Europe's finest opera houses.

She was much older than those two Yankee divas had been. Whatever strength a mother had given them, she must provide for herself.

❖

A strange hunched man met her at the Stazione Centrale in Florence. All day and all night, he must have haunted train platforms, on the lookout for a bewildered foreign face like hers. He saw her hesitate just after a cascade of luggage tumbled and landed around her.

"You want hotel? I find," he said in English, and made a grab for her valises.

A hard shake of her head did not sweep him away, this creature whose long yellow teeth reminded her of a mummy with its lips dried up and gone. The hunched man wore a dark, shabby suit. She did not trust him to find a clean mattress for her.

Erika beckoned a porter, who hauled her things toward a cluster of taxi horse cabs that waited in the street.

"You want nice, expensive? You want cheap? I find," the shabby man said, for he had followed her out to the horse cabs.

A mixture of weariness and anxiety filled her chest; the night appeared so black already. If only she had not boarded such a late train from Naples—if only she had arrived tomorrow instead. The little man to her right seemed to hear her thinking these things. He pointed to himself and batted the air with his sleeves, like an insect.

To escape him, she climbed into the cab and uttered a few words to the driver—the name of a random pension listed in the guidebook—"*Bianchi, Piazza dell'Indipendenza.*" When she had visited Florence previously, she and Peter had enjoyed the luxury of the Hotel Savoy, but she had to curb expenses now and could no longer stay at large, comfortable places.

When the horse cab drew up to the pension, a woman wearing a sprigged skirt came to a third-story landing, and she looked surprised by the sight of an American lady in fine clothes.

No, the pension owner shook her head. No more beds left. By this late hour, every bed in the city must have held a dozing body, Erika fretted; every hotel clerk had probably shut off the front-desk light and bolted the door, all booked up for the evening.

The next pension was full, too, when the horse cab paused outside. Did every tourist who came into Florence from the Central Railway Station carry the same British guidebook? The hordes must have arrived in the city earlier in the day, and claimed every room on the list.

At least Quentin wasn't enduring this with her. She would have felt dreadful, pulling him along by the hand, or wandering with the sleepy weight of him against her shoulder, unable to find a bed for him. If he were here now, he'd have grown too heavy to carry. If she let him slide from her arms, he'd have sunk to his knees, his breath sweet and sticky with candy.

When the coachman turned down a narrow, nameless street, Erika noticed a red carpet and potted palms through a glass doorway—a small hotel lobby.

"Only one room left," the clerk said. "I can give it to you for—" The man named a sum that sounded like a great quantity of lire, and while she stood and mentally calculated how many dollars that would translate into (she had always been slow at figures), he threw down his pen and halved the price.

"I'll take it," she said, relieved. The bed sagged and a faucet dripped behind the wall and kept her awake, but she felt lucky to have found it.

❖

The guidebook advised her to apply to a gentleman on the Via dei Pecori about furnished apartments for rent. He escorted Erika into a building whose corridors the sun never touched. A single gas jet burned all day and all night to illuminate the stairwell and the wearisome climb four flights up. The furnished apartments were situated under the roof, and the upholstery in each held the odor of burned stew or other stale smells of previous tenants.

Erika stood for a long while in one, attempting to envision a life here. She pulled open the shutters and found herself peering across a narrow alleyway and into the window of the opposite house, where a dog that sounded like a German shepherd gave terrible barks. She wondered if it would bark all night, a couple of yards from her pillow. "It won't do, I'm afraid," Erika told the agent, and she went away depressed.

The desk clerk at her hotel was a chubby, neatly dressed man. His dark hair grew thick around his ears and had broken off into thin bristles at the top of his head, where a round spot of scalp had worn through. He wrote in the ledger in such a precise manner that Erika asked if he owned the hotel.

"How I wish," he said, and laughed. Erika imagined him to be the father of young children.

He was patient with her efforts to converse in Italian. *"Per favore—"* she said. "How one might find a furnished room in Florence?"

"To rent by the month?" he asked.

She nodded. "Something pleasant but reasonable? I've come here to study—" She was surprised how she turned, almost pleadingly, to a stranger in this way, but there was no one else.

He was appalled at the price the agent had quoted for the apartment she'd seen earlier that day. "Such a man is a thief," the clerk declared. Little wrinkles worked into his forehead as they talked.

The next morning while she sat eating breakfast and studying her Italian language book, he approached her table in the courtyard.

"I know of a place," he announced. "Views of the Arno. Right near the Ponte Vecchio. Very beautiful."

"Is it expensive?"

"No," he insisted, both of his forefingers pointing toward his heart in sincerity. "Only forty lire a month, plus five lire a month for servants. Sunny. Perfect."

"What is the address? May I see it?"

He looked uneasy. The elderly proprietress was very particular in choosing her tenants, he had heard, and she might not care for foreigners, so perhaps he should go and vouch for Erika's character himself. He found his hat and went directly out, leaving a waiter in charge of the front desk.

While he was gone, she waited on a courtyard chair and studied Italian verbs. In a short time he returned, looking dejected.

"No luck?"

A servant had answered his knock, and had carried the message to the elderly landlady that a gentleman wished to rent the room for a lady, but the owner had refused to see him.

"Did you say that I am an American?"

"Only that you are a dignified lady, and a schoolmistress."

A schoolteacher. He must have fabricated that to furnish her with respectability, but perhaps the old proprietress had felt suspicious that a man had come to rent the place, rather than the lady in question.

"What is the address?"

Erika decided to wait until afternoon before paying a call herself at the house on Lungarno Acciaiuoli. She would have to pretend to be an entirely different lodger from the one proposed that morning.

When a horse cab drove her past the place, she could hardly believe how splendid it was. The façade was ochre-colored, the dimensions high and narrow. The upper-story rooms had wrought-iron balconies where one could stand and survey the river with its arched bridges reflected on the water. Less than a block away, jewelers' shops clung, like squatters' huts, to the sides of Florence's ancient bridge, the Ponte Vecchio.

The driver dropped her off. She worried that just in the past hour, the place had slipped away and been rented to someone else. Thank goodness she had worn her most impressive suit, the dove gray with the blue velvet collar, and her blue toque with the ostrich feather. The day was warm, and as she strolled toward the building, she fretted that she had become hot and unkempt in the heat. Perhaps the elderly landlady suspected that the hotel clerk wished to lodge his mistress in her house. Perhaps that was why she had turned him away. Or it could be that the old lady simply disliked men, or felt afraid of them.

From a street vendor Erika bought an orange and ate it to sweeten her breath. Afterward she regretted it, because her hands felt sticky from the rind and juice.

The house had an elaborate knocker on the front door. Erika lifted the large metal ring through a lion's brass nose and rapped against the wood. A fat servant who wore no corset answered. Erika explained that she was an American who had come to Florence to study opera, and that she was seeking a room. The maidservant looked at her and disappeared up a long, echoing stairwell. After a time she called from the landing that Erika was invited to come up.

She headed for the broad staircase. The foyer's red-tiled floor, the banisters, the walls—everything gleamed from the efforts of someone with rough hands and vigorous elbows who loved to clean. The window on the second-story landing was open. The afternoon light above the Arno was so brilliant that Erika expected to see the watery reflections mirrored in the highly glossed floors.

Upward, upward. As they passed closed doors, Erika feared that the room to be let faced the rear alleyway, where laundry drooped from clotheslines. The room might provide no panorama at all. She believed the stout servant was leading her to inspect the quarters in question. But no—she was to be interviewed first.

The owner of the Lungarno Acciaiuoli house lived in an expansive apartment that consumed the top floor. Erika was surprised that an elderly person would wish to climb four flights, but the views must be best here. As the servant unlatched the door and motioned for her to follow, Erika felt a flush of light and airiness, the sensation that she had entered a place close to the sky and clouds. This was the apartment farthest removed from the din of the street.

The proprietress, an old lady, did not turn as they came in. She sat in profile, like Whistler's mother, and faced the long balcony doors that opened to the river on this warm September afternoon. The elderly woman was fragile, her limbs as spindly as the arms and legs of the fine antique chairs that furnished the rooms. The apartment contained a beautiful grand piano, and carpets and dark oil paintings of such quality that Erika wondered if she had stumbled on a descendant of one of Florence's ancient banking families.

At first Erika was struck by the landlady's regal profile, by her nose with a small, stony bump in its bridge. Then, as the proprietress turned her head, it became obvious that she was blind.

Her old brown eyes appeared unfocused and coated with a peculiar film. The vanity Erika had felt over her fine suit, the fretting she had done about her perspiring forehead—it all seemed absurd now.

"You sing?" the landlady said in English. "Let me hear."

"Ah," Erika said. "You speak English. Where did you learn it?"

"I lived in London as a girl."

Days had elapsed since Erika had practiced anything, but she went to the piano. Her fingers felt numb on the keys. She sang softly at first, her voice very light. ("If you want to snare someone's attention," her Conservatory professor used to say, "sing quietly.") She knew she was executing it all very weakly, singing Rossini at half-voice. But her tone grew more secure by the end.

Afterward, the old Florentine landlady sat motionless in her chair, as though she could still hear the vibrations of Erika's aria after it ended. The blind woman faced the Arno, not seeing the river but perhaps sensing its light, its flow.

She instructed the servant to take the American lady downstairs and show her the room situated directly below this vast parlor.

The room was light-filled and empty, large enough for a piano and much else besides. Its red tile floor shone, and Erika heard her heels strike and echo against the surfaces. The servant explained that her mistress preferred each tenant to bring her own belongings and personality to it. Erika did not worry about how she would furnish it.

The maid unlatched a pair of shuttered doors and threw them open.

Erika stepped onto the balcony to view the Arno. The room had the same vista as the owner's apartment, just one flight above. She imagined one day showing this to Ravell, his spirits uplifted by it all.

"Well," the blind lady said when they returned upstairs. "What do you say? Will you take it?"

"Of course," Erika said. "It would be splendid." She could hardly believe that only forty lire per month were being asked for it.

"Good. I have one request."

"What is it?"

"As you practice, if the day is warm enough, I would like you to leave your windows and shutters open. A voice such as yours is something I want to hear clearly."

"That would be my pleasure." Erika suspected that the blind woman could hear a smile when a person spoke; the shape of smiling lips changed the sound of words. "You haven't told me your name."

"My name?" The old lady paused. "You can call me 'Donna Anna.'"

"Like the character in *Don Giovanni*."

"Exactly."

The apartment held masses of flowers, Erika noticed. Lush blossoms floated in bowls, and long-stemmed yellow roses and flame-colored gladioli thrust upward from vases. Dashes of color everywhere, all beautifully arranged.

As she and the servant descended the stairwell, the maid mentioned that her employer played the piano for long hours, music being a deep consolation in her old age.

"She loves flowers, too, I see," Erika said. In Italian she could not express the little mystery, the irony she had felt, being in the apartment of a sightless woman who surrounded herself with so many colorful blooms.

"She can smell them," the maid said.

35

"I am a busy man," he declared to Erika in a handwritten note. "Remember, I have only ten minutes to give you."

The most sought-after voice teacher in Florence, according to a friend of Magdalena's, was a man named Mario Brassi, who spoke excellent English. Students flocked to him.

A servant instructed Erika to remove her shoes upon entering the maestro's house. She had been forewarned about Maestro Brassi's passion for anything Oriental. He wanted all visitors to his Florentine home to imagine that they had stepped into a Mandarin palace. When Erika cast off her hard-heeled shoes, the servant pointed to an array of Chinese slippers of all sizes on the vestibule floor. Erika was supposed to choose a pair and wear them for as long as she remained in the maestro's house.

The walls were painted traditional Chinese colors—mustard gold, with moldings and doors that glowed fiery red.

Erika was told to wait on a hallway bench until he had a chance to audition her. Through the studio's open doorway she observed the maestro. He was a round, effete little man who crossed his arms over his chest. As he listened to others talk, he would sometimes give a laugh and a haughty jerk of one shoulder, and shake his head dismissively.

Half the morning she sat listening through the open doorway as he coached young sopranos through cadenzas with comet-tailed notes. As their upper registers shattered, the awful sounds made Erika think of birds that flew straight into windows and came out bloody. The maestro's fists would fall onto the ivory keys in a temper, or he would withdraw his hands from the keyboard and punish his failed coloraturas with long silences.

To his tenors, Brassi was kinder. "Whenever I bathe," Erika overheard the maestro advising a male student, "I always take my bath in a darkened room with incense and a single candle burning. It relaxes me, especially before a performance."

As she waited, Erika noticed through another open doorway that the dining room furniture had been imported from the Far East—one low table hewn of darkly oiled wood, encircled by floor cushions. Maestro Brassi evidently expected guests for lunch: the table had been set for eight.

For two and a half hours she waited on the bench. Students came and went, with scores pressed against their chests.

Around noon, aromas of fried pork and soy and sounds of sizzling vegetables invaded the house. The air tasted of ginger. Erika presumed that Maestro Brassi had hired a cook from Peking or Shanghai. She grew hungry for the food, smelling it.

Near lunchtime, after a young tenor exited, the maestro himself finally came out. He lifted a finger toward Erika and gestured for her to enter the studio. "Go in and wait for me. I need to check something with my chef. Remember—this must be quick."

Down the corridor he hurried away with rapid, mincing steps. If anything got in his path, Erika imagined he would flap his hands and swat it away.

Five more minutes elapsed. The room's red color affected her mood. She stood by the piano and decided she would sing one of the most furious arias she knew.

Framed photographs of Japanese Kabuki actors hung on the walls. The maestro tried to make himself up like a Kabuki figure, too, she realized. In the hallway, hadn't she noticed something like white flour dusting the wings of his nose? Perhaps he rubbed his cheeks with beet juice as well.

What a silly, infernal little man he was. Hadn't she sent him a note, requesting a formal time to meet? And hadn't he scrawled a reply, telling her to appear at nine-thirty in the morning? How dare he set an appointment and then make a show of having no time for her. She hated his pretensions.

He reentered the studio carrying a small platter of Chinese hors d'oeuvres. A young accompanist followed him into the room and took up his position at the piano while Maestro Brassi slid into a chair and settled the plate on his knees. He did not offer anyone else a taste of the food. Clearly he expected the audition to be dull, and Brassi had brought the morsels to amuse himself during her arias.

Before she began, Brassi placed a piece of crispy duck meat on a thin white pancake and rolled it up. A brown paste oozed from one end of the stuffed pancake as he munched. He dipped two fingers into his mouth and licked them clean.

She handed the pianist a score she'd brought along. "I shall sing 'Ah, fuggi il traditor' from *Don Giovanni*," she announced. "After that, I shall do 'Mi tradì.'" She did not want to allow Brassi to tell her what she would sing.

Hearing the finality in her tone, he made no objection. It suited her mood very well to open with an impassioned line, a musical scream, as Donna Elvira sang about her philandering lover. Ah, to sing of a traitor! Outrage warmed her chest, her throat, and her diaphragm.

The first notes thrust into the air like a gleaming sword. It went on like that, strong and deadly, straight through the second aria. The tones astonished her. Her indignation dispersed all nervousness. Let him deny that this was the best voice he had worked with all morning, Erika thought.

Once she started to sing, Brassi did no more nibbling from his platter of hors d'oeuvres. Taps came at the front door and flurried footfalls sounded in the corridor as his luncheon guests assembled. The studio door was ajar, and she sensed the respectful hush that fell out there—a churchlike quiet—because her voice commanded it. She knew they all sat out there wondering who was in here, vocalizing. A shrewd expression touched Maestro Brassi's face.

"A strong and natural voice," he admitted. Regretfully he added, "It is only too bad your training has been poor until now. Before you came to me."

His speech was loud and calculated, she surmised, especially for those listeners in the hallway. Brassi stepped toward her.

"Say the sound of the letter *h*," he ordered. "Aspirate!"

She did so.

"Now sing the first phrase of 'Ah, fuggi il traditor' again."

Erika repeated it. Midphrase, Brassi chopped the blade of his hand straight into her stomach. Pain bloomed behind her eyes. She could not recall any instance in her life when anyone had hit her so bluntly, so hard.

"Do it again."

"I will not."

"Ah," he said, his lips stretched to a sneer, "but you will."

"If you touch me again," she warned, "I shall punch you back."

He moved back a few paces. He could see that she meant it. "I do this to illustrate your faults," he defended himself. "If you had been breathing correctly, you would have felt no pain. The diaphragm muscles should be tough. Like a stone wall. As a student of mine, you must learn this." His jaw jutted upward.

Though Brassi was reputed to be one of the most celebrated voice coaches in Florence, she decided that this would be the only meeting she would have with him. She did not care how many impresarios came to his house to sample Peking Duck. The maestro picked up a Chinese umbrella and opened and closed it like bellows, with deep knee bends, in mimicry of what he considered her absurd breathing habits. In a high, splintered voice, he eked out the first phrase of the aria she had just sung.

A comprehension of his methods flashed into her head. She saw a pattern to all she had observed that morning. Each student was a victim he had alternately flattered and mocked. In order to keep each singer in his fist, Brassi had to affect a superior stance, and feed a student's doubts and inadequacies.

"After what I witnessed here this morning," Erika said, "I would never dream of becoming your student."

She fished a gold coin from her purse and placed it on the piano. Through the corridor, past a tunnel of shadowy figures, she rushed out. Sunlight stung her eyes. As she hurried across the piazza, she heard a door open behind her and the ting of a coin thrown at her heels. The door thundered shut.

Pride prevented her from glancing down at first, but then she thought better of it. Money was something she would need now. She stooped to retrieve the gold coin rolling on the paving stones, and replaced it carefully in her purse.

36

Another potential voice teacher—and Magdalena's sentimental favorite—was the man who had coached Magdalena during her own youthful days in Italy. But by now, he must be an octogenarian. The house where Maestro Piva lived faced a piazza with bougainvillea and a teeming fountain. On the morning Erika went to audition for him, she did not need to peer at house numbers to know which door was his. His windows were open, and from across the square she could hear the maestro playing something from Verdi's *Aida* as she approached. He played with such finesse that the music flowed across the piazza, a slender river of sounds that pulled her toward him.

It surprised her that he was not distracted by the cacophony of old men who argued over their card game on the cobbled pavement outside. Nor did the *thwump!* of a ball that some little boys bounced against a wall interrupt the maestro's playing. The music threaded between the muted murmurs of old women on benches; the strains of *Aida* outlasted the clangor of church bells that marked the hour.

The square was alive with so many pigeons that Erika feared she might step on them, and she expected birds to be caught under her skirt. She had the impulse to run, as her little son would have done, just to scatter them, but any hurry on her part would not be dignified.

A matron dressed in black came to the door, and introduced herself as Maestro Piva's daughter. Lines of displeasure framed her mouth.

"Magdalena's friend is here to see you, Father." In the parlor she called to her father in alarming shouts, but nothing interrupted his trance.

The white-haired gentleman continued his music, oblivious to them. The daughter crossed her big-boned wrists over her stomach and muttered to forewarn Erika: "He doesn't take students anymore." Only when the daughter placed a hand on her father's shoulder did he stop playing and glance up.

Was it the maestro's wish to discontinue teaching, or was it his daughter's preference? The latter, Erika suspected. Piva was an affable fellow. A pink delight quickened in his cheeks at the sight of this new American lady sent to him by his most famous pupil. Either Piva's skin had stretched, or his bones had shrunk; the two no longer matched well. A hollow of age had formed where his throat ended just above his collarbone, a cavity deep enough to store a chestnut.

Warmly he clasped Erika's hand, and released it only reluctantly, as they took their seats. "What will you sing for me?" he asked in eagerness.

She named several arias and told him to choose which he might like to hear. He grinned and regarded her with unwavering buoyancy, but oddly, he did not respond to the question.

"Father!" his daughter barked. "The lady asks what you want her to sing. Now, what shall it be? 'Caro mio ben'? 'Voi che sapete'? Or something from *La sonnambula*—'Care compagne'?" Impatience made her shouts more rapid, and her face looked tired. Clearly, it wore her out to have to prompt him.

Was he senile, then? Erika fidgeted uneasily on the antique velvet settee. How many years had elapsed since Magdalena had actually seen her former maestro?

"In his day," Magdalena had said of Piva, "he was a tenor of great repute. He can play all the operas from memory."

The white-haired maestro sat with crossed legs, and he leaned toward Erika as if nothing charmed him so much as the presence of an American lady who had come to the homeland of bel canto to study. "In six months, you will know our language like your own," he said. "After you study with me for one year, you will know five roles *perfettamente*. Cues, recitatives—not just arias. All of it will be here—" he said, making motions of inscription on his heart.

Erika found it premature for him to predict her progress when he had not yet heard her sing. Had her letter of introduction from Magdalena been enough to convince him? Or was he being wishful in his old age, and confusing her fate with that of his most successful student? A brilliant student made a teacher's reputation—or so the saying went.

They agreed that she should begin with "Caro mio ben." As Maestro Piva resumed his place at the piano, his daughter bent toward Erika. The daughter shielded her mouth with one hand and whispered, "He has lost his hearing."

As Erika rose to sing, her heart fell into her shoes. If he was too deaf to shape an opinion, why audition at all? Her vocal cords withered before the first notes emerged. He played. (How did he manage so well? From the habit of touch? From memory?) She sang limply while the daughter waited in a chair. As soon as it was done, Erika bowed and thanked him, and she hurried out, knowing she would not return.

❖

Later that afternoon, feeling somewhat dispirited, she went to sip a *limonata* at Doney's famous *caffè*. There, she saw children—English children—eating *cannoli*, their tongues licking long hollow tubes filled with sweet ricotta cream. She imagined the bliss that would come over her son's face if he tasted one.

Because she could not send Quentin spoonfuls of gelato or panna cotta, she mailed him a package of hard candies that she hoped he'd suck and swallow like love. She sent him a tiny carving of a terra-cotta angel that would fit in his palm. On the Ponte Vecchio, she bought a tooled leather birdcage—a new home for Quentin's parakeet—and she arranged to have it shipped.

But no note arrived to thank her for these presents. Quentin was so young, his skills with pen and paper so tentative, that someone needed to prompt him, obviously. But no one did.

37

On the morning Erika had spent waiting to audition at Maestro Brassi's studio, she'd taken a business card left on a vestibule table—that of an English-speaking accompanist advertising his services. Nobody answered Erika's knock when she went to inquire at his address. The accompanist lived in a neighborhood where wet laundry hung between the narrow houses and rained a few drops on the heads of passersby. The front door was dented and scuffed at the base, evidently having been kicked open on many occasions. She took it upon herself to go directly up. The business card indicated that he lived on the fifth floor, under the roof.

At two o'clock in the afternoon, Christopher Wise still wore his dressing gown and slippers. At first Erika presumed that he was ill.

"I'm sorry to disturb you," she said. "I've come to inquire about an accompanist. No one responded when I knocked downstairs—"

"That's quite all right," he assured her, and invited her in. "This is one of those days when I've been awfully slow about getting dressed."

He was a young American of about twenty-five, the first blond fellow she had seen for days. When he smiled, his nostrils flared, and one dimple was etched like a crescent in his left cheek.

His living quarters consisted of a single room. In order to change his clothes, he excused himself and disappeared behind a painted wooden screen. While she waited, she heard the pouring of water and splashing as he washed himself in a basin. He called out apologies for the disarray of the place.

The bed, which doubled as a divan, was unmade. So many books and opera scores lay upon it that Erika could not have sat down. She wondered if he survived on bits of bread and cold soup carried five flights up to his room.

"You'd like to hear me play while you sing, I suppose," he said.

Christopher Wise sight-read effortlessly. He kept the tempi brisk and firm, and still provided her spaces to breathe. His hands showed a surprising span—they arched like bridges and came down forcefully on chords.

"Your voice is awfully good," Christopher said. "You may think I'm flattering you, but I'm not."

She could tell that his enthusiasm was real. There was something unguarded about him. He shivered, as if he'd just felt a gust of good fortune.

"I am honestly surprised," he repeated, "at how marvelous your voice is."

His reaction buoyed her, and made her almost giddy. She felt closer to Christopher Wise, suddenly, than to any other person in Florence—closer than she had felt to anyone in weeks. His bow tie was askew. One end of it hung dog-eared. Impulsively she reached over—as she might have done with her son—and set his limp tie right.

"I haven't got a piano yet at my new lodgings," she said. "Would it be all right if I came here in the mornings?"

They agreed that she would come every morning at ten-thirty. He would drill her for new roles she wished to add to her repertoire. He would help familiarize her with entrances and exits of other cast members.

"I'm not a good sight reader," Erika confessed.

Christopher Wise assured her that they would repeat everything a thousand times, each little *parlando* stretch, until a new role became instinctive to her.

Light pervaded the room. His building stood a story higher than the other narrow houses in the neighborhood, and his windows overlooked the terra-cotta rooftops of Florence. With her head thrust through an open pane, she lingered, half-longing to fly out. Odors from the centuries-old streets rose up—scents of dust and cypress, of roses and wet stone.

He asked how long she had been in Florence. "Have you been to the coffeehouse at the Boboli Gardens?" he asked. "Why don't we go there right now for something to eat?"

Exuberantly he trotted down the stairwell steps, moving so fast that he might have been falling down—flight after flight—yet at each landing he turned to wait for her.

❖

They lingered at the *caffè* until late afternoon. "A husband and a son," Christopher repeated. "Was it difficult for you to leave them?"

"It was the most painful decision I've ever made," she said. She sank into sadness, and for the first time in days, she allowed herself the luxury of a few tears. She took the cloth napkin and blotted the dampness under her eyes.

He was so receptive a listener that he might have been a womanly confidante. Or did he seem more like a much younger brother? It was hard to know, because she had never had a younger brother.

To cheer her up, he plucked three fat strawberries from a plate and placed them in her palm. She sniffed them before tasting. *Fragoli*, she thought, reminded of the fruit's name.

From the gazebo-like coffeehouse they could see views of the Arno, the cupola of San Frediano, and the campanile of Santo Spirito, the Duomo, and the crenellated tower of the Palazzo Vecchio. Christopher Wise had no money, she knew, but he had a refinement that made it seem natural for him to be there, drinking dry white wine and biting the tips of wild strawberries with his even white teeth. A *caffè* suited him better than his shabby room.

As for his own story, Christopher explained that he had left Chicago about nine months earlier to come to Florence. His ambition was to compose or to conduct, though he had not yet decided which.

She felt faintly sorry for him when he revealed his aspirations, although she did not quite know why his dreams sounded doomed to her. Why did she have this vision of him in twenty or thirty years: for all his charms, still as an impoverished accompanist? By then he would no longer be considered a young man lit by hopes; by then he would be a sad, faded fellow in rumpled suits who lived for his own private appreciation of culture. Did he secretly believe her yearning for grand accomplishments a little hopeless, too? Why was it that others' dreams might sound ludicrous, but never our own?

"Every morning after practice," Christopher said decisively, "we should go to a different *caffè* on the Via Tornabuoni, or we should explore other things—like a few old curio shops I know about. In a few weeks, I will have shown you all the little treasures of Florence that have taken me nine months to discover."

Erika sighed. "You know, I still haven't found a good voice teacher."

"Maestro Valenti," Christopher said. "He's your man. Valenti must know every impresario from Naples to Milan. I'll take you to audition for him."

He announced this with such self-assurance that she realized his circle of professional acquaintances was far greater than she'd assumed. Later she learned that he worked with a number of talented singers. He was poor, perhaps, but ambitious.

Strolling back past the statues and cypress-lined lanes of the Boboli Gardens, Erika thought what a relief it was to be able to speak in flowing paragraphs to an American, and not have to grope for each sentence in Italian. "Do you ever feel lonely?" she asked.

"No," he said. "I have two very close friends, both Americans. They came to Florence around the same time I did. We see each other constantly. What about you? Are you lonesome?"

She had to admit that she was.

❖

At dusk, after she'd left Christopher, she stopped to watch a group of boys of various ages kicking a ball in a piazza. *Someday Quentin's voice will deepen and crack like that older one's,* she thought. *But I may not be there to see his calves lengthening, or the knobs of muscle forming in his arms.* Another boy raced so close past the bench where she sat that she smelled his raw animal scent. He retrieved the ball and hurled it. The boy's hair was damp; in the heat, his scalp glistened as he bent to tie his shoe.

As suppertime neared, the pack of boys thinned. The ball drifted, unattended for longer stretches. An impatient mother appeared, and she hooked her arm around her son's head, pulling him homeward.

Eventually the square was deserted except for Erika, who remained seated on the bench. No more boys yelled to one another, no ball resounded against the paving stones. Through open windows, the aroma of sizzling meats wafted toward her. During this hour when families gathered together, Erika felt the stone bench underneath her grow cold. On this warm autumn evening, no one in the city of Florence waited for her to return home.

38

Since her arrival in Italy, it was the memory of Ravell that gave her courage. On the morning she was hurrying toward her audition at Maestro Valenti's studio, with a portfolio of scores tucked under her arm, she imagined Ravell beside her. In her mind she planned a letter she might send to him. *I am alone now and living in Florence. Like you, I have left Boston—I've ended the old life, and begun another.*

In Italy, Erika rarely spoke of her son. In her thoughts, only Ravell understood her torment and her struggle; he forgave what few people could.

She reached Christopher's building very early. They had agreed to head to Maestro Valenti's studio together. On the stairs she passed his two American friends, who seemed to be leaving with terrible haste. Seeing her, they paused and tried to stifle their giddiness.

"Are you Madame von Kessler?" one of the young men asked. He introduced himself as Mark and the other as Edmund. The two had spent the night on Christopher's floor. After what must have been a late evening soaked in wine and endless talk, they had failed to carry themselves home until now. Mark's tie dangled like a snake from his pocket, and Edmund had thrown his vest over one shoulder and held it there by his hooked thumb.

"Christopher tells us that you're going to meet Maestro Valenti," Mark said. His long hair was whisper-fine, his shirt half-buttoned, a little fissure of flesh visible on his well-toned chest. He stood in a languorous way, with his weight leaning into one hip. He was clearly aware of his good looks.

The shorter man, Edmund, had the homeliness of a Hapsburg monarch with his narrow head and slack jaw, and his red, protuberant lower lip.

Erika felt a faint dislike for both of them—they, unlike Christopher, struck her as insufferably young. Mark and Edmund acted excessively polite. No doubt they viewed her simply as their friend's employer. Their presence reminded her that her accompanist's situation was not as solitary as her own.

❖

"You are silent this morning," Christopher said as they walked through the Oltrarno and a street shaded by ancient trees toward the master teacher's house.

"I'm thinking—" Erika said.

"Of what?"

"You must see me as very old. What age do you suppose I am?"

"Twenty-nine," he said at once.

"I'm far into my thirties."

"The perfect age for a mezzo," he said.

With the flicker of a smile, she pointed at his bow tie, dog-eared once again. Despite his elegant hands and manners, there was always something askew about Christopher, as if he'd just been napping on a sofa, fully clothed.

Tucking his chin into his collar, he looked down to inspect himself. "Oh, dear," he said, trying to pat his bow tie smooth.

It was not yet seven-thirty in the morning. When had she ever been summoned before a voice teacher at such an hour? According to Christopher, Maestro Valenti was the most dedicated vocal instructor in Florence. Opera was a religion for him.

"Valenti wastes no time on small talk," Christopher said. "Relentless work—that's all he cares about. Valenti won't speak of anything personal or trivial except—"

"Except?"

"Except that Valenti is a sort of hypochondriac. He has a passion for people's little ailments. He can't hear enough about yours, and he'll confide in you about rashes he has found on the most private parts of his body. You'll see all his powders and pills. Homemade potions, I think."

A maid escorted them into a studio with an amber-tiled floor where the maestro—sixty years old, perhaps—sat hunched at the piano, playing something modern by Puccini. He did not glance up as they entered.

Maestro Valenti wore a suit of summer white, his silver hair swept off his forehead, ending in a long wave that touched his back collar. All of this contrasted with his dark eyes and smoky complexion. Black eyebrows hinted at the color his hair had once been.

Wordlessly, the maid handed Erika a tall glass of water and went out. Erika sipped and felt a cool river move down her gullet to her stomach, where a hollow of hunger had carved itself. She thought of the chocolate and bread she'd left standing on the table in her room. Why had she not made herself eat something before coming here? Light-headed and suddenly nervous, she wanted to sit down.

"What role do you know best?" Maestro Valenti called out, not bothering to look at her as he continued with whatever he was playing.

"Amina," she said, "in *La sonnambula*."

He hummed as he played, the music a hive that enveloped him. It broke off abruptly.

"'Care compagne'? Will you start with that for me?" From a cupboard he retrieved the score and dismissed Christopher, indicating that it would be no problem to accompany her himself.

The maestro's olive complexion had charcoal nuances, with smudges of half-moons below his eyes. As he resumed his seat at the piano and flexed his fingers, the wrinkles at his knuckles appeared dark gray.

"Care compagne" . . . The first time she had sung it at the New England Conservatory, she had been fourteen. Each time she sang it—or any aria—she was never absolutely certain what tones she might float. At first her voice sounded faded to her, but as she and Maestro Valenti eased into the next part ("Come per me sereno"), the phrases came with more surety, and she let the loveliness Bellini had composed—the legato beauty of it—carry her.

The studio's shutters had been thrown open like arms to the warm autumn morning. Birds flitted from twig to twig along the shady boulevard. As she sang, she saw a single rose in a tubular vase on a nearby table. Erika imagined herself inhaling its fragrance, the promise of its unfolded petals, its mysterious crevices.

For the audition she had worn a décolleté dress, for she could never bear the restriction of a high-necked blouse as she vocalized. The balm of early morning light caressed her neck and upper chest. The pouf sleeves she wore made her feel youthful—as if she were dissolving into the happiness of the village girl Amina.

Silence followed her singing. After a pause, the maestro's fingers sought the keys again. Valenti waved a hand and encouraged her to go on being Amina—all the way through the next part, "Sopra il sen la man mi posa." He hummed and played and called out entrances and exits and cues for other, imaginary cast members—as if the room had filled with unseen villagers. She saw that Valenti wished to measure her stamina. It was not a couple of arias he wanted her to sing, but the entire opera.

While he called out lines and played, in a kind of shorthand, the music that ran between Amina's parts, she grabbed her glass of water and gulped. The water lost its chill as the scenes rolled on. Her eyes shut as she drank the water like a fast prayer, letting it moisten her tongue and throat before continuing.

Finally she had sucked the glass dry. As she set down the empty glass, it knocked against a shelf with a hollow echo. Valenti rang for the maid to bring more water, and the music went on.

Occasionally, when Erika pronounced an Italian word badly, the maestro's spine tensed and his fingers flinched from the keys. "Your Italian is not so bad," he said, "but for the stage, every word must be perfect. Repeat after me, '*Sono innocente*.'"

"*Sono innocente*."

"That's right. '*Innocente*.' Take a little bite out of the middle of the word—that's how we pronounce it." He shook his head. "You don't realize how cruel Italian audiences can be about foreigners' mistakes. If you mispronounce something, they will laugh you right off the stage."

Later he cried, "Hit each note cleanly! 'D,' then jump—as the composer wished—neatly up to 'C'."

Twelve times he made her redo a particular phrase. He seemed not to mind how long it took her to perfect it.

After that he did not interrupt her again. While she sang, his strange little humming continued as he played. She heard strains of the opera's other, unseen characters that were so alive in his head.

How stupid she had been not to eat anything. By now her exhaustion was such that she felt she had become—like the heroine Amina—a sleepwalker herself. Her vision dimmed and the studio's amber-tiled floor blurred. She heard her voice, but it came from afar, like tones from under the piano's lid. Would she last to the end of it? She tucked one curl behind her ear and her fingers came away wet with sweat.

"*I am going to faint*," she considered telling him, but they were too close to the end not to keep on. Her shoulders swayed, and her legs felt as though they were melting. Only the music carried her through it—no food, no nourishment, left inside her at all.

With the final part— "Ah, non giunge"—over at last, Erika dropped against a black satin sofa.

At first Maestro Valenti said nothing about her singing. Instead, he tapped his knuckles lovingly against the pages of the score and sighed, muttering in wonderment over Bellini's genius, as though the composer—dead eighty years by now—were his close friend.

"Are you ready to sing a couple of arias from *Il barbiere di Siviglia* for me now?" Valenti asked. From the couch Erika must have given him the stare of a dead woman, because he swung his head back and laughed.

"Every diva must learn to stay fresh," Valenti teased and shook his finger. "She cannot let herself be wrung out after a few arias. Even after a whole opera, you must be ready to sing more—still more."

She wondered if he intended to take her on as his student. Clearly her stamina had failed to please him. Her fatigue was so huge that it might not have mattered, in that moment, if he had said no.

When she put the question to him, he glanced at her, astonished. "Do you think I would have kept you here all morning," he said, "if I did not find your voice beautiful?"

She did not have the energy to smile at him. She slid deeper against the black sofa, expressionless.

"You have done a wise thing by moving to Italy," he said. "Two years of work, and you will have a career."

"I must use your water closet," Erika confessed.

He rang for the maid, who ushered Erika down a dark hallway into a cubicle where a pale gas jet glowed like a divine finger pointing upward in a da Vinci painting.

With her skirts lifted, Erika sat on the commode, her head in her hands, elbows on her knees. How could she manage to come here daily, and work that exhaustingly with him? Her own undisciplined past shamed her now. She saw how frivolous and how easy her training with Magdalena had been. Years of laziness seemed irreversible. How could she—a dilettante with a pretty voice—endure hours onstage in sweltering cloaks and heavy costumes? Valenti warned that she must withstand fifteen piano rehearsals and five orchestral rehearsals before ever performing her first real opera in Italy. How would she last through it all?

How would she keep on doing it for years? As a way of life?

When she returned, the maestro frowned and moved closer to peer at her. "Is there something wrong?"

"I'm afraid I'm feeling very weak."

"Palpitations?" His uneven black eyebrows flitted upward with interest, and he patted his heart, as if he knew such sensations well.

His solicitous manner made her want to laugh. She wished Christopher had been present to see Valenti at that moment. For the first time she noticed that the silver-haired man kept a collection of antique glass vials on the windowsill beside the piano—bottles of blue juice and pink crystals and noxious-looking liquids.

Maestro Valenti pulled up a chair beside her. "Here." He showed her a pillbox nestled in his palm, and offered her one of the white tablets contained inside, as if with one swallow, the pill would transform her misery into pastoral serenity.

"Do you feel feverish?" he asked. "A dryness of tongue?"

"I'm only hungry. I had nothing to eat this morning."

He had his servant bring her grapes and olives and cheese and thick slabs of bread. Valenti watched as she seized a whole cluster of red fruit, popped one chilled grape after another into her mouth, and crushed them with her teeth. "Better?" he asked. He studied the impact on her as if the food had been a prescription.

"Don't you have other students today?" she asked, strengthening.

"Not on Thursday morning. That is why I had Signor Christopher bring you today."

The maestro seemed friendlier now that she had experienced her spell of illness with him. "Erika von Kessler." He repeated her name while staring through the window toward a full-bodied tree.

She tore a shred of bread with her hands and continued to eat while he sketched out a full year's worth of projects he envisioned for her, seven roles he wanted her to master, in *La sonnambula, Le nozze di Figaro, Nina, Il barbiere di Siviglia, Carmen, La cenerentola, Rigoletto.*

She set each olive like a bead on her tongue and chewed, plucking the pit from her mouth before she swallowed. Listening to his panoramic plan of how he intended to direct her work, she sensed that she could depend on him. Valenti was close to her father's age; his calm and deliberate speech rhythms reminded her of Papa. And she thought: *If I lose hold of his hand, I am lost. But if I stay close to him, he will get me to the place I long to be.*

❖

Christopher was not at home. When he did not respond to her knock, Erika scribbled a note and slid it under his door. *"Un colpo di fortuna, a stroke of luck!* The great Valenti has agreed to take me on."

To celebrate this success, she went to a restaurant and ordered her favorite dessert, *millefoglie alla crema.* She bit into the flaky layers of pastry and licked the whipped cream from her lips. She felt an inward sweetness, thinking that while her time of greatest striving was only beginning, her future would unfold as planned.

It was a day to rejoice—or so she'd thought. But when she returned to her room near the Ponte Vecchio, a bleak note from her father awaited her.

> *My darling daughter,*
> *Peter has asked me to tell you that the very nice gifts and letters you sent Quentin have had unfortunate consequences. When any reminder of you comes in the mail, the poor little boy becomes tearful. I was present when he opened the leather birdcage you shipped, and the initial excitement was soon followed by sobs, and questions about your whereabouts. He is still very young and cannot understand his mother's absence.*
>
> *Peter asks that you refrain from sending Quentin any more treats or correspondence. Certainly you don't want to make your little son miserable.*
> *Your loving Papa*

After reading the letter, she was too upset to stay in her room. She put on her wraps, and for the rest of the afternoon she strode through the streets, wandering everywhere and nowhere. From the Lungarno Acciaiuoli she crossed to the Oltrarno again, and drifted through unfamiliar neighborhoods.

In an alley she passed a small child, a pathetic thing with knees and shins so filthy, they looked charred. He was crying.

In that little boy's cries, she heard the misery she must have caused everybody, especially Quentin. In the bloody scabs on the boy's face, she saw neglect. Where was his mother? Had she left him and gone away? Or had she sent him into the streets to beg, with orders not to come back without money?

A smear of fresh blood glistened on his elbow. Dust from the paving stones darkened his feet. She had an urge to scoop him up and take him home for a bath.

Instead, Erika opened her purse and gave him a coin. The boy sucked in his breath, and the sobs stopped for a moment as his dirty fingers opened and closed over the money. He broke into a stumbling run and made off with the coin, but as he disappeared around a bend, he was still crying.

Returning to her room, she closed the shutters and lay down on the bed, fully dressed. She crossed her arms over her chest.

Leaving Quentin was the most grievous thing she had ever done. She loosened her shirtwaist and rested her hands against the smooth skin of her abdomen, just as she'd done during pregnancy, her fingers just above her navel. Here, she used to feel her son's movements under her skin. One night when she was six months along, she'd felt the same tiny twitch of movement repeated more than ninety times before she stopped counting. The baby must be hiccuping, she had thought. Now it was as though she could still feel him inside her—except that now she was feeling only her own bright pulse.

Behind the shutters, the day dimmed. Night came. Hunger made her roll from the bed. The room was so black that she crawled to the table and struck a match, lighting a candle. The glow washed the walls with warm ochre hues. From inside the cupboard, she took a piece of focaccia and paper-thin slices of prosciutto, and she set these on the table.

With its sparse furnishings, the room felt empty. Bits of song, a little humming—that was what she needed to lift herself from the gloom. But she couldn't sing, or stop remembering the small boy she'd met in the alley. She wondered if the sound of his crying would ever leave her. In her heart, he went on weeping.

39

My darling daughter,

. . . Peter says he'll change ships in Naples around mid-May. He'll visit Pompeii and Vesuvius before proceeding on to Alexandria to do his cotton buying. . . .

Erika was not certain why her father's letter offered such information. Perhaps a warning lay beneath it. Peter was more determined and persistent than any person she had ever known. Did he plan to take a train north from Naples to Florence? Would he stand before the door to her building, grasp the brass ring that fitted through the lion's nose, and knock?

As the time neared, she expected him to come. In seven months, Peter had sent her no sort of personal message, communicating with her only through her father, requesting her signature on various documents. By now, his flaring pride must have receded a little. It would be quite like him to appear. He'd ask if he might come up to her room to speak with her. After she led him up several flights, he'd admire her view of the Arno. Quite self-righteously, he'd try to persuade her that she was making no visible progress toward anything here in Florence. He'd speak of Quentin and spark guilty tears in her. When he walked toward the door, preparing to depart, he'd spin around suddenly and try to engulf her in his arms.

By May, she was ready for him to appear. And then one afternoon, as she walked through the Piazza della Signoria, near the place where the monk Savonarola had been burned centuries before—an area where tourists frequently passed—Erika saw him.

She saw him from afar. Peter wore a brown herringbone suit, and looked thoroughly British. From the instant she noticed him, fear jumped inside her chest; sounds of surprise threatened to leap from her mouth.

She glimpsed his profile just as he was turning a corner. Briefly she followed him, just to be certain. His long, trim back spoke to her with frightening familiarity. Though her father had hinted about Peter's possible arrival, the sight of her husband in Florence shocked her nonetheless.

In less than a minute, she headed back to her room. After closing the shutters, she lay down on her bed, shoes still on, hiding herself. She regretted sending him her address. If the bell rang and the maid brought word of a gentleman caller, Erika wondered what she ought to say. What did she want to have happen?

If he stepped into her room, she worried that loneliness would pull her backward like the tides. His presence might wash away everything she'd worked for.

While she waited on the bed, her blood coursed faster, and the heat of worrying left her skin moist. Did she want to see him, or not? Finally she got up and removed her blouse; patches of the fabric were soaked through by then. Draping the garment across the back of a wooden chair, she poured water from a pitcher into a bowl, and washed her underarms.

If he comes here, she thought, *I will pull him straight onto my bed, and afterward, I will insist that he leave. His body, a man's body. That is what I miss most.*

Half-dressed, she went to the window, cracked open the shutters, and looked out, expecting to see Peter in the street below. He did not materialize that day.

But during those moments while she waited, as it dawned on her that he would not be coming, she found herself mourning the past. She saw before her a thousand mornings when his foot had touched hers in bed, and she had woken beside him, happy. She no longer loved him or wanted to be with him, but it was unbearable to think that those times were lost and would never come again. Only he remembered the day they'd ridden by camel into an Egyptian desert on their honeymoon. Only he could recall with her the terror of that storm at sea, and laugh about Mrs. Bickford with her pickles.

It felt strange to deny his prominence in her memory, but now that he was no longer her husband, she must do just that, in order to forge on.

Later that summer her father wrote:

It's a pity that Peter never made it as far as Florence on his latest trip. Forgive me for saying this, but I'd hoped the two of you might have experienced a reconciliation. If he'd knocked on your door, he might at least have assured me that my beloved daughter is well and thriving in Florence.

Your sentimental old Papa

So the person she'd seen that day at the Piazza della Signoria had not been Peter after all. After one glimpse of a man in a herringbone suit, she'd gasped at his nearness and fled, but it had only been her mind conjuring him up.

❖

But it was not Peter, really, who walked beside her, as close as a shadow, through Florence. It was Ravell. At night, through open windows, he flowed into the room on a river of air.

When she slid from bed on a dim morning and lifted her shoes from a cold floor, she felt the chill of the leather, and sensed his presence. When she bathed, Ravell sank alongside her into the water's heat.

Her father sent her a small drawing of a horse that Quentin had sketched. No note had come from her son since she'd moved to Italy, only this, but the words "For Mama" moved her to tears. Under the pressure of Quentin's small hand, the paper had curled as he filled in the mane and the tail. *Look what he drew,* she wanted to murmur to Ravell. *Look what our son drew.*

She tried to envision herself on Ravell's island, but she did not see how she could make a life with him. Her voice would be lost in the canopy of tropical foliage, her arias blending with the cries of macaws and scarlet ibises.

If Boston had felt limiting . . . how long could she be happy there, in that wild place?

❖

Now her days had become more regimented than any she had ever lived. At nine every morning, she had a lesson with Maestro Valenti. Between ten-thirty and noon, she worked with Christopher to learn the notes of new operas. Lunch followed—the one frivolous hour of the day, during which they would go to a *caffè* on the Via Tornabuoni, or to a restaurant where Erika would order her favorite dish, *coscia di vitello con maccheroni,* and Christopher his *petto di pollo* or his fish.

By one o'clock he hastened away, because Christopher had other aspiring opera singers whom he had to accompany.

During the afternoons she was invariably alone. The one glass of Chianti or *vino bianco asciutto* she had drunk at lunch would make her drowsy, and she would lie on her dark red sofa and doze while studying Italian grammar in her room. When the book slid to the floor, the thump woke her. Determined to be more diligent, she shuttered her room against the afternoon sun that always deepened her lethargy. She made herself sit upright at a table while translating whatever libretto she was learning line by line. Valenti had encouraged her to do this. "Don't let the meaning of a single word mystify you," he said. "You should know this opera's story like the story of your own life."

After taking a long, exploratory walk around Florence, she often returned at dusk and caught succulent whiffs circulating through the house's stairwell: the aroma of sautéed onions steeped in red wine sauce being cooked by the landlady's servant. From five to seven in the evening, Erika stayed in her room and sang. When the weather was mild, she opened the windows, as her blind landlady had requested.

As the singing began, Erika heard the old woman dragging a chair across the floor overhead in order to sit closer to her open balcony doors. It helped Erika vocalize with more hope and seriousness, just to know that *la padrona di casa,* the landlady Donna Anna, might be listening.

❖

In the landlady's apartment, Erika and Donna Anna sat together one evening, listening to Caruso on the Victrola. It was dusk. The watercolor skies washed above Florence, mauves that darkened into purples.

"You and I have both heard Caruso sing in person," Donna Anna said. "This is hardly the same experience, but—"

As the great tenor's voice swelled through the funnel of a Deluxe Talking Machine, the recorded orchestra sounded vaguely like a circus band; Caruso might have been shouting through a drainpipe.

"Still—" Donna Anna remarked with awe. "To be able to capture even a scratch of Caruso's sound—"

"It's a feat that stops one's breath," Erika agreed. Just to bring a trace of the great man into the room on a late spring evening—this was a God-like accomplishment.

Together they sat by the window. The moon came up and made the landlady's lace collar a sharper white. Donna Anna did not notice the sky blackening, of course. All on her own, she walked over to the Victrola and changed the recording. After Caruso, they listened for a while to Nellie Melba, until no light was left in the apartment except that reflected from the street.

Erika made no move to turn on a lamp. She felt closer to Donna Anna in the darkness, sitting there as the old woman always sat. While they talked, Donna Anna explained that she had not always been blind. A fever had stolen her sight when she was twenty-two.

"Sometimes as I listen to you singing," Donna Anna said, "the sounds that flow out of you are so beautiful, I can hardly believe they are real."

Erika smiled, and then she frowned, thinking of an unrelated concern. Every day after the post arrived, a maid sorted the letters and packages and placed them into piles on the foyer table, where the various tenants retrieved them. Erika wondered aloud if pieces of her correspondence might have gotten lost in the blizzard of the Italian mail system.

"Have you been expecting a particular letter?" Donna Anna asked.

Erika was glad the landlady couldn't see the look of distress that must have flitted across her own face. She confessed that she had expected her husband, Peter, to write at least one letter—if only to persuade her to return.

Not a single word had arrived from him. His silence, his rage of pride, surprised her. He had certainly not come to Florence, as she'd imagined he might.

"And your son?" Donna Anna asked.

Erika recalled singing Quentin to sleep, his hair like dark feathers against her hand. She explained how her son had just been learning to form letters of the alphabet with his pen when she left for Italy. "If he were older, I would have made him promise to write me letters," she said. But Quentin was too young. Already her son must have half-forgotten her.

The blind woman listened, her head bowed as though she were studying Erika's feet, and the unevenness in the tiled floors. Donna Anna rose from her seat and motioned for Erika to join her on the balcony. "Remember why you came here," Donna Anna said as she pointed upward. Even if she couldn't see the night sky, she knew what existed there. "You came here to reach the stars," Donna Anna said. "To touch the moon."

40

TRINIDAD

1911

Ravell dropped Peter's letter onto the desk, having reread it several times. He got his rain slicker and walked down to the beach. A late morning shower had just finished. The water looked dark, and the sand felt gritty as it sank underfoot. As he stared into the waves, he thought about what the letter meant.

> *My dear Ravell,*
> *My apologies for not having written for so long, but the news is bitter from my end. It saddens me to report this, but since you are like a brother to me, I don't wish to hide the situation from you. Erika has left me and moved to Florence, Italy, with the hope of developing her operatic career. After three years have passed, the law will permit me to divorce her, and I intend to do so.*

Pulling off his shoes, Ravell tossed them onto the damp sand. During the months after Erika and Peter had left the Cocal, Ravell had waited and hoped for any news, but since the day the steamship had taken Erika from Trinidad six years previously, there had been not a single word from her—only a few rare letters from Peter.

With his trousers rolled to his knees, Ravell stood at the shore and let the coolness and foam wash over his feet. This was the Atlantic—part of the same sweep of waters that reached through the Strait of Gibraltar and licked the boot of Italy, only to reverse and mingle with this vast ocean, traveling thousands of miles before it rolled up here, all brine and breakers. The tide tugged gently at his ankles, and he suddenly felt closer to Erika than he had been in years.

Perhaps I should go to Florence, he thought, *and search for her.*

Before Erika's departure from Trinidad, she had intimated that she might send him a safe address—perhaps that of a friend—where he could write to her, but she had never done so. The cold wake of silence she'd left behind had hurt and bewildered him. He had not been in a position to write any sort of private message to her—as she well understood. From a hundred street corners in the city of Boston, she could easily have slipped a brief note or a farewell letter into a mailbox. Once when an envelope arrived addressed by her husband, Ravell put the letter to his nose, hoping for a whiff of the lilac sachets she kept in her drawers, but the paper smelled instead of pencil shavings and stale tobacco.

About a year after Erika left, he had gone into the forest one day and reclined on the ground where he had made love to her. Lying on his back, he heard wind pass through palm fronds. He remembered her soaked white shirtwaist and her walking skirt, limp with rain.

❖

On the veranda at Eden, Ravell sat one night with Hartley and his wife, Stella, sharing Peter's news. The drama of it impressed them. In the darkness, dressed in their white clothes, they held themselves as motionless as the wicker chairs they sat upon.

"Does she plan to support herself by singing?" Hartley asked. "Or is her poor husband paying for her upkeep?"

Ravell had no answer for this. Stella Hartley's tone became lofty and knowing. "Erika always struck me as fiery. Desperate."

"Desperate?" Ravell said.

"Restless. You could call it that," Stella said. "She'll make a perfect prima donna."

"They had no children," Hartley said. "That's always hard on a woman."

Stella gave a start, remembering. "Didn't they—did they never have another baby?" she asked with a lilt of sympathy, but that note of hope died before she finished the question, because the answer seemed already obvious.

"No," Ravell said. "I don't believe they did." He puffed on his cigar and released a wreath of smoke into the air, obscuring everything.

❖

At the coconut plantation, Ravell sat at his desk and began a letter.

Dearest Erika,
It is now spring at the Cocal. Yesterday as I walked through a clearing in the forest, I pictured your husband racing after butterflies with a net, and it was impossible to forget—

He shredded the page. Such words—reminding her of her husband—were not a good way to begin. He dropped the torn bits of white paper into the wastebasket, and started again.

Dearest Erika,
The news has reached me that you have moved to Italy, and I am glad that you have succeeded at last in throwing off everything that must have held you back. Your art is the essential thing. . . .

He wanted to praise her bravery, to applaud her for freeing herself from the judgments of gentlemen in starched shirts, and from the stifling opinions of Yankee matrons laced so tight they could hardly breathe. He wanted to laugh with her and say, *You've wrestled free! You've flung the weight of them from your shoulders like a great musty coat.*

Then he pushed away from the desk, got up from his chair, and paced the room wondering where he would even send such a letter. He had no address for Erika. How could he ask Peter for his estranged wife's exact whereabouts? The notion was ridiculous. Nor could he make inquiries to her father or brother about how to contact her—not after the disgrace of his last days in Boston—and he could think of no other way to reach her.

So Ravell crumpled that page and threw it away, too.

Now that she was a free woman, he wondered if she would write to him. Even after so many years, he was convinced that she had not forgotten him.

❖

Months passed, but no letter came from Erika. Hartley and Stella brought their children to the plantation for a few days. The boys and girls had gone down to the lagoon hoping to catch tarpon in a net. On the front porch at the Cocal, Ravell sat with Hartley and his wife. They drank green swizzles. They rocked in chairs, they watched the surf.

"Don't you think it's time we found a proper wife for you?" Stella asked Ravell.

Once at a dinner party at the Eden estate, a married acquaintance of Stella's had pressed up against Ravell in an unlit hallway, and the lady had hinted that he should meet her at a hotel room in the capital, but he'd declined. Her breath smelled of the lamb they'd just eaten; he knew he did not love her and never would.

"I'm beginning to side with my wife about this," Hartley said, leaning back deeply in his rocking chair.

"Next month we are going to have another garden party," Stella said. "Several attractive young ladies are bound to be present."

They understood his loneliness. Ravell wondered if he had referred too frequently to Erika in their presence. He worried that the memory of Erika was ruining his life. When he wandered through the coolie village at the plantation, he saw laborers surrounded by their little ones, and he yearned in a simple, aching way for children he could call his own. If he could not bring himself to forget about Erika, he would remain alone, living on a plantation in a remote part of the world.

"All right," he told Stella. They agreed that Ravell would spend several days at Eden, where Stella would oversee his search for a wife.

A couple of weeks before the Hartleys' garden party, Stella decided to arrange a series of dinner engagements for him, so that he could meet his prospects in a leisurely way, one or two ladies at a time.

On a Wednesday, two very young sisters appeared at the Hartleys' table. Both were blonde, their twisted curls elaborately pinned and dangling from their temples. They were pretty enough, but as they ate their roast pork, they had little to say until Ravell inquired about their fashionable hairstyles. The sisters glanced at each other, unable to stop giggling and chattering after that. It sounded as though they mainly liked to spend their days arranging each other's hair.

"Am I expected to marry them together, as an inseparable pair?" Ravell asked after they departed, and Hartley laughed. Ravell did not want to tell Stella how depressed the young sisters had made him feel, how very old and somber.

The following evening Stella invited a pale young widow who had lost her husband so recently that tears welled in her eyes, and she kept reaching for her glass of white wine and taking hard swallows. Ravell felt ashamed sitting across from her, as though he'd rushed in like a grave robber.

"I'm afraid this was all too soon for her," Stella apologized afterward.

To cheer him up, Hartley went into another room and reappeared with a cue, which he handed to Ravell as he challenged him to a game of billiards.

On Saturday, Ravell's final night at Eden, a mother and her very tall daughter descended from a motorcar. Both wore feather boas. When the daughter shook his hand, he felt as though ice had been rubbed against his palm.

The daughter, who was in her midtwenties, had a lovely face. He admired the balance of her features, but when he looked closer, he noticed that she had red eyes (an allergy to her feathers?) and a habit of dabbing her thumb under her runny nose.

"I understand you lived in Boston previously," the mother said.

"I did," Ravell said.

"Tell me." The mother leaned toward him and spoke in a quiet tone, clearly hoping to be subtle. "Did you live in a pleasant neighborhood? What sort of house was it? Did you rent or did you own?"

As the evening wore on, the tall daughter kept inquiring about the price of things—the Hartleys' fringed lampshade, Stella's high-heeled, buttoned shoes. The conversation bored Ravell so much that he wanted to bolt across the Hartleys' great lawn and lose himself in the wild forest.

After the tall one rode away with her mother in their motorcar, Stella took a breath and turned toward Ravell expectantly. "Well?" she said. "What do you think?"

His gaze flitted away at that moment. Surely Stella guessed that he couldn't marry that one, either. After each carefully hosted encounter, he felt he was failing her.

"I'm impossible, I know," he said.

❖

After his return to the Cocal, Ravell went for his usual evening walk along the beach. He found himself talking to the waves, to the night sky, to Erika. Many months had passed since she had left Peter, yet still no word—not even a postcard—had come from her. Ravell felt sure that she must have taken another lover—a leading man, a tenor or a basso profundo, whose vocal cords were long and whose limbs were long, too, because (as Erika had once told him) all men who sang bass were invariably tall.

I have faded into her past like a face in a forgotten audience, Ravell thought.

He reached for fistfuls of sand and threw them at the white foam spreading along the shore. Instead of Erika's voice—which he still recalled so keenly—he heard his own wails. Toward the moon he pitched more sand, but drafts of wind blew it backward, blinding him for a moment until he staggered sideways, rubbing his eyelids to wipe away the grit. He told himself he must no longer think about Erika. He decided he ought to attend Stella's garden party in a few weeks. Until he'd let Stella introduce him to every available woman on the island, he should not resign himself to loneliness.

Walking back to the house, he turned his back on the sea.

41

ITALY

1911

Dear Erika,

I am frankly alarmed, her brother Gerald wrote, *that you have lived in Florence only eight months, and yet your expenditures have far outpaced your share of the quarterly income from the Bell Street rental property. Before you decided to move to Italy, I warned that if you planned to live on the proceeds of our mother's estate, you would be forced to endure a very simple—even meager—existence.*

Erika threw her brother's note into a cupboard drawer and slammed it. "*Excessive,*" he had called her expenses. Sunlight streamed through the French doors and reflected so brightly against the red-tiled floor that the color burned painfully in her head. She pulled a hard wooden chair up to the simple table she had bought, took paper and a pen, and wrote back.

Dear Gerald,

If you and your wife saw the Spartan furnishings surrounding me in the single room that I rent, the two of you would be shocked. Thus far I have purchased a narrow bed, a wooden cupboard, a rather crudely constructed table, and a couple of chairs. My only extravagance has been a rather pretty sofa. . . .

She glanced at the sofa, with its carved frame and plush wine-colored upholstery, the fabric soft against her cheek when she napped on it. From the moment she saw the sofa in a dark shop, she'd felt that it belonged in this room, the same red as the tiled floor. She wrote,

I have bought a good piano, but that is a necessity for my career. There are set-up costs when one moves to a foreign country and arrives with nothing. I am living in a room with no carpet, no paintings on the walls—no sort of decoration, not even a proper coverlet to hide the sheets on my bed.

If you and Thea are worried that you may end up supporting me one day, let me assure you that I don't intend to depend on anyone financially.

❖

To conserve money, she tried to go less often to the Teatro Verdi and other local theatres. Instead, on Saturday evenings she swaddled herself in a white mohair shawl, its lacy crocheted folds slung over her shoulders, and she sat alone on her balcony. A line of electric streetlamps illuminated the Arno's black channel and the ochre-colored buildings on the opposite bank.

"Allow the vocal cords a rest after a hard week's practice," Maestro Valenti had advised, so on Saturday and Sunday nights, Erika did not sing at all.

On Saturday nights in particular, the panorama of lights and the rattle of carriage wheels in the boulevard below reminded her of her own isolation. She imagined that all over Florence, people were rushing to one another's houses to eat bowls of *ribollita* or veal saltimbocca. She watched couples step into motorcars bound for theatres, gentlemen in tall hats and ladies with long pearls that swung from their necks to their hips.

Where was Christopher on Saturday nights? With his American friends, no doubt. She never knocked on his door on weekends because she did not wish to appear too needy. Instead, she waited for the hastily jotted notes that occasionally came from him. "A stroll in the Boboli today at three?" he would write. Or: "Save next Sunday afternoon. We'll go to Fiesole by tram."

Her loneliness was her own fault, she knew. Other lodgers at Donna Anna's had been friendly, but Erika had gently shut the door on their overtures. She had introduced Christopher as her "brother" as well as her accompanist, to ward off any disapproval about a man occasionally visiting her room. One had to keep a distance from neighbors, especially in a house where so many lives emptied into one stairwell.

❖

On a street corner the roses waited, dark red and long-stemmed. On a Friday evening, she paused and brushed her nose against their velvet petals, inhaling a sweetness that traveled along the arc of her spine and reached her toes. It was the sort of extravagance her brother, Gerald, had warned her against. The vendor came right over, ready to lift them, dripping, from their pail and wrap them in thin paper. She shook her head and backed away.

I cannot afford such things, she reminded herself, and resumed her walk home. Soon she would climb three stories and open a door to a room where nothing waited to welcome her. Christopher was off with his friends; even Donna Anna had gone to the countryside to visit relatives. In this ancient city where artists had been living and dying for centuries, she had no one to converse with. A completely unknown singer, perhaps she would always remain so.

The roses, she thought, *will keep me company.* She wanted them beside her on this night. So she went back and bought an armload, carrying their weight and rich hue up to her room.

She placed them in a vase until the air thickened with their dark fragrance. Before leaving Boston, she had bought herself a crimson dress and matching shoes that she intended to wear one day for a recital. Now she put them on. She pinned up her hair and placed clustered diamonds on her earlobes. In the mirror she studied herself, trying to see the woman Ravell might find if he stood here now. Her earrings captured and reflected pinpricks of color—yellows, greens, and blues.

Alone in her room, she opened the long windows, and sitting at the piano, she sang her favorite arias—those that suited her voice best. She sang for only herself. She sang for the day when others—besides her blind landlady—would hear her. Although no man had touched her in months, her body burned, never more alive. Music streamed from her throat and fingers.

Sounds floated through the open windows and she went with them, over the Arno, across terra-cotta rooftops and the Duomo, across every beautiful thing that men long dead had created here in Florence. Someday she, too, would be dead, but for now that did not matter; for now she was as alive as every light that glimmered and reflected against windowpanes in Tuscany. As she sang, she was not sorry that she had brought herself here to add her voice to all the rest—her singing passed across frescoes and statues, across towers and all the architectural dreams that rose in giant silhouettes against the horizon.

No one in Florence—apart from her maestro, Donna Anna, and Christopher—listened to her with real pleasure yet, but Erika sang as if she stood in their theatres, as if the people of Italy were already hearing her.

She sang until eleven-thirty at night. Surprisingly, no sleepy neighbor begged her to stop. When cool drafts of air entered through the pair of open balcony doors, she realized it was raining. She couldn't smell the roses anymore, only the odor of rain wetting the dust on the pavement. She closed the lid over the keyboard. When she went to latch the doors, she leaned over the balcony rail and noticed two women and a man huddling below in the rainy street.

When the man saw her at the window several stories above, he removed his hat and waved it high in the air, calling out, *"Eccolà! Here she is!"* The women, who had been covering their heads with shawls to fend off the rain, looked up in sudden surprise, tilting their heads to gaze halfway to the sky. Rain wet their faces. One woman danced in a circle, her skirt whirling around, while all three cried out, *"Brava! Brava!"* as they thrust their arms upward toward Erika.

42

∾❦∾

My dear brother,
The funds you promised to send have still not arrived. It has now been
three months. Even after making allowances for the slowness of the
Italian postal system, there can be no excuse for this.
>*Your loving sister,*
>>*Erika*

Gerald must be behind in his bookkeeping, she told herself, irritated that
he had forgotten her.

"I'll pay," she said when Christopher hesitated outside a restaurant
with brass lamps. "Consider it part of your salary." Apart from their
weekday luncheons, Erika worried that Christopher didn't get enough
to eat.

She did not want him to sense her concern about the delay in receiving
her brother's check. Although Christopher served as an accompanist for
other singers, she suspected that they did not compensate him well because they were struggling themselves. Probably none of them had a
brother like hers, who—at least until now—sent regular income from
their mother's estate.

For her birthday, Papa had sent a postal order—a generous sum—so
she wasn't low on funds yet. To celebrate, Erika invited Christopher and
his friends to Doney's busy *caffè,* where they all ordered *zuccotto,* a Florentine version of a trifle, and she licked the rich chocolate that stuck to
her spoon.

From time to time Erika would leave a basket of citrus fruits and strawberries in Christopher's room. "How long has it been since you've eaten?" she'd ask gently. He would say that he had coffee earlier, but nothing else. He'd reach at once for the fruit. With his thumbnail he would poke into an orange's rind, his delicate hands turning the fruit and peeling back the skin, and he'd pop the segments into his mouth as eagerly and furtively as a squirrel.

Christopher's family sent him nothing. He wore trousers that were frayed at the hems. One ghastly hot morning in May, while Christopher sat at the piano accompanying her, perspiration gathered on his forehead like moisture condensing on a windowpane. It flowed in tiny rivulets down his temples. Twice Erika begged him to take off his suit jacket, but he refused. Only when he could scarcely go on playing due to the heat did he remove it. Underneath, Erika saw what he had not wanted her to notice: the fabric of his shirt had grown thin after so many washings, and the back was torn.

❖

The money from her brother had still not arrived ten days later. At that point Erika became alarmed. It occurred to her that Gerald and his wife, who had vigorously disapproved of her move to Italy, meant to exert leverage somehow.

> My dear Gerald,
> You know how I depend on the Bell Street rents to survive here. Do you intend for me to starve in a room in a foreign land? Is that what you and Thea believe I deserve? Do you imagine that if you withhold income that is rightfully mine, I will give up my music and all I have worked for, and return to Peter?

After mailing this letter, she paused at a storefront window and stared at a mannequin elegantly buttoned into a moleskin coat. Such a coat— long and dark—might become her; it had a slimming effect. It was a coat she might have bought if she'd stayed with Peter. The mannequin's shining silk hose and pumps were lovely, too. Now she stood before the window in worn-down heels in need of repair. She did not have the money to leave them at a cobbler's shop.

The worst thing was this: she owed Christopher his fee, but could not cover the payment.

Just hours after she sent one letter to her brother, she began another.

Dear Gerald,
Must I hire an attorney to sue my own brother? One-half of the rental
income from our late mother's Bell Street property is due to me. This
is an inviolable fact. You have no right to decide otherwise.

She opened drawers, placing bracelets and diamond earrings and pearl necklaces across the surface of her bed, and thought about which jewels she might sell. *I could give voice and piano lessons,* she thought, *for the young daughters of British and American expatriates.*

From the array of jewelry on the bed, she chose a pair of diamond earrings and felt their weight, one glittering cluster in each hand. The next day she took the earrings to a pawnbroker and sold them for a fraction of their worth.

There were a number of ways she might survive. Even without a husband and a brother.

❖

The following morning she decided to write to her father about engaging a lawyer on her behalf; she could no longer allow Gerald to serve as executor of their mother's estate. The worry of it unleashed unhappiness about everything, especially Quentin.

Dearest Papa,
What has become of Quentin? You say that Peter has asked that I not
write to my son because reminders of my absence are upsetting to a

*young child. Still, I cannot go on being punished like this, and left
without any word of him.*

I know what my own brother and his wife must think of me. . . .

A crinkled envelope arrived soon after that, addressed in Gerald's
small, tight penmanship. He had mailed it several months previously.
The letter looked as if it had fallen from a postman's sack and blown
into a gutter, or behind a bush. Perhaps it had remained there until
someone noticed it, and placed it, for a second try, into a mailbox. The
envelope remained sealed. It was dry now, though clearly it had been
soaked—the paper rippled, the blue ink of the address blurry. The letter
looked as if it had been dragged under the sole of a stranger's shoe.

Inside she found the check her brother owed to her. When she opened
it, she was aghast at herself.

All those withering, accusatory notes to him and Thea . . . Erika put
the check for safekeeping in a drawer. She ran upstairs to Donna Anna's
apartment, where the blind woman sat calmly in a chair.

"Send a cable to your brother," the landlady advised. "Maybe it will
reach them before your letters do."

Erika hurried off to arrange for the cablegram.

DOCTOR AND MRS. GERALD VON KESSLER
176 COMMONWEALTH AVENUE
BOSTON

YOUR LOST LETTER AND CHECK OF APRIL 30
FINALLY ARRIVED.
WILL YOU EVER FORGIVE ME?
ERIKA

43

Erika arrived at Christopher's building on a Thursday afternoon carrying a basket of salami, prosciutto, provolone, and pears. The foyer and stairs were as dark as a church's interior, and she groped for the banister, half-blinded by the sudden dimness. A box of newborn kittens had been abandoned on the bottom step, and one furry creature brushed her ankle, then slinked away. The old newspaper they nested upon smelled of cat urine.

A desolate quiet often ran through the building at this hour, when Christopher tended to be gone. But today she heard the sounds of a gramophone at the top of the stairs, the voice of a countertenor coming from Christopher's quarters, under the roof.

She ascended, and rapped her knuckles noisily against his door, hoping to be heard above the flourish of the orchestra. No stirrings from within. She tried again. Still no response. Had he left in a hurry, she wondered, and forgotten to shut off the gramophone? That would be typical of him. Erika scoured her memory to reconstruct what she knew of Christopher's schedule. Hadn't he mentioned something about going to audition for a man who was arranging a party at a palazzo on the Via Maggio? Or perhaps he had gone to Mark's place, a rented room near the Duomo.

Fishing in her bag, Erika searched for the key Christopher had given her. She would step inside, just for a moment, and deposit the basket on the table. Just as she took hold of the doorknob, the recording reached its rousing finish; the gramophone music died and the air became quiet. Her chain of keys jingled as she inserted one in the lock. A drowsy mumble came from within; she worried that the sounds of her entering might have awakened him. Apparently Christopher had fallen asleep while listening to music, as he was apt to do on a hot afternoon.

The dangling keys swung from the door's lock; she caught and squeezed them silent in her hand. Not glancing over at the bed at first, she tiptoed inside and set the basket down. Then Erika turned. She hardly moved or breathed as she surveyed the room. Her eye followed the odd trail of clothes strewn across the floor—Christopher's shirt and trousers, and also Mark's high-collared jacket, a distinctive dark maroon. A shoe of Christopher's, lopsided and worn at the heel, lay upside down on top of one of Mark's buffed boots. The mates—one of Christopher's and one of Mark's—had been kicked halfway under a chair, and those were touching, too.

In the bed, in the unpleasant heat of the afternoon, the two men lay together, asleep. Their backs were turned toward her, the sheet half-shrugged from Christopher's shoulder, exposing a golden shoulder with a sprinkling of freckles, like sand, upon it. Suddenly, without opening his eyes, Mark rolled over. Reaching out an arm, he grasped the sheet and flung it off. Both men lay there nude. The bed linens exuded smells of salt and perspiration, semen and sweating feet.

The room enclosed her in its odors. With his eyes still closed, Mark scratched his groin.

Her footsteps were fleet, her respiration softer than a gasp, as she turned and fled.

Later, she had no recollection of how she had gotten down four flights; she might have been dropped, like a parachutist, down the empty well.

Outdoors she went, straight into sunlight, and crossed the river. She found herself wandering into one of those nameless, innumerable churches that waited with open doors all over Florence, as silent as caves harboring frescoes and statuary.

Just a handful of shrouded old women were present, their heads bowed, rosaries twined around arthritic fingers. Erika sat in a pew, trying to gather the quiet of the sanctuary inside herself.

Two men in love—yes, her heart was hitting hard from the shock of that. Never before had she thrown a door open to the sight of a man she'd not expected to see naked. And there had been *two* of them lying there relaxed and languorous, at their most private. She could still hear the sound of Mark's fingernails as he scratched himself. If they had opened their eyes at that instant and seen her, what could she have said? She might have given a small strangled cry. Should she have apologized to them? Or they to her?

Two men, friends of hers, in love. How very peculiar that was—contrary to nature's laws, for no child could ever be born to them.

When the stillness of the church failed to calm her, she left and went to the Accademia to gaze at a painting she loved more than any other—Botticelli's *Primavera*. People talked of moving the painting to the Uffizi, where it might be displayed alongside the artist's other masterpieces. She entered the building and headed straight toward *Primavera*, its vast canvas spanning a whole wall, its backdrop a dark forest, as mysterious as night.

Against that dark screen, eight figures danced and lifted their limbs as if lit by music, their long hair and whisper-thin gowns floating with wind. One blond figure with a beautiful, triangular face reminded her of Christopher—the features not quite those of a woman or a man.

The three Graces joined hands and danced in a circle, transparent costumes showing their long legs. The painting made her remember the smells of sweat and sex in Christopher's room; she'd entered before the scent had evaporated. The air had been drenched with it, an atmosphere she had not stood inside in a very long time.

❖

"I wanted to tell you about Mark and me, but I didn't know how," Christopher said the next day. "And Edmund, too—he's one of us."

She said nothing.

"Let's go for a walk," Christopher suggested, "along the river."

They crossed a bridge built from a sketch by Michelangelo. Erika leaned her elbows against the arched stone rail. At this dusky hour, reflections of the ochre buildings that lined the Arno lay on the surface, as if their façades had fallen into the water. Their lovely, liquid images wavered and dimmed with the day.

"I hope things won't change between us," Christopher said. "Now that you know."

"Why," she said, "should anything change?"

In only a day, the shock had lessened, and she suspected that it would soon fade and not matter to her what the two men did. It wasn't as if Christopher might have become *her* lover. She had always known, as women often do, that he would be a neutral presence in her life. Toward him she felt the same absence of tension that existed between her and female friends, no matter how attractive their faces.

How did one sense this? How did one understand, before any words of explanation came?

She envied what he and Mark had, that raw bliss. The sweep of a man's breath against her spine, a man's hand resting against her hip as they both faded to sleep: when would *she* know such rapture again?

❖

"If I tell you something I've told no one else," Erika asked softly, "will you keep my secret?"

The blind landlady nodded. In Donna Anna's apartment, gilded frames held ancient paintings the old woman could not see. Here at last, so far from Boston—where gossip could not travel from tongue to tongue and harm her son—Erika found herself free to confide.

"Quentin is not related to my husband by blood," she said. "The man who fathered my son—that man lives on an island near South America. I've never told him that my son is his."

She swallowed, her words fading to whispers, her cheekbones warm

284

with tears. "I'm a terrible person," she said. "I left my child. I've done the worst things a woman can do."

Donna Anna listened for a long while without speaking. In the darkness of evening, she shifted skeptically in her chair. Her small shoes retracted under her skirt. From the recesses of her bodice the old lady drew out a clean, folded handkerchief and handed it to Erika.

"Believe me," Donna Anna said finally, "there are women who have done worse."

"What could be worse?"

"There are women in jails in Florence who have murdered their own children." Donna Anna waved a knotted hand dismissively, impatient with this opera of tears.

"Tell me," the old lady said. "Do you still love him—the other man?"

"Yes," Erika whispered. "I think about him constantly." She described the coconut plantation—its bats, quicksands, and lights that glowed like messages across the water. But she explained that the Cocal was not a place where she could stay forever; she couldn't live there, not even for Ravell.

"Maybe you'll take a trip to see him," Donna Anna said. "Or persuade him to visit here."

In bed that night Erika flexed her toes, smiling in the dark. The sheets almost smelled of Ravell, his heat. In her excitement she slipped from the bed and sat at the wooden table, caught by the urge to write to him.

My dearest Ravell,
I have given up my life in Boston and come at last to Florence to sing.
The hardest thing for me has been leaving Quentin. He is a sweet
child, small for his age, with a thatch of dark hair rather like
yours. . . .

Ravell could probably guess what she was telling him—if he hadn't surmised the truth already. But for her son's sake, she realized that she ought to be cautious and vague in writing about him. She had already caused enough distress in her little boy's life. ("Always be careful what you put in a letter," Papa had once warned her.)

She lay down her pen. It was really too much to confess—the complications too extraordinary and dangerous to introduce into all their lives just now. Who knew how Ravell might react to the news that he had a child? What if he wrote to Peter, and begged to see Quentin? Suppose Ravell felt disappointed in her? Disapproving? What if he wrote to her saying: *It grieves me to think of our child growing up on another continent, apart from his real father and mother.* . . . *Erika, how could you have left him?*

In a letter, there was little she could possibly say that would make the situation forgivable, or even comprehensible. If she saw Ravell again, if she discussed it with him over many days, surely she could make him understand why she'd come to Italy.

No, she wouldn't tell Ravell just yet. She couldn't unleash havoc now, not while she was working toward what mattered so much—her *prova*, and winning over an impresario.

So she folded up the letter and tore it into halves, quarters, eighths.

44

"I haven't seen Venice in years," Erika said, "and I want to go back."

"It's smelly," Edmund said.

Mark tossed aside a magazine he'd been reading. "What's smelly?"

"Venice. Last time I took a gondola along the Grand Canal," Edmund complained, "the water was green, with muck floating past. I had to hold my nose shut."

"Well, don't come along with us, then," Christopher said.

In the end, because Edmund couldn't stand to be left out, he packed a valise. All three of them (Christopher, Mark, and Edmund) accompanied Erika to Venice.

They found an enormous room in a decaying palazzo so full of atmosphere that they could not bear to search for any other accommodation, even though it meant the four of them would have to stay together. They agreed to split the cost four ways. When a gondolier dropped them at the palazzo's water gate, the entry was so low that Erika's skirts dipped into the canal as they hopped out.

"I can smell it, too," Erika said the first night, as they settled themselves under blankets in scattered corners. "That odor Edmund was talking about. But it isn't unpleasant." Moss-covered pilings held the buildings up. She sniffed again and there it was: the aroma of wet wood and ancient stone.

The Gothic windows framed views of the Grand Canal, and the tiled floors felt sunken under their feet. The furnishings were glorious—tapestries that cloaked the walls, and vermilion chairs with carved, gilded legs.

"An opera ought to be staged here," Christopher said. "In this very room."

"We've got to see that our prima donna is outfitted properly," Mark said. "For future concerts and recitals."

The three men took Erika to a dressmaker Mark had heard about. As one particular bolt of Italian fabric was unfurled, with bits of gold woven through its shimmering folds, they all lost their breath for a moment. It reminded them of a Byzantine mosaic. Mark walked in a circle around Erika, draping a length of the fabric against her. "Imagine Erika standing there in the footlights," he said, "with the gilded bits reflecting."

They danced around her, as though it made them half-drunk, the fun of costuming her.

❖

While the men were out exploring and losing themselves in the labyrinth of Venice's canals and streets, Erika got a chambermaid to fill a metal tub so she could bathe. She lolled for a long time in the warm water, a rolled towel cushioning her neck so she could gaze at the great room's painted ceiling.

The men had not taken a key, knowing that she remained in the room. When they returned, they rattled the wrought-iron latch and banged impatiently. They could not fathom why she took so long to let them in.

Half-panicked, she dried herself with a fat towel and searched for her clothes. Over and over, like a chorus, they called her name, bending their mouths to the keyhole as they continued to thump on the thick door.

"Erika—ERIKA!"

"MADAME VON KESSLER, are you in there?"

When she finally opened the door, they fell into the room and Mark glanced around with wicked amusement. "What's been going on in here?" He peeked under a bed, and playfully opened an armoire to check for a possible lover she'd taken care to hide from them.

"Where is he?" Mark asked. "Is he handsome? Would *we* like him?"

"I was having my bath." Erika pointed at the tub.

"You were having a bath," Mark said, "and what of it? You didn't have to lock the door." He lifted his nose and pretended to be miffed. "Listen," he added jokingly, "if you happen to think that Christopher or Edmund or I have *any* interest *whatsoever* in seeing you—" He laughed.

❖

At night a gondola carried them along the Grand Canal, and they glided past Venetian palaces that glowed from within. Through arched Gothic windows they saw how chandeliers gleamed above tables lined with candles and guests. Erika felt both close and distant from the lives they glimpsed.

The coolness of night rose up from the water and blew across their faces as the gondolier steered. On a passing boat a bass-baritone sang, "Se vuol ballare, signor Contino," to the rousing delight of his friends. The other gondola wobbled with applause as he finished.

Not a bad voice, Erika thought.

"Sing something back," Christopher begged her, leaning forward.

He called to the bass-baritone across the water, prompting him: "Sing—'Là ci darem la mano, là mi dirai di sì—' "

The bass-baritone launched into Mozart's famous love duet from *Don Giovanni,* and Erika, to her own surprise, heard herself singing in response. Suddenly the bass-baritone's gondola turned and headed in their direction, drawn toward the lady who sang in the dark. Several other boats followed his.

"My God," Mark hissed in excitement. "It's an armada coming after us!" He flapped his arms at the man who steered them. "Slip away—fast!"

To elude their pursuers, their gondolier maneuvered the boat into a smaller waterway. Erika, thrilled by the nearness of those who gave chase, let her head drop back and she heard herself laugh at the sky. As their gondolier wrestled the boat around another corner, steering them from sight, she opened her mouth and again announced their whereabouts to all of Venice as she sang another aria from Mozart, "Un moto di gioia."

Along the smaller canal, shutters swung open and heads poked out.

Listeners clapped and whistled. Someone tossed a flower that landed at her feet. When Erika and her friends turned to look behind, the flotilla of pursuers had found them—so many followers that they feared their gondola might soon be surrounded, tipped over in the heat of the chase.

As soon as she finished, Mark cupped his hand over her lips to shush her—just until they'd escaped through the silent canals.

Then she sang again. She could have sung all night, her head leaning back, her mouth opening wide. The stars and moon could have fallen on her tongue; she could have swallowed them.

PART FIVE

45

BOSTON

1912

Quentin did not go for a walk with the other boys. All Sunday afternoon he sat in the window seat at the boarding school and waited for his father to come. Earlier that week he had sent his father a letter begging him to drive down from Boston in the Haynes Touring Car. *Dear Pappa*, Quentin had written. *Please bring your atomobile and kum to see me on Sunday. I want the other boys to see it.* Quentin knew the stir the sight would cause as his father motored through the school gates, riding upon the Haynes's quilted seats and shiny wheels. Papa would step from the Haynes in goggles, cap, and duster, and when he pulled Quentin close—just for a moment—Quentin's face would press against the cold crevasses of his father's coat with its smell of crisp, decaying leaves. The other boys, who'd been waiting in the parlor, would rush out, too, and surround the car.

His father was so long in arriving that Quentin laid his head against the window seat cushion and closed his eyes until the matron came by and told him to straighten up. Lifting his head, he saw mothers drive up, their slender ankles stepping down from carriages or purring motorcars. Boys in short trousers and dark jackets flew toward doorways, and they were caught up and tossed into a blur of furs, hugs, perfume, skirts. From the bow-front window he watched them, thinking of his own mother until his throat went sore.

The roads beyond the wrought-iron gates of the school had been hard and frozen, and quite dry in the morning, but by late afternoon, the snow whirled as if the air thickened with white, battling flies. "Come away from the window," the matron who had been monitoring the parlor said to Quentin. "Perhaps your papa will come to see you another Sunday." She closed the draperies and led Quentin away.

The stairs to the alcove where he slept were so steep, his shoes felt weighted as he climbed. That evening he wrote:

My dear Pappa,
Why didn't you kum to visit me today? I waited for you all after-
noon . . .

Between sentences he put his head down on the desk and rubbed his eyes until his knuckles grew wet, smeared with blue ink. His cursive grew larger, the letters crossing the page in big loops, becoming more reckless.

WHEN IS MAMMA KUMING BAK?
I WISH YOU WOULD TELL ME.

For more than a year, this was the question he'd continued to ask. Sometimes during his vacations in Boston, he thought he heard her in various parts of the house. He expected that he might awake one morning to find her lifting the shades in his bedroom. His father said only, "Your mother has hopes of becoming a better-known singer. She has gone off to Italy to study opera." This did not explain why she did not send him any letters while he was away at Mowgli Camp last summer, or why— after he wrote and told her about the mole he and another boy trapped— she did not reply.

Because he had been sent to the school not long after she left, it was possible that she did not know his address. On a fresh sheet of white paper he scratched a message with his pen: *My dear Mamma, I wish you would rite to me. My address is the Chadsworth Skool. . . .*

During Easter vacation, behind a fourth-story window of his father's Back Bay house, Quentin pressed his forehead against the glass pane and peered out. Below, cherry blossoms whitened the street. He pretended he could see his mother on the sidewalk, scurrying. Her lavender skirts swished past tall brick row houses, darkening and lightening as she moved under trees.

At the window he blinked twice; his mother's lavender skirts were gone. Cherry blossoms still fluttered white in the sunlight; the sidewalks emptied, nothing there but dull red bricks. Quentin retreated from the window, a terrible and familiar tightness beginning in his chest. No matter how long he watched the street, no matter how acutely he remembered or imagined her, his mother did not return.

He walked from his bedroom into the hallway and leaned over the banister. He peered down four flights, staring into the spiraling loop of stairs where the abyss was frightening. What would happen, he had asked his father once, if somebody fell into the stairwell? Papa said that surely a neck would be broken; if you were lucky, just an arm or leg.

A wine-colored carpet covered the stairs, laced by a pattern of scrolls and flowers. The landing used to be a favorite spot of his for playing. Here on the landing, he used to make his little lead soldiers climb the steps and form barricades. From this position, sounds in the high, narrow house rose up to him—the tinkle of silverware being polished and replaced into drawers in the dining room. The high notes of his mother's arias used to mount and glide up here until the walls shivered. He used to pause sometimes, listening to her. She sang in a foreign language—Italian—that he did not understand. But when she sang, something made him stop. The skin behind his ears tingled.

Since she'd gone away, he no longer liked to play on the stairs so much because the house seemed too empty and silent there. So Quentin went down to his father's study. Though his father had been abroad for weeks now, the study still smelled of leather and cigar smoke. On Papa's desk, a real butterfly lay preserved and embedded inside a magnifying glass.

When Quentin had been much younger—before he'd started school—he'd heard his parents argue many times. The terrible sounds had made him bolt upright in bed. He'd sobbed noisily until they heard him, and that made them stop because Mama had rushed into his room. She wore a hat and long cape and gloves, as if she were going out. Her dress made stiff, crinkly sounds as her weight fell lightly against the bed. She removed her gloves and stroked his face with her fingers, and he kept very still and pretended to be asleep. For a long time she remained with him in the darkness, as if his room were a place to hide. Finally she rustled toward the door and he saw her face by the hall light, her cheeks wet, her eyes squeezed tight.

❖

The housekeeper, Mrs. McMannis, put her hands on her hips and let out a gusty breath when she found Quentin writing a note in the study. "I don't know why you scribble so many letters," she said. "A big strapping boy like you ought to be outside enjoying yourself on a bright afternoon."

He knew a boy from school who lived nearby at the Lenox Hotel. They had planned to play ball together in the Boston Common, but that morning the other boy had felt poorly and could not go out. So Quentin kept on with the note:

> Dear Uncle Gerald,
> I wish you would give me the photograph you have got on your piano.
> I mean the one of my mother wearing her opera kostume.

When Quentin had told his cousin Susan that he wanted that framed picture, she told him that Uncle Gerald wouldn't want to let him have the photograph because Papa would probably burn it.

"Why would he burn it?"

His twelve-year-old cousin had made her eyes large with surprise. "Your father is going to *divorce* her, don't you even know?"

I promise nothing bad will happen to the pikture, he wrote to his uncle. *Becuz I am going to keep it in a secret place in my room.*

When he finished the letter to his mother's brother, Quentin hunted through his father's desk drawer for a stamp. At school they put stamps on your letters for you. He found ink bottles, rulers, a compass, and elastic bands in his father's top drawer, but no stamps, so he opened the next one. A sheaf of pages was stored there, tied with a ribbon, with his handwriting across the papers. These were letters he'd composed at school. *My dear Mamma,* one began. Another said, *Dear Mamma, Did you get my letter I wrote about the skunk?* A third said, *Do you love Italy?*

Every letter he'd written to her was here. No one had mailed them.

46

EGYPT

1912

I n Cairo, after Peter had finished his business, he hired a guide to take him into the bazaar on Mousky Street. His dragoman Abdou spoke smooth English, but their passage through the bazaar was hardly easy. Twenty thousand people flowed through it. One had to squeeze past other bodies. First came silver merchants, followed by vendors selling amber, then candles, then ostrich feathers, then ivory, then slippers, then scents. Roses and spicy incense tinctured the air.

A caravan of camels moved down the thoroughfare and blocked the road, setting off skirmishes and bursts of complaints. Peter found himself backed up into an open-air shop. It was there that he noticed a young woman who was perhaps seventeen standing in the shade.

The thing that struck Peter first—apart from her delicately shaped face—was the fact that she was not veiled. He'd become used to seeing Egyptian women with nothing more than their eyes showing. The young woman did not appear to be Egyptian, though he could not be certain of her origin.

Peter pretended interest in the atomizers and glass vials arranged on the tables. A fat Arab with steely curls and coarse features rose from a cushion and came to assist. This proprietor, a man in his forties, beckoned the young woman and she came forward like an obedient daughter. She pushed up the sleeve of her loose cloak, dabbed a fragrant oil on the inside of her smooth forearm, and held it up for Peter to sniff.

"Do you like it?" Abdou translated. "Would you like to try the musk?"

The girl upended another vial, moistened her finger, and rubbed the oil against the crook of her opposite arm. Hands behind his back, Peter bent over politely, careful not to touch her, only to sniff. The girl had a silvery scar, the size of a minnow, on the underside of her wrist. He could have stationed himself there all day, if only the young woman had a thousand arms.

Peter handed his guide a number of piastres and let him do the bargaining. "Ask where the young lady comes from," Peter told Abdou.

After an exchange in Arabic, he learned that the girl was from Tangier, though no explanation was given about how she got here. Like most Moorish women, her eyes and hair were black, yet her skin was as white as a European's.

❖

That night at his hotel, he could not stop thinking of the Moorish girl, how she'd held her slim arm only inches from his lips. He remembered the silver minnow scar on her wrist.

A strange whim took hold of him. What if he returned to Mousky Street, offered her Arab master a healthy sum, and asked if he might borrow the girl for a day?

The next morning a different guide accompanied him to Mousky Street. The Arab in charge of the girl seemed perfectly willing to pocket a considerable amount of money. What was he—her husband? Uncle? Godfather? Paramour? Peter did not want to think about it.

The dragoman led them to a side street where a coachman and a fine carriage waited. Then the guide departed.

First they stopped at a dress shop for English ladies, where a seamstress agreed to take charge of the Moorish girl. She was escorted to an upper-story room and bathed until the sweat and stale perfumes of Mousky Street evaporated with the steam. The seamstress saw to it that the young woman's hair was done. Finally the girl was fitted for slippers and a white eyelet dress, and fixed up with a parasol.

Within an hour the girl no longer looked Middle Eastern, but instead like a thoroughbred European. She could have been mistaken for a native of Britain. The dark hair had been drawn off her neck and lifted, fixed by a curved pompadour comb.

Through the streets of Cairo their carriage rolled at brisk speed. Her high-necked gown was white—the color that his wife had usually worn. Like his wife, the young girl had ringlets. Like Erika's, her throat was long.

As she sat across from him, her pompadour jiggled slightly from the motion of the carriage. What he wouldn't give to see inside her silent head, to know what sort of life she came from, how she got to be here. Peter had once seen a snake charmer in Tangier, and wished he could ask about her knowledge of such things. A serpent had bitten the man's tongue; Peter had seen for himself how the blood flowed. Then the snake charmer had stuffed his mouth with hay. Peter had inspected the man's mouth, tongue, hands, and the straw itself, but saw no gimmick. The performer had pushed more hay into his mouth, and then exhaled fireworks of smoke and flame.

Peter wanted to tell her, *"I have been to your country. I know something of life there—"*

He took her to a fine restaurant known as the English Tea Room, where she ate like a perfect lady. Peter doubted that the other fashionable patrons of the dining room guessed that she was not of their class.

When the last cake was done, she licked whipped cream from the tines of her fork and looked up at him demurely. He gave her his own two finger cakes and she finished them, too. Her hunger touched him.

Outside, the air grew cooler, the afternoon waning. The sun was losing its bright power, and he realized with sadness that in an hour or two, the stalls in Mousky Street would be closing, and he would have to return the girl. But first he wanted to buy her flowers—pink, to match the satin ribbon at her waist. They walked several blocks without any sign of a florist or curbside flower vendor.

In his hotel room he had flowers—irises and delphiniums in a tall vase. Not pink, of course, but for lack of any others, he decided to go back for them. He intended to leave her seated in the hotel lobby while he went upstairs, but when they reached the Hotel d'Angleterre, he did not know how to communicate his plan to her clearly. He was afraid that if left alone, she would vanish before he returned. So he took her upstairs with him.

When they entered his room, the Moorish girl looked flustered. She said something quickly in Arabic, and shook her head.

"Don't worry," he said, to reassure her. "We've just come to fetch the flowers. I won't harm you." He opened the shutters and let sunlight rush into the dim room.

Two chairs faced the long window. Peter settled into one, and motioned for her to be seated in the other. He took the purplish-blue flowers from the vase, shook water from them, and dried each long stem with a towel. Wrapping the flowers in a silk scarf, he placed them in her lap.

The window before them overlooked a bridge that crossed the Nile. On that bridge every motley mode of transportation could be seen: camels, wagons, fellahin on foot, fashionable French motorcars. Sunlight burned red glints into her hair. She looked out the window at a minaret.

"Let me show you a picture of my son," Peter said. He went to his steamer trunk and fished out a silver frame.

He wished he could tell her how Quentin's small face would appear at the window, two palms pressed against the glass, waiting for his father's return. As Peter entered the house, Quentin stood at the top of the staircase. The child hyperventilated and ran toward him in such excitement, Peter was afraid that the little boy might tumble down the steps.

Pappy, Pappy, Pappy, Papa—!

To no other person, Peter realized at such moments, *does my existence matter so much.*

The girl took the silver frame in her hands and smiled in tender recognition. She pointed to Quentin's mouth, and then touched Peter's mouth with her fingertips—to show a similarity. Surprised and confused by this, Peter felt the muscles in his shoulders tense; he was not certain how he ought to respond.

He opened the back of the silver frame and removed another photo-

graph stored behind the one of Quentin—an engagement portrait of
Erika. The Moorish girl took the photograph of his wife and walked over
to the room's full-length mirror. The young woman touched her pompadour with one hand, comparing her image to the American lady's, like a
little girl consulting a fashion magazine.

"My wife left me," Peter said bluntly. He pointed to Erika's face and
kept shaking his head. "My wife did not love me." His eyes watered as
he said it. The room had grown so hot that Peter loosened his tie, and ran
his hand inside his stiff collar.

The pain in his voice increased. The Moorish girl sat motionless in her
chair, the insteps of her white pumps drawn together while she listened.
"My wife never loved me as I loved her," Peter went on. He described
how Erika had gone to Italy and left Quentin motherless.

The room filled with stark brightness, the last harsh rays of the day.
Atop a minaret a lone man chanted prayers from the Koran, calling others
to face east and touch their foreheads to the ground. Peter felt overcome
by despair. Why was he reciting his heartbreak to a strange woman who
did not know the words he used? What did he expect from her? He had
expressed more of his anguish to her than to anyone. Why was it easiest
to be open with a stranger whom one would never meet again?

This young woman with her glossy pompadour would soon leave his
life forever, just as his wife had done.

The girl touched his knuckles, and let her head fall sideways to show
that she respected his sorrow. She stood up. He assumed that she was
worried about the hour, signaling that they should leave. Then she surprised him by settling herself on the arm of his chair. She slipped her cool
hand against the back of his neck. The hairs on his nape stood up, tingling.
He waited for a long moment, and then he put his mouth against hers.

When he led her to the bed, she did not resist. He helped unfasten her
corset, for he knew how to unlace it better than she. Her back flexed into
a cool little arch as she let the undergarments drop to the floor. Her
breasts were small and cone-shaped. He drew one into his mouth and
tasted a strange fluid that came from the nipples. He sucked harder—

there wasn't much of it, just a sweet flavor, like dew on a leaf. Against the bed, her arms were flung over her head in surrender, her eyes closed. He heard air catch in her windpipe.

He had not been with a woman in the eighteen months since Erika left. Remembering things that had pleasured his wife, he now did them to the Moorish girl. Startled, her eyes blinked open. She was very young, and perhaps no one had cared about her enjoyment before. Eyelids shut, her head fell back against pillows, her dark hair unspooling from its knot. A humming sound came out of her as they rocked.

Eventually her head thrashed from side to side against the pillow and she let out sharp cooing cries, her black hair loose across her shoulders, her body coming to rest after one final, delicious twitch. Triumphant, he let the girl from Mousky Street recover her breath, and he restrained his own pleasure in order to do it to her again. The second time he imagined that his wife lay under him, and he pumped with vengeance, each pump inflating her with gasps. As long as he was inside her, he controlled the helpless curve of her throat. As long as he stayed inside her, she could not go anywhere.

47

BRITISH GUIANA AND TRINIDAD

My dear Ravell,

Years have elapsed since we last saw one another, and I feel the urgency of so much to say and discuss with you that little of it can be contained in a letter. In fact, I have something important to tell you, but would prefer to talk in person. Let me propose that you and I journey together deep into the wilds of Guiana, as we once spoke of doing, to see the highest waterfalls in the world. Only forty white men have seen the Kaieteur Falls, and it has always lured me, despite the difficulties of reaching such a place. . . .

Three years have passed since Erika moved to Italy, and the divorce is now final. . . .

Ravell had heard nothing from Erika in eight years. He did not know what information Peter might offer about his former wife, but if he joined Peter on such a journey, he felt certain that he would learn more about what had become of her—perhaps even her exact whereabouts. A simple remark might lead him solidly in her direction. Maybe as they traveled upriver, Peter would name a maestro with whom she was studying, or refer to a theatre in Florence where she performed.

Ravell wondered, with trepidation, what exactly Peter wished to discuss with him. For once he was glad that he had never sent Erika a letter, and that she had never corresponded with him. No love letters existed for a wronged husband to stumble upon.

They arrived in British Guiana feeling anticipation, and much curiosity. As he and Peter walked together through the capital, Georgetown, Ravell felt he had never seen such a potpourri of humanity. Along the streets they saw copper-skinned Indians with scarlet loincloths, Hindus with topknots, and Chinese workers with pigtails—not to mention the Portuguese and the British.

They were on their way to meet a fellow named Manthorne, the person in charge of mail delivery to remote destinations in Guiana's interior. A friend of Peter's from the Colonial Bank had suggested that Manthorne might help arrange their expedition to the Kaieteur Falls.

So far Peter had said little about Erika, his allusions to his former wife so fleeting that Ravell wondered if he should dare to ask about her. He felt an unbearable curiosity welling up.

When he and Peter paused at a street corner, a Hindu with his whiskers dyed magenta rode by on a bicycle, but nobody else's eyes lingered on him. Then a naked man passed by—with hair that stood on end, as if he'd been electrocuted—and not a single citizen of Georgetown turned to gape.

"If Erika were meant to be famous," Peter said suddenly, "don't you think it would have happened long ago?"

Ravell did not reply. He hardly knew what to say.

As they hurried toward Mr. Manthorne's office, Peter's pace was so vigorous that Ravell had to double his steps to keep up. The drought that plagued Trinidad was worse in Guiana, and they both wondered how this might affect their journey.

❖

"The problem is this," Mr. Manthorne said. "In this country where rain normally falls every day, we have had scarcely any rainfall in six months."

"In Trinidad we've been luckier," Ravell said. "Although the drought has been quite serious there as well."

"I would strongly advise you to postpone such a trip," Mr. Manthorne said. "Such travel would be most difficult. In certain places rivers are shallow. Even if you did manage to reach the falls, it would hardly be worth it. They've slowed to a trickle, eyewitnesses say."

"How long does it take to reach the Kaieteur Falls?" Peter asked.

"Ordinarily a week. These days—who knows? Rivers have dried up, and crops have been ruined. The country is headed for much suffering."

Peter was hardly daunted. "I'm afraid we're a rather determined pair," he said, and he shot Ravell a conspiratorial smile.

"All right, then." Mr. Manthorne slapped both of his palms against his desk. "I will get you up as far as possible." He pulled a blank paper from his desk drawer, ready to list the provisions he'd arrange. "Brace yourselves for a bit of discomfort. Despite the drought, in some spots you're liable to be thrown out of the boat. You may find yourselves standing on your heads in the midst of rapids."

"I'm an excellent swimmer," Peter said. "And so is Doctor Ravell."

❖

A ghostly mist rose from the river on the morning they started up the Essequibo. Ravell and Peter stayed in the forward part of the launch; the after part carried the engine and crew. To either side of the main launch, another bateau was tied, weighted down with a half dozen black passengers and cargo.

They felt their way slowly at first. On either bateau a man with a pole took soundings. A black boy named Thomas had been assigned to serve Peter and Ravell. The boy prepared a luxurious breakfast for them—with tea, bread and jam, sweet potatoes, and even a chicken that had been roasted earlier.

Even in a season of drought, the river spread a mile wide. Out of the dense forest, a figure in a canoe would appear, and that person would retrieve a fistful of letters.

The crew consisted of two blacks in charge of the engine, two who steered, and a man stationed on each parallel bateau. All of them shouted orders and suggestions. The crew member whose voice blared loudest had skin as dark as oil, and a neck and shoulders so powerful that he awed Ravell. "That one's built like a gorilla," Peter said under his breath. Ravell stepped hard on Peter's foot and glared at him in warning. Did Peter think, in these close quarters, that he could mutter what he liked, and not be overheard?

In the afternoon they struck a rock. Havoc and shouts from the blacks ensued. They reached an area so shallow that crewmen got on either side and pushed and hauled the boat upstream, until they reached a second, smaller launch. Ravell and Peter were transferred into the next little boat with their luggage.

Ravell stared at Peter's canvas bundles. Inside those bags, along with his pen and writing things, did Peter carry a small book that listed Erika's address?

Ravell pictured himself waiting on an Italian street corner. When she approached her front door and paused to open her purse and fish out a key, she'd use her teeth to tug the tips of her long gloves from her fingers.

"Erika?" he'd say, stepping out from the shadows. For the first time in eight years, her face would turn toward him.

❖

More trouble came. Rocks studded the stream. Rapids rushed everywhere. Only one bateau at a time could pass through. They eked by, only to find the launch soon wedged between rocks. The crew strained, shoved, and grimaced as they loosened it. Perspiration ran like rainwater down the black men's necks.

Later, the launch jammed between rocks and would not budge. A cry came: "All men overboard!" Ravell and Peter jumped, their shirts rising like balloons in the water.

The shouting was continuous as the white water roiled. After a black steersman grabbed Ravell's arm and helped him climb back on board, Ravell shook himself and spat out the taste of the river.

At six in the evening they reached more placid waters, and the sun fell behind the forest wall.

Night made the journey too difficult to continue, so they soon made fast to the banks and prepared to camp. While Peter disappeared through trees to relieve himself, Ravell moved stealthily toward Peter's old leather valise, and carefully opened it. His nose filled with the sour smell of rumpled clothing. He searched for anything that might resemble an address book, but there was nothing.

Quickly he shut the luggage, his heart punching against his chest. *What has reduced me to this?* he wondered. *Rummaging like a petty thief through another man's things?*

Mr. Manthorne had sent two folding beds for Ravell's and Peter's comfort. The ingenious construction of these beds impressed them: each fit into a portable case, each case compact enough to be stored in the bottom of the launch. Mr. Manthorne had also provided mosquito netting for them. The boy Thomas hung his hammock at the foot of their beds.

After supper, Thomas built a small fire for them. The boy helped pull off Ravell's boots, and then Peter's. They dismissed the boy for the remainder of the evening so they could be alone.

❖

From time to time, Peter had been taking out a portfolio filled with loose pages and making notes. By the firelight he scribbled a few more lines.

"Are you keeping a diary?" Ravell asked.

"I'm writing a letter to my son," Peter said.

Ravell sat stupefied. His tongue went dry with the shock of this, and he struggled to continue speaking. "You have a son?"

"Quentin is eight years old," Peter said.

"Why did you never tell me that you'd had a child?"

Peter sat on the side of the camp bed, his face orange in the firelight, and gave Ravell a look. "I think you—of all people—can guess how complicated that might have made everything."

Ravell sat on his own bed. He held himself as still as an animal that senses danger, hoping that if he doesn't move or breathe, and just plays dead, the threat will pass.

"You've never had anything to hide from me," Peter said. "Whatever secrets you thought you were keeping, I always knew."

Ravell felt his bones lock in place. His neck became a solid pillar, so that he could not turn his head if he tried. His breaths became thin.

In those seconds, Ravell feared that Peter understood even more—a sin far worse than those cuckolded husbands of the Back Bay ever guessed. Even when Ravell became intimate with Erika, he could not bring himself to tell her how profoundly he had deceived her and Peter. Ravell felt it unforgivable, what he'd done. The terrible result still returned to him like the grimmest dream—a dead daughter, a baby whose eyelids remained sealed.

❖

Under the darkness of night in Guiana, down by the banks of the Essequibo, the crewmen had begun drinking. While Peter and Ravell sat facing each other on parallel folding beds, the crew made alarming noises in the distance. The black men laughed and insulted one another. Overhead in the trees, a howler monkey let out a voracious roar. While Peter talked, Ravell glanced at the dark sky, and tried to keep his heart calm.

After the baby girl died, after Ravell fled from Boston . . . Peter explained how he and Erika had consulted another doctor. When that specialist had proposed a semen examination, Peter found his previous resistance to the procedure gone. After all, he had fathered a child by then, hadn't he?

When the physician shared the results with him, he'd been confounded.

"But how is that possible?" Peter had asked the specialist. "My wife and I just had a baby girl."

The doctor had looked uneasy and stopped swiveling in his chair. The specialist asked if Peter had been ill, or if he'd experienced extreme fever in the past year or so. That could have brought on sterility.

Peter had shaken his head, and the doctor became quiet. Together they had felt the implications hanging in the air. Peter inhaled and exhaled and knew that moment would be etched forever in his mind—the fortress of medical books on the surrounding walls, the specialist sitting motionless in his chair, the tufts of hair that grew along the man's folded hands. The physician decided to say nothing else, so Peter rose and was gone from the office.

Ravell, he had realized at once. Ravell.

Peter remembered the delivery, those moments when the dead little girl was brought forth from his wife's body. Even in his own grief, Peter had felt a sharp surprise at glimpsing Ravell's face: never had Peter seen another man look so sad. Ravell's glasses had been spotted with water until he pulled them off and put his fingers to his eyes. Ravell's lips had grown wet and he bit down to stop them from quivering.

❖

"Until I saw your grief over the first baby," Peter said, "I never suspected that you were in love with my wife. I never realized that Erika was infatuated with you."

"She wasn't in love with me. Not when the little girl was born."

"So why did she sleep with you? Because she was desperate for a child?"

Ravell sat up and swung his legs over the side of the folding bed. He went over to the fire the black boy had built for them and threw dirt to extinguish it.

"Don't make me answer," he said to Peter finally. "Don't make me explain."

❖

Neither of them could sleep after that. The crew had shared their liquor with Thomas, and the boy was soon vomiting against a tree. Ravell and

Peter helped the boy into his hammock that hung at the foot of their beds. Thomas fell into a heavy, drunken slumber but Ravell and Peter lay there, unable to rest, listening to the crew catcall and howl by the riverbanks.

"I'm afraid I shall have to assert myself," Peter announced finally, as he prepared to head toward the smell of the whiskey.

Ravell felt it unwise to say anything. "Don't go down there," he called warningly to Peter. They were a long way from any settlement, a world away from other white men.

But nothing stopped Peter. As Ravell watched his old friend move down the slope toward the drunken men, he wondered at Peter's sense of invincibility.

After Peter made his complaint and turned away from the crew, the unruliness only worsened. Near the riverbanks, a large object was hurled through darkness into the water. A great splash could be heard, and angry shouts. From his camp bed Ravell watched Peter slowly returning uphill. Behind him, men raised their fists as they dodged and shadow-boxed. In their drunkenness Ravell feared that they would lunge after Peter, and then him.

He realized they might die here together tonight. Had Peter brought him here as a kind of vengeful wish? A handful of inebriated men might leave them for vultures and animals, until nothing remained except the whiteness of their bones. Their bodies might vanish into the forest, disappear into the darkness of the soil, and feed the shrieks of hungry birds. No acquaintance of theirs would realize what had happened. Perhaps nobody would ever know the fear he felt, waiting there.

48

At dawn, like a mercy, the sun came up and the expedition continued.

Farther upriver a smaller stern-wheeler awaited them, allowing them
to pass through shallower depths with ease. The engine resembled a toy.
A broad-ribbed Negro fed wood into the miniature furnace. Each time
they transferred into a new boat, signatures were exchanged for a receipt
to be sent back to Mr. Manthorne.

By afternoon they reached Tumatumari, where a rest house sat on a
hill overlooking the river. The front door had a pointed arch. Inside, Ravell and Peter shed their moldy clothes that smelled of fish, mud, sweat,
and the river. After they took turns lowering themselves into a bath, they
got up from the hot waters refreshed, and put on clean bush clothes.

Outside they went to inspect the giant bleached boulders that blocked
the river. The grand cataract had dried up, reduced to nothing more than
the force of a few bathtub faucets. In Tumatumari everyone told them
that the Kaieteur Falls had waned, and now barely dripped.

Peter said, "I'm afraid our journey must end here."

"Perhaps we could hire Indian carriers to help us reach the Kaieteur
Falls," Ravell said. Only forty miles remained.

"We haven't got proper supplies for an overland journey," Peter
pointed out.

Ravell's heart shrank in disappointment. What had been the purpose
of having fought their way so far upriver, if they would never see the
marvel they'd struggled to reach?

At Tumatumari he and Peter sat on boulders to view the cataract, now a cascade of nearly pure stone. Sun warmed the rocks and heated their backsides. "With a thriving river," Ravell said, "the waterfall here must be glorious."

And then, to Ravell's surprise, Peter's forehead became furrowed and he said: "When I left Erika with you at the coconut plantation and went off to Venezuela, I knew you'd sleep with her. I fully expected it."

Ravell turned his head and stared at Peter.

More loudly Peter said, "I wanted you to have intercourse with my wife."

The shock of it marred Ravell's vision; he saw splotches before his eyes. "Why?"

"Because I wanted a child—and I wanted to keep Erika. I understood that I'd never make her pregnant myself."

Ravell heard the frustration in Peter's clipped words.

"Well," Peter said. He lifted his head and scanned the uppermost reaches of trees. "I suppose it's all irrelevant at this point, whatever you or I wanted, isn't it? She's gone off to Italy and left us both."

❖

Hidden in the forest near Tumatumari, he and Peter found a cluster of Indian huts, all deserted. "The owners can't be far away," Peter concluded, noting fires blazing and pots boiling. Then they saw an old Indian who'd been left behind. He lolled in a hammock, flesh hanging from his bones as if he wore a suit that stretched.

Each hut had four posts, the roof thatched with palm leaves. When Peter noticed a few weapons tucked under the rafters, he pulled down a bow and one six-foot-long arrow, handed them to the old Indian in the hammock, and pointed to a large lizard fifty yards away. The old man took the bow. Without leaving the hammock, he shot the arrow and it pierced straight into the lizard's head.

"You see the skill of these people," Peter said.

Walking back to the rest house at Tumatumari, Ravell could not resist asking Peter, "If you wanted a child so much . . . and if you were willing to use another man's sperm . . . why didn't you make discreet arrangements with a specialist? Why did you have your wife sleep with another man?"

Peter's words sounded emphatic. "I didn't want to use a stranger's seed, someone I knew *nothing* about."

"Weren't you worried that Erika and I—" Ravell hesitated. "That we'd fall in love? That she might stay with me?"

"I suppose, in a way, I counted on your honor—" Peter shrugged. As a last thought, he added: "I'm a businessman. I know when a very hard bargain must be made."

That night at the rest house, Ravell lounged on a bed while Peter continued his long letter to Quentin. At every opportunity he found, Peter took out his pen and wrote to the boy. He read parts of the letter aloud: *If I'd asked the old Indian lying in his hammock to shoot a fish far downstream, I am certain the old man would not have missed. . . .* He wrote as though the boy were always at his side, accompanying him.

He is writing to my son, Ravell thought. *A boy who stands at a window watching snow fall. A boy with a face I have never seen.*

❖

Upon their return to Trinidad, they both stayed overnight at the Queen's Park Hotel before Ravell headed east from Port of Spain. It was turning out to be a very good year for Peter's business, he told Ravell, and messages from his partner awaited him at the hotel, urging him to return to Boston as quickly as possible. Peter would not have time to come to the coconut plantation.

Before a tender arrived to take Peter away to his steamer, anchored a couple of miles offshore, Ravell suggested a stroll through the Botanical Gardens.

He showed Peter the rare bloom on the Trinidad bamboo, a flower that appeared only during times of devastating drought. Shopkeepers displayed it in their windows, and old men claimed they could not recall having seen the flower before.

Peter peered at the bloom. "I suppose there's always something beautiful to be had, even during a drought," he said. "Even when crops are failing, and people are suffering."

Ravell asked, "Do you have a picture of him?"

Peter's eyebrows twitched quizzically.

"Quentin, I mean."

They sat down together on a bench and Peter pulled a billfold from his suit jacket pocket. "He's got dark hair. Big eyes, rather like yours."

In the photograph the boy posed with a violin, although Peter said that Quentin did not like to practice. The child wore a sailor suit. Ravell studied the image, looking for traces of Erika in the child, but the boy did not resemble her.

When they got up to resume their walk, Ravell held on to the photo and halted twice to stare at it. "Why did you want me to know of his existence?" he asked.

"I'm a man who believes in the truth," Peter said. "I've always felt it fair for you to know."

"But why now? Why were you so careful not to tell me until now?"

"Because the divorce has become final, and I've got legal custody. Nobody can take him from me at this point, not even Erika."

Ravell handed back the photograph. "I'm sure he's very attached to you."

Peter replaced it in his billfold. "Oh, he is."

PART SIX

PART SIX

49

CAPE COD, MASSACHUSETTS

1913

My dear Pappa,
Please I don't want to go back to Mowgli Camp this summer. I'd
rather be with you. . . .

His father was far away again. Quentin wriggled down and closed
the hamper lid over his head and waited for the others to find him. He
pressed his teeth against his knees and closed his lips to keep from laughing, because it was very funny when the others raced into the room and
he could hear every sound they made as they peered around. "Look
under the closet, look under the bed," said Margaret, the eldest girl. Inside the hamper Quentin fell sideways and wondered if they would see
the bulge his body made against the wicker sides. The lid lifted slightly
as Quentin's head pushed against it. "Open the drawers," Margaret ordered. Drawers slid open and banged shut again before they ran out,
thinking they had searched very thoroughly. Nobody thought to look
inside the hamper filled with dirty clothes that smelled.

❖

"He lives here with us now," Margaret explained. "At least for the
summer."

"Are you an orphan?" her friends asked.

"No," Quentin said.

"What happened to your father and mother?"

"My father is in Egypt buying cotton," he said. "And my mother is a singer in Italy."

They stared at him for a moment, as if they were unsure whether to believe him. Their faces looked grave, as if they did not envy him for whatever circumstances brought him here, without parents. He asked if they wanted to see a thirty-foot anaconda skin his father had brought back from the jungle for him, and they nodded.

"I will even let you touch it." Quentin said, and drew the special bag his father had given him from under the bed. He brought the snakeskin along everywhere he could.

❖

His father's business partner, Mr. Talcott, had five children and a summer house on Cape Cod with a roof so steep it looked like a witch's hat. Papa thought Quentin might be happier here, with a family, rather than at camp.

The house had a hundred dark corners and tiny doors in the wainscoting that opened into cupboards and low closets to crawl inside and hide. The Talcotts had cousins who also liked to visit here. Two of the oldest boys brought sticks like swords into the attic to attack a squirrel that lived up there, but the squirrel sneaked away through a hole under the eaves.

Whenever Quentin and the others returned from the beach, they carried towels so twisted and dirty and heavy with sand, they were told to drop them at the back porch. Nobody was allowed in the house with a damp towel.

At night he would lie in bed and feel sand silted between his toes. The rush and fizz of waves stayed in his ears, like sounds caught inside a conch shell. High up in his nose, the sharp scent of the beach stayed alive.

When Quentin had a cold, Mrs. Talcott poured him a glass of vinegar to purify his system. None of her own children could bear to drink vinegar for their colds, she said, because the taste was so terrible, but Quentin braved it. He gulped the full glass, got it all down in one long swallow, and though he grimaced and shuddered right afterward,

Mrs. Talcott petted his shoulders and told him he was exceptionally strong.

On Sundays she asked her children to learn a psalm and repeat it to her, but they studied the verses half-heartedly and slipped away to the beach or the rowboat before finishing. He was the only one who stayed beside her on the porch until he got a whole psalm learned. When he was done reciting, she got up from the divan where she liked to sit with a book and an open box of chocolates. She let him choose a piece of candy, and then she pulled him against her waist and rubbed his head. People made jokes about her eating so many chocolates, and they called her fat, but he liked the feel of her. She had soft parts, like a bed with feather pillows you fell upon. He sniffed a sweet powder through her clothes.

She said it would not do for him to call her "Mrs. Talcott" anymore; he should call her "Mother," like the rest of them.

❖

One evening he sat on the porch swing with Mrs. Talcott. It was so dark they couldn't see the lawn, but he smelled the grass; if he ran across it barefoot, the newly mowed blades would smear his soles green.

"Did something bad happen to my mother?" Quentin blurted suddenly.

"Something bad?" Mrs. Talcott said with hesitation, and used her heels to brake the swing. They stopped rocking.

At school a boy once said that he'd heard Quentin's mother was dead. The rumor had startled him, and now he felt an odd urge to confront Mrs. Talcott with the same strange words.

"Heavens, no!" Mrs. Talcott sucked in her breath and exhaled quickly when she heard this. "Your mother is living in Italy, last I heard."

He knew this all very well. But it still troubled him to think of his unmailed letters to her, hidden in his father's desk. Quentin told Mrs. Talcott how he'd found them.

"Unless Mama died . . . why didn't Papa send them to her?" Quentin asked. "After I'd gone to the trouble of writing them?"

"I can't speak for your father," Mrs. Talcott said. "But I would imagine that your mother's absence has caused him a good deal of grief. Maybe— maybe he thinks it's better for you to carry on, and not be frustrated by things that can't be changed."

❖

Several nights later, after a game of freeze tag, Quentin flopped on the lawn, panting. He noticed how his heart hopped like a small animal caught inside his chest, until he had rested enough. After the others had scattered and gone into the house for card games and checkers, Quentin remained there, the ground cold against his back. Dew dampened the lawn, and stars glittered like the heads of pins.

He heard Mrs. Talcott on the porch, behind the bushes, talking to another lady. No doubt they were passing the box of chocolates back and forth, although it was dark so he couldn't see the ladies, and they did not see him.

Mrs. Talcott was saying, "Everyone asks me: 'You already have five children, so why would you take in another?' The simple answer is that it tugs at my heart to see that little boy so alone. His father is always crossing the ocean, whether for business or pleasure or adventure. . . ."

"Quentin hurt his knee the other day," she went on. "I brought him into the bathroom to wash and bandage it, and when I saw that blood flowing from his knee, I thought: *Where is his mother? What can that woman be thinking? Where is she?*"

PART SEVEN

50

ITALY

1913

Onstage at Montepulciano, Erika stood incandescent, the sounds of Bizet's *Carmen* passing through her. Arms horizontal, she stood there with her tongue releasing beauty.

During rehearsals, members of the orchestra applauded and cheered her. They had been hired to play at her *prova,* and they owed her nothing apart from a decent rendering of their services, but thanks to them, anticipation had begun to spread through the ancient hill town. The new singer, they were telling everyone, has a beautiful voice, *una bella voce.* You must come to her debut.

❖

The night Erika had first headed from the railway station toward the fortressed city where she was to make her *prova,* things had not seemed quite so promising. The train that delivered them was horrendously late, and she and Christopher discovered that the station was far from Montepulciano. Darkness and slanting rain had taken hold as they found themselves being jostled uphill inside a covered carriage. A steep embankment rose up on one side of the road, and the silhouettes of olive trees fell away on the other.

Lightning split the sky, close enough to touch. Erika watched the storm and worried. They would never reach the mountaintop city before restaurants locked their doors for the evening, and they were both famished. The ascent became steeper and the carriage moved in a cumbersome, treacherous way, on great waterwheels. She prayed for the horses not to lose their footing.

Beside her Christopher napped, as he often did when a situation felt overwhelming. The road's angle became so sharp that his head fell back and his mouth opened, his thin nose tipped toward the carriage roof.

When they reached the inn at Montepulciano, only one room remained. The manager showed them to an odd corner chamber, hardly larger than its single, narrow cot.

"It won't do for my sister and me both to stay here," Christopher declared, and Erika turned her face away to hide the mirth that rippled her lips. How could anyone really believe them to be brother and sister? They did not resemble each other in the least.

"Surely there are other rooms available in town?" Christopher insisted, flustered. His sealskin coat dripped and water shook from his fingertips.

At such an hour? The inn's manager doubted it. Christopher went out into the rain again and left Erika staring at her water-stained luggage. She removed her cape, suspended it from a hook, and watched a tiny pond form on the floor below the hem.

Twenty minutes later Christopher returned, having found no alternative. The innkeeper dragged in a spare mattress that consumed nearly all the small chamber's floor space.

Erika took a towel from her bag and pressed moisture from her hair with it. "I don't mind at all—really I don't," she told Christopher, but two prongs of irritation appeared between his eyebrows. Clearly he didn't relish the prospect of spending the night on a pallet on the floor.

For their supper the portly innkeeper set down plates filled with long noodles. The aroma of the food improved their mood. The pasta sat pooled in a sweet and sour tomato sauce, thickened by red onions and currants, and flavored by hints of vinegar and red wine. "You have tasted our *vino nobile*?" the innkeeper inquired, and he filled their glasses from a big carafe.

The wine ("the king of Tuscan wines," as the innkeeper called it) moved down their throats like a cleansing fire. Two things made Montepulciano famous, he claimed: its wine, and the grand vistas visible from this mountaintop by day.

The dining room was dim as a cave, with two gas jets like torches against the wall. While they ate, the proprietor told them about his city and its history.

After they'd finished dinner, Christopher opened a window and stuck his head out. The rain had ceased. "Go put on your coat," he called excitedly to Erika. "Don't you want to have a look around at the town?"

At midnight, after so many stormy hours, they found almost no one about on the slick black streets. Together they went out like children, giddy from the wine and the sense that this whole deserted, fortressed town was theirs to explore like a darkened stage.

As they climbed a stone staircase toward the piazza, they saw chasms of blackness between the houses and dripping ivy on walls. On the steps Erika stopped. "Don't you just wonder what's out there?" she asked.

By dawn a landscape of fifty miles would be visible from here. For the moment, darkness obscured the panorama of Tuscany. What exactly lay before them out in that abyss—other than a few lights, which they managed to discern like faraway stars? Were there also rivers, hills, towns, lakes—or endlessly terraced slopes of olive branches and vines?

At the piazza, they felt they'd reached the top of the world. By the glow of streetlamps, they saw that it was all here, surrounding them—the tower of the Palazzo Comunale, the Duomo, a fountain, the Renaissance palace that had once belonged to the Del Monte family. All hers now, and Christopher's—only a backdrop for them.

Perhaps it was the *vino nobile* they'd drunk that made them feel playful and frivolous, or the hope that if her *prova* were a success, their lives might suddenly change. Christopher took a flamboyant leap over a wide puddle. Lifting her skirts, Erika swung around and around until she was dizzy. The pavement glittered where shallow depressions had been filled by water. Moisture seeped into her leather shoes. Her toes grew wet, but she didn't care.

On this night, in this hill town, they were both unknown, and as free as they would ever be. In these silly, capering moments, Erika could almost imagine that it was not Christopher beside her but a lover who had accompanied her to Montepulciano.

Suddenly he reminded her of an off-duty sailor, skipping across the midnight piazza like that, his sealskin coat slapping his calves. "Can you snap your fingers and click your heels together at the same time?" he asked, and jumped high to demonstrate, both legs thrown to one side as his ankles touched midair. Erika laughed. She hoisted her skirt to her knees and tried the same, but landed—*splat*—with her right foot steeped in a puddle.

As their voices reverberated against the gloomy medieval stone façades and she danced in circles, he must have noticed the flirtatiousness in her laugh, and sensed her craving for intimacy.

At the inn that night, Christopher was excruciatingly proper. While she changed into her nightgown, he waited downstairs. When he came up, she lay on her nun-like cot and listened to him remove his boots and wet socks in the darkness. When the sounds ceased, she knew that he planned to sleep in his damp trousers.

"Christopher," she whispered, "haven't you brought any pajamas with you?"

"No," he said. He settled on the floor mattress, a blanket drawn over him.

His trousers had been drenched, she recalled, when she'd mounted the inn's staircase behind him. The wet cuffs of his pants were pasted to his boots.

"Christopher, you can't sleep in those trousers. They're soaked through." His modesty seemed absurd to her.

Discomfort soon got the better of him. She heard a rustling under his blanket as he stripped off the damp trousers and tossed them over a chair, all without exposing his unclothed legs.

A stark square of moonlight shone through the room's one high window. In the dimness Christopher settled on his back, his hair a pale-colored patch against the pillow.

Wordlessly she got up and knelt on the floor beside him. "Would you let me try an experiment?" she asked. "Close your eyes."

Christopher obeyed. His head lolled against the pillow, his arms fixed against his sides.

"Sometimes I try to imagine what the world must be like for my blind landlady. Donna Anna was curious about what I looked like, and she asked if she could touch my face."

"Did you let her?"

"Of course. Would you mind if I did the same to you?"

"All right." He relented.

For the first time in almost three years, she felt the sweetness of placing her hands on another human face. She didn't intend to seduce him, of course—only to play, and continue the lark of the night. She shut her eyes, too, her fingers exploring the contours of his cheeks. He lay completely still. With her index finger, she traced the length of his thin nose. Her thumbs followed his jawbone, and she felt the coarse grit he'd shave away tomorrow. Like a sightless woman she examined his firm lips, the sad pouches under his eyes, until his face became like something sculpted by her own hands.

"That's enough," he said crisply, and flipped onto his side, away from her.

"Sorry," she said. "I didn't mean to annoy you."

"No harm done," he said, "but we both need our sleep."

Like a child chastised, she found her way back to the cot and pushed her bare feet deep under the covers, pulling the sheet as high as her neck.

She had touched his face, wishing it were Ravell's. If only Ravell lay beside her in this odd cell of a room, ready to share her victory or her folly, or whatever her *prova* turned out to be.

❖

Erika sat on a sloping pasture outside Montepulciano's walls, with a writing board resting against her knees. Sheep fed on the hillside grasses as she addressed an envelope to Ravell. The sun was so strong it had dried the ground after the previous night's rain.

She folded a copy of the program that announced her debut and tucked it into the envelope, along with a small photograph of her dressed as Carmen, in ruffles, a shimmering Spanish shawl, and a bodice that cinched her waist. The photo and the program would tell him everything, really—how, on the twenty-third of July, at nine o'clock in the evening, she would sing in full opera regalia from a mountaintop city in Tuscany.

MONTEPULCIANO

R. Teatro Poliziano

Questa sera 23 Luglio 1913 a ore 21 precise
Prima Rappresentazione Straordinaria
dell'opera in quattro atti

CARMEN

di G. BIZET
con i seguenti artisti:

Erika von Kessler
(Carmen)

Edoardo Audia
(Don José) . . .

No need to say anything else.

Still, it did not seem right to moisten the envelope's seal with her tongue and send it off without adding a few words, composed in her own hand.

My dearest Ravell,
As I write to you, I am sitting on a grassy slope in Tuscany, with the ruins of an old castle around me, buried in ivy. Pink geraniums grow out

of the soil where blood was once spilled. The old Castello walls fell in 1232, the year rivals from Siena murdered half the population here.

I live in Italy now, and I send you this program hoping that no matter how far away you may be, you will share the joy of my singing debut in Italy—also known as my prova, my test performance.

Papa has loaned me three hundred lire in order for me to sing in Carmen, the role of my choice. It is not cheap to hire a theatre, an orchestra, and a cast. Papa and my former voice teacher Magdalena wanted to come, of course, but I discouraged them. If the performance is a fiasco, I do not wish them to see it, and if it proves a success, there may be future (paid) engagements for them to witness.

I have so much more to tell you, dearest Ravell, but will do so in another letter. With greatest hopes of hearing your news—

My fondest love,

Erika

❖

Ten piano rehearsals, five rehearsals with full orchestra.

As the night in question grew closer, she fretted over anything that might affect her vocal cords. She tossed a jet of pungent roses from her room. Cigar smoke made her hurry through hallways. To protect herself against filaments of fog, she knotted a white scarf around her throat and covered her mouth and breathed through the scarf's gauzy tail.

❖

The house was full, Christopher reported with glee.

Just before the curtain rose on the evening of July 23, Erika opened her Spanish fan. The night was warm, but at precisely nine o'clock, she waved the fan lightly and a chill of nerves passed over her, like an icy breath against her décolletage.

Applause for the conductor as he marched to his stand. Then a hideous quiet from the draperies' other side. Why, Erika wondered, had she chosen this torture for herself? The morass of possible disasters that awaited her . . . As many dangers as strangers' judgmental faces on the curtain's opposite side. Suppose the lyrics died in her memory? Suppose she opened her mouth to find her voice gone like a ghost? Three times since she had eaten her early supper, she had checked to be sure the voice had not left her.

The overture reassured her with its rousing, festive air. As the curtain swept upward and she waited to make her entrance, a draft cooled her half-nude shoulders, the sleeves of her gypsy dress hardly more than puffs of fabric that clung to her upper arms. *Your aim,* Magdalena used to say, *is to make the audience fall in love with you.* Erika leaned her head far back and swiveled it to lessen the tension in her neck, conscious all the while of her throat, the plush scarlet of the silk flower she carried, her fissured bosom. Herself, exposed.

Nearby, just around a corner where she dared not look, the audience waited like a darkened forest.

"But we don't see La Carmencita!" the soldiers cried.

She made her entrance with the long-stemmed flower in her mouth, with young men surrounding her from all sides, their voices adoring. At their center she rose up like a lick of fire, the highest flame.

She sang the "Habanera," not in the French language of the composer, but in Italian, so that the good people of Montepulciano would understand.

E l'amore uno strano augello . . .   Love is a rebellious bird . . .

As the footlights met her eyes, she shed her old self and *became* Carmen. It was Carmen's golden hairs that glistened on her bare arms, the gypsy girl's nonchalance that roughened the edges of her song. Such gorgeous indifference Bizet had infused into the music. . . . The composer released his heroine's allure like the taunt of a charming, vicious bird. The aria flew out as though it had been caged in Erika's chest, and yes, she realized with certainty—her voice was soaring tonight. She knew the part so well that she did not have to think; she drew breaths and exhaled the purest music.

In that aria she heard herself flying, unattainably, just above the reaches of young men's hearts.

Silence followed the last lyrics. Then a figure shot up from a seat in the audience and shouted, *"Brava, brava!"* The violence of the stranger's cries sent a startled shudder through her. A throng of others rose to their feet, and they made her repeat the aria twice more.

If Italians like your singing, Maestro Valenti said, *they will always let you know.*

She sang like a woman balanced on the blade of a knife, the music keen and seductive. The melodies passed through her as though they had always existed, even before the composer happened to write them down.

When she sang the "Seguidilla," the phrases skipped like sweet laughter around the yearning tenor Don José. More applause followed, along with the thunder of feet so loud that the floor planks shook and she smelled the rising dust. Four curtain calls followed Act I. Her head fell forward and she curtseyed so low that she worried her breasts might fall out of her dress. Tears of gratitude wet her lashes. Finally she was able to get away and hide in her dressing room. How, after that, could she expect to do so well through the rest of the opera?

"Ice water," she begged her voice teacher in a whisper as he met her backstage.

Maestro Valenti quickly brought a crystal pitcher of ice water. He said very little, as overcome as she was. As he poured, Erika noticed that his face was mottled and pink, for he must have been as concerned as she was about how well she would survive the next three acts. He squeezed her shoulder as though to imbue her with courage.

She refused to receive anyone in her dressing room except for her silver-haired voice teacher and Christopher. There, she lost all modesty. Right in front of them, she pushed a handkerchief between her cleaved bosoms and wiped dry the crack of sweat.

You always know if a performance is a triumph, Magdalena used to say, *by the end of the first act.*

Christopher brushed back his hair with excited rakes of his hands, and his forehead shone. "You should have heard the man next to me. He cried out so loud I don't know if I'll be able to hear the rest of the opera through my left ear!"

Erika sank onto a velvet settee, dazed. The ice water flushed coolness into her and strengthened her vocal cords. She caught sight of her underarms in a long mirror on the far wall. During the next acts, she warned herself, she must not lift her arms too high or with too much abandon, particularly as she danced with castanets—or the audience would notice the dark moons of perspiration that stained her dress.

❖

She feared she would not last, but she did.

The "Gypsy Song"? They encored that aria, too, with a mad stomping of feet. Through beams of stage light Erika saw dust showering from the rafters.

When Don José stabbed his beloved Carmen to death at the end, the women of Montepulciano wailed.

The final curtain rose and fell, rose and fell, and rose again. The audience kept her singing half the night, her voice spiraling toward heaven.

❖

Backstage, Maestro Valenti kissed his fingertips and bowed low, and when he straightened up, the moisture in his eyes surprised her. Just behind him was another of his former students, a man who had come up from Naples to play Escamillo and sing the "Toreador Song." The bass-baritone kissed her hard on the mouth and fell back, as though drunk with the taste of her.

Christopher rushed toward her, laughing at her victory, his neck red with emotion, his arms outstretched for an embrace, his ribs bumping hers. Bodies crowded into the dressing room, fans bearing bushy bouquets in both fists. A stranger pushed his way forward, sniffed her bare shoulder, and ran out before she could swat him away. Mark and Edmund had traveled to Montepulciano with Donna Anna; now they formed a protective tunnel so that the blind woman, whom they guided inside, could come close to Erika's ear.

"You sang *divinamente*," the elderly lady whispered with heat. *"Che bellezza!"*

As the room emptied slowly, Maestro Valenti took Erika aside to say, "There is an impresario from Milan here who wishes to speak with you."

Erika turned, aware suddenly of a broad-shouldered gentleman whose silk cravat gave him an air of importance. An impresario from Milan? But why would he come to this obscure performance, in such a small city? A very plump, expensively outfitted lady stood beside him. They reserved their comments until the others had departed.

"May I present Signor Lorello and his wife, Signora Lorello?" Maestro Valenti called loudly, and then, with great sweeps of his arms, her teacher shooed stragglers from the dressing room. He bowed, drew the door shut, and left the two visitors from Milan alone with Erika.

Lorello clasped his hands behind his back, his lips pressed together in a secretive yet pleasant manner. His heavy-set wife was more effusive. "We have heard many Carmens," the signora said, "but never in Italy have we seen anyone who suits the part as beautifully as you." The wife had black hair and currant-colored eyes that glinted in a face of white skin. An overwhelming fragrance of gardenias emanated from her.

"You're too kind," Erika said.

"You have," the impresario noted with a sober expression, *"grandissimo talento."*

"We are on holiday," Signora Lorello explained. "We rarely attend opera in a provincial city like this, but when everyone told us about the new mezzo-soprano—" She smiled. "We realized this might be the exception. We never expected to come to Montepulciano to *discover* someone."

The wife's gaze slid to Erika's waist. "Tell me," Signora Lorello said, "did you diet for the role, or are you naturally so slender?"

"I had to study Spanish dancing for the part. It's wonderful exercise—"

The impresario mentioned the name of a Milan theatre where he assembled opera casts—not La Scala, of course, nor the Teatro Lirico, but Erika knew it to be a reputable place to obtain a contract.

Could she meet with them to talk over breakfast?

Breakfast? Of course, she said.

❖

At the hotel she pinned up her hair, preparing to head downstairs to greet the Lorellos, when she heard a commotion under her window. Three men with rough, untrained voices burst out singing the "Toreador Song," while a little assembly of other citizens waved their arms at her.

"Erika von Kessler!"

"*L'Americana!*"

"*Bellissima Carmen!*"

Erika pulled a bouquet from a vase and threw handfuls of dripping flowers down to them. The Lorellos, who were just stepping into the hotel, paused and glanced up, smiling.

Perfect, Erika thought. *Just the scene for them to witness.*

❖

"I have no agent," Erika said cautiously. "Surely I should find one before I sign anything?"

"We can introduce you to agents," the impresario offered. "We know many in Milan."

His wife's quick currant eyes lingered over Erika's dark curls, the lace cuffs on her lavender dress. "I can tell you one thing," Signora Lorello said. "There is no agent in Milan who would refuse you as a client."

Was she joking? Erika wondered. As the impresario and his wife verbalized the sort of praise Erika had always longed for, their comments sounded oddly false.

"We have in mind an important role for you," the impresario said, "as

Suzuki in *Madama Butterfly*." They warned her that the publishers of Puccini's operas, the managers of the Ricordi company, maintained the right to veto any singer whom they did not care for, should that person be under consideration for a Puccini production. "But in your case"— impresario Lorello relaxed an arm across the back of his chair—"this will present no problem, I am certain."

If Erika came to Milan, the Lorellos said they would present her as a singer of rare ability—as a potential star—to the owners of the theatre where impresario Lorello arranged productions. The Lorellos would press the owners to compensate her handsomely, because such an investment would force them to promote her name.

Erika sensed that the impresario and his wife were not quite as important as they hoped to become. The Lorellos intended to cling to her, to ride her toward future success.

When they finished breakfast, the impresario held the door for the two women, and his wife turned to Erika as they exited. "How unusual," Signora Lorello said with slyness in her eyes, "that a lady so young and beautiful should sing with such fever and passion."

Erika did not want to mention that she was probably older than the signora herself.

51

Milan's Galleria had an enormous glass and steel roof that arched over *caffès* and restaurants and offices and shops. This was a place where singers' tours were conceived, where contracts were signed, where operatic careers were made.

Erika and Christopher strolled past marble-topped tables where opera house managers, conductors, and librettists gathered. The Lorellos were due to arrive shortly. Two months ago, Erika thought, no one in the Galleria would have noticed or spoken to her. A striped cat slinking under a table or a waiter would have attracted more attention than she did.

If she'd come here then, if she'd thrown back her head and sung upward at the Galleria's glass roof, no one would have listened. The business people of the opera world would have gone on spreading pages of proposals across circular marble tables, and ignored her. Hands would have gone on scribbling contracts. Once signed, the pages would have been folded up—just as she saw happening now—and tucked into breast pockets as carefully as money.

But today an impresario expected to meet with her, to hire her.

Suddenly Signora Lorello hurried toward them, just ahead of her husband. The loose ruffled dress she wore to hide her corpulence swung wildly around her body, and she could not stifle her excitement.

"Pietro Palladino is here," she announced, seizing Erika's arm. "My husband and I have just spoken to him." Pietro Palladino was an agent, it seemed. "In the past he has handled tours for Caruso. Come," Si-

338

gnora Lorello insisted, hooking her fingers through Erika's, "you must meet him."

"Like this?" Erika glanced down at her plain gray traveling clothes.

"Yes! Just come." The signora beckoned Christopher as well. "You come, too."

At a corner table sat a large man with an extravagant moustache. Behind his table, an enormous potted palm fanned to the left and right of him. This corner of the Galleria seemed to be reserved for Pietro Palladino, the place he often held court at midday. Flanked by two charcoal-suited assistants, the agent sat like a man enthroned.

A river of men circulated around him. One bent and spoke into his right ear, while another slapped Pietro Palladino's left shoulder before moving on. Others tipped their hat brims and waved to the agent in passing, and he laughed and called out to them in man-to-man jocularity.

As Erika approached, he stood up—a tall, stately man. The edges of his lapels were carefully pressed. "The Lorellos have been so enthusiastic," he said, smiling. "I must say I look forward to hearing you sing."

One felt quick intelligence in Pietro Palladino's glance, in the penetration of his eyes. The Lorellos and Erika and Christopher settled into chairs that the assistants pulled out for them. After ordering desserts and cups of bitter-tasting *Americanos* for them, the pair of lackeys withdrew.

While Pietro Palladino questioned Erika politely about her *prova*, Christopher bit into the creamy layers of a pastry. His nostrils flared in jest and he made big eyes at her from across the table, as though to say: *Can you believe that we are actually sitting here?*

The agent invited them all to come to his apartment for light refreshments. He wanted Erika to sing for him.

"We leave for New York in ten days," Signora Lorello reminded everyone. "We'd love to have everything settled before then. I loathe the anxiety of waiting."

"*She* loathes the anxiety," Christopher said later, laughing.

Pietro Palladino's apartment consisted of the entire top floor of a palatial building not far from La Scala. The arched doorways and ceilings were so high that Erika felt she ought to be riding a carriage, not walking, through such rooms. The vast spaces made her feel dwarfed, inadequate.

Pietro Palladino led them to a smaller, more intimate sitting room that contained a grand piano. An assistant closed the glass balcony doors to shut out the noise of traffic from Milan's streets.

A maid brought in platters of white grapes and Gorgonzola, green and potent, and a rectangle of mascarpone to spread across bread like butter. Erika ignored the food, but Signora Lorello took a full plate onto her lap and relaxed against an antique chair. Her husband sat in an antique chair, too, and he cupped his palms confidently over one knee.

Before the little audition began, Pietro Palladino poured tastes of a black grape juice he loved. Erika did not sip from her glass, because she did not want to discolor her teeth just before she sang.

When Christopher went to the piano to accompany her, he turned as pale as his shirt. Erika sent a twist of a smile in his direction, as if to say: *My poor boy, why be nervous now?*

The pair of assistants in dark suits lounged against a peach-colored sofa, ready to render their judgments. The impresario's wife grinned encouragingly at Erika. As the first aria began, Signora Lorello licked her lower lip, and her currant eyes shone.

No matter what the celebrated agent decided to do, the Lorellos intended to hire her, and the certainty of her position made Erika confident. She sang "Una voce poco fa," followed by the "Seguidilla"—both nearly flawlessly. What agent could fail to be influenced by the Lorellos, who lifted their faces toward her as if transfixed?

("A lovely-looking lady, don't you think?" Erika had overheard Signora Lorello murmur to the agent as they were being ushered down a hallway to this sitting room.)

When the last vibrations of song dissolved into silence, Pietro Palladino and his assistants excused themselves and stepped outside into a hallway. After a moment, the famous man returned, smiling, and he bent to kiss her hand. "Yes, yes. Definitely yes," he said. "We want to represent you. We must represent you."

The following day in the Galleria, Erika signed a contract with Pietro Palladino. From adjacent tables, men with thinning hair watched and smiled, expecting to soon learn who she was. Long ago her vocal teacher, Maestro Valenti, had told her: *An impresario hires you to sing in a certain operatic production, but it is the agent who will protect you and shape your career. If an impresario does not treat a singer well, a brilliant agent will simply take you elsewhere.*

"I have never dealt with the Lorellos before," Pietro Palladino said, "but their enthusiasm, their willingness to champion you—this is a crucial thing."

His underlings stood behind the fanning screen of a great palm while he spoke with her. "If we don't like the offer that the Lorellos make," Pietro Palladino said, "I have some ideas about where we might go for a better sum." To what other cities might he lead her, Erika wondered— Brescia, Modena, Rome, perhaps? The unseen entrées this powerful agent might provide were beyond her knowing.

She sent a letter to her master teacher in Florence, telling him that she had signed an agreement with one of Milan's most illustrious agents. Maestro Valenti wrote back, "Every student who has a *prova* dreams of this. Such a victory comes to few!"

❖

The Lorellos had assured the agent that Erika's audition before the other opera house managers and Puccini's publishers would take place within a few days.

The delay was fortuitous because Erika knew she would need every hour between now and then to refresh her knowledge of *Madama Butterfly*. Her one qualm during all of this, which she had shared with no one except Christopher, was that she had always disliked Puccini's modern music and preferred old-fashioned *bel canto* roles. But who could be choosy? She had been trained to sing different styles, and sing she would.

The Lorellos had booked a suite of rooms for Erika and her accompanist at a hotel where operatic performers frequently stayed. The dense walls made the rooms as sound-resistant as caves. Each suite had a piano with a vase of flowers.

"I can't believe this is all really happening," Christopher said. "I've known so many opera students, and I've never seen this happen to anyone."

At twilight Christopher raised a foot and hoisted himself up onto the sill of a window so tall that he actually stood up in it. Framed against the evening coolness, he looked as if he might stretch out his hand and touch constellations that were just beginning to show. "You're the chosen one among thousands! You're the example that will give rise to people's dreams."

She had never seen him so jubilant. A breeze lifted his tie. He clutched either side of the window frame and rocked forward, ready to fly.

"A thousand lire per night—that's what they'll offer you!" he said, laughing.

"Be careful," she said. "If you fall out, our good luck will end."

❖

"I loathe the music I am going to sing," she told Christopher. "Surely they will hear that in my voice. I can hear it." On the morning of her audition, Erika was convinced that it would be a fiasco.

"Where is the actress in you?" he argued. "Put yourself in a trance and fall in love with Puccini, at least for today."

Just before her audition, the nearly deserted opera house smelled of cold, dead smoke. It was a huge theatre, though not as celebrated as the Teatro Lirico or La Scala. Two rows of men had come to hear her. In their demeanor Erika detected harshness, a consciousness of exactly how many seats had gone unsold at their most recent productions. She could not discern who among them represented Ricordi—Puccini's music publishers—and which ones owned the opera house. Their faces had the blankness of morticians.

The opera house at Montepulciano had been of more modest dimensions. Here, huge, sprawling balconies rose like terraces toward the gilded ceiling. She sensed the weight of echoing, invisible places, corners where seats ranged that she could not even see. To expect her talent to fill this entire space, and stir every particle of air with vibrations of sound!

Impresario Lorello and his wife appeared nervous as well. Signora Lorello wore an ice-blue satin gown meant for evening and looked overdressed. She fidgeted and flashed her rings, her fingers like fat little sausages choked off at the knuckles by silver bands. The impresario stood with hands clasped behind him. Did he ever venture anywhere without his fussy, beribboned wife?

The Lorellos, Erika had come to realize, were the newcomers here, their uneasy smiles betraying their longing to please. Just two years ago, Lorello had managed an opera house in an Italian city so minor that Erika had never heard of it.

The hall was dark, the men in dark suits ready to listen.

Why could she not vocalize a few arias of her choice? Why not "Una voce poco fa" or "Habanera"? If they heard her do those, they would realize the diva she was capable of becoming.

But no. The Ricordi publishers were here to assess what she would do to their precious Puccini.

Of the ten people present, surely only she had the awful, coppery taste of anxiety in her mouth. She felt as if she had sucked on a filthy penny. Only she had to sing, of course. The others were merely expected to utter an opinion.

Christopher positioned himself at the piano. She had been wrong about one thing: she was not the only one suffering. On his stool he sat cane-straight, and his torso lengthened as it always did when he was on edge, his neck so thin that he looked hungry. He shot her a smile that twitched.

Out it came, then—Suzuki's first phrases from *Madama Butterfly*. Erika's true voice fled like a frightened cat through a hole in a fence; what was left, what they heard, she could hardly guess at. Erika dropped her eyelids for a second, wanting someone to wake her after she had gotten to the end of it. After this, more singing from other scenes—just as bad.

Before any objection could be interjected, she announced, "I am going to sing "Una voce poco fa," and she launched into Rossini to save herself.

She walked out knowing that she had done badly, though Christopher assured her that the Puccini had been passable, and the Rossini ravishing.

❖

Silence for three days thereafter. "How long can they expect us to sit around at this exorbitantly priced hotel, waiting for their verdict?" Christopher said. The Lorellos had recommended these accommodations, though no one had volunteered to shoulder the bill for them.

To distract themselves, they crossed the square in front of the Duomo, admiring the variously colored tiles in the pavement. They studied the cathedral's marble belfries, gables, and pinnacles. They discovered a restaurant where espresso was priced nearly as modestly as water, where they whiled away the afternoon reading Milanese newspapers. Not once during those three days did they venture into the Galleria's glass-roofed arcade, so as to avoid seeing anyone from the opera industry.

At last a summons came in the form of a note from Pietro Palladino. He was lunching on *risotto alla certosina* in the Galleria when they arrived. Though they declined his offer to join him for a plate of rice with crayfish, mushrooms, and peas, he insisted that they eat something. His assistants ordered them *panettone*—a fluffy currant cake—and the pair of underlings distanced themselves.

Pietro Palladino turned to Erika in a measured way. "It seems—" he said, "that impresario Lorello and his wife have changed their minds about casting you in *Madama Butterfly*. Instead, they've offered you a

344

booking for a recital." The agent mentioned the sum they planned to pay her—a meager fee.

Erika glanced across the table at Christopher, who pressed the tines of his fork aimlessly against the cake crumbs on his plate, his face devoid of expression. To the agent she said, "So what would you advise me to do? Accept their offer?"

Pietro Palladino sipped his water and patted his moustache with his napkin before answering. "You're a gifted singer just beginning her career," he said with great seriousness, "and everything must be handled very carefully."

Did he honestly admire her voice? Erika wondered. Or had he been fooled by the Lorellos, whose effusions had died the more they heard her sing?

"I suppose I should take it," she said. "I don't want to quibble over money."

The agent nodded. He appeared tired, and his oversize shoulders no longer looked so powerful to her.

He drew a gold watch from his pocket and peered into it like a polished mirror. "The Lorellos will be here in about fifteen minutes to speak with you," Pietro Palladino said, and stood up. "Unfortunately, I have an appointment myself at the Teatro Lirico. Stay at this table for as long as you like. I've reserved it for all of you."

"What shall I say to Signor and Signora Lorello?" Erika asked.

"Tell them you'll think about their proposal over the weekend and respond on Monday."

After the agent departed, she and Christopher remained at the table. The previous day, Christopher had his hair cut. An unskilled barber had left his hair too short, in bludgeoned, uneven shingles. Why did the bad haircut pain her so? With too much hair snipped off, he looked skinnier, weaker. She could hardly bear to look at him.

"Shall I meet you back here in an hour?" Christopher said. "Perhaps you'd like a little privacy with the Lorellos?"

"Don't leave me alone with them," she begged.

A slate-gray poodle jumped from Signora Lorello's arms as she and her husband strode up; the little dog went straight under their table and rested there as though the pet were accustomed to being encircled by people's shoes. Why had the impresario's wife brought her pet dog to the Galleria? To relieve the unpleasantness of such a meeting?

"After the way we acted in Montepulciano," Signora Lorello began, "we find it very difficult to say certain things to you." Her upper and lower teeth met in a neat, even line, and she smiled so hard her eyes slitted.

"We are candid people," her husband said. "We must be truthful with you."

Erika waited, her neck rigid.

"We are concerned," Signora Lorello said, "that you simply do not have the stamina to endure a long performance."

Christopher uncrossed his legs. "How can you say such a thing?" he demanded. "You, who heard her vocalize for a whole night straight at Montepulciano?" He moved so suddenly that Signora Lorello's poodle, which had been resting like a fluffy slipper against his foot, was roused and began to bark.

Signora Lorello gathered the poodle into her lap. Her eyes cut toward Christopher, then away from him.

"You have a lustrous voice," Signora Lorello assured Erika. "With luck, if we choose your repertoire correctly—you'll give a nice little recital."

Did they care for her talent at all anymore, Erika wondered, or had they simply trapped themselves into offering her *something*? Certainly they did not want to appear unreliable in Pietro Palladino's eyes.

"We're just as enthusiastic about your future as we were at Montepulciano," Signora Lorello insisted.

"Are you?" Erika said coldly. It was a bad tone to have used. "What did you think of the Rossini—my version of 'Una voce poco fa'?"

"It was lovely," the impresario admitted.

"Certain *passaggio* problems," his wife added.

"That's ridiculous," Christopher said bitterly.

The impresario's wife cast him a look that begged for a waiter to clear him from their presence like a soiled plate.

"Listen," she snapped finally at Erika, "do you want to be a singer or not?"

Erika told them she would consider the proposed recital, and let them know her decision on Monday.

❖

By Monday morning Erika had convinced herself that she must be humble and not arrogant; she must do the recital for them, of course. After Christopher had headed off to a *caffè* to enjoy an espresso and a newspaper, she finished her toilette, and prepared to call Pietro Palladino. *Accept their offer,* she would tell him.

Erika had just fastened the last hook of her white dress when she heard a brusque whack on the door. Signora Lorello strode into the hotel suite, and the tails of her sash flew around her like whips. It was the first instance Erika had ever seen her alone.

"Signora von Kessler—" The impresario's wife's tone was harsh. "My husband and I have thought about it all weekend, and we do not wish to engage you for any performance. We're uncomfortable working with a person like you."

Erika heard a plea escape from her throat. "Please don't say this. Please! Just listen to me." She gestured for the impresario's wife to be seated in a gilded chair carved with cherubim. The woman sat, while Erika took a similar chair nearby.

"I was ill on the day of my audition at your opera house," Erika said. "Besides, my voice is not suited to Puccini. Believe me, if you hire me to sing the music of a different composer—"

"Your ambitions are far grander than your voice," the signora said.

"I tell you, I can do better on another day." Erika knew she had fallen to begging now.

"We don't wish to work with a singer who brings her silly young boy-friend along to defend her."

Erika decided to ignore this.

The plump woman slid her hips to the edge of the chair, preparing to leave. When she spoke, her syllables were hard. "You can say what you like, but your voice is not smooth across the three registers. Your top notes are faked, metallic! No amount of study or rehearsals can resolve that."

Behind this Erika heard the ugly concurrence of a whole committee. She had humiliated the Lorellos before their associates; she saw that in the tiny muscles that tightened bitterly around Signora Lorello's eyes.

Signora Lorello got up. "I will tell Pietro Palladino." She announced this as if it were the last dreaded task that remained.

Erika gave a soft wail—a plaintive sound she had not made since she was a child.

The impresario's wife hastened to the door, pulled it open, and fled.

After she left, Erika dropped onto the divan. Inside her came a hardening. For months, for years now, she had figured: if my *prova* fails, if all my sacrifice and training come to nothing, I will throw myself from a high tower, or the roof of the Duomo.

But now she thought: *Who would commit suicide for the sake of such a flighty, silly woman?*

For an hour she remained on the gray divan and waited for the thing that would surely happen next. A messenger from the agent's office would knock on the door to inform her that the great man had abandoned her, too.

Instead, the telephone rang. Pietro Palladino's voice came on the line, sounding soothing and assured and paternal. The decency and fairness in his response surprised her. "Well," he said, "*I* love your voice and *I* want to find a good home for your talent at a fine opera house."

Over the weekend, the agent confided, he had learned that Erika had not been the first singer to whom Signora Lorello had made extravagant promises that were later forgotten. "Her infatuations," the agent observed, "extinguish themselves as rapidly as they ignite.

"I've already sent my courier to deliver a letter to another impresario," he added. "We'll march onward, and arrange other auditions for you."

But Erika worried that Signora Lorello had spoken the truth. Perhaps her own aspirations reached far beyond where her voice could carry her.

52

Everyone in her neighborhood—the fruit vendor at the corner stand, her blind landlady, the new charwoman on the stairs—all of them were curious about what had happened in Milan. Would she now sing from grand stages? Each time Erika shared the disappointing news, she felt even more depressed.

Thus far, her famous agent had found her nothing. He was trying, that she knew, but it was not easy to sell an obscure mezzo-soprano. Opera house managers preferred vocalists whose names were securely familiar. Pietro Palladino had tried a little bargaining with impresarios, telling them that he would let them have a certain well-known baritone they coveted if they would agree to hear his new mezzo-soprano. Auditions were scheduled; Erika traveled to small cities to sing before coveys of men who smelled of cigars and old creased bills passed from wallet to wallet.

In the end, only one hired her—as an understudy for the leading role in *La Cenerentola*. An understudy must be present always—at every rehearsal, every performance, ready to glide onto the stage at any moment. Erika tried not to lurk, and tried to remain unobtrusive, but the prima donna glared at her during rehearsal one day and pointed a finger and shouted, "She'll bring me bad luck. Get her out of here! I don't want to lay eyes on her again." The singer was famous, and she shuddered with such distress that everyone rushed to calm her.

After only three days, Erika was dismissed and sent back to Florence.

Sometimes in the streets, or at a *caffè* on the Via Tornabuoni, she encountered one of Maestro Valenti's other students, who would inevitably inquire if her illustrious Milan agent had yet found her a booking. If she noticed one of these students from afar, she ducked her head over her cappuccino or turned inside a shop to hide.

"You need a vacation from all of this," Christopher remarked as they were strolling over a bridge that crossed the Arno. "It's a pity you can't simply get away." He sucked the last juicy threads from a peach stone, and with a grunt of satisfaction, he took the clean pit from his mouth and tossed it from the bridge.

To cheer her, Mark and Edmund invited her along to Miss Maude's English Tea Room. "This is the only place in Florence where scones can be had," Mark said, opening a menu. "And the equivalent of Devon cream."

"I never cared much for Devon cream," Erika said.

"Not the sort of thing one comes to Florence to sample." Mark caught sight of his reflection mirrored in the window, and his gaze lingered there as he studied his own smart looks. Legs crossed, he stroked his trousered thigh almost lovingly, and bobbed his foot.

Erika described to them how, for months, she had been approaching each new audition with senseless hope, preparing for it for days. Past disappointments hardly mattered, she tried to persuade herself—only reaching for the next opportunity.

The men had already wearied of her angst, she knew, and now that weeks and months had gone by, they barely listened. A slim-hipped waiter brushed past their table and Mark and Edmund stared after him.

"Another bugger," Mark said. "Like us."

"Nice-looking," Edmund nodded.

"Take him." Mark winked at Edmund. "He's all yours."

"I am running out of chances," she cried to Christopher upon returning from yet another failed audition. She worried that before long, Pietro Palladino would give up on her and quietly cease his efforts on her behalf.

Her anguish grew so extravagant that Christopher bent under it, as if her gloom were a whip hitting him. One day he ran out of her room saying, "What is the point of talking? Nothing I say ever cheers you."

Erika leaned her head over her third-story balcony and called to him in the street. He pretended not to know his own name. In his unpolished shoes he rushed along the Lungarno Acciaiuoli and disappeared into a tunnel of tourists buying fruit. She picked up an embroidered cushion and crushed her face into it.

"Why didn't you answer?" she asked later, painfully.

Softly he replied, "Because I didn't hear you." But she knew otherwise.

❖

A postman pulled the bell one morning. When Erika peered down from the balcony, he called out that she must sign for a registered letter. Her feet tripped down three flights, and her heart flew with the silly, impossible hope that an opera house manager had reconsidered and written to Pietro Palladino. Perhaps she was running toward the news that would save her.

She wondered, too, if the slow mail that crossed oceans might have finally brought Ravell's response to the letter she had sent.

As she scratched her signature on the postman's pink receipt, she saw that the large envelope had been sent from the States, from the Suffolk County Courthouse in Boston. She passed the new charwoman in the foyer, a rough, unpleasant woman who twisted her washrag and gave long, suspicious stares whenever Christopher or Mark or Edmund ascended for a visit to Erika's room.

The legal document notified her that three years had passed since she had "willfully and utterly" deserted her husband. Peter's petition to divorce her had been finalized; custody of their one minor child had been granted to him.

It was hardly a surprise, but it saddened her. It marked a kind of death. Finally, irrevocably, her marriage was over; her son was gone.

She recalled what her brother, Gerald, had recently written to her:

Quentin, it seems, is spending his summer on Cape Cod while his father is away traveling in England. The wife of Peter's business partner—mother to a large brood—has decided to take on Quentin as a kind of foster child.

Why did her brother feel the compulsion to tell her this?

If she threw her capes, dresses, slippers, and opera scores into a pile of trunks and went back to Boston, the court would not allow her near Quentin again—not without permission, not with any ease. She could approach her former door and hammer with the brass knocker, but if the servants peeked out and saw her on the step, they'd probably let the window drape fall. No doubt they'd been warned against opening the door to her.

The court did not know about her and Ravell, how their bodies had made that little boy, how Quentin belonged to them as much as to Peter.

She read the documents thoroughly, and then placed them at the bottom of a drawer. No judge knew how strangely exquisite Quentin had looked to her when he'd been ill with diphtheria, during those nights when she held him and whispered prayers into his sleeping face. Very softly she'd parted her lips and blown cool air across his feverish forehead, scattering his fine dark hair (*Ravell's hair!*). *Let him live*, she'd prayed.

On the afternoon that Erika received the divorce papers, she walked for miles through Florence, covering much of the city.

She went to the Piazza della Santissima Annunziata, and stood before the Hospital of the Innocents. Over centuries, until just thirty or forty years earlier, mothers had come here, shawls over their heads to obscure their faces, carrying infants in their arms. Some had hesitated, and turned back. Some had rushed boldly—desperately—forward before they could change their minds.

Erika glanced up above the nine arches where terra-cotta medallions pictured babies in swaddling clothes, their plump, outstretched arms imploring their mothers not to desert them.

She saw the window that framed the special wheel—the *ruota*—where mothers placed their infants, and with a spin, passed them anonymously to a stranger's care on the wall's other side.

And she thought: *Where are they now, those ghostly mothers who came here in centuries past?* At this hour she was the only woman who stood staring at the *ruota,* but she felt the spirits of those other mothers around her. Many of them, like her, must have returned here, sorrowful and regretting what they'd done.

❖

The charwoman eyed Erika with wrath not long after Christopher paid a call to her room. Erika had gone out for lunch and come back. As she tiptoed up the cascade of freshly washed steps toward her room, lifting her skirts and smiling an apology for the spots her shoes might leave, the servant stopped her.

Holding a string mop aloft, letting it drip rivulets into a bucket, the charwoman said, "People tell Donna Anna the kind of woman you are, but she doesn't listen. She is old and blind and she will stand for the worst, just to have a singer around to listen to.

"Your singing," the servant said, "has gotten worse."

❖

"Dreadful woman," Donna Anna said. "I will give her notice."

A driver brought Donna Anna's motorcar around and chauffeured them into the hills behind Florence. Erika and the landlady sat at the rear, swathed in tulle and veiled in chiffon to keep the dust away.

They parked at a curve overlooking a villa nestled in a dip of land. Soft hillsides ringed the house, and as they sat in the open-air automobile, Erika described the view of it to Donna Anna—the villa's red-tiled roof and the walled gardens. Box hedges defined the estate's perimeter, and stone benches stood in shady corners where the dark earth remained moist. Erika loosened her veils while a breeze toyed with the ends, blowing the chiffon tails.

Donna Anna lifted her nose and sniffed. "Jasmine," the old lady said, before Erika even noticed the hedge ornamented with white petals.

"I wonder what it would be like to live in a villa like that," Erika said. From their aerial perspective, she could see a glass-roofed courtyard where a fountain gushed and oleanders bloomed. She described it all to Donna Anna.

"That sort of house is usually filled with tapestried chairs and tapestried fire screens," the old lady said. "And the doors are locked by great iron bars at night."

As they motored farther, Donna Anna tilted her face to the sky, absorbing the sunlight and rush of wind across her skin. *Look at her,* Erika thought, *alive to every pleasure, while my ambition cripples me.*

"You were not wrong to come to Italy," the old lady said. "Not with talent like yours. It would be against God's wishes not to try to bring that voice before the world."

"Sometimes I feel that God is against me," Erika responded. Why had she been blessed with a gift, if upon every attempt to release sounds from her throat, the world silenced her?

The chauffeur stopped the car at an overlook. They got out and sat on a stone bench to view the panorama of Florence with its Duomo and tiled rooftops.

Erika said, "I've cast away everything. I have nothing now."

Donna Anna said, "You have money saved, don't you? Christopher is right—you should take yourself on a journey, get away."

A letter finally came—the very letter she'd most longed to receive. When she saw Ravell's handwriting on the envelope, she mounted the stairs with haste, and sat by the window and held it in her hands for a long while before opening it. It was a reply to the one she'd sent, just before her *prova*. Mail moved slowly across the seas, his words seven weeks old by the time she read them:

> *My dearest Erika,*
>
> *You have never been gone from my thoughts since you left Trinidad eight years ago, and it gave me deep joy to receive your letter.*
>
> *By now you must know whether your operatic debut has turned out to be a victory or a disappointment (the former, I suspect). One thing is certain: you moved to Florence for the sake of your passion, and few have lived as fearlessly and vividly as you. . . .*
>
> *Perhaps you know that Peter and I traveled to British Guiana earlier this year. Due to a severe drought, we never reached the Kaieteur Falls, as was our plan. The journey was memorable nevertheless. Peter told me about your son and showed me his photograph. Quentin is a handsome boy, and I was deeply moved and happy to know about him. It would mean everything to me to meet him.*
>
> *I long for the day when we'll see each other again, and I wish you every good fortune on the opera stages of Italy.*
>
> > *With greatest love,*
> > *Ravell*

After rereading the letter several times, she took a vial of musk from a drawer. It was almost Christmas, and she'd bought the little bottle as a holiday present for Christopher. Now she uncapped it. Musk was the scent Ravell used to slap on his jaw after shaving. With the vial drawn close to her nose, it seemed to her that his jawbone was within the reach of her own fingers.

She screwed the glass bottle shut, and then uncapped it a second time. When she inhaled, it was as if she had drawn him into her body again. Her head went light. She closed the vial's cap to stop the swoon.

After finishing her supper, she took a hot bath and hung up her robe. She pulled a long, translucent nightgown over her head and reached for her jar of Glycerine and Rosewater, spreading cream onto her hands.

When he was still a toddler, Quentin used to stand close to her, his tummy pushed against her leg while she sat at her vanity table. He had watched her rub the white cream into her skin until the iridescence vanished. "This makes Mama's hands soft," she had explained. When she held out her hands, her son had put his nose against her knuckles to sniff. She daubed a bit of Glycerine and Rosewater onto his arm and he rubbed and stared, fascinated, as it disappeared.

Often at night when she unscrewed the jar, out came Quentin, like a genie appearing in the fragrant vapors.

Now it was Christmas, and she was alone. Every person who had mattered deeply to her, she had deserted. *Utterly and willfully,* the court papers said. None of them had ever entered this building overlooking the river, or seen this room where she lived.

And yet they were here with her, all of them. She was in Florence, in Tuscany, but if she uncapped a vial or unscrewed a jar of hand cream, two of them in particular floated into the room—Ravell and Quentin, a mirage of them in the scents.

She lit a lamp and sat at a table and wrote to Ravell, picturing him as he unsealed the letter at a coconut plantation, far away.

My dearest Ravell,
  . . . No matter what the law may prevent me from doing, I intend to see my son again. I will steal him if necessary, and before long I am going to bring him to meet you. . . .

PART EIGHT

53

S he stood at the iron gates of her son's school, uncertain as she pushed the grille open if the directors of the Chadsworth School would allow her near him.

"Family visits normally occur on Sundays," the secretary said. Three pearl buttons fastened her dress shut at midthroat.

This was a Tuesday, as Erika well knew. In the long window behind the secretary's desk, snow flurried like white moths melting against black branches, leaving no mark on the frozen ground.

"The headmaster is not in his office," the woman said. "Perhaps he's in another building. Why don't you have a seat in the parlor while I check to see if an exception can be made?"

From the parlor window Erika watched boys in knickers playing football in a distant field. If she stood at the spiked iron fence, close to them, would one boy in the pack look up, recognize her, and stop hurling the ball? But the swarm of boys appeared too old—they were eleven, perhaps, and Quentin was not yet nine.

She settled into a chair. While waiting, Erika removed a long glove and examined the sparkle of her amethyst ring. She reminded herself not to rush at him, or clutch him too desperately. On her lap rested a box of dried apricots glazed in bittersweet chocolate. After more than three years, Erika hoped they remained his favorite.

And his face . . . at eight and a half years of age, how changed would his face be? In height he might reach her chest by now.

The wait continued so long that Erika grew curious about the great building she stood inside, so she took a few steps into the long, vacant corridor. The place was reminiscent of a small castle, with its turrets and unseen wings. Doors at one end opened to a dark, beamed dining hall, and an aroma of boiled potatoes wafted through the hallway.

From down a stairwell she suddenly heard a horrible shriek. Another scream sounded like a plea for someone to come. As she raced down the steps, her heart hurt in fear of what she would find. Why—it made no sense—but why did she think she might find her own son there?

"Off with them!" Down a basement corridor a *"THWACK!"* resounded—the echo of a cane struck once, for practice, against a massive desktop. "Drop them. To the ankles!" As Erika headed toward an open door, she saw a stick slice the air. A boy's yelps took bites from her heart.

When she reached the basement room, the master had his back turned to her. The man thrashed fast and with such vigor that the victim hardly had a pause to cry out between blows. The boy was very small, his hair rust-colored, his face and bare calves freckled. His shirttail quivered, and his naked backside and legs were already striped red. To protect his buttocks, the boy's hands flew to cover them. Then his hands flinched away in order not to be stung, too. Before the next impact came, his feet did a strange, twitchy dance to shy away from the blow. Knowing the master would be incensed if he missed, the boy sidestepped only a few inches left or right.

"Don't you think that's enough?" Erika said loudly.

The master wheeled around, his lower lip wet, agleam, a relish for the task brightening his eyes before his cane faltered. He was a burly man with a ginger moustache. At the sight of Erika, he reddened from his neck to the top of his hairless head.

As the boy spun around, his small penis shook beneath his shirttail. Instinctively, he cupped his hands to hide his privates.

The man put down the cane and dismissed the boy. While Erika continued to stand there, the child dressed hastily and picked up a satchel of books and exited from the basement through a side door.

Without saying another word to the man, she followed the boy. Outdoors in the frigid air, the boy did not seem aware that she walked behind him. He sniveled, rubbing his knuckles against his nose.

"Darling," she called out, "I have something for you." She folded her skirt carefully over her knees as she squatted down beside the child. Then she opened the box of chocolate-covered apricots she had brought for Quentin and handed a few to the boy.

"I'm not permitted to have any candy," he said, lowering his head.

"Take them," she said. "Take two right now and eat them while I'm standing here."

He obeyed. He chewed and wiped the mucus from his face with the dark blue sleeve of his school jacket.

"What's your name?"

"Oliver Madsen."

"Where do your parents live?"

"In Chestnut Hill."

The February air felt fierce and wonderfully cold on their faces after the heat of what had happened. She slipped him another candy and let him go.

When she returned to the main building, she went directly to the office. The secretary with the pearl buttons raised her head and said, "The Headmaster is back. He'll see you now."

The man in the basement had worn a shirt with the sleeves rolled up, but when she entered the Headmaster's office she encountered the same man wearing a tweed suit jacket, his suspenders nicely covered up. He looked taken aback when she entered, and he tidied his ginger moustache with his fingers before he spoke.

"Mrs. von Kessler?" He did not sit behind his desk. He stood. "According to our files, you no longer have custody of Quentin."

"I'm not asking for custody. I am his mother, and I wish to visit him."

"Is the boy's father aware that you've come here?"

"As you may know, Quentin's father is an importer. He happens to be away in England at the present time. I'm asking for only a little time alone with my son in the school parlor, and a short stroll around the school grounds with him."

The Headmaster clasped his hands behind his back, his tone sharpening. "Do you have the court's permission to see the boy?"

Erika strode over to the window and reflected for a moment, and then she turned to the Headmaster, her wrists firmly crossed. "It would be most unfortunate for you, sir, if young Oliver Madsen's parents over in Chestnut Hill were informed—in the greatest detail—about the scene I just witnessed downstairs."

He reddened again, from the edge of his collar to the curve of his balding crown.

She plucked at the fingertips of her long gloves, and pulled the gloves tighter at the elbows, straightening them.

"I'm sure it won't take long to locate Quentin," she said.

❖

When they brought her son into the parlor, Erika did exactly what she had vowed not to do—she leaped at him too quickly. At first sight he looked strange to her, not as sweetly plump in the neck or limbs as she remembered. But his eyes, hooded by his dark eyebrows, stared at her with a familiar seriousness, like Ravell's. As she thrust her fingers into the thick wings of his dark hair and kissed his forehead, he stepped back and stood numb. Her heart dipped, and she opened the box of chocolate-glazed apricots and apologized for the few that were missing, though she did not explain what had happened to them.

"It must be quite a surprise for you—seeing me," Erika said brightly. She patted the brocade cushion of the settee so he would sit beside her.

"Why are you here?" Quentin asked. He moved stiffly, the mistrust evident in him.

"To visit." She leaned toward him and straightened his tie. "Because I've missed you and wanted to see you."

"Did Father send you?"

She noticed that he called Peter "Father" now, not "Papa," as he used to. "Your father," she said drily, "has no idea I'm here."

Quentin drew back his chin to show his unease. Erika closed the parlor door and slid closer to him. She glanced at his wrists and knuckles and searched for any bruises or discolorations a long stick might have made. "Quentin," she said solemnly, "don't be afraid to answer me truthfully. Have you ever been punished here at school?" She paused. "Physically, I mean? With cruelty?"

Quentin looked baffled. He did not appear to understand what she was alluding to. After he had eaten several candies and licked the chocolate from his fingers, she suggested that they take a stroll around the grounds and tour the Chadsworth School. They passed the playing field, where Quentin's gaze turned toward boys in heavy sweaters and knickers, all tumbling in a muddy heap around a football. He watched them with more interest than he showed in her.

"I'll be staying in Boston for a while," Erika said. "Next time you visit Grandpapa, maybe I'll see you there."

Quentin halted. He bent down in the cobblestone driveway and retied his shoe. "I don't think Father would be happy about that. I think he'd be angry to know you came here."

"I *am* your mother," she said firmly. "It's natural for me to visit you." She asked if she might see his room.

"I don't have a room," he said, "just an alcove—which I like better."

"Your alcove, then?"

Her son guided her into a dormitory where walnut wainscoting darkened the hallways. Quentin put one hand on the oiled banister and faltered. "I don't know if you are allowed."

"Are boys up there now?"

"No. They're doing their lessons before supper."

At her prodding, he showed her upstairs. The youngest boys, who were only six or seven, slept on a dozen beds in a dormitory room that lacked ventilation, its dark green shades depressingly drawn in the late afternoon.

She felt faint passing through it. A staircase almost as narrow as her hips led upward to a third story resplendent with light, even on this February day. A ring of windows opened to treetops—the branches stark now, but she imagined thickets of leaves would grow upon them in the spring.

His alcove was there, and she understood why he liked it: the small space was his alone, with no roommate crowding him. Its tiny window pointed in a Gothic arch. The alcove had a bookcase recessed into one wall where he kept his collection of lead soldiers. Quentin had made his bed so carefully that an iron appeared to have passed over it. A half-finished letter lay upon the desk.

"How tidy you keep things," she praised him.

While Quentin went to the lavatory, she spied around a bit. *My darling Mother*, the letter on his desk began—and her pulse leaped with the shock of seeing that. When he was younger, he had always referred to her as "*Mama*." She sat on Quentin's bed and pulled the letter's loose pages into her lap. He'd composed it like a diary.

February 15

My darling Mother,
I miss you so awfully I cannot think strait. Yesterday three boys in the class had dredful headaches and I got one myself and my eyes drooped and my forehed hit my book, so Mr. Taylor gave me leave. I stayed in bed all afternoon and the kittchen ladies brought me soup with carrots floating in it.

February 16

My hedache is not so bad as yesterday but it is bad enuf. As you know, I have got the stamp craze and so I stayed in bed all day and did my stamp catalog. It was dull with nobody to talk to except Percy the cat that one of the boys snuck in. . . .

February 17

My freind Nigel is teaching me to box . . .

Erika skimmed the parts about ball games, lessons, the skunk caught under the dormitory wing. Her eyes slowed over lines that seemed to address her directly.

> *. . . Sometimes at night I wake up and forget that I am not in the Boston house with you. I listen and think you are close by and that you may come into the room. . . .*
>
> *I have been wearing my hat and boots and learning my verses just as you would want me to do. I have finished the psalm you gave me and have gone on to Psalm 148. . . .*

Psalm 148? Erika eyes stumbled over the passage, perplexed for a second, for she had never been religious herself. Other odd references and strange names littered the letter—"Margaret" and "the sailing races" and "playing hide-and-seek in the big house at Buzzard's Bay." Then Erika recalled her brother's report that Quentin had passed the summer with the Talcott family, and that Mrs. Talcott doted on him like one of her own children.

My darling Mother, Quentin had written. Erika felt her breath halt in shock, knowing that Mrs. Talcott must have encouraged him to call her that.

When Quentin returned from the lavatory, drying his hands against the sides of his pants, the pages dropped from her hands. Her son froze at the alcove's entrance, as if he understood his own infidelity.

Erika went to him. She knelt, holding him by the shoulders. "You probably thought I was never coming back, didn't you?"

Quentin looked uncomfortable, chin down, staring at his shoes. He slid one shoulder loose from her grasp and walked over to the window. "The boys are lining up for supper," he said, pointing. "I'd better go back now."

❖

Her father's walrus moustache had whitened during the three and a half years since she'd gone away, and she worried at the stiffness she saw in him. As the motorcar dropped them in front of his Back Bay town house, her father failed to see the curb. He stumbled, falling into a bank of snow.

"Are you all right, Papa?" Erika scurried to help him to his feet.

"Nothing serious." He rubbed his hip and backside. "The worst part is always the embarrassment."

He had aged at a rate that surprised her. Magdalena told her that Papa would be hastening down a street with his black medical bag, and he would halt suddenly, as though lost. More than once he had stepped inside Magdalena's house to telephone his office so that his nurse could remind him of his destination. Her brother claimed that Papa had missed appointments. For the first time, their father had begun to lose patients.

Yet the old man still exuded warmth. When her father's chauffeur drove them to the Chadsworth School to pick up Quentin for the Washington's Birthday holiday, Quentin sprinted down the school steps, happy to be pulled into his grandfather's arms. On the veranda, the Headmaster stopped greeting parents and ducked back into the building when he saw Erika.

They rode directly to her brother's house, where they'd been invited to dine with Gerald and his family. Quentin shot up the stairs, eager to disappear with his cousins.

After dinner Gerald took Erika aside into his study to review financial matters with her. As he closed the door, they heard the rumble of children's feet overhead.

"Erika." Her brother set a green leather folder on his desk and swung around in his chair to face her. "May I inquire about your plans?"

"My plans?"

"Do you intend to return to Italy? Or has that phase of your life been 'played out,' so to speak?"

"'Played out'?" she said.

"You seem more interested in your son these days. I was simply wondering."

"I don't plan to live in Boston again, if that's what you mean. I'm here only for a visit."

"I see."

"You and your wife disapprove of me entirely, don't you?" she asked. "If there's anything you'd like to say—why don't you go ahead and say it?"

"I don't think it would have the least effect." Gerald turned back to his desk, and finished writing the check he'd promised her from their mother's estate.

❖

Almost from the moment Erika returned to Boston, she longed to escape. In the Back Bay, she could hardly walk two blocks without seeing stunned looks of recognition from people she'd known all her life. People regarded her differently now, since she'd gone away.

On the main floor of a department store, she met two ladies she'd first encountered as girls at primary school. Amid the tables of dry goods, they whirled around, incredulous at the sight of her.

"Erika!"

"Are you famous now, in Italy?"

"Hardly." Erika gave them a small smile.

"It must be lonesome, living by yourself in a foreign country," one prompted her.

"Not really." Erika would have made an excuse and fled quickly if she'd been able, but the sale was being rung up, and she had to wait until a basket riding an overhead trolley clacked and returned with the receipt and her change.

She hoped that her two acquaintances had not noticed the odd purchases she had just made. She did not want them to guess the next part of her story. In Boston it was still winter, but she had asked the clerk to search the storeroom for a boy's white sailor suit, and lightweight things more suited to summer.

The two ladies scrutinized her for regrets and shreds of remorse.

"Is it official, then—the divorce?" One lady spoke the question in a hush. They must have seen the legal notice the court had required Peter to run in the *Boston Transcript* for three consecutive weeks, in order to finalize his proceedings against her.

"Yes," Erika said. They waited to hear more, but she lifted her eyes to the basket being lowered from the ceiling. "Lovely to see you," she said, smiling. Taking her package and her change, she headed for the street.

Behind her, she knew, their huge hats must have drawn close. As soon as she left, they must have exploded into discussion about her.

❖

"I'd like to take Quentin to New York with me for a few days," she told her father, "just so he and I can become reacquainted."

Papa understood that in New York, she would feel freer to stroll down the streets with her son without the burden of explaining herself to old acquaintances.

"Go to New York," her father said, and gave a limp wave. "I will notify the school."

Papa did not seem to notice that she had bought a new valise for the child, or that she'd filled it with new clothes for him—summer-weight fabrics in cotton and seersucker. The sailor suit was probably too large, but such things were not easy to find in Boston stores in February.

"I'm sure Quentin will cherish every moment you're willing to give him." Her father stood by a window as he said this. Light shone on his aging face, and there was a trace of sadness in him.

Quentin, too, liked the idea of an excursion to New York. What boy wanted to miss the chance to slip away from a few days of school? In New York she would take him to Central Park and the Museum of Natural History, where he'd see a dinosaur assembled with all its bones.

On the morning Quentin was due back at school, they waited for Papa's chauffeur to take them to the train. Erika overheard her father downstairs in his office, almost shouting into the telephone.

"Scarlet fever," he was saying. "That's right. This is Doctor von Kessler, Quentin's grandfather. He's come down with scarlet fever and he won't be returning to school for a while. . . . Yes, we'll keep you informed."

❖

In New York City she and Quentin sat at a soda fountain while he drank an egg cream and she sipped a sarsaparilla. She'd just bought him a new pair of lead soldiers.

"What have you liked best about New York?" she asked.

"The dinosaur skeleton at the museum," he said. Perched on a stool, he sucked through a straw and swung his legs in contentment.

"Would you like to go to a tropical island?" she asked. "One with monkeys and alligators and palm trees?"

He pulled his lips away from the straw and made his eyes big and nodded.

"We could take a ship," she said, "and visit a coconut plantation. A place where you can watch coolies climb palm trees and cut down coconuts with their machetes."

"Father told me about it. They've got quicksands there. Your horse could sink in and you'd disappear."

She smiled. "That's the place."

"And they've got mysterious lights on the water," Quentin went on. "But I think that's caused by phosphorescent fish."

"So you'd like to go?"

He nodded. Erika gave a soft laugh, and tousled his hair with her fingers, feeling his reserve and mistrust of her ebbing. She took a swallow of sarsaparilla and let the sweet tang wash over her teeth. "Your father and I have an old friend who manages the plantation. Doctor Ravell. I was thinking you might want to meet him."

Quentin finished his frothy drink. He sucked bubbles from the very bottom of the glass. By now he had forgotten about the Chadsworth School and his lessons and his alcove and the playing fields. She could have persuaded him to go anywhere.

At the passport office, she made inquiries. Did a young child require a separate passport? Not if he was less than twelve years old and traveling with his mother, the clerk said.

In a photographer's studio she posed with her arm around her son. At the passport agency, after handing over a large bill to expedite things, she asked for her passport to be reissued with the new photograph that included him.

Before leaving Boston, she'd taken a copy of Quentin's birth certificate from her father's drawer. In the event of an emergency, Peter had left it with Papa, along with a written statement appointing his former father-in-law to direct Quentin's medical care.

Erika Myrick, her passport read, still issued in her married name. *Quentin Myrick*, his birth certificate read. The clerk glanced at their faces and stamped various documents and handed over the new passport as if no case could be simpler than that of a mother leading her young boy onto a ship.

"Where are you off to, young man?" the clerk in suspenders asked.

"We're off to a coconut plantation," Quentin said.

Back at their hotel room, she sat across from him at a table, playing a game of checkers. Quentin picked up a black checker and leapfrogged twice across the board, snatching up two of her red pieces.

"Were you angry that I went away for so long?" Erika asked.

"I knew you were coming back." He smiled rather smugly, and drew himself up straighter in the chair, pleased that he was winning. For such a young boy, he carried himself with an air of manly confidence that seemed faintly comical.

"How did you know I'd be back?"

"I just did." His nostrils flared as he gave one quick laugh. His shoulders twitched.

She laughed, too, and went around the table, hugging him from behind, burying her face in the side of his neck. She kissed his cheek rather loudly.

"Why are mothers always doing that?" he asked.

"Doing what?"

"Giving their kids great big smackers."

Before they embarked from New York, Erika posted a letter to the parents of young Oliver Madsen, whose address she'd found in a municipal directory, stating what she had witnessed in the basement room of the Chadsworth School. A second letter she mailed to her father: *"Quentin and I have set off on a small adventure,"* she wrote. *"He's in my safekeeping, and no one should worry."*

54

TRINIDAD

1914

"Erika?"

She heard Ravell call her name before she saw him paddling toward them through the mirrorlike stillness of the lagoon. (**QUENTIN AND I WILL VISIT COCAL SOON**, she'd warned him in a cablegram from New York, but she'd given no exact date for their arrival.)

The dugout cleaved the water. Ravell happened to have a small boy with him as well, a child as light-skinned as a European, except that it was obvious from his dress that the boy was a coolie.

At the sight of her, Ravell stood up in the boat and teetered and laughed; she thought he might fall backward into the water. He swept his hair back from his forehead with his fingers, his shoulders moving fast from a shortness of breath. He wrestled the dugout onto land, his boots still half-submerged, shirtsleeves rolled to his elbows. As she and Quentin walked closer, Ravell stood with hands on hips, feet wide apart in his boots, gazing at them.

He looked at her, then at Quentin, and then at her again.

"By God," he said. "You've actually done this mad thing. You've actually come and brought him here."

"I always do what I say."

Children were present, so he and she did not so much as shake hands. Instead, they could not stop smiling.

"Quentin," she said, touching her son's shoulder. "This is Doctor Ravell."

"Hello, Quentin." After a vigorous handshake, Ravell stepped back to stare at the boy. "Tall, aren't you?" he said. "Much taller than I was at your age."

A crush of new wrinkles had appeared around Ravell's eyes, and to Erika's surprise, she saw sharp tears in them. She could not tell what overwhelmed him more—the sight of her, or Quentin. At that moment she thought, *He knows that Quentin is his.*

"Well," Ravell said, composing himself. "We were just setting out to find a manatee or an anaconda, if we get lucky." He turned to Quentin. "Would you and your mother like to hop in a boat and come along?"

They traded the dugout for a dinghy to better fit the four of them. Ravell put the oars in the water and rowed to a dark quarter of the lagoon where the mangroves grew thick. Insects speckled and marred the surface, like pulled threads in a silk stocking.

Ravell pointed out the mangroves' deep roots growing underwater, with shells clinging to them. "Oysters grow on trees here," he told Quentin. "We'll eat those for dinner."

Afterward, Erika thought how fortuitous it was that the coolie boy should have been there with them, because the small boy's presence relaxed everyone. His name was Ajeet, and though he was half Quentin's age—only about four—the children eyed each other with awkwardness that lasted only a minute. The two of them soon hung their heads over the sides of the rowboat, peering into the water in the hope of sighting the great body of a manatee that might be passing under the surface. It didn't matter that the shadows darting below the surface turned out to be ordinary tarpon, nothing more. The boys raised their heads and pointed in excitement at peculiar movements in trees that might be an anaconda dangling from a limb. They ignored the adults and spoke to each other in the secret language of boys.

In a densely forested part of the lagoon, water penetrated far into the woods. The depths were dark brown and shadows touched their faces. Quentin jerked in his seat and pointed upward when he caught sight of two monkeys springing through trees.

"My feet are a bit damp," Erika said.

"Take off your shoes." Ravell rested the oars on their metal locks and drew a dry towel from a wooden box. Facing her, he beckoned her to extend her right leg. He captured her foot, rubbing gently with the towel's soft folds.

As he massaged her one foot and then the other, chills shot up her legs and opened a channel of warmth inside her. Gooseflesh spread to her upper arms. She gave a shiver, bent her knees, and slipped both feet back inside her soft leather shoes.

"You're cold," he said. He reached inside the wooden box and took out a navy blanket and unfolded it, careful to avoid making the boat waver. He laid the blanket over her lap and helped tuck it under her hips. He knew, with alarming precision, exactly where to place his hands.

When he raised the oars and resumed rowing, there was no ambiguity in the look he gave her. "How long has it been?" he asked. "Nine years?"

❖

The saplings planted at the Cocal nine years previously had become immense trees now, thousands upon thousands of them, all heavy with coconuts. Ravell suggested a tour, so they drove past in a wagon. "I call this area the Madame von Kessler Plantation," he remarked, "because these began to grow the year you were here."

He stopped and split a coconut open with a machete, and gave Quentin a taste of its sweet milk.

When they dropped the boy Ajeet at the village where the workers lived, Quentin hopped from the wagon and ran off to join the children playing there.

At dinnertime, both boys returned. The cook fed Quentin and Ajeet in the kitchen, while Erika and Ravell were served in the dining room. One surprise was this: it was not Munga who waited on them, but the lovely, green-eyed coolie girl who had worked at the Eden estate long ago. Erika still recalled the girl's name—Uma. The servant girl carried in a platter of fresh oysters served over that rarity in these parts—a bed of crushed ice.

The girl appeared to be in her late twenties, a woman now, but she still carried herself with the same mute, remote air. As she reached to arrange dishes on the table, her forearms stretched long and smooth, her skin tan and polished, as if with a hint of curry. The fragrance of coconut oil emanated from her. Barefoot, she moved around the table. Even after she left the room, they heard the faint jangle of silver bands around the servant girl's ankles.

After the door to the kitchen had swung shut, Erika leaned forward and said, "I remember her. Wasn't her father the one who—?"

"The one who tried to poison Hartley's father's soup?" Ravell nodded.

Their voices shrank to whispers, their eyes huge as they stifled awkward laughs over the horror of it. Ravell refilled her glass with green swizzle.

"She works at the Cocal now? Not for the Hartley family?"

"Mrs. Hartley grew uncomfortable with Uma's presence." Ravell kept his tone low, and glanced at the kitchen door, lest it open again. He tapped two fingers against his temples and looked at Erika meaningfully.

Uma's mother had gone mad, Erika remembered. Something about a fire and an asylum . . .

"One can't just turn someone like Uma out, you know," Ravell explained in a hush. "One feels an obligation, and as long as she does her work—"

Ravell interrupted himself as the kitchen door breezed open, and Uma came in bearing finger bowls of rainwater. One end of her lavender sari trailed over her shoulder like a long scarf. Her face was expressionless and serene, but there was something haunting about the girl. Erika could not recall having heard Uma utter more than two syllables, or ever having seen her smile.

"Your father and I are wonderful friends," Ravell told Quentin. That evening in the parlor the boy listened with his mouth agape as Ravell described the expedition he and Peter had attempted to the Kaieteur Falls.

"We had no moon the night we made our way back down the Essequibo River," Ravell was saying. "We grew desperate to reach Rockstone by midnight. The water and the forest around us were so black, we all got a little . . . afraid. Men had to stand at the bow and hold up reflective lights to help the steersman find the way."

"Did you get there?" Quentin asked.

"We did." Ravell spoke of an Indian woman they'd seen on the dock the next day. She carried a baby on her back whose forehead had been painted vermilion, and she had a pet monkey coiled around her neck. A black man bought the monkey from her for five shillings, and the poor little monkey wailed as his new owner carried him off. This had greatly upset Peter.

Quentin pressed his mouth against the padded arm of his chair, rapt, still listening.

He lifted his head suddenly. "Why didn't my father buy it? He's got a craze for animals."

"I think he was tempted," Ravell said, nodding, "but the monkey might have died during the Boston winter."

Erika observed the two of them. "All right, darling," she said to Quentin. "Time for sleep. Enough adventures for today."

❖

After the boy had been put to bed, she and Ravell walked down to the beach, and breezes found their way under her white skirt, rippling the hem like a wave. They sat down on the sand and watched the stars. He wanted to know more about what had happened to her in Italy.

"For about two days after I sang *Carmen*," she said, "I thought the people who heard me would devour me with love. One man burst into my dressing room and sniffed my bare shoulder! A trio of men sang under my window the next morning, and crowds threw flowers at me.

"And then it all stopped. I auditioned everywhere for six months, and nothing came of it."

"Perhaps you left too soon," he said.

"I needed to breathe new air. It's not as if I've quit singing—I could never live without music."

"Do you plan to go back to Italy?"

She shook loose grains of sand from her hair. To her, the breakers sounded restless. "I haven't decided. My landlady, Donna Anna, is saving my room until I make up my mind."

When they got up, she turned to him and lifted her arms. The wind seemed to push them together, the heat of his body against hers while gusts snapped their white clothes. His tongue tasted of the sweet plantains they'd eaten for dinner.

When they returned to the house, it was empty of servants. She paused in her own room before going to Ravell's bed. Her robe, just laundered, was gone, still drying on the line. In a playful mood, she shed her clothes and pulled a long sheet from her bed, wrapping her body tightly in its pleats. She tiptoed through the dark house, still bound in the sheet.

On his bed the linens were pristine, almost lovingly folded back. Candles glowed and painted the walls with amber light, and orchids—the kind of orchids that spilled in profusion in the forest—floated in a bowl on his night table.

He stepped back when he saw her, watching with amusement as she twirled in a slow circle while unwinding herself slowly from the cloth— shoulders first, then breasts, navel, and hips.

"You shine," he said softly. "Your skin still shines."

As they slid against the bed, her hands gripped his haunches, still lean and hard, slippery with sweat. She smelled musk rising from his pores.

When they were done, she rested her palm against his heart. She heard the breakers outside beat and spread; in nine years the sound had never stopped.

❖

When Quentin was missing at lunchtime the next day, Erika went to the workers' village to look for him. Ravell had gone off earlier with the overseer to attend to a drainage problem. Everywhere Erika heard coolie children calling to their mothers in Hindi (*"Ma! . . . Ma!"*), and it amused her to hear a foreign syllable that she so easily understood.

She happened upon Uma, who sat on the stoop of a hut, balancing a toddler by his underarms to prevent him from tumbling. The tiny boy wore no diaper, only a loose shirt, and was clearly just learning to walk. He went forward a few feet and fell in the dust, picked himself back up, and wobbled a few steps before stumbling again.

"Is that your baby?" Erika asked. The servant girl nodded. It had not occurred to Erika before that Uma was a married woman with a child.

"That's a beautiful sari," Erika said. The girl's sari was the color of saffron, bordered with a brilliant turquoise design. Uma beckoned Erika into the hut and opened a trunk to show her others—an astonishing assortment of saris, fabrics the colors of jewels, lengths of garnet, emerald, and amethyst.

Inside the dim hut with mud floors, Uma showed Erika her other treasures. She drew long, fringed earrings from pouches, and she pushed silver bangles halfway to her elbows. The interior of the hut smelled of incense, cumin, sandalwood.

In Italy Erika had come to adore costumes. How strange it was to stand next to a thin-boned girl who inhabited a hut with dirt floors . . . and to long, suddenly, to drape herself in the scented garments of a Hindu coolie woman.

"Would you show me how to wrap myself in a sari?" she asked Uma.

Erika forgot that she had come to call Quentin to lunch. While Uma's baby played at their feet, rolling the husk of a coconut back and forth like a ball, Erika let herself become transformed. She selected the most daz-

380

zling sari that had been folded into the trunk—the fabric the color of lapis lazuli, with gold threads woven through it—a sari intended, no doubt, for festival days.

Silently, expertly, Uma spun the long banner around Erika, winding it around her hips. Uma formed perfect pleats in front with her nimble fingers, tucking the folds here and there, passing a length of cloth between Erika's legs. Erika felt shivers of coolness as the coolie girl's fingers nipped and grazed her form.

Finally Uma held up a mirror to show the banner of deep blue across Erika's chest. A long glimmering tail fell from Erika's shoulder to her knee.

The door of the hut opened and light flooded in. Quentin and four-year-old Ajeet halted at the threshold. Ajeet came inside and rubbed his head against Uma's hip, begging for something to eat. *Ma,* he called her. *"Ma."*

"I didn't realize that Ajeet was also your son," Erika said.

❖

She asked if she might borrow the sari, and wore it to dine with Ravell that evening. He was stunned when she appeared.

"Well, look at you," he said.

Across the table, he could not wrest his gaze from her. They lifted their glasses of green swizzle and laughed at her new persona.

"To the diva in her sari," he said, toasting her.

At one point during the meal, Uma stationed herself in a corner of the room. She held a serving platter, and studied Ravell with an intensity that seemed strange. When he addressed her, Uma lowered her eyelids, but when he continued to converse with Erika, the servant girl looked at him with a yearning that hinted of pain.

After dinner, he closed the doors to the parlor, so that he and Erika could be alone.

"I was surprised to see how many saris she had to choose from," Erika said. "Such a feast of luscious colors. And the jewelry—all those little pouches she kept opening, with bracelets and anklets and nose rings."

"The workers are like that," Ravell said. "Their women are regarded as princesses. Husbands funnel their wages into their wives' adornments."

Erika smoothed the long scarf of the sari draped over her shoulder. On the divan she lounged with bare feet. The doors were shut, but she softened her words nevertheless, so as not to be overheard.

"I see that Uma has a baby. Did you deliver her younger child?"

He nodded. "It was fortunate that I was there." Uma's younger son had presented feet first, so Ravell had been forced to reach up and turn the child's body completely around.

Erika remembered herself in the aftermath of giving birth, the mystical figure Ravell had become for her.

"You know, I think Uma is in love with you."

Ravell turned his head away in embarrassment. "That sometimes happens with servant girls. They form a fixation on their master."

Later that evening, Ravell shut the curtains that hung like white veils at his bedroom windows. Erika's backside fell against the bed as they went down together. As Ravell unwrapped her body from the sari, they smelled spices wound up inside the cloth—ginger, cardamom, and hints of coconut.

❖

"Which of the coolies is her husband?" Erika asked him another night, as they lay in bed.

"She doesn't have a husband."

"Who fathered her children?"

"That's a source of speculation. I never ask about such matters." Ravell got up to use the outhouse.

The older boy, Ajeet, was light-skinned, the younger one much darker. Erika wondered if Mrs. Hartley had viewed Uma as too much of a temptation to keep at the Eden estate. Perhaps Mr. Hartley had become overly fond of the girl, and that was why Uma had been exiled to the Cocal.

"How long has Uma been here?" she asked when Ravell returned to bed.

"Five years," he said. He turned on his side, away from her.

She bent an elbow and propped her head against her hand. With one finger she traced the outline of his shoulder, bared above the sheet.

"Have you slept with her?"

A pause. "Why do you ask?"

She did not repeat the question, and he said nothing more at first. Her head slid against the pillow and she watched shapes shift against the ceiling and walls. Wind bent the tall stalks in the garden. The next time she saw Quentin and Ajeet playing together, she would look at them differently. It had not occurred to her before that they might be half-brothers.

Ravell turned, and they lay on their backs in parallel. "You're angry," he said, and sighed.

If it had been daylight, he would have seen how flushed she'd become, her neck and face reddening in the darkness. The servant girl's beauty used to intrigue her, but now it felt ominous. When Ravell reached for Erika's hand, she withdrew it.

She had expected that other women might pass through his days and nights, like waves that washed away. It had not occurred to her that Ravell would have fathered two children—a choice on his part, clearly, because as a doctor, he knew how to prevent such things.

"Were you in love with her?" Erika asked.

"Not in love," he said. "But I felt . . . well, compassion for her. Her parents were dead, she had no family . . . and she was happiest around children. It was obvious that she wanted a baby. . . . And to be honest, I longed for children myself."

Ravell sighed. "You never wrote," he said. "In all those years, you never so much as mailed a postcard to me. . . . How was I supposed to guess that you'd ever come back to this island?"

It was unfair of her, she knew. Why had she imagined that this man understood how often she thought of him, even while she had avoided him for years?

Yet knowing she had a rival only sharpened the edge of their lovemaking. Now something dangerous lurked, and that figure of loveliness must be kept from the bed. But how had it come to this? Erika also wondered, as she straddled Ravell and rode him hard; or as she paused to touch his navel with the tip of her tongue. She was warring against a servant, a young woman who had no voice at all.

❖

They had been at the plantation about ten days when Ravell took Quentin on horseback with him to collect the mail. Fifteen miles along the hard beach they traveled, all the way to Sangre Grande.

Ravell was writing a book about the history of obstetrics, and he was pleased to receive two yellowing volumes from a London bookseller for his research.

A letter had also arrived from Christopher.

Dearest Erika,

. . . Signor Nardini, the impresario for whom you auditioned in Perugia, has made inquiries regarding your whereabouts. Nardini is gathering a cast for a summer production of Il barbiere di Siviglia, *and he wishes to consider you as a possible Rosina. . . .*

Inside her chest she felt a burst of vindication, her body summoning up its familiar and wild readiness for flight.

Then she read further.

If you can catch a ship fast, auditions are to be held on the first of March. . . .

But the first of March had come and passed, and Christopher must have known that his correspondence would never arrive in time. So why

384

had he told her about an opportunity that had already expired? Erika wanted to wad up the letter. A cry of anguish came out of her.

Ravell tried to console her. "If one impresario still remembered your voice months after you sang for him, others will," he said.

To amuse Quentin, Ravell took the boy to hunt butterflies the next day, while Erika took opera scores to the beach. She held up a parasol and faced the Atlantic and practiced her scales. Every morning, she promised herself, she would go to a spot of shade where palm fronds blew. She would sing until her powers came fully back. She would perform for the Portuguese men-of-war with their purple and blue streamers, and for fish that floated and listened under the waves.

Every day the housemaids swept the bungalow. They waxed the floors and changed the bedding and bleached the mud from Quentin's sailor suit. It was Uma who laundered Erika's undergarments and soaked her hairbrush in ammonia, Uma who tended Erika's personal things. The servant girl entered Erika's room only during her absence. When Erika returned, her perfume atomizers and tortoiseshell hair combs had been neatly shifted to the left or right on a table; her silk stockings had been folded over the ladder-back of a chair. The white coverlet on the bed looked as smooth as freshly fallen snow.

One morning when she returned to the room early, before Uma had left with her broom, the servant girl glanced up. Uma's eyes formed two slits of resentment, and then she was gone.

Later that day Erika told Ravell about the spite she'd seen in Uma's eyes. He lowered his head, sighed, and ran his fingers roughly through his hair. "I'll have to say something to her," he said. "Do my best to apologize."

Through a window Erika saw Ravell in the yard behind the kitchen, where he'd gone to speak with Uma. His face looked pained. Whatever he was saying, whatever words of reassurance he meant to offer her, Uma would not listen to any of it. She stood with her back to him, bending to fill pitchers from canisters of rainwater. When he patted Uma's shoulder, she flinched, and left the filled pitchers on a bench, her long braid swinging along her spine as she made her way back to the village.

Ravell took Erika to Esmeralda, the other estate he managed for Mr. Hartley, where the house stood on stilts, high off the ground. They sat together one evening on the high steps that led inside, and listened to the animals and parrots hidden in the forest that encircled the house.

Ravell liked to come to the smaller estate to work on his book. Here, he found fewer interruptions from workers, servants, and the overseer. Last time he visited, he'd finished a chapter on the history of contraception. Across a long table inside she'd seen his piles of notes.

He told her how the kings of ancient Egypt had ordered girls in their harem to have their ovaries removed, in order to prolong the time of pleasure that might be had from them.

A thousand years ago, an Islamic physician had written down twenty recipes for birth control. "Sneezing was one method," Ravell said.

"Sneezing?"

"After coitus, he said a woman ought to sneeze to expel semen. He also advised a woman to jump backward seven or eight times right after sex, so the sperm would fall out."

Erika laughed at that. "What would happen if she leaped forward?"

"That was the worst possible move—that would cause her to conceive."

They fell into silence, letting the forest speak for them, listening to the crack of wings and the shiver of leaves as monkeys leaped from one branch to another.

Erika said quietly, "Quentin is your child, you know."

Ravell nodded. His dark eyes held on to hers, absorbing her words with tenderness. "I've been aware of that. Peter told me that while we were in Guiana."

She stared. "Peter told you? How would he have known?"

"Apparently a fertility specialist told him that he was incapable of impregnating you—but that was something I'd always known."

"Well," she said, gazing into the blindness of the nighttime forest, "he did make me pregnant once."

"No, he didn't."

The air thickened with the humid perfumes of the forest. She listed to one side, sensing something awful coming, a terrible duplicity. She struggled to breathe, and when she wiped her brow, water ran from her fingers. "What are you telling me?"

"I was the father of the baby daughter you lost."

She got up and went into the house. The house was built in a hexagon, and sticks propped open the windows on all sides. She staggered around in a circle and felt herself growing dizzy, as if she were riding a carousel.

"I was your *patient* then." She stopped walking and braced her legs a stride apart. "You never asked, you never *told* me?"

"It was the only time I ever did such a thing to a patient."

"Why did you do it?" She peered into his face.

"I wanted you to have a child." His tone grew desperate. "It was the only way."

She gripped the back of a wooden chair and sat down hard. "My God," she whispered. She put her fists against her temples and widened her eyes, staring at nothing.

"Do you hate me for it?" Ravell sat down on the bed and waited.

"I don't know what to say. . . . Violated—I feel violated," she said loudly. "For a woman to believe she's carrying one man's child—and then to find out. . . . It's the worst kind of lie, to dupe a woman like that!"

"I did it because he was incapable—" His words diminished to whispers as he pleaded with her. "I did it because I loved you. I couldn't bear to have you gone from my life."

Erika swiveled her head from left to right, collecting herself. "It's just a shock," she said matter-of-factly. "Now I have to view the story of my life differently."

For a while she was silent, thinking. "I suppose, looking back—" She gave him a nod. "I guess I'm glad you did it."

"Mama?"

Back at the Cocal on another night, she reared up from the pillows. She fled from Ravell's bed, shoving her arms through the sleeves of her dressing gown.

Quentin stood in the hallway, a small figure in pajamas too short for him, ending halfway up his calves. Normally he was a heavy sleeper. During their voyage to Trinidad, he'd dozed off in a chair while the ship's band was playing. She was startled to see that he'd found his way down from his attic room.

"Where did you go?" he asked, his tone sharpened by fear. "You weren't in your bed."

"I couldn't sleep," she told him. "I got up to get something to drink."

She was afraid that he recognized the falsehood. Had the noises she'd made with Ravell and the greed of her enjoyment awakened her son? She sometimes worried about this.

"I heard a bird," he said in a plaintive way. "It was in the house, very close by."

He cooed—giving high little pants that got faster and changed from quarter notes to eighth notes and erupted into long, delirious squeals. It was a pitch-perfect imitation of how she sounded as her head tossed from left to right against Ravell's pillows. It amazed her, the accuracy of her child's ear.

"Maybe it was the red howler monkeys in the trees behind the lagoon," she said quickly.

"It wasn't," he insisted. "It was a bird in the house."

"Then it was me," she said. "I cried out—I had a terrible dream."

Quentin put his fists against his ears. "Please don't do that. Please!"

"All right." She steered him by the shoulders to the wicker settee on the front porch, where they sat down. She kept an arm around him, and pulled him against her side.

"Listen to the breakers," she said. "That's always soothing." From the porch they heard the tumult of the sea that never rested, even while they slept, and she hoped the explosions of the surf would wash the fright from him.

"When are we going back to Boston?"

The question caught her off guard. The Cocal had seemed a paradise for him—Ravell had taken Quentin for treks through the forest, and her son had come back elated over the wildlife they'd sighted. (Hadn't he been thrilled by the iguana he'd seen? And by the hoofed, piglike peccary? And the agouti that skittered away like rabbits?) Before breakfast, he'd bounded toward the beach and ridden Ravell's shoulders into the surf. (What boy would not love to begin the day with a good, salty soaking of his hair?) In the village, the workers' doors hung open, with more than enough playmates for him.

"Don't you like it here?"

"I'm homesick," he said.

"What do you miss?"

"Everything." His face fell into his palms as he wept.

She heard a noise behind them. Ravell stood in the doorway in a striped dressing robe.

"I miss the Talcotts and their big house on the Cape."

Her heart dropped and beat dully. *Mrs. Talcott,* she thought, with a hard knot of bitterness. She pictured the matronly Mrs. Talcott as she'd always been: with a book open on her lap, lifting her fat wrists to reach into a box of chocolates. Erika recalled the letter in the form of a diary that Quentin had been keeping for Mrs. Talcott. *My darling Mother,* it began.

Ravell pulled up a wicker chair and placed one hand on Quentin's knee.

"What else do you miss?" Ravell asked.

Quentin rested his head against the back rim of the settee and closed his eyes, wetness caught between his lashes, settling there, crystallized.

"I miss my father," he whispered.

After Erika and Ravell rode horses down the beach to Mayaro and back, she dismounted and headed into the house. A groomsman led their horses away while Ravell went off to tend to patients in the plantation's infirmary.

The house felt changed from the moment she entered it, though she could not have said why. Servants chattered in the kitchen, and she caught sounds of someone tipping a bucket and sluicing the floor, dragging a mop. Nothing unusual there. But as she turned and entered the hallway to her room, she saw that the door had been left open. It was never open. Three of her shoes had been flung in her path—heels upside down, a buttoned boot collapsed on its side. She could have tripped over them. One of her petticoats had been dropped there, too. It had landed like a parachute.

In Erika's room, Uma stood at the mirror, brushing her hair upward, holding it off her neck with one hand. She was wearing one of Erika's corsets, her silk stockings, and other undergarments of hers.

The lid of the trunk yawned open, every private thing removed. Dresses and shirtwaists had been tossed on the bed, or cast on the floor. Perfume had been dumped from bottles.

"What have you done?" Erika heard herself blare. She gripped the crown of her head, and swayed as though onstage.

The other servants' feet pounded toward them, but Uma did not even turn her head. She went on stroking her hair with the silver brush.

❖

"She's raving—like her parents!" Erika told Ravell that night.

They stood on a promontory overlooking the sea.

"It's not a healthy situation for her—or for us," he said, "to keep her on here. I'll ask Hartley to make inquiries among his friends about another position for her."

"What about Ajeet and her baby? They're your children. You can't send them elsewhere."

Ravell looked at her. "Do you expect me to separate them from their mother?"

Erika said nothing more. It would take time, of course, to secure a new situation for a servant. Such a change could not happen the next day, or the day after that.

❖

Uma did not return to the house for the rest of the week. Then the cook, who suffered from headaches, took to her bed. Munga stepped in to take charge of their meals, and he must have ordered Uma to help carry plates to and from the kitchen.

On a Saturday evening Munga concocted a stew of lamb, plantains, and spiced yams—a favorite of Ravell's. Erika remembered the sweetly flavored meat from long ago, how Munga splashed the lamb with a minty marinade. But that night after they put the first forkfuls to their mouths and tasted, Ravell pressed his napkin to his lips and spat into it. "Soap," he said. "The food tastes of soap." Erika, too, was sorry that she had swallowed.

Ravell pushed his chair back and stomped into the kitchen to find Uma.

"Are you trying to threaten us?" he cried.

"I'm sending you away!" he shouted. "Do you hear me? We can't have you here any longer, lurking and distressing people!"

55

Quentin went down to the lagoon to search for a dead toucan some-body told him they'd seen by some bushes. He thought he would wrap it in a pillowcase and arrange for it to be stuffed and preserved. He would take the toucan back to Boston, as a gift for his father.

From beyond the thickets of mangroves where he stood, his ears caught the sounds of a little boy's shrieks and protests and desperate hollering.

Quentin lifted his head and walked toward the commotion. In the middle of the lagoon, Uma stood in the rowboat and Ajeet leaned over the side, straining and reaching his small arms in vain to catch hold of the baby, who had fallen into the water. Uma grabbed Ajeet and lifted him up. Her four-year-old son squirmed in her arms. He wriggled down the front of her, hammering at her thighs with his fists.

She threw Ajeet into the deep water.

Quentin froze. Only then did he realize that she had also deliberately tossed her own baby into the lagoon.

Uma pushed off with the oars, turning her back on Ajeet as he strug-gled and flailed. In the rowboat she headed around an island, and was gone around the bend.

Quentin ran closer to where Ajeet and the baby were. While the four-year-old thrashed and tried to keep his head above water, the baby floated facedown, not moving at all. The lagoon was deep and Quentin had not yet learned to swim in water over his head, but a dugout waited on the bank, so he climbed inside it and paddled sloppily toward them, as best he could.

Ajeet saw him. The lagoon must have felt black and thick and bottom-less to his struggling legs, but he was a strong little boy, and his arms flew like small windmills, his neck high out of the water as he fought his way in Quentin's direction.

Quentin wanted to help the baby first, because he was so tiny, so help-less, his shirt drifting like a shroud over his head. The baby's bare bottom appeared yellow under the water, his small legs motionless, floating be-hind him.

Quentin would have tried to go straight to the baby, but the baby drifted at a distance, and the dugout reached Ajeet first.

When the canoe neared Ajeet, Quentin extended the paddle like a long stick. "Grab hold!" he shouted to Ajeet.

The four-year-old caught the oar, and Quentin tried to reel him in. But when the younger boy reached the boat, Quentin leaned too far over the side, pulling Ajeet by both wrists. The dugout flipped over, and they both descended into watery darkness.

❖

Munga was the first to notice the empty canoe. As far as he could see, there was no one to save, but the capsized dugout made him worry.

He led Ravell and Erika down the path, all three of them running. When Ravell ran around the lagoon's perimeter, he noticed what ap-peared to be a piece of laundry floating near the bank. Coming closer, he saw a little body rotate, softly turning, with one tiny arm flung east, the other west.

Ravell jumped into the water and scooped up the baby, brought him to land. Water streamed from the toddler's shirt and Ravell's clothes. He took the baby's body firmly and flipped him over. Ravell knelt and low-ered his face close to the child's. He pinched the baby's nostrils shut as he turned his head left, inhaled, and pressed his mouth against the child's, blowing air.

When his efforts came to nothing, Ravell set the baby's body on the ground. As the tiny, lifeless boy lay on his back, Ravell placed the child's hands neatly, one on top of the other, across his little chest. Crouching beside him, Ravell kissed the child's forehead and bowed his own head in grief.

A spear of sadness went through Erika. The sight of that blue-faced toddler made her think of the stillborn daughter who had passed through her own body, and she sensed that Ravell must have been reminded of that loss, too.

But then another emotion flashed through her, and that was fear. Erika knew that Quentin had gone down to the lagoon after breakfast, and now it was long past lunch. Her neck grew stiff as she surveyed the lagoon, not wanting to scan for the sight she dreaded, but forcing herself to hunt with her eyes.

She stood on the bank and called her son's name. She screamed for him to answer, and Munga called out a phrase loudly in Hindi, hoping for Ajeet to scamper from behind a tree on the opposite shore.

Ravell stood up, put his fists on his hips, and looked out over the water. "The other children might have been in the canoe with the baby. We've got to keep searching," he announced. The words rushed out of him.

He swam out to the capsized dugout, righted the canoe, and brought it back. The paddle had already drifted to shore. As Erika and Munga climbed into the boat, their heels knocked the bottom with the sound of wood on wood. If they hoped to find anyone alive in this vast lagoon—anything besides an anaconda coiled around a tree trunk, or a rare manatee—they had to glide quickly. It was a matter of time.

Her hand was a visor, the sun a blade in Erika's eyes, as she squinted through the mangroves. She must not think about the lifeless infant. The baby could not be saved. Her breaths hurt as if she were sprinting, but the dugout moved slowly—far too slowly, as they all knew.

A huge trunk lay like a fallen bridge across the water. As the canoe neared it, Munga took the paddle from Ravell and pushed against the great log for leverage, and they got past.

Erika turned completely around to look backward, wondering if they had overlooked any human shapes in the dark depths behind them.

Noises. The screams of birds. Erika rose unsteadily to her feet, the better to survey the islands and bends. The water seeped endlessly between trees, overtaking the land. Erika called to her son, and to Uma's four-year-old boy:

"QUENTIN! AJEET!"

Ravell lifted the oars from the water and they all listened in vain for a small voice to respond. They heard nothing, only the soft splashes as Ravell resumed rowing. In long, searching syllables, Erika wailed to the children again:

"QUENNNNTIN! AAAAAJEEEET!"

Only her sorrowful voice echoed back. The men let her emit the mournful syllables. She cried out the boys' names until her voice broke like a snapped string. The dugout swayed, and the men warned her to sit. As she collapsed back down, her hip bones fell hard on the plank seat.

When their canoe rounded the next bend, the lagoon widened and spread like a lake before them. They saw an empty rowboat surrounded by blooms of color, banners of saffron, celadon, magenta, royal purples, and blues.

"Saris—!" Erika said in disbelief.

Uma had flung her saris from the boat—every one of them, it would appear. Erika suspected that Ravell had bought the poor girl many of these saris as gifts. Some dangled from trees. Most drifted in the water, the fabrics crisscrossed in places, stripes of red over gold.

They wanted to gasp—it was almost beautiful, until they noticed Uma floating facedown, her garments swelling to the surface like a balloon. Uma's hair was undone, trailing as dark as the depths of the lagoon.

❖

The laborers carried two more old rowboats that had been stored in a shed down to the lagoon. They searched all afternoon, but located no more bodies.

The two children had hidden. It was growing dark and they were lost in the forest. Earlier, just after Quentin had fallen into the water, he'd risen to the surface and clung to the side of the capsized dugout. "Hold on to my shirt!" he'd yelled to Ajeet. "Hold on!"

While Quentin kicked and pushed the canoe toward the muddy bank, Ajeet had clutched his shirt so tightly that Quentin's vision dimmed and he felt his face reddening, because the younger boy was nearly choking him.

When the boat finally rubbed against the shallow bottom of the lagoon, Quentin struggled to his feet, carrying the terrible weight of Ajeet piggyback. They wobbled, lunging in the muck. With every step, Quentin's soaked shoes sucked mud. The moment they reached land, he let the younger boy slide from his shoulders, relieved to drop Ajeet on the ground. The younger boy sat in the dirt, sobbing. *He's crying, but he's alive,* Quentin thought.

At first he believed that they were safe. Then he heard a woman's strange, raging sounds not far away, and great splashing as things were being hurled into water. Finally, from an unseen place in the lagoon, a great swash echoed, as if a huge fish, or a manatee maybe, had fallen into the depths.

It was Uma he heard, and he knew they must hide from her. Ajeet sprang up, muddy-kneed, and raced through the trees with him. For a long time they knew she could be close. Twigs crackled and broke behind them—it sounded like footsteps. From behind every creeper-laden tree, it was possible that Uma, swaddled in her sari, would appear.

By late afternoon they were completely lost. At the edge of the forest, they wandered into a clearing. A worker saw them and dragged them homeward, pulling them by the wrists. Both boys were crying. The man spoke Hindi, and Quentin felt helpless, trying to explain why Ajeet must not go back to his mother's house in the village.

Only when they saw Erika hurrying and stumbling in their direction did the boys cease resisting. They reached out their arms, and ran toward her.

❖

The boys were given supper and baths, and Erika and Ravell helped them into their pajamas. That night Ajeet would sleep in the attic room, in the big bed with Quentin.

In the tub Quentin recounted every detail of his bravery. How he'd fallen into the lagoon . . . how he'd grabbed on to the overturned canoe, how he'd ordered Ajeet to hang on to his shirt . . .

Erika took Quentin to her room while Ravell spent time alone with Ajeet. She rubbed Quentin's damp hair with a thick towel; she brought a dish of peppermints for him to eat.

When she told him what had happened to Uma, Quentin asked worriedly: "Who will raise Ajeet? Who will look after him now?"

"Doctor Ravell is Ajeet's father," Erika told Quentin quietly. "Doctor Ravell will take very good care of him."

56

⌒∞⌒

"A doctor takes an oath to do everything in his power not to do harm," Ravell said. "Now a woman has ended her life because of me."

Seated on the bed, he took hold of his head, with shreds of his dark hair caught between his fingers. Against his white shirt, his black vest looked as if it were binding him.

Erika's mouth filled with liquid. More than her eyes, it was her mouth that was running with grief. She swallowed, and wiped her nose with the end of the bedsheet.

"I should have sent Uma away on the day you arrived," Ravell said.

"She wouldn't have survived being banished."

"At least I might have protected the children from her." He got up from the bed and pushed aside the long drapes, letting moonlight burn through. "I've fathered four children," he said suddenly.

Erika realized he was including their stillborn daughter in the count.

"Four children," he said. "And I haven't been a true father to any of them."

Ravell tiptoed to the attic to check again on the boys. When he returned, he beckoned Erika upstairs to look at them. Side by side, the boys were asleep. Quentin had fitted his arm under Ajeet's neck, and their foreheads were nearly touching, as if they were accustomed to lying there as brothers.

But later, a cry of distress tore into everyone's sleep. Ravell ran up the attic stairs, and Erika rushed after him, clutching the sides of her nightgown.

Quentin stood on the mattress, doing a short mad dance in his pajamas. "Help me!" he cried out in terror. "Somebody help me!"

Erika caught Quentin by the arms and tried to calm him, but she was unable at first to rouse her son from his nightmare. In his blind dance, he batted the air with his arms and turned in a circle. Slowly she eased him down onto the mattress and rubbed his back with long, soothing strokes. Ajeet was also whimpering in the dark, and Ravell knelt to quiet the younger boy.

Later, in their own bed, Ravell said to Erika: "I can't stop thinking of Peter, and what he must be going through. Tomorrow I'll write to him. We must give Quentin back to Peter."

❖

Ravell liked to give others what they wanted; he tried to say yes as often as he could. In Trinidad, cremation had been declared unlawful, but here at the Cocal, miles from anywhere, Ravell decided to let the villagers do what they considered holy.

Surely this was what Uma would have wanted. A Hindu priest had explained to him how Uma's soul and the baby's soul had flown away, suggesting that the most sacred thing to do would be to destroy their bodies. The blessed thing, the Hindus felt, was to make bodies disappear.

So one morning Ravell dressed in white like all the rest, and went to join them at the place where they'd stacked the wood. The villagers stood ready to pour sugar and ghee—a type of liquefied butter—under the bodies to help them burn.

On the day they cremated Uma and her baby, Erika walked for miles along the beach. Though Ravell attended the ceremony, she stayed away. If she appeared, the villagers might close their eyes in prayer, but in their hearts, she knew they blamed her.

Her nostrils caught the smell of what was happening. No matter how far she walked, the wind brought the odor her way. She wondered if they had dried out Uma's saris and thrown them on the pyre, too. By noon, the sky and air held fingerprints of hazy smoke that drifted over the sun. In the air she detected ash and burning colors—vermilion, marigold.

❖

After that, she no longer wanted to remain at the coconut plantation. Ravell longed to leave, too—at least for several months. Neither of them could bear to follow the footpath adjacent to the lagoon, or see the ghosts that floated there.

Ever since Christopher's letter had come, informing her that at least one fine impresario still remembered her singing, her hopes had been rising; if she went back to Italy, her career might actually take wing. She told Ravell that the number of English-speaking expatriates in Florence was huge. If he came along with her to Florence, he could easily practice medicine there.

"*If I had been a better man—*" Ravell kept saying in a remorseful tone.

If I had been a better woman—Erika thought.

In Ravell's sins, she saw her own—he, like she, had longed and reached for ruinous things. Ravell was similar to herself; that was why she had yearned to see him; that was why she found herself in his bed again after so many years. She did not want to return to Italy without him.

She told him, "If I ever earn enough money from my singing, we could bring Ajeet to Florence. We could hire a servant to mind him."

"Perhaps that will happen," Ravell said.

For the first time, she imagined that she could have love, and give herself fully to her music, too. Until now, she had not been able to envision how that might be possible.

❖

One morning when the sky was still softly colored with dawn, Erika and Ravell and the two boys sat on the beach wearing their pajamas and dressing robes. A week had passed since the awful day at the lagoon. Quentin lolled in the sand with his head against his mother's lap. Ajeet sat crouched between Ravell's legs, the man's knees braced on either side of the boy, sheltering him. Since the drownings, Ravell had talked of taking Ajeet traveling with him when the boy grew older, and of sending the child to his old boarding school in England. Ravell planned to raise Ajeet as his legal son.

"I don't want to go back," Quentin said.

"I thought you missed Boston," Erika said.

"I do, but I don't want to go back."

Ravell loosened the belt of his robe, and he patted Quentin's ankle. "Your father must miss you, Quentin."

"He's always away," Quentin said, "on voyages."

"That's his job, traveling," Erika pointed out. "He's an importer. Just like my job is singing, and that's why I have to return to Italy soon."

Her son's future was in Boston, Erika believed—Quentin would probably attend Harvard like her brother and other men from the von Kessler family. She had not yet told her son that Ravell had agreed to accompany her to Florence and stay for three months while he worked on his book. In his absence, he'd leave the plantation to the overseer's care.

Ravell had written to Peter, asking him to come to New York to meet their ship, promising that in New York, they would return Quentin to him.

Along the horizon, a breach appeared in the silvery blue, and Erika gazed at the flames of gold and magenta that separated sky from sea.

"Why must we leave the Cocal?" Quentin asked.

"Places and people always seem particularly beautiful when you realize you'll be leaving them," Erika said, and she ruffled his hair with her fingers.

57

NEW YORK

1914

From the ship's railing in New York, Erika saw Peter standing below on the quay. He took a gold timepiece from his pocket and checked the hour. It was her first sight of him in four years, since she'd left Boston. Peter wore a tall hat and a tweed overcoat, and he looked as elegant as ever. For years she had chosen almost every shoe and shirt he owned, but today everything he wore was new to her, including his gloves and tie. Even his hair was styled a little differently. Each change in him seemed a sign of things they no longer shared, markers of the time they'd been apart. If he'd had an interesting conversation with a stranger this morning, she was not aware of it. She did not know if he'd ridden a camel on his last trip, or if his business this year was thriving or faltering, or if he'd found love again.

Nor could Peter imagine all that had happened to her.

They had not spoken, nor would they speak now.

She rested a hand on her son's shoulder as he stood beside her. Leaning against the rail, the boy propped his chin upon his crossed arms as he stared down at the dock. Quentin hadn't yet noticed his father. In the crowd below, people jostled one another and raised their faces, their eyes searching for loved ones about to disembark.

Quentin appeared bored by the tedium of waiting for one thing to be over and another to begin. Lines formed at the stairwells. Suddenly the ropes lifted. Shoulder to shoulder, passengers herded toward the exit.

Ravell's eyes met her own, like a signal.

She bent toward her son, the velvet sleeve of Quentin's jacket soft under her touch. "It's time to meet your father now."

"I'll take you down," Ravell told Quentin.

Her son turned to embrace her, his head butting her in the ribs. She crouched to kiss him.

"Give me a few good smackers," she said.

His chin bumped her face as he gave her kisses that were noisy and enthusiastic, his breath smelling of the sticky, banana-flavored candies that Ravell had fed him as they entered the Narrows and New York Harbor. She wondered if Quentin would be as tall as a man before she saw him again.

"Give your letters to Grandpapa," she said, "and he'll be sure that they reach me."

Nodding, her son lowered his head, watching the feet of passengers shuffling past. She wondered if he would cry, but Ravell said, "Hurry now," and Quentin merged into the crowd of bodies as he broke away.

At the rail she waited while Ravell and Quentin descended. On the dock Peter stared at the emerging passengers. He squinted slightly, his features tensed. Perhaps he worried that Erika and Ravell had changed their minds, and would not appear or return the boy as promised. Until the new arrivals had passed through customs, the passengers were being cordoned off and kept separate from those who had gathered to welcome them.

When Quentin saw Peter, the boy let go of Ravell's hand and charged, ducking under a rope and leaping past officials who twisted in surprise. The guards laughed and shrugged when they realized it was only a young boy who'd gotten loose.

When her former husband finally noticed Quentin sprinting toward him, Peter's relief was visible. He gave Ravell a small wave—a salute of thanks—and then turned to the boy and flung his arms wide. In just seconds Peter would catch and lift his son, arching back, smiling. *All three of us created this boy who is alive and exultant,* she thought. She and Peter and Ravell.

From the ship's rail, Erika watched Quentin running toward his future.

58

FLORENCE, ITALY

1914

Several months later—in the late spring—the taxicab pulled up at the Teatro Verdi. As Erika and Ravell stepped out, one of the managers rushed toward them, his chest heaving with anxious breaths.

"You must come at once," the man said to Erika. "Your husband, the doctor, is needed in Signora Lanza's dressing room."

In Florence Ravell had begun caring for expatriate ladies, British and American, but his Italian was still faltering, so Erika followed to translate. The door to the renowned diva's sanctuary opened, and after they'd entered, someone discreetly pulled it shut behind them. The large woman reclined against a violet sofa, the crook of her arm covering her eyes. She groaned and twisted against the upholstery, her knees flinching as she writhed. Ravell found a stool, drew it close to Gabriella Lanza, and sat down. He held his palm against the singer's forehead, and he lifted her wrist to count her pulse.

"Il bambino," Gabriella Lanza said softly, mournfully. Turning her face toward the ceiling, she blinked, tears sliding from her eyes into her hair.

Eight days earlier, Erika had auditioned to become Gabriella Lanza's understudy. Erika suspected that part of the reason the acclaimed diva had favored her presence, and encouraged the managers to hire her—despite her inexperience—might have been because Ravell had accompanied her on the morning she had tried out for the role of Rosina in *Il barbiere di Siviglia*. When Erika had introduced him (*"Mio marito fa il medico. . . .* My husband is a doctor, an obstetrician. . . ."), Gabriella

Lanza had turned to Ravell as though he were lit from within—as though nothing could reassure her more than to keep a doctor close, almost as a member of the cast. Smiling, she had guided him and Erika for a tour backstage, petting their hands and waving away any doubts from the impresario and the managers of the Teatro Verdi.

Later, at rehearsals, Gabriella Lanza greeted Erika with a kindness that seemed rare for a prima donna, and she asked, "How is your husband? Has he delivered many babies this week?" She always spoke his name reverently: *"Il dottor Ravell."*

"When did the pains begin? How long have you been bleeding?" Erika knelt at the mezzo-soprano's side, repeating Ravell's questions in Italian.

Gabriella Lanza was four—no, five months pregnant, Ravell concluded. This did not surprise the great singer. (*"Mio bambino—"* she murmured again, her head leaning far back against the pillow, the hair at her temples darkening with tears.) The singer always kept her large figure swathed in shawls or richly embroidered tunics, and until now, she had not mentioned her condition to anyone.

❖

It was less than an hour before curtain time. The impresario, who was the tallest man Erika had seen since arriving in Italy, led her into a smaller room. His forehead glistened; he pulled a handkerchief from his pocket and wiped his brow. With his tie loosened and yanked to one side, he told Erika—rather gruffly—that she must prepare to sing. Then he rushed away down the corridor, his trouser leg crooked, caught up in his sock.

Just ten days earlier, the previous understudy had quite suddenly broken her contract and left for Verona, where she'd found a more promising engagement. In the impresario's eyes, Erika was only a temporary substitute, to be used as a last resort. If he had been able to send for a more celebrated singer to stand in as Rosina—if he had been able to arrange for another revered mezzo to rush in from Milan or Rome to satisfy the audience—he would have done so. But at this hour, on such short notice? That was impossible.

In the smaller room, a wardrobe assistant slipped one of Gabriella Lanza's gowns over Erika's head. The fabric felt damp, the puffy sleeves still warm from a steam iron. The dress smelled of the vanilla-like cologne of the woman who had worn it the previous night. The seamstress pulled the bodice—which was far too loose—closer around Erika's waist and ribs. With pins clamped between her lips, the seamstress worked with thread and needle, basting the darts until the fabric hugged Erika's form. Another assistant knelt at Erika's feet, shortening the hem. They made her step out of the dress while their fingers flew and scissors snapped, finishing the adjustments.

Through the walls she heard the theatre abuzz with sounds of arriving musicians who were soon plucking and tuning their instruments. In the adjacent room, a tenor was warming up by vocalizing a few phrases. He accompanied himself on a piano, stopping repeatedly to praise or chide himself. "That's it," he called out happily, or he cried out, "Awful! Come on, let's try that B-flat again."

Before a brightly lit mirror Erika sat while another attendant combed her hair and pinned it severely against her head. A long, curly wig was lowered and tugged tightly against her hairline. Her scalp grew warm, as if covered by a winter cap. A makeup man wielded his thin brush, his breath smelling of salami as he leaned close to paint her eyebrows into sable arches. He daubed color onto her lips until her mouth shone like cherry candy that had been licked.

While the wardrobe assistants made her stand and turn sideways like a mannequin, or while the makeup master took hold of her chin and tilted her face, Erika closed her eyes, going deep into herself, preparing to become young Rosina. ("The prompter will be there," the impresario had assured her, but Erika knew the role very well.) Earlier that week, when Gabriella Lanza had failed to appear at two rehearsals (the diva's fatigue must have been real—not a result of laziness—Erika realized now), the director had called upon Erika to sing phrases from the wings. At the time she'd felt as insignificant as a prompter herself, serving only to cue others and help them recall their lines.

In the hallway she heard a commotion. Later she understood that must have been the moment when a group of men lifted the ailing prima donna from her sofa and carried her to a waiting motorcar. Gabriella Lanza needed to remain on strict bed rest, Ravell had told the managers and the impresario. Erika presumed that Ravell would escort the singer back to her hotel room.

Tonight Ravell had accompanied Erika to the opera house to see *Il barbiere di Siviglia*, but now he would miss it. No one close to her would witness tonight's performance; none of them would remember how the next hours proved either a little miracle or a fiasco for her.

Out of respect—just in case Gabriella Lanza was still present nearby—Erika stayed hidden in the small dressing room, fully costumed and coiffed, until the overture began. When she heard it, she opened the door and eased her head into the corridor, which was eerily empty and filled with chilly night air because, as someone later told her, a back door had been left open after they carried Gabriella Lanza out.

It was possible that the great singer might lose her baby tonight. Erika told herself she must not think about that.

❖

When the moment came for the heroine's grand entrance aria, Erika glided across the stage holding a letter, and she felt herself swell from within. Beyond the footlights, the theatre opened before her like a cavern of terraced seats. Ladies wearing feather boas raised their lorgnettes in anticipation. Gentlemen in stiff collars waited for her to begin. Their presence expanded her. *All my life, I have been walking, singing, sailing toward this moment*, she thought. By the end of this aria, the audience would know who she—the character Rosina—really was.

Before she sang a single note, the orchestra foreshadowed everything about the heroine. The opening notes sounded imperial, commanding; but that effect was soon mixed with a flirtatious flourish of strings. Rosina was coquettish and alluring, but she had fierce power, and she could bite like a viper if that was required of her.

The conductor did not take his eyes off Erika, not for a moment. It was a great risk they had taken, letting her go on. As she began the *andante* from "Una voce poco fa," he followed her voice with cautious flicks of his baton.

By tomorrow, the famed mezzo Gabriella Lanza might recover and stand once again in this wig, in this gown. *But for tonight,* Erika thought, *this stage and this theatre and the wild sparkle of this aria are mine.* Even if such an opportunity never came again, Rossini's music was filling her now, and she felt herself flying. As she sang of her would-be lover, Lindoro, her tongue caressed his name. Tension eased in the impresario's face as he listened from the front row.

As Erika continued to sing, the conductor's eyes grew huge, the swipes of his baton more bold. The heroine Rosina was at the center of this opera; she brought fiery playfulness to everything. When Erika came to the line she loved most—the phrase that exposed Rosina's steely spirit— the conductor's mouth opened and his eyes seemed to ignite, as if he could hardly believe the sounds coming out of her.

Lo giurai, la vincerò.   I swear, I will win.

An extreme stillness settled over the audience.

The next part of the aria—the moderato—echoed the sweet harmonies of a popular song. The conductor's coattails swayed as though he were dancing—a marionette animated by her voice. Smiles crept into the listeners' faces; they might as well have been humming along.

Toward the end of the famous aria, she remembered the gesture Magdalena had taught her long ago. ("You send up the last note like this—" Magdalena used to say, demonstrating the pose.)

And so it happened. Just as Erika released the last high, flourishing note, she raised her right arm in triumph, as though she were holding a torch. When the music ended, a roar rushed toward her from the audience. A man sprang into the aisle, ran halfway to the stage, and hopped around like a crazed monkey. She laughed and touched her heart; she bowed her head and curtseyed. When she looked up again, even the members of the orchestra had risen to their feet. Men bellowed, *"Brava!"* Ladies shivered in their satin sheath dresses and raised their clapping hands above their heads. They made her sing "Una voce poco fa" all over again.

❖

The shiny black taxicab carried Erika and Ravell through the ancient streets of Florence. Light from lampposts flashed against the glass windows, illuminating the car's interior. Their faces darkened as they turned a corner, then brightened and dimmed again. Flowers that people had brought to toss at Gabriella Lanza now belonged to Erika; the taxi moved carefully, weighted down with sprays. Bouquets quivered against the windows. As they motored through the streets, a bunch of long-stemmed roses rolled from the seat and threatened to fall; Erika caught them with one hand and pushed them back.

"A happy night," Ravell said.

An Italian doctor had finally appeared to tend to Gabriella Lanza, so Ravell had not needed to accompany her to her hotel room after all. From a loge overlooking the stage, Ravell had been present for the entire performance. "It was thrilling," he said, "from beginning to end."

Before they'd left the theatre, Ravell had telephoned Gabriella Lanza's hotel and spoken to the other doctor. The singer's pains had eased; she had gone to sleep.

Ravell took Erika's gloved hand and gazed through the taxicab window. They still struggled for money and had not married yet, although they told everyone in Florence that they had, because that made their lives here simpler. On her left hand, she already wore a gold band. She expected that they would marry soon.

The lights on the Arno looked like small comets that had fallen from the sky; the bright streaks now lay on the dark water, cooling. The blaze of each would be gone by morning.

"Things won't be the same now between Gabriella Lanza and me," Erika said.

"Why do you say that?" he asked.

She had not forgotten her brief experience as an understudy for another well-known mezzo-soprano; that singer had glared in Erika's direction, telling the management, "I don't want to lay eyes on her," until they sent Erika away.

"Gabriella must have considered me a novice," Erika said. "She never expected me to perform well."

"She heard your voice," Ravell said. "Shouldn't she have known?"

After the final curtain fell, the impresario had bounded backstage, his face florid with delight and relief. He bent his tall body in half, bowing. He caught Erika by the wrists, saying, "We will talk. We must talk."

Gabriella Lanza had begun bleeding that morning, and yet she had come to the theatre anyway. Erika wondered about this. It made no sense that the other singer had been so determined to perform, or that she had delayed so long in telling the impresario and the managers about her incapacity. But if Gabriella had not created such an emergency . . .

Tears spurted from Erika's eyes. On one of the happiest nights of her life, she wept into her gloves, wanting to go to Gabriella Lanza's bedside and thank her—for what? Erika knew that her own night of triumph had been made possible by another woman's suffering.

A phrase from *"Una voce poco fa"* kept going round and round in Erika's head:

Lo giurai, la vincerò.   I swear, I will win.

The taxi rolled closer toward Donna Anna's house—toward the rented room with the red-tiled floor that overlooked the Arno, a place much too small to accommodate two people. If she and Ravell continued a life together in Florence, they would need to find more spacious quarters, and perhaps one day they might bring Ajeet from the Cocal to live with them.

In the dark cab Erika leaned against Ravell. She pressed her nose into his neck, just below his ear. Instead of the flowers, she smelled him. When she entered a room and caught a whiff of the bedsheets he'd risen from, she noticed it. A sweet smell. At the coconut plantation, when she'd helped little Ajeet into his pajamas, she'd sniffed it again on the small boy's skin, as familiar as baking bread. Quentin did not smell like Ravell, but this second son did. Until then, she had never known that a particular child could inherit his father's smell.

Ravell looked again out the taxicab window, fingering her rings through her glove.

"What are you thinking?" she asked him.

"I was remembering that day in the cemetery, riding in the carriage with your brother," he said. "The first time I heard you sing. The snow on your face, your white furs."

"And now we are here," she said.

"Yes," he said. "Now we are here."

When the taxi pulled up in front of the house, they tried to be as quiet as possible as they hurried up and down the staircase, carrying armloads of flowers. Even the driver assisted. Blossoms and petals dropped on the steps, the stairwell filling with so many fragrances that it smelled like a florist's shop. At the very top landing, a door opened. Dressed in a white nightgown, Donna Anna appeared, steadying herself against the banister. Erika suspected that before they left the theatre, Ravell had telephoned the old woman to tell her the news.

"I know what has happened," the landlady called gaily down to Erika. "I can smell it."

Laughing, they rushed upstairs to the landlady's apartment, their arms laden with several bouquets to give to her. Her parlor was dark as they entered, with light from streetlamps streaming across the floor, because the blind woman had no need to close her shutters.

"Ah, lilies," Donna Anna said, plunging her nose into a spray of white flowers. "Lilies to trumpet your night of glory."

The old lady took the armful of lilies and stepped onto the balcony. With a strength that surprised Erika and Ravell, Donna Anna made a great sweep with her arm and flung the lilies, letting them arc into the air. They landed on the dark waters of the Arno, where the white flowers scattered and floated like swans.

A Further Historical Note

Even in past centuries, certain bold doctors experimented with fertility treatments now regarded as modern. They undertook such work behind veils of secrecy and at the risk of moral disapproval. An illuminating moment in the scientific understanding of human reproduction occurred when sperm was first viewed through a microscope invented by a Dutchman, Anton van Leeuwenhoek, in the late seventeenth century. This opened a window through which early pioneers in gynecology began to see endless potential and possibilities.

Artificial insemination, which can be achieved by relatively simple technology, has long been practiced. In 1785, the revered Scottish surgeon John Hunter recorded a case in which he successfully inseminated a female patient with her husband's sperm, and the birth of a living infant resulted. In 1866, the brilliant American physician John Marion Sims—referred to as "the father of modern gynecology"—reported a similar accomplishment.

By the mid-nineteenth century, it had become clear to Dr. Sims that infertility—which had historically been blamed solely on a "barren" wife—might also arise from a husband's reproductive difficulties. Based on his clinical investigations, Dr. Sims proclaimed the radical notion that a sexually potent man could be sterile. He performed fifty-five artificial inseminations for six couples. Sims and other innovative gynecologists of the nineteenth century invented variations of the "impregnating syringe," as well as other tools and implements, so that sperm could be strategically stored, manipulated, and optimally positioned for the purpose of facilitating conception.

In his many clinical attempts to assist conception, Dr. Sims used only a woman's husband's sperm—and that stirred moral controversy enough. But in 1884, the first successful insemination with donor sperm reportedly took place. A Quaker couple consulted Dr. William Pancoast, a professor at the Jefferson Medical College in Philadelphia, to help them conceive. When the husband's semen was examined, he was found to be "azoospermic" (i.e., sterile). Dr. Pancoast allegedly turned to his circle of six medical students, and they agreed that one of them should serve as a sperm donor. Under the guise of performing some other treatment on the wife, the doctor then chloroformed the woman and artificially inseminated her with the sperm of the medical student deemed to be "the best looking." A baby boy was born to the woman nine months later. The mother was never told what had happened, although the doctor supposedly informed her husband. Only in 1909, after Dr. Pancoast's death, did one of the medical students who had been present reveal the story.

By the 1890s, other medical experts performed treatments with donor sperm. Such procedures had to be undertaken on such a clandestine basis that one physician, Dr. Robert L. Dickinson, did not publish reports of what he had done until another forty years had passed.

Apart from the fear of moral condemnation, early fertility specialists may have preferred to keep the exact nature of their procedures veiled for another reason: their statistical rate of success was undoubtedly low. Many doctors found the treatment of infertility the least rewarding aspect of their practice. Their clinical trials and experimental work were hampered by a couple of key issues. First, many male patients were sensitive to any questioning of their "virility", and found the act of submitting to a semen analysis repellent, so physicians did not require them to do so. Second, the timing for ovulation was poorly understood during the nineteenth century. In the 1870s and 1880s, a woman was thought to be most fertile during the time of menstruation. (This notion was soon questioned as medical experts noticed that breast-feeding mothers, in the absence of their periods, sometimes became pregnant.) It was not until well into the twentieth century that medical investigators determined that ovulation occurred at mid-cycle.

The possibility of freezing sperm has long inspired the medical imagination. In 1866, the Italian physician Dr. Paolo Mantegazza suggested that before soldiers went off to battle, they should leave behind frozen sperm, so that in the event of their deaths, their widows might bear them posthumous children. Effective methods for cryopreservation (freezing sperm) were not perfected, however, until the 1950s.

Read on for an exclusive
interview with the author of
The Doctor and the Diva

An Interview with Adrienne McDonnell

What is *The Doctor and the Diva* about?

The story begins in 1903, in Boston. A young Harvard-educated obstetrician who is a rising star in his profession becomes dangerously attracted to a patient – a lovely opera singer. She turns to the doctor for help in conceiving a child. The doctor becomes so drawn to her that he takes a great moral risk – a secret he can share with no one.

The novel is based on ancestors, and hundreds of pages of family letters. Who were those ancestors?

The married couple in the novel, Erika von Kessler and her husband Peter, were inspired by my son's paternal ancestors – his great-great grandparents. They lived in Boston at the beginning of the twentieth century, and they were an extraordinary pair. Even by modern standards, they dared to live in bold, highly adventurous ways.

What moved you to write about them?

I can remember the moment I first heard about the great-great grandmother, the woman whom I call 'Erika' in the novel. I was nineteen years old, living in Santa Barbara. A friend had gone away for the weekend, and she'd loaned me her beachfront apartment. It was around midnight, and I was lying there in the arms of a young man I barely knew. He later became my husband, but at that moment we were just beginning to know one another. He talked about his grandfather, who had recently died.

Suddenly he said, '*When my grandfather was a little boy, his mother deserted him and her husband and moved to Italy to develop her career as an opera singer.*'

The idea of a privileged woman in early twentieth century Boston who abandoned her husband and small child for the sake of her art . . . the thought of it amazed me. Then I couldn't decide: did I admire her and want to applaud her courage? Or was it heartbreaking that she'd deserted her little boy? The tension of all those conflicting feelings drew my imagination to her.

How did you manage to learn more about her life?

Early in our marriage, my husband and I moved to Boston. Every day on my way to work, I walked through the Back Bay neighbourhood where these ancestors had once lived. Erika's childhood home stood on Commonwealth Avenue. Her father was a famous physician, and they lived in a rather grand house with two archways.

When I went up to the front entrance and cupped my hands against the glass pane to peer inside, I saw that much remained the same as it had been in the late nineteenth century. The wide staircase was still panelled in black walnut, and I imagined her fiancé Peter mounting the steps and her voice echoing down to him while she sang from the parlour upstairs.

Why did their story seem so haunting to you?

When I stood across the street from 'Erika's' house, I could almost see a young girl's face – her face – staring back at me from an oval window on the third story. I had a strange sense of god-like omniscience, because I knew things about her life that she couldn't foresee – how her husband would one day be forced to divorce her and take custody of their small son; how she would sing in *I Puritani* from Montepulciano, Italy; how her little boy would write her letters that were never delivered to her.

What about her husband? How was he unusual?

Her husband was a fascinating person as well. He was British, a highly successful international businessman – an importer of Egyptian cotton, among other things. 'Peter' was a man of voracious curiosity, a naturalist, a lover of flora and fauna. He imported the first chimpanzees to the London Zoo, where he later became a Director. He travelled across four continents, and ventured into remote places, keen on seeing and experiencing everything. And he wrote prolific, richly detailed letters.

He was the sort of man who'd ride a camel through the Egyptian desert to visit a tribe of Bishareen nomads, where he'd move from tent to tent, tasting their dried bread and goat's milk.

Or he'd head to a friend's lush Caribbean coconut plantation, where they'd ride at midnight in a buggy along a beach, with vampire bats flying overhead . . . He'd slash a path through a rainforest with his machete, or he'd travel upriver in South America toward a waterfall that few Europeans had ever seen.

A third character in the novel – the fertility doctor Erika and Peter consult – becomes a crucial figure in their lives. Many readers may be surprised to learn that fertility specialists existed in 1903. Were their treatments effective?

Certain procedures that many people might regard as 'modern' – such as artificial insemination – were actually being practiced more than a century ago, but doctors had to conduct such work surreptitiously. They risked grave moral condemnation.

The Doctor and the Diva takes place at a real turning point in medical history. Prior to that era, if a couple were unable to have children, the fault was always placed on the woman. The problem was always thought to be due to a 'barren' wife. In the latter half of the 19th century, physicians began to discover a startling truth: *a man could be virile – he could be sexually potent – and yet he might also be infertile.*

What led to that discovery?

As far back as 1677, a man in Holland named Leeuwenhoek looked through a microscope and saw sperm. By the mid-nineteenth century, physicians had begun to study human sperm with real scientific scrutiny. An American physician named Dr Sims became known as 'the father of modern gynaecology'. Dr Sims would follow married couples into their homes. He'd wait behind a bedroom wall while a couple had intercourse, and then he'd rush in and probe and take measure of things under the microscope. He invented an instrument known as the 'impregnating syringe'.

During the Victorian era, how was he allowed to do that kind of research?

Dr Sims shocked and appalled many people. But the majority of patients who filled gynaecologists' consulting rooms during the nineteenth century came there because of infertility. Some were so desperate to conceive a child that they were motivated and willing to cooperate.

There's some statistical evidence that infertility was more prevalent during the 19th century than it is today. One cause was gonorrhoea, which was epidemic and incurable then. During the 1870s, there was one rather sad and touching case that convinced a professor of obstetrics at the University of Pennsylvania that husbands – as well as wives – were part of the equation. A female patient came to him, begging for an operation to help her conceive. While the doctor was trying to decide if he ought to perform the procedure, the woman's husband presented himself, feeling very guilty about all his wife's anguish and distress. He told the doctor that he believed his gonorrhoea – from which he'd been suffering for many years – must be the root cause. So, after an examination of the husband's semen under the microscope, it became evident that the man was sterile. This proved a revelation for the professor of obstetrics. Afterward, he told his colleagues, "I beg of you, be sure to examine the husband, as well as the wife."

A century ago when doctors performed artificial insemination, did they use a husband's sperm, or a donor's?

At first, during the mid-nineteenth century, they relied on the husband's sperm. But by the 1880s and 1890s, certain gynaecologists did begin to use donor sperm – although they rarely revealed what they'd done until decades later.

Older women in the family shared their memories with you, and rumors they'd overheard. What else did they say about the real Erika?

One elderly cousin, born in England in 1898, came to visit the US. As a child, she'd heard a lot of whispering about her American aunt. She'd heard that 'Erika' had a baby daughter fathered by a man who was not her husband . . . She'd heard that long after 'Erika' had deserted her son, she'd appeared one day, unannounced, at her son's boarding school.

The novel draws upon hundreds of pages of family letters. Where did you find those letters?

After my husband and I had lived in Boston for nine years, we decided to move back to the West Coast. We drove cross-country and stopped at his aunt's ranch in the Sierra Nevada foothills. Like me, she had a passion for genealogy. From the moment you stepped into her house, you felt the presence of the ancestors . . . Huge family portraits stared down at you from her living room walls. She had a little gallery of framed butterflies – a dozen exquisite butterflies that her grandfather 'Peter' had meticulously painted with hair-thin brushes.

'Where are the letters I've heard so much about?' I asked her. The aunt brought out hundreds of pages of correspondence. Reading them just amazed me. I realized that these ancestors had led far bigger lives than I'd imagined. Their voices could be heard in those pages. There was so much detail and adventure – nights spent exploring winding streets in Tangier, or visits to a coconut plantation in the Caribbean where the guests told ghost stories after dinner . . .

If 'Erika' were alive today, do you think her career vs. motherhood conflicts would be any different?

Her guilt and anguish would probably be very similar to that described in the novel. But I think that today the courts and society would have allowed her more flexibility with respect to staying in contact with her child. In those times, transatlantic airplane travel wasn't an option. She couldn't fly back and forth to visit her son for a few days. In that era, if a mother moved across an ocean and settled in another country, that was it – she was *gone*. And from a legal standpoint, she surrendered her rights to custody.

It's interesting to think about her husband 'Peter' and his mode of parenting. In real life, 'Peter' was often an ocean and a continent away from his young son, and he did a lot of his parenting by letter. At the age of seven, the boy was placed in boarding school, and during vacations, his father arranged for him to live with a family like the 'Talcotts' (as described in the novel). The boy was basically 'mothered' by a colleague's wife. But despite his father's long absences, the real-life Quentin always regarded his father as a towering, loving figure – and as an extraordinary man.

And long after 'Erika's' death in 1918, her son remembered his mother with a certain pride and respect. His daughters told me that as they were growing up, 'Quentin' always kept a framed photograph of his mother on top the Steinway piano – a picture of 'Erika' dressed in her operatic regalia.

What did you enjoy most about writing *The Doctor and the Diva*?

Apart from the joy of composing the fictionalized story, I loved doing the research. It was deeply pleasurable to steep myself in another era, and revel in all those exotic lands described in century-old family letters.

Learning about the history of medicine and the working life of a 1903 obstetrician like Dr Ravell – that was also fascinating. And the music! I cannot tell you how it nourished my soul and my senses, to listen to the gorgeous arias that 'Erika' sang. Had it not been for my son's ancestor, I might have missed out on a whole domain of thrilling and lovely music.

How long did it take you to write *The Doctor and the Diva*?
About six years. I wrote a first draft of the novel in the mid-1980s, but the result was lifeless and stale. I packed up those pages and stored them in a box for twenty years.

Then, after a couple of decades passed, I envisioned an entirely new way to frame the novel. This time I would begin Erika's story not through her own perspective, but instead through the eyes of the young doctor who was becoming obsessed with her, a man who would take a terrible risk and jeopardize his career because of her.

How did you research the novel, and balance factual information with storytelling?
First, I read the family letters with great scrutiny, always on the lookout for material that might be transformed into a scene. I imagined the exotic locales as stage sets where dramas might unfold.

Like any good student, I brought home musty books and old recordings from university and public libraries, and while I pulled out my pen and took careful notes, my conscious and unconscious mind were both at work. I was constantly on the hunt for just the right, historically apt detail. For example, when 'Erika' is confined to her bed during childbirth, Doctor Ravell puts a ball of cotton soaked in chloroform into a tumbler, and he tells Erika to place the glass over her nose. After she breathes its vapours, the tumbler slides from her hand and rolls along the carpeted floor. That's all you need to evoke pain relief during childbirth in 1904 – one detail like that, just a whiff.

What was the creative process like?
I researched for a couple of years before the formal, serious writing of the novel began. While I was gathering the historical facts, an entire scene would often come to me. Whenever I 'overheard' conversations between

the characters I'd grab scrap paper and capture their dialogue quickly. I jotted down whatever the characters were saying, even when I had no idea where in the novel that exchange might occur. I tossed the wildly scribbled scenes into a box and saved them. As I researched, the dramatic scenes accumulated, and the story line began to take shape. (Later I found that the dialogue I'd 'overheard' barely needed revision. It came out clean, and sounded natural.)

For many months I refrained from doing any 'real' writing. Instead, I kept listening to ravishing arias and consuming a feast of fascinating information – about the history of medicine and opera, about the training of vocal artists, or about apartment hunting in Florence a century ago.

When I finally sat down to begin the newly envisioned novel in earnest, I pulled out that box of spontaneously scribbled, random scenes and saw very quickly how they ought to be sequenced. Even before I began to compose the first page, my unconscious had already done much of the work. A new draft erupted from me with great speed and excitement.

On a deeper, thematic level, what is *The Doctor and the Diva* about?

The themes are too many to count, but I will say this. Several characters in the novel commit unthinkable acts. I've always been interested in the challenge of seeing a character's situation with empathy, so that even the most shocking choice or appalling actions might become understandable.

Acknowledgments

The Doctor and the Diva is a work of fiction, filled with countless dramatizations of incidents, characters, and scenes that are purely imaginary. Yet the inspiration for the story was sparked by my son's paternal ancestor—a great-great-grandmother who lived a century ago. The novel would not exist had she not led an extraordinary and unconventional life. In the early twentieth century, Alice Wesselhoeft Haserick deserted her prominent husband in Boston and sailed to Italy, where she settled in Florence to further her operatic career. Among others, she left behind a small son who wrote heartrending letters to her from boarding school.

In equal measure, I am beholden to Arthur A. Haserick, the remarkable man she loved and later abandoned. British born, he was a highly gifted entrepreneur and international businessman whose far-ranging curiosity and intrepid wanderings took him into remote places on four continents. As I read his exquisitely detailed letters about surviving violent storms at sea, or taking a moonlight buggy ride along a hard beach in Trinidad, or sharing dinners at his friend "Ravell's" coconut plantation, the novel began to take shape in my imagination. (In fairness to Arthur Haserick's memory, I would like to point out that there is no evidence that his sons were fathered by anyone but him.)

Long after their deaths, Alice and Arthur lived on quite vividly in the minds of their descendants. Alice and Arthur's two granddaughters, Polly Brockhoff and my former mother-in-law Barbara Dodge, always felt intrigued by their grandmother Alice, and were haunted by the fact that she had deserted their father when he was a small boy. When I started writing a novel inspired by their grandmother, Polly and Barbara generously shared mementoes and photographs with me, as well as stories, anecdotes, and an abundance of family letters. To those two marvelous women, my abiding love and thanks.

An elderly cousin from England, born in 1898, once came to visit the United States, bringing with her rumors she had overheard as a child about her American aunt, including whisperings about Alice's love life. Whether those rumors were true or not, I am grateful for the recollections the cousin shared.

Alice Wesselhoeft Haserick was born into a family of illustrious Boston physicians. To re-create the milieu in which she lived, as well as to capture the work life of the character "Doctor Ravell," I relied on many sources, notably *The Empty Cradle* by Margaret Marsh and Wanda Ronner; *Brought to Bed: Childbearing in America, 1750 to 1950* by Judith Walzer Leavitt; and *A History of Women's Bodies* by Edward Shorter. To set the stage for my heroine's performance at the Isabella Stewart Gardner Museum, I found that *Mrs. Jack*, Louise Hall Tharp's remarkable biography of Mrs. Gardner, was essential. To understand how an ambitious American mezzo-soprano might move to Italy, find a maestro, make her *prova*, and enter the world of professional singers abroad, I depended greatly on Ira Glackens's exceptional biography *Yankee Diva: Lillian Nordica and the Golden Days of Opera*. (Lillian Nordica's "Hints to Singers"—included as an appendix in Glackens's biography—provided the basis for the advice she offered my heroine early in the novel.) Geraldine Farrar's autobiography, *Such Sweet Compulsion*, also enlightened me about my heroine's training and experiences as a singer—as did biographies and memoirs of other vocalists, especially those of Enrico Caruso, Nellie Melba, Kiri te Kanawa, Luciano Pavarotti, and Renée Fleming.

The immense beauty of certain recordings gave rise to whole scenes and chapters in this novel; I only wish I could thank the composers who created certain arias, and the vocalists who sang them. For example, as I listened to Frederica von Stade's meltingly beautiful rendition of Paisiello's "Il mio ben quando verrà," I envisioned the scene when Doctor Ravell sees the diva "Erika" for the first time—the snow, the ice skaters, and the woman in white furs stepping from the black motorcar. When I heard Cecelia Bartoli's astonishing "Agitata da due venti," the storm-at-sea chapter broke loose in my mind. (I realize that Vivaldi's music had fallen into obscurity during that era, but I couldn't resist having my heroine sing that aria.)

As I wrote the novel, a number of people sustained me with their precious friendship, and by reading and reacting to early drafts: Elizabeth Fishel, Janet Peoples, Linda Williams, Mollie Katzen, Mary Ellen Geer, and Christine McDonnell. My deep thanks go as well to my fellow workshop members at three writers' conferences—Bread Loaf, Sewanee, and Napa Valley; and to faculty at those conferences who critiqued excerpts of the manuscript with keen insight and encouragement—particularly Tim O'Brien, Jill McCorkle, Erin McGraw, Samantha Chang, and Margot Livesey.

Above all, the novel owes its entry into the world to two particular women—my phenomenal agent, Lisa Bankoff, and my legendary editor, Pamela Dorman. Lisa Bankoff's clarity of thought, finesse, charm, and literary discernment make every interaction with her a joy, and that pleasure is enhanced by her stellar assistant, Elizabeth Perrella. My editor, Pamela Dorman, has brought her passionate involvement to the novel, and I have marveled at her artistic instincts and her gift for catching every wayward word or phrase. As an editor, she has stayed attuned to every nuance in the evolving psychology of the characters. I will be forever grateful for all she has done, and how she has helped to strengthen the novel. Her assistant editor, Julie Miesionczek, has been a truly nurturing and outstanding partner in the process; no detail eludes her. From Little, Brown in the UK, Rebecca Saunders has also offered a wise and wonderful editorial voice, and has left her distinct mark on *The Doctor and the Diva*.

My appreciation goes as well to my parents. I will simply say that the luckiest thing that has ever happened to me was to have been born and raised as one of their eight children. I thank my son, Colin, for the adventure of mothering him, and for connecting me with the ancestors who inspired this novel. To my husband, Barry—man of unflagging humor, huge warmth, advice, love, and vitality—let me say: I am happy to finally place this book in your hands. At long last you can open the novel, and read this story.

Also available from Sphere

THE RUSSIAN CONCUBINE

Kate Furnivall

'Wonderful, a gripping love story . . . A hugely ambitious
and atmospheric epic novel'
Kate Mosse, author of *Labyrinth*

1928. Exiled from Russia after the Bolshevik
Revolution, the beautiful and fiery Lydia and her aristocratic
mother, Valentina, have taken refuge in Junchow, China.
With destitution looming, Lydia realises that she must use
her wits to survive and resorts to stealing.

When a valuable ruby necklace goes missing,
Chang An Lo, a handsome Chinese youth who is under threat
from troops hunting down Communists, saves her from certain
death. Thrust into clashes with the savage triads of Junchow and
the strictures of the white colonial settlement, Lydia and Chang
fall in love and are swept up in a fierce fight against prejudice and
shame. Forced to face opium-running, betrayal and kidnap, their
compelling attraction to each other is tested to the limits.

978-0-7515-4042-0

UNDER A BLOOD RED SKY

Kate Furnivall

Davinsky Labour Camp, Siberia, 1933. Sofia Morozova
knows she has to escape. Only two things have sustained her
through the bitter cold and hard labour: the prospect of one day
walking free; and the stories told by her friend Anna, beguiling
tales of a charmed upbringing in Petrograd – and of Anna's
fervent love for a passionate revolutionary, Vasily.

So when Anna falls gravely ill, Sofia makes
a promise to escape the camp and find Vasily; to chase the
memory that has for so long spun hope in both their hearts. But
Russia, gripped by the iron fist of Communism, is no longer the
country of her friend's childhood. Sofia's perilous search takes her
from industrial factories to remote villages, where she discovers
a web of secrecy and lies, but also bonds of courage and loyalty –
and an overwhelming love that threatens her promise to Anna.
But time is running out. And time, Sofia knows,
is something neither she nor Anna has.

Under a Blood Red Sky is a breathtaking epic novel – a tale
of love, escape, revenge and redemption.

'Breathtakingly good'
Marie Claire

'Escapism at its best'
Glamour

978-0-7515-4044-4

Other bestselling titles available by mail

☐	The Russian Concubine	Kate Furnivall	£7.99
☐	Under a Blood Red Sky	Kate Furnivall	£6.99
☐	The Concubine's Secret	Kate Furnivall	£6.99

The prices shown above are correct at time of going to press. However, the publishers reserve the right to increase prices on covers from those previously advertised, without further notice.

──────────────── sphere ────────────────

Please allow for postage and packing: **Free UK delivery.**
Europe: add 25% of retail price; Rest of World: 45% of retail price.

To order any of the above or any other Sphere titles, please call our credit card orderline or fill in this coupon and send/fax it to:

Sphere, PO Box 121, Kettering, Northants NN14 4ZQ
Fax: 01832 733076   Tel: 01832 737526
Email: aspenhouse@FSBDial.co.uk

☐ I enclose a UK bank cheque made payable to Sphere for £ . .
☐ Please charge £. . . . . to my Visa/Delta/Maestro

☐☐☐☐☐☐☐☐☐☐☐☐☐☐☐☐☐☐

Expiry Date ☐☐☐☐   Maestro Issue No. ☐☐

NAME (BLOCK LETTERS please). . . . .

ADDRESS . . . .

. . . .

. . . .

Postcode. . . . . Telephone. . . . .

Signature . . . .

Please allow 28 days for delivery within the UK. Offer subject to price and availability.